The Fireblood Betrayed
By Kathe Todd

I0676554

The Fireblood Betrayed (The Fireblood Chronicles, Volume 3) by
Kathe Todd. Copyright © 2013, 2016 by Kathe Todd. Published by
Kalefaction Press, an imprint of Rip Off Press. All rights reserved.
No portion may be reproduced by any means without the permission
of the copyright holder. Visit KatheTodd.com for contact
information and the full list of titles available. First print edition
March 2016. ISBN: 978-0-89620-026-5

Chapter 1: Drakespring Farm, Year Five

Bernadette was in the middle of the trickiest part of crafting a daimonic sword when the crisis erupted. "Mama! Mama!" was the cry, as Andreas, age four, came barreling up to the forge they had built in the yard to the northeast of Drakespring Farm's millhouse. Eyes darting to the side to take in her son and assess his level of agitation, and glancing around for but not yet finding the woman who was supposed to be looking after him, she continued hammering the daimon blood together with the sablium. To stop now would mean throwing her work back into the smelter and losing the most valuable part of it.

Andreas stood, feet planted, his warm brown eyes boring into her with intensity. "Crackclaws!" he exclaimed. "Crackclaws in the Drakespring!"

Not ceasing her hammer strokes, perspiration breaking on her brow, Bernadette asked "Where are Larissa and Riki?" At that moment the objects of her inquiry arrived, the tall and slender elf woman with Bernadette's two-year-old Erika and her own daughter, big-eyed Sintra, on either hand. Sintra was a year older than Riki and somewhat taller, but so slender she likely weighed less. As Erik's daughter, Riki would probably someday tower over her mother.

Continuing her hammering, beginning to feel pressured, Bernadette asked "Larissa? What's Andi talking about?" Larissa looked a little embarrassed.

"He's right," she said. "There are crackclaws in the Drakespring Water." Larissa was beautiful, a gentle soul, and a good sometimes-nanny for the children of The Fireblood. But she was not a warrior.

Andrion was at the Mages' Academy in Eisenstag at the moment, and Erik was in Waterdon with Gerard delivering her most recent consignment of arms and armor to Valkyrie; so it fell on Bernadette to handle any threats. Those came so seldom to them these days, she had not really expected to have to deal with any.

"They're just sitting there, right?" Bernadette asked, her hammer completing the final blending that would enable the hunk of metal on her forge to be transformed into an article of daimonic arms or armor. Once the sablium and daimon's blood were blended, it could rest for a while before finally being hammered into whatever shape she intended. Setting it aside, Bernadette picked up her bow and a quiver of arrows. She'd found elven armor to be ideal garb for smithing, light yet protective. Sparks ran off it and it did not conduct heat well; so she was already as armored as she needed to be for dealing with a surprising incursion of crackclaws in the tiny rivulet on the western side of Drakespring Farm.

After her years in Iscandia battling dragons, aptrgangr overlords and master vampires, Bernadette scoffed at the idea of dispatching a few crackclaws. But there was no question they were dangerous. She not only needed to eliminate any that might be lurking in their little stream, but find out how they'd gotten here. Perhaps an expedition to the Brightwater, a half mile or so to the east, would be in order. If you killed off every threatening creature in the vicinity, it might be weeks before they became a problem again.

Andreas, Sintra, and Riki, expressions of awe on their little faces, trailed behind her under Larissa's arms as, bow in hand, Bernadette stalked toward the western side of the property. Two pregnancies had made her body a little more lush, especially as she was still nursing Riki; but she was an athlete, still an impressive warrior as she bore down on her target with deadly intent. Her kids knew Mama was a force to be reckoned with.

Bernadette bit her lip, struggling not to laugh out loud as, bow drawn, she confronted the menacing crustaceans lurking on the shores of the tiny stream known as the Drakespring Water. She'd always wondered where juvenile crackclaws went. Most of the places they lurked, you only saw the adults – three feet across and with claws that could crush a human leg bone like it was a twig. They were probably at the very outside edge of size and mass possible for an exoskeletal creature that spent a lot of its time on land.

These were… a lot smaller. Actually, they were a very likely size for the cookpot. She'd been wondering what to serve for supper tonight. Releasing her bow's draw and unstringing it, returning the arrow to her quiver and slinging the bow behind her back, Bernadette said "Larissa, could you fetch me a large bucket please?" Larissa took the two younger children with her but Andreas stood firm. A mature young man, now, he was not to be cowed by threats that might cause babies like Riki and Sintra (older than Riki, true, but a whole *year* younger than him!) to cry and scream. He wanted to see what Mama was going to do about the situation.

Larissa soon arrived with a wooden pail, of a size used by farmers for gathering cabbages. Those crabs looked as if they might still break a finger if you weren't careful, but she was coming to see that they weren't truly a mortal threat. Meanwhile, Bernadette had enlisted Andreas' help as well. "Bring me the tongs from the forge, Andi," she ordered. He leapt to obey. His Papa Erik and his Papa Andrion were authority figures in his life, but no other person on Terris had quite the power to galvanize him into action that Mama did.

With pail in one hand and tongs in the other, Bernadette approached the rivulet with a mother's wrath in full flood. This tiny streamlet was where her beloved children played, along with Lifa and Bjorn's two, Drelos and Larissa's little girl and, on occasion, Alessia and Wolaf's daughter Julia – of an age with Sintra. No bloody crustaceans were going to turn this pure and innocent stream into a hazard on her very doorstep!

While her cheer squad looked on and exclaimed with excitement at each thrust of the tongs, Bernadette wrested half a dozen of the little crackclaws from the banks on which they'd chosen to take up residence. When she had them all, they very nearly filled the pail. She hammered down on the top one where it waved its claws threateningly, and carried them inside the house.

Hours later, the family pushed away from the table. The crabs had been served in a style that, according to Uncle Lev up at the Maiden, was called "cioppino." There was a tangy tomato-based sauce, with lots of salad greens and bread toasted with butter and garlic to go along with it. Somewhat to Bernadette's surprise, even the younger children had enjoyed the savory mudcrab meat. She had the feeling that if the majority of Iscandia's human population were to learn just how tasty those oversized crustaceans were, they'd soon become extinct.

Larissa set to work cleaning up. She'd be taking Sintra, probably asleep, back with her to Drelos at the Maiden as soon as she finished that task. Gerard had gone out for the evening, no doubt up to

Waterdon or over to the Maiden. Andreas sat in Erik's lap, gazing into the fire and being told a bedtime story, as Bernadette snuggled Riki into hers and nursed her.

The girl was just two, and her mother was thinking that soon Riki would be weaned. She felt a little wistful at the thought of her baby moving on to the next stage of life. Her enormous, milk-filled breasts would soon be returning to their former size. After that, should she dig her amulet out of the chest she kept it in, and put it on again?

As Riki suckled, drifting off toward sleep, Bernadette stroked her slightly waving red-gold locks and thought back on the events of the past five years. She wished Andrion were here, so that she could consult with him (and Erik) on the issue of having any more children. Their farm was small, and they already had all the help they needed. The only reason for them to keep having babies was that they loved them so much.

Chapter 2: Drakespring Farm, Year One

Bernadette, Andrion, and Erik had been married for only a few months, and spring was here. So far, their three-way relationship (which had, after all, been going on for the better part of a year) was working better than ever. They were growing ever more committed to it, and the future seemed to be reaching out to them and promising better and better things to come.

Bernadette had menstruated once, after removing her amulet on her wedding night. She had paid close attention to the details when she'd received it all those years ago, and she knew this likely meant she had passed through a cycle and not become pregnant. Given how much seed her two husbands had expended, this was something of a surprise. But she wasn't worried. It would come when it came.

Only a few weeks later Bernadette's menses failed to appear on schedule. She'd counted the days, and was not surprised that her breasts had become tender. She had watched her mother through two pregnancies between her sixth and ninth birthdays, and had become wise in the ways of things that until now had never applied to her own life.

Which of her husbands was the father? Did it matter? Bernadette concluded it did not. They were all in this together. Knowing also that not every early pregnancy would result in a child (a reason why there'd been a seven-year hiatus between her and her younger brother, Gerard), she held her peace. Time enough to tell the men when she began to swell.

There'd been little in the way of questing to keep Andrion occupied, and he was beginning to feel as if it were time for him to move on to a new project. Already, they'd reconfigured the kitchen water system so that the main water supply split to two valves above the sink. One delivered cold water only, at all times. The other could (if the on button was pressed, triggering the heating element) produce water almost hot enough to burn you. The two in combination could deliver a sinkful of water at a pleasantly warm temperature.

Andrion was thinking of adding another unit to deliver hot water to the bathroom sink. But that would require questing in a dypalfar ruin to obtain more materials. He sensed that huge strides could be made in providing creature comforts to homes throughout Iscandia with this technology – and huge amounts of money could be garnered, as well. But this was like mining, taking what was in the ground and putting it to one's own purposes. When that was gone, there would be no more. What they needed to do was penetrate the mysteries of dypalfar technology, understanding how it was created and duplicating it from scratch.

All this weighed on Andrion's mind, and he was thinking as well of his failure to come up with a solution to the issue of producing plate glass in sizes suitable for the wonderful windows in Drakespring House. He really needed to journey to the Academy at Eisenstag and make the elderly uruk librarian Mhyrzon din-Tzrek his new best buddy.

Andrion raised this subject one night while he and Bernadette were sharing their enormous central bed. Erik had opted, this night, to leave it to the two of them. He'd been getting more and more into crafting projects, and had decided to spend the evening working at the Maiden's basement forge – followed by an evening of convivial entertainment at the Maiden and a return to sleep in his own room at Drakespring Farm.

Knowing she was likely pregnant had not dimmed Bernadette's carnal fires. If anything, she felt slightly hornier than usual. "We're alone," she murmured. Andrion smiled down at her, as he was holding her in his arms. Since their marriage, they most often slept all together – and though the three of them frequently had sex together, an opportunity for one-on-one intimacy was not to be missed.

He kissed her passionately, his hand moving between her legs to cup her sex. Two fingers moved deeper, dipping into her honey-pot to sample her nectar. Oh yes, she was ready! He worked his way down her body, planting sweet, hot kisses during his passage. Her chin, her neck, her breasts, her navel; eventually he had worked his way down to her crotch, and his tongue dipped deep where his fingers had been a short while before.

Bernadette spread her legs wide, her hands stroking Andrion's head (he'd grown his hair longer, and now habitually wore it tied back with a leather band) as he began pleasuring her with his mouth.

Her head was thrown back on the pillow, eyes closed, soaking up the sensations as his talented tongue found the spots that would send her soaring.

"Ah, ah, AUGH!" she cried, climaxing. Then she pulled him up her body, dragging him by the armpits until Andrion was once again at eye level and his rigid cock was nosing inside her slippery, still-throbbing cunt. Soon he was plunging deep inside her, harder and faster, as she wrapped her legs around his hips and pulled herself up to meet him as he was thrusting down.

It was not until the tenuous threads of the afterglow were fading that Andrion broached his subject. "Berni, I need to borrow the map." She flinched very slightly. Erik had taken to the daily chores of farm life as if born to them (which was not the case; he'd grown up in a small town, son of a fisherman), but she'd sensed more and more that Andrion was beginning to chafe at the lack of a central purpose in life. How he'd survived even two years as a "hospitality specialist" at the Maiden, she could not imagine.

Bernadette pulled closer. She loved this man deeply, might be carrying his child. And above all else, she wanted him to find happiness. She could hardly expect him to hang around doing nothing, riding on the coattails of her fame as The Fireblood. Kissing him, she said "Okay... Where are you going?" He hugged her tight. He knew already that she would support him no matter what he wanted to do.

"I need to go to Eisenstag," he murmured close to her ear. "Well," she murmured back. "That's definitely a case for the map. I'm guessing even in summer that place is abysmal. You wouldn't want to walk there." He kissed her deeply.

"I'll leave in the morning. I need to do some research in the library. You're still looking for an 'instant hot bathing pool spell,' right?" He grinned into her ear. She shook with silent laughter.

"I thought now you've figured out how the dypalfar did it, you could just build one wherever you wanted to," Bernadette teased. Now it was his turn to laugh.

"If your definition of 'instant' is a couple of months, I'm there..." Andrion rolled over onto his back and Bernadette tucked herself into his shoulder. In this enormous bed, they felt like comfortable castaways on a good-sized island.

After a while she murmured, "I'll miss you. Don't be gone too long, eh?"

Early in the morning, Bernadette awoke to find Andrion already sitting up, rubbing his eyes in an attempt to achieve full consciousness. She rolled over to throw her arm around his hips, feeling his half-hard cock. "Where do you think *you're* going?" she purred.

"Got to get an early start," he replied, not making the least attempt to engage her in sex even though she was there, naked and alone in bed with him, and he already very nearly had an erection. She was a bit offended, but understood. Whenever Andrion got both feet into a new project, he might well focus on it to the exclusion of all else. She sighed, and rolled out of bed.

Nobody lived in their enormous house but them. The nursery was completely empty and the crafting room was only gradually beginning to accumulate furnishings: chemia and enchanting stations, a workbench for making jewelry (Erik's interest more than hers). Bernadette had not yet decided what else to put in there, but having all that space was a huge luxury.

In any case, no one was to see or care whether she put on a robe – so Bernadette went across the hall naked and slipped into the hot bathing tub after using the water privy to relieve herself. The water system Andrion and Diane had crafted worked wonderfully well. When Bernadette climbed out of the bath, she wrapped herself up in a towel. They'd had Arngeld's "girls" weave them some towels that were a lot bigger than the Maiden towels, thicker and more absorbent. She found Andrion coming out of the master bedroom full dressed, so she stepped over to him and kissed him. Then she went into Erik's personal quarters.

He'd had a late night, apparently, and was sacked out on his double-plus bed face down, the covers thrown over the lower half of his body. Arngeld and his family had done another custom job for them here, as well – the bed was more than seven feet long, room enough for Erik to stretch out in completely. Bernadette had come in to let him know Andrion was leaving soon, so he wouldn't miss the chance to say goodbye; but on seeing her golden, godlike husband sprawled there she was seized by a lustful and mischievous impulse.

Dropping the towel to the floor, Bernadette slipped into bed beside Erik and pressed her body (still warm and glowing from the bath) up against his naked skin. Her influence had spread to the extent that both the Drakespring men now habitually slept in the nude. She put a hand over his back and stroked down it below the sheet, caressing his firm buttocks. He awoke in an instant and seized her, a grin spreading over his somewhat sleepy, angelic-looking face.

"Well, look what I found in my bed!" he rumbled, sounding immensely pleased. Bernadette smiled at him in turn.

"Missed you last night," she murmured, kissing him. Then on a more serious note, she added "Andrion says he needs to go to Eisenstag. So I'm letting him borrow the map again." He had used it for two round trips to Daywatch in the weeks before their wedding, leaving her and Erik stranded in the Waterdon area for a few days.

Erik didn't release his grip on her, but he looked thoughtful. "He mentioned there were some things he wanted to study," he said. "We were supposed to have glass in these windows," he added, gesturing toward the shuttered windows on the south side of the door that led from the room out onto the veranda. Bernadette looked at him questioningly, but it occurred to Erik that continuing the discussion might lead to the loss of an opportunity he didn't want to pass up.

"I'll explain more later," he promised, before seizing her mouth in a deep kiss, his hands roaming over her body to stroke and fondle. Soon she had temporarily forgotten the subject at hand, and was lost in his body. Being in Erik's arms, and knowing that he was hers forever, filled her with a special joy that had not faded with time.

They emerged from Erik's room sometime later and Bernadette went back into the pool, this time with Erik. She always liked having a quick bath after sex if she was going anywhere afterward. They dressed and joined Andrion in the kitchen, where he was (much to their astonishment) making them all some breakfast.

Andrion's culinary skills were far below those of his wife or his co-husband, but he could produce a perfectly adequate panful of scrambled eggs. The toasted bread wasn't terribly burnt. He'd even gone to the trouble of grating a little soft cheese over the eggs. After they had eaten, Bernadette got the map from the chest in the master bedroom where she usually kept it. She was questing so little these days, she didn't want to carry it around with her all the time. If Andrion wasn't gone too long, she probably wouldn't even miss it.

"Any idea when you'll be back, dear?" Bernadette asked, as Andrion shouldered his pack and prepared to leave.

"Oh!" he said, recalling something he'd intended to do. One of their more extravagant acquisitions for their home had been a clock, which had pride of place atop the cookfire's mantelpiece. "I need to find out how long fast-traveling takes to the Academy," he pointed out, making note of the hour. "If my research takes very long I'll be wanting to return home from time to time, so it'd be good to know what that's going to cost in hours." Fast-traveling with the magic map seemed to take only seconds, but during those subjective seconds hours of local time would elapse – sometimes making for awkward arrivals.

Bernadette and Erik each hugged Andrion before he took his leave, walking down to the road before wishing himself to the Academy so many miles to the north. He was so connected to them emotionally, he wanted to be sure the map did not accidentally bring them along. He arrived in late afternoon.

Chapter 3: The Academy at Eisenstag, Year One

Hmm, Andrion thought, calculating. It had been around 7:45 when he left Drakespring Farm. From the apparent height of the sun (near as one could ever tell, with the Eisenstag region's charming weather) something close to ten hours had elapsed. That wasn't bad, less time even than a trip to Sylvanian. And, he hoped, he'd still be in time today to consult with din-Tzrek if not to spend much time researching.

Andrion made his way across the central courtyard and through the doors into the foyer. The door on his left, usually to be found locked, led to the Magister's quarters. The door on the right led to the library, while through a set of openwork doors straight ahead was a large room often used for conducting magic classes where a great deal of space was needed.

Andrion hurried up the stairs to the library, and found the elderly but still fearsome-looking uruk librarian, Mhyrzon din-Tzrek, seated behind the desk. It felt so strange to be here, without Berni at his side. The uruk looked up, eyeing Andrion suspiciously. It was his usual approach to anyone entering the library. The books here were his children, and woe betide any who harmed them or attempted to steal them!

"You look familiar," he said. "Andrion, somebody…?" "I'm Andrion Drakespring," Andrion told him. "I've been here on several occasions." "Oh wait," Mhyrzon said, his memory kicking in. "You were always with that young woman, Berni-something… The Fireblood, right?" Andrion nodded, smiling. "My wife, now. She's been too busy to come, but I'm here on a quest for certain books."

Andrion had hoped that establishing his association with The Fireblood would smooth his path, but Mhyrzon squinted at him from beneath his fierce brows, tusks gleaming faintly in the library's dim lighting. "Are you a student here?" he asked. Berni had technically been enrolled, not that she'd begun attending classes regularly or anything. She'd had nothing more than a rudimentary ability in battle magic when they met and was now probably better at healing than at anything else, after the better part of a year in Iscandia. She'd never really expressed a desire to study magic in more depth, other than that occasionally-voiced wish to find a spell that would conjure a hot bath to the location of your choice.

"Does that matter?" Andrion asked Mhyrzon. The uruk frowned. "The Academy's library is intended only for the use of its staff and students. I can't let unaffiliated people just walk in here." Now it was Andrion's turn to frown. He recalled now that Berni had had to go through a whole ritual to get past the mage student who'd been guarding the entrance to the Academy where it adjoined the village of Eisenstag. Only after she'd proven her magical abilities (slim as they were, at that time), was she allowed to enter. And then she'd been welcomed as a new student.

Since then, she'd been able to fast-travel direct to a spot just before the Academy's central courtyard. And as he had been along for the ride, Andrion had also been able to come here directly – without proving his abilities to the guardian. Yet he was four times the mage Berni was, and had had years of training in Auverne as a youth. An unexpected hitch. "I'm not a student, but I'm a journeyman mage," Andrion told Mhyrzon firmly.

Mhyrzon considered this. This man was the companion of a woman he'd come to trust, and the two of them had been here doing research a couple of times in the past year. But still, there was protocol to be gone through. "I'm sure it's just a formality," he told Andrion. "But I would appreciate it if you would check with Faramund, first. You need some kind of Academy credentials before I can allow you to use the library." Andrion recalled Faramund as a kindly old fellow, whom they'd met briefly during one of their previous visits. He should be easy enough to deal with.

"Where can I find Faramund?" Andrion asked.

"Oh, he's out at Gryndhaal, at the excavation. They've been digging there for months. You'll likely find him down in the works with some students."

"Thank you, Mhyrzon," Andrion said politely as he turned away. This was a bit of a setback. He sighed. Nothing for it but to go out to Gryndhaal and talk with Faramund, he supposed.

Andrion felt caught in the familiar time shift that fast-traveling always brought on. He'd eaten a hearty breakfast almost immediately before leaving, and it was now approaching suppertime in the vicinity of Eisenstag. He felt both more tired than he ought to have, and in need of a little lunch – or whatever meal this might be.

Stepping back out the doors into the Academy's main courtyard, Andrion pulled some trail rations from his pack. He'd brought along a number of bars of trail bread – nutritionally dense, and baked to a hard consistency that would keep it edible for weeks if properly stored. The stuff was a workout for your mouth, but it really quieted those hunger pangs.

Andrion and Bernadette had passed through the outer workings of Gryndhaal months before, on their way to the tower of Alzhenten as they searched for the dragon scroll. Wishing himself there was the work of a few moments, and as it was geographically only a few miles away from his starting point not that much time had elapsed. The sun was still above the horizon, barely, as he made his way down into the entrance to the workings.

Chapter 4: Gryndhaal, Year One

Within the excavation, Andrion found himself looking at a series of ramps going down. Despite the hour, workers were still bustling around here and there and it took him some time to locate Faramund. Finally, he found the man directing a group of students who must be new to the project.

"As some of you may know, Gryndhaal was one of the earliest Norse settlements in Iscandia," he told them. "It was also the largest. Sacked by the elves in the infamous 'Day of Dread,' not much is known about what happened in Gryndhaal. This is an exciting opportunity for us, to be able to study such an early civilization, and the magics they used."

Andrion waited politely for Faramund to finish. Shortly, the group of students dispersed, and the old man was alone. He looked at Andrion inquiringly. "You look familiar, young man... but the name escapes me?"

"Andrion Drakespring," he said. "Bernadette Drakespring, The Fireblood, is a student at the Academy – and my wife."

Faramund looked slightly nonplussed. Then he nodded. "Ah, what can I do for you, Mister Drakespring?" Andrion considered the best approach, and decided to take a cue from Berni and just plunge ahead.

"I've come north from our home near Waterdon to study at the Academy's library, but Mhyrzon din-Tzrek requires that I have some official standing at the Academy in order to use the facilities."

"So, you would like to enroll as a student?" Faramund asked.

"I am already a journey level mage, probably close to master level in the field of battle magic," Andrion replied. "I was hoping that you might grant me some... other status. Maybe Visiting Mage? I'd like to be recognized as someone with knowledge and ability in magic, with official privileges at the Academy, but without any... obligations."

Faramund was a little put out at this request. "Well, if you want those sorts of credentials, I think you're going to have to prove yourself. I tell you what, why don't you go find Robert Dumas, and see if you can assist him?" He could see that Andrion was well above the age of the usual student, so it wasn't unreasonable to believe that he might be as experienced as he claimed. "I expect he'd appreciate some help in locating any artifacts here in the ruins. I'm particularly interested in anything with an enchantment on it. If you find anything, the class can look it over."

Andrion was a little annoyed, but he couldn't blame Faramund. For all the ability he'd demonstrated so far (and massive applications of battle magic seemed like a bad idea in these close quarters), his request to be treated as a respected colleague could only seem impertinent. So, he began nosing around the works, bumping into other students in his search for Robert Dumas.

Andrion headed deeper into the ruin, a fairly typical ancient Norse site in his experience. In a passageway west of a second chamber he encountered the scholar in question. The old man greeted him sourly. "You're going to help? That's fine. I'm working in this area, so you can look around in the chambers over there. Be careful not to damage anything."

Sighing silently, Andrion continued on to the area Robert had directed him to. His eyes were darting from side to side and top to bottom, searching for any artifacts whatsoever. Perhaps if he found something, it would prove his experience – though a thuggish tomb raider was as likely to have such expertise as a trained mage.

As Andrion continued north up the passage he spotted an arched metal door to his left; and set into its surface where you might expect to see a keyhole was a gleaming metal plaque, around four inches in diameter. Its design reminded him of the door to the laboratory in Faastenberg. The project of excavating that ancient Norse stronghold, the upper levels of which had been collapsed millennia ago in an earthquake, was still being held hostage by Eorl Gjyrmund of Icemarch.

Hmm, this place was supposedly far older than Faastenberg, which had been built early in the Norse Uprising. But the underground cities were not that far apart, geographically. Probably less than twenty miles separated the two. Might the ancestors of the Faastenberg architects have already developed the same sort of locking mechanism he and Berni had found on that lab door?

Andrion turned and peered down the corridor. He spotted Faramund approaching. "Hey, over here!" Andrion cried out. Faramund came up to stand behind him.

"Oh, this?" the old man asked. "This door appears to be sealed, but we haven't yet figured out how to open it. There's no keyhole, and we haven't determined the locking mechanism."

"I know," the younger mage replied. "I saw something similar when my wife and I were exploring Faastenberg last year, searching for the spell to defeat Tarragin."

Faramund stared in astonishment. "That was you?" he asked.

"Right, Berni and I were at the Academy library for a couple of days researching the location. That was right around the same time she enrolled as a student," Andrion explained. The old mage dropped his gaze, then held out a wrinkled hand.

"My apologies," he said. "I should have recognized you. And Mhyrzon should certainly have allowed you access to the library. When next I see him, I'll tell him you're all right."

"Thank you, sir. I appreciate that," Andrion said suavely. But inside, he was bubbling with excitement. The possibility of discovering hidden knowledge was as big a thrill to him as the lure of treasure was to Bernadette, and he was eager to see if he could open this door – and what he might find behind it. "I wanted you to see this," he went on. "Is it all right for me to try to open it?"

"Certainly, if you think you know how," Faramund replied. "We've been working on this dig for over a year, and no one has figured it out yet." Smiling slightly, Andrion pulled his dagger and ran the ball of his left thumb over the blade. As blood welled out, he pressed his left hand to the door panel. There was a click, and the door swung open.

"Amazing!" Faramund cried. "You used this same technique in Faastenberg?"

"Exactly," Andrion replied, as he used a minor healing spell to close the bleeding cut. He'd finally borrowed one of Berni's spellbooks to learn it, as it seemed absurd for a mage of his abilities to be resorting to potions to heal minor injuries. But it would be a long time before he could approach his wife in healing magic – even though she'd been practicing it for only a few months. Berni seemed to have a natural affinity for that branch of the magical arts.

"In Faastenberg, where the leaders of the Uprising had built their stronghold against the dragons and their priesthood, I reasoned that my lack of any affinity with those dragons might be detected by the door spell and it would grant me entry," Andrion said. "But this place is from thousands of years before, isn't it?"

"Not all *that* much before," the old mage replied. "We believe that the ancient Norse first settled here no more than two thousand years before the arrival of the dragons in Agena."

"Well, shall we see what's on the other side of the door?" Andrion asked, as he stepped through the opening. He and Faramund proceeded down a short corridor, only to find themselves in a small burial chamber. Disappointingly, it looked little different from dozens of others Andrion had seen.

"I think we should examine these coffins," Faramund went on, gesturing to sarcophagi mounted vertically on the walls of the chamber. His years of experience raiding Norse barrows gave Andrion a pretty good idea what to expect, and he was not surprised when they proved to contain aptrgangr – who immediately wakened from their long sleep to attack them.

Andrion's recent discoveries with the focusing of destruction spells to produce a narrow beam capable of cutting through dypalfar metal with ease had given him a devastating new weapon in his arsenal. Dual-wielding fire and lightning, he punched a fist-sized hole through the face of the first aptrgangr – dropping it in its tracks.

Though he had come to the Academy as a scholar, Andrion had not come unprepared for fighting. Berni had provided him with superb protection from head to foot, each piece of armor imbued with enchantments that enhanced his abilities at battle magic. In addition, should his magic fail him, he had a number of top-quality weapons at his disposal. It was nice being married to one of the best smiths in Iscandia.

Faramund was seriously impressed, even as he applied his own powers to taking down the second of the attacking aptrgangr. When both lay motionless once again, he turned and looked up at Andrion with an apologetic gaze. "I was clearly mistaken in doubting your abilities," he said humbly. "And I would greatly appreciate it if you could accompany me further so we can investigate the ruin."

Andrion felt a grim satisfaction, and a sensation as if a small, precise hook had been inserted into his mind and was drawing him on. He could never resist exploring ancient ruins and discovering long-forgotten secrets. Smiling graciously at Faramund, he said "Certainly. Shall we go?" He gestured through an opening in the wall that had been revealed behind one of the no-longer-occupied sarcophagi.

They came into an antechamber with some urns in it, and then into a large room ringed with sarcophagi. One aptrgangr, bow in hand, was already patrolling it but did not immediately spot them as they came quietly inside. Andrion performed a surgical strike on the undead warrior with a beam of focused energy, small as an arrow shaft, that raked it from left shoulder to right armpit and left it in two pieces. Whoa! To think he'd been using battle magic for years and had never figured this out until a few months ago.

As the two mages stepped onto the room three more aptrgangr burst from their coffins. Andrion blasted two of them with his deadly combination of flames and lightning, as Faramund dealt with the third. Soon they stood unopposed and were free to explore the room. Faramund was entranced, and wanted to engage in a detailed examination of this area. But a door on the far side of the room opened on a pathway leading deeper into the ruins.

"You go ahead," Faramund told him. "I'll be along in a while, but I need to spend some time studying this room." A man of action despite his scholarly bent, Andrion was eager to see what else the tomb might have to offer – aside from more undead guardians. Most of these places, he knew, usually held some fantastic prize if you penetrated to the heart of them. And this was supposedly the oldest Norse tomb complex in Iscandia. Who knew what wonders he might find? "I'll see you later," he told the old man, and stepped through the gateway.

Chapter 5: Drakespring Farm, Year One

Bernadette awoke in Erik's arms, snuggled together in the master bed. Oh, he was so wonderfully solid, so deliciously warm. Even now, with sunshine smiling on the land and spring flowers riotous in the meadows, it got cold at night. She had just about gotten over her pique at Andrion's abrupt departure, but a hint of it lingered on.

Intellectually, she knew that Andrion needed to find a place for himself, an identity beyond "husband of The Fireblood." He was just a late bloomer, she told herself. For someone his age to have parked himself at the Maiden, he must have been having trouble finding a direction in life. Now he had what he'd said he wanted: the woman he loved in a committed relationship, property, a family in their future. But he was still missing a piece of the puzzle. She hoped more than anything that he would find it at the Academy. Not that she looked forward to any long absences.

But emotionally, Bernadette still did not feel right. All her patient understanding of Andrion and his need to be his own man failed to relieve her sense that he had abandoned her. She sighed, and shrugged it off. If one of her men had escaped her grasp, the other was right here with his powerful arms wrapped around her, and he was delighted to have her to himself for a while. Their unconventional relationship had many facets, and one was that it kept them hopping. The little bit of tension saved their passion from growing stale.

Bernadette had the usual sorts of chores on her schedule, the list of which had increased manifold since they had begun living on the farm. She considered whether they should hire someone to help out, freeing them up for some questing; but if her suspicions were confirmed, she'd likely be out of action for some time to come. So the cow needed to be fed and milked, the recently-planted fields weeded and kept watered (if not enough rain fell, they had Andrion's hose and dypalfar-powered pump to supply irrigation water from the Drakespring Water), the chickens fed and eggs harvested.

Erik was more than glad to do the bulk of these, enjoying the work with the same simple happiness he seemed to find with everything in life. This still left her with meal planning, cooking, cleaning, laundry and other familiar chores she'd performed since she was a child – and had not minded leaving behind her when she came to Iscandia. Maybe they *should* hire someone. They had plenty of income from her crafting and the Maiden's profits, after all. Perhaps a woman who could come in a few hours per day…

After all these thoughts had cycled through her mind, Bernadette concluded that she did *not* need to jump right out of bed and get to work. And that meant… Rolling over, she wrapped her arms around Erik's neck and kissed him firmly. Those summer blue eyes opened, a little sleepy but already lighting with desire. "Good morning, sweetheart," she murmured as he bent his head to kiss her neck where it joined the shoulder. A tingle ran through her, driving away the malaise with which she'd awakened.

Some while later, after they'd bathed and dressed, Bernadette was in a much better mood. "What culinary delights would you like me to prepare for breakfast, O my husband?" she asked, smiling flirtatiously at Erik.

"How about if I prepare breakfast instead, O my wife?" he rumbled, smiling back. Her smile got wider, and she plopped herself down on a chair. Rather than the usual farmhouse benches, they'd gotten a full set of comfortable chairs crafted by Arngeld and sons for seating around their long dining table. It would seat eight with ease, and when the Steadfasts or Alessia and Wolaf came for supper it was handy to have. For bigger parties, they'd need to move outdoors.

Erik set to work in the kitchen area. He got the cookfire roaring, and began mixing up some flour, lard, salt, and leavening in a bowl to which he then added a little milk. With his powerful arms and shoulders the kneading tasks of a baker came easily to him, and he soon had biscuits baking on a rack inside a large, covered cast iron pot. The entire fireplace could be converted to an oven of sorts by closing the iron doors, but this feature was rarely used.

While the biscuits baked Erik took some pork sausage from a cold-storage chest under the counter. They'd crafted a smaller version of the huge chest used at the Maiden, and in Andrion's absence there were a couple of frost staffs kept handy so they could renew the ice that kept the insulated chest and its contents cool. Erik fried the sausage up in a pan and added some flour and milk, plus a few seasonings, to produce a rich brown gravy.

The gravy went over the hot fresh biscuits, which were accompanied by some eggs fried in butter. Bernadette had been enjoying the entertainment of watching Erik cook, her stomach growling increasingly as the smells of cooking tormented her. He was a good cook and enjoyed it, so it was not every night she got stuck with that chore. But he hadn't often cooked her breakfast. Oh, she loved him so much!

Erik presented the plate to her, a small sprig of blue wildflowers from the patch growing outside the front door serving as a garnish. Bernadette smiled up at him, delighted. She could hardly wait to dig in. Her appetite had always been hearty, her active lifestyle and natural high metabolism letting her eat pretty much anything she wanted without getting fat.

Erik laid his own plate on the table opposite her and the two of them set to. As Bernadette used a knife to slice through an egg, the still-runny yolk oozing across the plate to join with a pool of gravy, she had a sudden uneasy moment. What? She loved runny eggs. Swallowing, she used the side of her fork to break off a chunk of hot biscuit, soaked with the slightly glistening, meaty gravy. She took a bite, and found it delicious.

Abruptly, turning white as a sheet, Bernadette stood and bolted from the room. She dashed down the hall to the bathroom and hurriedly shut herself into the small room where the water privy sat. Down on her knees, she hurled up the small amount of food she had just eaten – and possibly, everything she had eaten for the last week, as well. Gasping, swallowing the saliva that was filling her mouth and then retching it up again, she stayed there for a couple of minutes.

Oh shit, Bernadette thought. I guess that makes it official. She'd seen her mother in similar circumstances for months during each of the pregnancies that produced her younger siblings, and a couple that ended in miscarriages as well. She felt simultaneously pleased and deeply annoyed. Damn, that breakfast looked so delicious! And now, the mere thought of it sent her into fresh spasms. Urgh.

On the other side of the door, Erik was knocking gently. "Berni, are you all right?" The concern in his voice was deep. In the nearly a year they'd known each other, he had never seen her knocked down by anything for long. With healing spells and potions, she'd never had more than a few minutes' discomfort. But such things were not a good idea with a baby on the way. Their effects might alleviate her nausea, but could damage or even kill the fetus within her. She was just going to have to tough it out.

"I'm fine, Erik," she croaked through the door. "Just a little stomach upset." Feeling better now, she emerged from the privy room and went to the basin to wash her face and hands and rinse her mouth out with a little cold water. It was no use – she was going to have to tell him. She'd wanted to wait until she was beginning to show, when there was less chance of a miscarriage. But she was never going to be able to hide this if she was puking all over the place and refusing to heal herself or take a potion.

When she'd finished cleaning herself up Bernadette turned to find Erik standing there looking at her, radiating concern. "Oh, I'm sorry, Erik!" she moaned. "That breakfast looked so good!" He stepped closer, taking her hands and peering down into her face.

"What's wrong, love?" She gazed up into his blue eyes. "It's no big deal, sweetheart. We're just going to have a baby…"

Erik's eyes lit with delight. "A baby?! Berni, that's wonderful!" She smiled lovingly at him.

"It's early days yet," she pointed out. "It'll be next year by the time the baby arrives, assuming everything goes all right." She wanted to be sure he was mentally prepared against the possibility of disappointment. Her mother's miscarriages had made a big impression on her as a child.

He smiled down at her, and hugged her gently to him. "Let's hope for the best, then."

Speaking into his chest, Bernadette replied wryly, "It'll be best, for starters, if I'm not spewing my guts out for the next six months… I think I'd better have some dry toast." Erik gave her a little squeeze, then hastened to return to the kitchen and produce a small plate of dry toast for her.

Meanwhile, Bernadette walked down the hall to the crafting room and began rummaging through her stores of chemia ingredients. She had them all in covered ceramic jars, each neatly labeled and arranged alphabetically on shelves. It made it so much easier to find what she was looking for. The hours she'd spent in childhood and adolescence with Selene, Pied-de-Puce's "Wise Woman," had taught her many bits of herb lore. She found one that would make a tea that was useful for reducing the nausea of morning sickness while being safe for a developing fetus. It didn't taste too bad, either, if sweetened with a little honey.

Bernadette soon sat sipping her herbal tea and carefully munching on thin slices of dry toast. She was beginning to feel a lot better. After assuring himself that she was doing all right, Erik plowed into his own neglected breakfast, cleaning his plate – and then going on to finish hers, as well. Waste not, want not. She smiled fondly at him, pleased that she could observe his prodigious appetite without any renewed bouts of nausea.

When they'd both finished their breakfasts, Erik was anxiously bustling around. He cleared the dishes and washed them, in the shallower of their two sink bowls filled with a sudsy mixture of hot tap water and lye soap flakes. Bernadette sat sipping her tea and watching him. She knew that he was galvanized by the revelation of her condition, and that this solicitousness would likely wear off in a while; but she planned to enjoy it while it lasted provided he didn't go too mother-hen on her.

The kitchen chores concluded, Erik kissed her and hurried out to deal with the farm chores. Livestock could not be consulted and asked to rearrange their schedules to suit yours. They needed to be fed and cared for daily, whether you had something else to do or not. Bernadette washed up her tea mug, feeling really a lot better now, and considered. This was ridiculous! She could not sit around on a cushion, being waited on hand and foot, for the next eight months! For one thing, she'd likely end up doubling her weight and having a delivery that might kill her.

Almost her old self, Bernadette went back to the master bedroom and donned her smithing gear. She might as well walk down to the Maiden and make a few pieces for sale, as long as Erik was taking care of the animals.

Chapter 6: Under Gryndhaal, Year One

Andrion continued through the labyrinthine tomb, alert for danger. He'd already killed off a couple more aptrgangr, and while he was feeling increasingly confident in his ability to send those accursed warriors back to their well-deserved rest he could not help wishing Berni were here. She was deadly with that bow of hers, and her dragon spells came in handy when foes suddenly loomed up out of the darkness.

Well, Berni wasn't here, and neither was Erik. Time to man up. Down a staircase, Andrion pushed open an iron door. There were fewer aptrgangr here than he'd feared, and he was not sorry. As powerful a mage as he was coming to be, it was nice to have backup – especially as he had not yet managed to grow eyes in the back of his head.

Throughout the tomb complex Andrion had seen pressure plate traps, and these he'd handily avoided. You learned to look for these things. As he was working his way carefully down the next corridor, he was surprised to find that Faramund had caught up with him. A bit relieved, too. One old mage was better than nobody at all.

After the immediate area had been explored, Andrion opened an iron door before them with the elder mage at his elbow. Inside, they found a large chamber lit by glowing crystals in metal cages. They bathed the room in a blue-green light, but at the far end of it they could see a curious blackness. Was there a hole in the floor there, leading down into some remote depth?

They approached cautiously, afraid to step too close. It looked more as if a disk of darkness had been spread across the floor in a circle four feet in diameter, darkness that no light could penetrate. The eerie glow of the crystals illuminated the walls, the ceiling, and the floor – but if that blackness was a void, no light fell within it.

Andrion crouched near the edge of the mysterious black circle and prodded it with the tip of his sablium longsword. There was a "tick" sound, as if the blackness were merely paint on the stone floor. But he wasn't quite ready to walk out onto it!

As the two mages stared in fascination at the phenomenon, they suddenly found themselves assaulted by a powerful aptrgangr overlord. Andrion had defeated more than one of these high-level aptrgangr in his time, more frequently over the past year as questing with Berni had accelerated the development of his battle skills. There was just the one enemy, and he didn't anticipate a problem. But when he hurled a focused bolt of his lethal entwined "plasma" spell at the figure, the energy seemed to be deflected somehow.

Did it have a powerful ward spell in place? Andrion drew his sword again and swung a mighty blow. He might be older and less massive than his brother Erik, but he had kept in shape and that blow should have cloven the walking corpse like a balk of soft timber. Instead, it skittered off somehow – and in the next moment the sword went flying as the aptrgangr hit him with what he knew from past experience was the Repel Weapon dragon spell. Damn!

The aptrgangr attacked his temporarily weaponless enemy, and Andrion staggered back bleeding. "I think there's some kind of connection with the disc!" Faramund shouted. "He seems to be drawing power from it!" The old man's magical senses, no doubt finely tuned after decades of spellcraft, seemed to have detected something Andrion – busy in fight for his life, after all – had not noticed.

"Can you ward it somehow?" Andrion shouted back, dodging out of the way of the overlord's attacks. It was wielding a magical staff, and sizzling bolts of energy were flying from it. Fortunately the room was crowded with stone architectural elements that offered him some protection.

"I'll try!" Faramund called back. "Keep him busy, and I'll tell you when…" Hoping it was going to work, Andrion withdrew – encouraging the overlord to follow him by hurling lightning bolts at it. They splashed harmlessly off whatever was shielding it, but did serve to hold its attention as Faramund approached the disc and cast a magical barrier spell. Suddenly, one of Andrion's bolts got through just as the older mage cried "There! Now attack it!"

No need to tell him twice. Andrion shifted from broadly-aimed lightning strikes, requiring only a small portion of his available magical energy, to an all-out concentrated bar of glowing force that punched into the attacking aptrgangr and burned straight through his withered body to dig a small indentation in the rock wall behind. The creature swayed, the light of the crystals visible through the sizeable hole in his chest, before collapsing with a clatter to the stones of the chamber's floor.

Andrion stared at the corpse for a moment longer, chest heaving, until he was convinced it was well and truly dead. Then he approached and searched it, before examining the rest of the room. It was clad in sablium plate armor, worth a fortune – but he didn't care to lug it with him. He did take its staff, a useful-seeming weapon. What he'd expected to find, and did not, was a dragon spell stone.

How was it that this undead creature could cast such spells without the stone to power them? Had the ancients known some technique for embedding the stones in the flesh – or had this man been fireblood? He was not about to start excavating the mummified flesh, searching for stones embedded beneath the skin, at least not right this moment.

Andrion pulled a powerful healing potion, crafted by Berni, out of his pack and downed it. His nascent ability with healing spells wasn't quite up to dealing with the injuries received in the scuffle with the aptrgangr. Finding his sword, he slipped it back into his sheath and went to consult with Faramund.

Andrion stopped in amazement, staring at the spot where the black circle had been. It was now aglow with swirling blue energy, casting a flickering illumination on the walls and ceiling of the chamber that far outshone the light crystals. "Isn't that a magic portal?" he asked. Though it was slightly larger in diameter, it looked more or less exactly like the one opened by the Arch Protector Duraenis to admit him, Berni, and their friend Nerissa to the precincts of the Eparchy – in a hidden arctic valley hundreds of miles away.

"It can be nothing else," Faramund replied. "But what is it doing here, down at the bottom of Gryndhaal? And where does it go? That overlord must have been guarding it, somehow. And now that we've killed him, anything might come through here."

"Won't your magical barrier work to prevent that?" Andrion asked. This was not a spell he'd studied, and he didn't know the details of its effects. But clearly it had prevented the aptrgangr from drawing energy from the masked portal to fuel his own barrier spell.

"It won't last," Faramund told him. "I must renew the barrier every couple of minutes, or almost anything might come through here from whatever's on the other side of the portal. The Magister needs to be informed of this immediately. He needs to see it for himself, and perhaps he knows a more permanent spell we can employ. Can you return to the Academy and inform Dalandrin of this discovery? Please, hurry."

Huh, Andrion thought. After his exploration of the ruins and fight with the overlord, he was feeling a little let down to be dispatched on an errand as if he were one of Faramund's junior students. But on the other hand, the situation seemed to be critical. "I'll report to him as soon as possible," he told the older man.

He had spotted a door at the rear of the chamber – and as he'd hoped, it gave on a tunnel leading up to a part of the Gryndhaal ruins near the entrance where he'd come in. Within moments of subjective time he was standing, once again, near the entry to the Academy's central courtyard.

What time might it be? Andrion had no way of knowing, but it felt late. It had been only around the dinner hour when he'd entered the ruins, but surely hours had passed since then. He guessed there was not a lot of time lost passing between Gryndhaal and the Academy, a distance that could be walked in an hour or less; so likely it was now in the wee hours of the morning.

And he felt incredibly tired and hungry. Andrion decided that this was no time to be hammering at the Magister's door; so instead he made his way to the room Berni had been assigned all those months ago. It was empty, which he took as a likely indication it had not been reassigned to someone else in her absence. Pulling some trail rations out of his pack he ate until the gnawing in his stomach had eased, then removed his armor and stretched out on the bed. In moments, he was asleep.

Chapter 7: The Academy at Eisenstag, Year One

Andrion woke, uncertain of the time. He'd had trouble arising in the morning since he was a child, though he'd noticed a change in this since starting his relationship with Berni. Whatever time it might be, he felt he'd had enough sleep – and he suspected the hour was now more appropriate for delivering his message to Dalandrin, the Magister of the college.

Splashing his face with cold water from a basin in Berni's residence hall quarters, Andrion ran a comb through his hair and tied it back again. Donning his armor and shouldering his pack, he exited the student quarters on the hall's ground floor and walked across the courtyard to the entryway.

He found the door to the Magister's quarters standing open. Perhaps Dalandrin left it that way as a clue to anyone wanting to consult with him that office hours were open. Andrion climbed a long flight of stone stairs, and walked into a comfortable apartment. It appeared to occupy one whole floor of the square tower. Dalandrin, the elderly but dark-haired head of the Academy, was sitting at a simple wooden desk writing in a large notebook. He looked up as the visitor appeared, peering at him as if in puzzlement.

"Do I know you, young man?" the old elf asked.

"We met briefly several months ago," Andrion told him. "My wife Bernadette, The Fireblood, is enrolled as a student here."

"Ah," Dalandrin replied. "Well, what can I do for you?"

"I was conferring with Faramund out at the Gryndhaal dig site," the younger man explained, "and we discovered a way down into the depths. We found what looks like a portal down at the bottom of it, one that was being guarded by an aptrgangr overlord, and Faramund needs your help with it."

The nachtalfar mage flushed slightly beneath his deep gray skin tone. His tip-tilted almond eyes widened slightly, but there were no other signs that Andrion's message had riveted him. "Could it be?" he murmured, so softly that his visitor wasn't sure he'd heard it. The magister closed the notebook and got to his feet. "Thank you for bringing this information to me," he said. "Come, we must get to Gryndhaal as quickly as possible."

Andrion and Dalandrin arrived outside the entrance to the Gryndhaal dig site a few moments of subjective time later, and hurried inside. "There's a shortcut down to the chamber where the portal is located," Andrion told him. He led the old elf to the door through which he'd emerged a few hours ago and they wound down the tunnel to the room where Faramund still stood guard.

The old man's wrinkled face gave him an air of great age, but he seemed to be physically – and magically – vigorous. Though he must have been standing here, casting his magical barrier spell every two minutes for all of the hours while his young colleague was taking a nap, he seemed no less energetic and alert than he had when Andrion had left him.

"At last! I was beginning to wonder if you'd been eaten by a bear on the way back to Eisenstag!" The old man said with a touch of annoyance.

"Sorry, it was the middle of the night when I got back and I didn't want to drag the magister out of his bed…" Andrion responded lamely. How could he have been so thoughtless?

As this interchange was going on, Dalandrin's face had taken on a look of wonder as he walked slowly around the chamber, peering into the portal. Abruptly he turned to Faramund and said, "Remove your barrier. I need to see something." Andrion felt a shifting in the magical ambience and guessed that the old mage had cancelled his spell. Permanent spells usually required a counter spell, but one with a limited duration could be cut still shorter by the will of the one who'd cast it.

The portal looked no different than it had before, like a pool of swirling blue light. But now, Andrion could sense energies emanating from it – or perhaps, from what lay beyond it? Prior to that first trip to the Academy with Berni, he'd had no experience of magic portals – though he'd read what little he could find on the subject. They'd been in use for thousands of years, and could provide instantaneous transport between spots on Terris – or between the plane of existence that Terris occupied, and planes of the Netherworld.

A look of happy excitement had come over Dalandrin's face. "It is as I thought!" he said eagerly.

"You know where this portal goes?" Faramund asked. He was old, but the elf was far older. "Yes, yes," the magister answered with a trace of impatience. "You need not fear anything coming through from the other side. I am going in."

"But Magister, do you think that wise?" Faramund asked. "I'll be right back, I assure you," Dalandrin said curtly. He didn't like having his authority challenged by this upstart, who'd probably been soiling his nappies at a time when the magister was already a powerful mage. Andrion and the old man stood side by side, watching as Dalandrin stepped forward into the pool of light and vanished.

"It seemed as if he knew where he was going," Andrion remarked when they were alone.

"There are ways to recognize the energy of a portal," Faramund replied. "I assume if one had prior experience of one portal, one might be able to recognize that another portal led to the same location."

"Two portals leading to the same spot?" Andrion asked. "Why would you do that?"

"My personal experience with them is quite limited, of course," the old man replied. "But suppose you had the need to regularly travel between, say, your home and several different cities. Assuming you had the ability to create these portals, the making of which has of course been lost for thousands of years, you could place a ring of them around a central location. Step on one to travel to Eisenstag, another to go to Sylvanian, and so forth."

"And at the other end of each of those portals, the energy would be the same?" Andrion asked, intrigued. Perhaps he *should* consider enrolling in the Academy as a student. It was clear there was much he might yet learn. But there was no way he wanted to be away from Berni, and Erik, for weeks at a time. He already missed them and their wonderful home.

"That's my understanding," Faramund replied. "But I haven't been able to put the theory to a test. This is only the second magic portal I've ever seen."

"It's my third," Andrion offered. "But I'm afraid I don't know any more about them than you do…"

The minutes went by, and Dalandrin did not return. Andrion took some trail rations out of his pack, along with a skin of water, and shared them with the old mage. They dragged some ancient but still-sturdy chairs in from the front of the chamber and sat in them while they had their refreshments. More time went by, as the two grew increasingly more anxious.

When Dalandrin had been gone for more than three hours, Faramund couldn't stand it any longer. "Something has gone wrong," he said firmly. "The magister would not have told us he'd be 'right back' if he planned to spend half a day on the other side of the portal. Something has befallen him. Andrion, do you think you could go after him?"

"Not without some help," he replied. Dalandrin, a mage of presumably incomparable power, had vanished in there without a trace. Before Andrion tried to follow him, he needed more information. "I'm going back to the library, and find out if Mhyrzon has some more information about this place," he told Faramund. "Depending on what I find, I may need to go home for a while and get some reinforcements. But I'll be back."

Faramund had to acknowledge the wisdom of that approach. "Could you ask a couple of the students to come down here as you're leaving?" he asked. "We're going to need to post a guard here until Dalandrin comes back, and probably barricade the doors to the outside as well. If the magister was wrong about what he'd find on the other side of that portal, he might have been wrong about the dangers we face as well."

Getting Faramund to jot him a quick note to Mhyrzon and then, bidding the old man farewell, Andrion sought out Robert Dumas and explained to him what was happening. The middle-aged, balding Galise drafted the tallest and most muscular of the students on site to accompany him, and went to answer Faramund's request himself. Andrion showed them the door to the shortcut before leaving.

Back at the Academy once again, arriving in the midst of a swirling snow storm, Andrion made his way into the central hall and up the stairs to the library. Mhyrzon was once again behind the desk. "You talked with Faramund?" he asked.

"And then some," Andrion replied – handing over the note. It was a good thing he'd thought to have the old man write it!

"Beautiful handwriting," the librarian remarked. He smiled, an expression that was far from reassuring. "You're good with me," he went on. "What can I help you find?"

Andrion told the uruk, "We discovered a portal to somewhere down at the bottom of Gryndhaal. I need anything you've got on magic portals in general, and anything on Gryndhaal specifically."

Mhyrzon's expression had gone from a smile to a frown. "Can't help you with that," he said gruffly. "Not anymore." Andrion was surprised.

"Nothing on either of those subjects?" he asked.

"I *said* not anymore," came the reply. "A former student here, Mindhal, stole a number of books when he ran off to Sindrendell. One of those volumes was on the subject of magic portals, and another was the only known history of Gryndhaal. Find him, and bring back the books if you want to learn more." Andrion got the librarian to give him a list of the missing books, then turned on his heel. He felt it was time to go home.

Going out through the front doors and stepping into the courtyard, Andrion wished himself back to Drakespring Farm. He found it both curious and pleasing that the name had changed on the map.

Chapter 8: Drakespring Farm, Year One

Having left the Academy's courtyard fairly early in the morning, Andrion found himself standing outside his home in the golden sunlight of late afternoon. Was it his imagination, or were the smells of supper wafting from the smoke that arose from the chimney? After their renovation the house at Drakespring Farm was far too large to be called cozy, but it had certainly begun to seem homey. Here were his heart, his love, his best friend, and the focus of his dreams for the future. He stood for a few moments just savoring it before striding up the walk and opening the door.

Inside, Andrion found Berni at the cookfire stirring a pot. The cooking grates had been pulled out to allow a large stewpot to be set on a hook, and something savory was simmering within. "Hi honey, I'm home!" he chirped, unable to resist. She dropped the spoon on the table and rushed to him, her face glowing with joy at the sight of him. It was almost worth leaving, just to experience it.

By now Bernadette had pretty well gotten over her bad feelings about Andrion's departure, and was just glad to see him back so soon. He'd been gone less than 48 hours. Knowing now that she was pregnant for sure, she'd begun taking her feelings with a grain of salt. Carrying a child had a way of sending a woman's emotions on a ride that made passing through adolescence seem tranquil by comparison. She squeezed up to her husband as much as she could, given he was wearing armor and she was in street clothes, standing on tiptoe to kiss him.

"Did you find what you were looking for already?" Bernadette asked. She'd feared he would be gone far longer than this. Andrion grinned down at her wryly.

"Not exactly," he said. "I dropped into the middle of a quest, instead. Where's Erik?"

His wife dimpled at him. "Down the hall, in the crafting room," she said, a hint of pride in her voice. The skills Erik had taught himself for fine crafting so that he could create her wedding bands were proving to be source of pleasure for all of them.

"Let me get out of this armor, and I'll tell you both about it at supper," Andrion suggested. Now that he was home, he was eager to unburden himself and just relax. Tossing his pack on the bed in his private room, he removed his armor and placed it on a wall-mounted rack. Then he put on some clean underwear, soft trousers, a tunic, and some soft shoes. A sniff of his armpit revealed it might be time for a bath, but he didn't want to delay eating. Bathing could wait until later this evening.

Andrion walked across the hall from the door of his room and in through the open door of the crafting room. The unoccupied space remaining was big enough they could have had fencing practice in here, if the weather outside was wet. But they'd found little enough time for such things so far. Running a farm was more work than he'd realized, and he was glad that both Berni and Erik seemed to take to the chores with such enthusiasm. He had to admit, as much as he loved living here, he was not cut out to be a farmer.

Not that they couldn't have afforded to hire someone. Perhaps they should. They'd already borrowed one of the Maiden employees to fill in for them when the three of them went questing together a couple of times since the wedding, and if this was going to become a regular thing maybe they should just have a permanent farm hand. The spare bedroom was fully furnished and ready for someone to move in.

These thoughts occupying Andrion's mind, he approached Erik where the larger man sat working with some small crafting tools at a workbench. What would it be this time – a ring, a necklace, perhaps a circlet or jeweled bracers for some rich warrior? As he got close enough to see what Erik was working on, he was surprised and delighted to see that apparently Erik was trying to replicate the dypalfar pen Diane had shown them several months ago.

"Erik!" Andrion called as he approached. Erik looked up from what he was doing, and a huge grin split his face as he stood and seized Andrion in a bear hug. Andrion returned the hug. Erik was his co-husband, and dearer to him than any other person on the planet save their mutual bride.

"Back so soon!" Erik boomed. "Did you find what you were looking for?" Andrion shook his head, smiling.

"I'll tell you at supper. Say, is that what I think it is?" he gestured to the small, cylindrical metal object clasped in a vise on the work table.

Erik looked a little rueful. "I hope it is," he said. "But I'm having trouble figuring out how the dypalfar got the tolerances so tight. I'm having to design my own tools and build those before I can build the pen." Andrion nodded.

"I sure wish we had a living dypalfar mechanist to pump for information," he said. "I talked with a living white elf, so who's to say there aren't dypalfar out there somewhere too?"

"We'll just have to keep exploring those dypalfar ruins, I guess," Erik smiled. Aside from working with his hands, he got great enjoyment out of a good fight – and such were usually to be had when you went down into the depths of those not-quite abandoned cities.

"Well, see you at the supper table," Andrion said, heading for the door.

"I'll be along in a couple of minutes," Erik replied. "I need to put my tools away and wash up."

That seemed like a good idea to Andrion. He stopped off in the bathroom, used the privy, and washed his hands with soap and cold water before going back to the kitchen. Bernadette, meanwhile, had taken the stewpot off the fire and replaced the cooking grids, on which she was toasting some bread rolls to warm them up a little. They had been baked this morning down at the Maiden and kept in a bread box to help preserve them, but were still a little on the stale side now. She was setting the table with three places and humming a tune to herself as she worked, a smile on her lips.

Andrion came up behind her and put his arms around her as she bent over the table, squeezing her to him and kissing her hair. "It's good to be home," he murmured. She rotated in his arms and gave him a deep kiss. This man could be so high-maintenance sometimes, but she loved him so!

"Well, have a seat dear. I assume Erik should be appearing shortly?" Andrion nodded, just as Erik came through the doorway. He, too, enfolded Bernadette in a hug and received a kiss.

The two men sat and Bernadette used a pair of kitchen tongs to transfer the now-warmed bread to a platter, setting it on the table beside a small plate with a hunk of butter on it. Then she seated herself as well, and the three of them helped themselves to the simple supper. On nights when she cooked, Bernadette generally drew the line at serving everyone their food – nor did she expect to be cleaning up, afterward.

After everyone had had a few mouthfuls of the delicious, savory stew and hunger had been blunted, Andrion asked "Well, anything exciting happen around here while I was gone?" Bernadette and Erik exchanged glances. Erik felt it was up to her to break the news, and she wanted to wait until they'd finished eating. She also wanted to hear about this "quest" Andrion had mentioned.

"Why don't you tell us about your trip, first?" Bernadette suggested, and Andrion was happy to oblige. He was eager to share these experiences with the people he loved and relied upon most, and get their insights. Bernadette and Erik had relatively little to say as he told of Mhyrzon's rebuffs, the trip through Gryndhaal, near death at the hands of that unusually powerful overlord, and the mysterious disappearance of Magister Dalandrin. "And now," he said finally, "we need to go to Sindrendell and find the student that stole the books I need, before venturing into the Portal of Doom." His grin told them he was up for the challenge.

Bernadette looked a bit unhappy. "Oh, it's all right!" Andrion told her. "Why don't we just get one of the guys from the Maiden down here, or maybe see if the Steadfasts could come stay for a few days. Then we can *all* go. It'll be fun, and easy with all three of us. I have the feeling this is going to be big." Bernadette and Erik exchanged glances, and this time Andrion caught it. He looked from one to the other, then back again. "Okayyy…" he said. "*What?*"

Bernadette bit her lip, then smiled at him somewhat apologetically. "Andrion, this sounds like the most exciting quest we've found in ages, and I would love to go… But I can't, because we are going to have a baby!" Andrion looked momentarily poleaxed. Of course, he'd been there when she ceremoniously removed her amulet. And she'd explained to him some months previously that once the amulet was removed it would take a month or more before she could conceive a child. Gods knew, he'd contributed plenty of semen to her in the months since the wedding.

Yet all that knowledge had somehow failed to translate into an expectation that she would shortly become pregnant, changing their lives forever. Just as he'd wanted, of course. But still! From surprise and puzzlement Andrion's features transformed to joy overlaid with a hint of concern. He and Erik were seated on the opposite side of the table from Bernadette. He stood and came around to lift her from her chair and look her in the eyes.

"Darling, that's wonderful! But I guess it means no more questing for a while?"

"I'm perfectly fine except for a little morning sickness," Berni admitted, "but yes – it would be crazy to go on any quests while I'm pregnant. I have no idea what effect a healing spell or potion would have on our baby. I guess I'll be off *all* potions for the next eight months. So I need to avoid getting severely injured or infected with any diseases." She sighed.

Sitting back down, Bernadette swabbed her stew bowl with the last bite of toasted bread and ate it. Fortunately, her appetite seemed fine after around eleven o'clock in the morning. Otherwise she might waste away to nothing and give birth to a baby you could hold in one hand. She washed it down with a mug of spring water. The rivulet running behind their farm provided water that was delicious and safe to drink, there being no livestock pooping in it during its short journey from its source in the rock above them. The rainwater in their cistern was fine, too, though it didn't taste as good.

Bernadette wrestled with her own thoughts and feelings for a moment, then said "There's no reason you and Erik couldn't go together." They both looked at her with concern. She turned, looking each of them in the eye to show she meant it. "Look at me! Except for having lost the ability to quickly recover from injury or disease, I'm exactly the same person I've been since you met me! It's not like the chores around here are so arduous. And what are we talking about initially, a couple of days?"

The two of them considered. She was right, of course. Their ability to realize this boded well for a long and happy marriage. But it still seemed wrong, somehow, to abandon their darling so soon after the revelation of her delicate condition. Had either of them had more experience with such things (Andrion was an only child; Erik the youngest in his family) they would have realized that now was the *best* time to abandon her if they were going to do it at all. Later on, her pregnancy would begin to erode the competence they had come to expect from her.

Bernadette sensed that if she were to pull this off, she needed to seize the initiative. She didn't want her two husbands hovering over her for the next eight months, chafing the while at their "confinement." She wasn't eager to see both of them go off and leave her alone, either, but she knew this would be for the best in the long run. And she had plenty of friends near at hand. "Erik, could you please clear the table?" she asked in a voice that was sweet as honey and brooked no argument.

Erik whisked away the plates, cutlery, and the stewpot, which held about enough stew for someone's lunch. He put it in a covered crock and stuck it in their cold storage chest, to be reheated the next day. Next Bernadette said, "How about fetching the map, Andrion, and let's see where Sindrendell is." Neither of them had ever been there before, apparently. At least she had no memory of it.

Andrion went and retrieved the map from his pack, where he'd tucked it after arriving home. He spread it out on the now-clean dining table as Erik was running some hot water into the sink to soak the bowls, plates, and cutlery with soap. The cast-iron stewpot would be washed with hot water only and dried over the fire before being stored, lest its protective coat of ancient baked-on grease be destroyed.

Bernadette came around to Andrion's side and they studied the map. "I'll be!" Andrion exclaimed, managing to avoid profanity. "Erik, you and I and Diane could have stumbled over it while we were on the way to Bzaltham! It's just a little to the northwest of that bandit-infested tower alongside the Brightwater." Erik shut off both the water heater and the tap and came over for a look. The place *was* remarkably close to where they stood, probably no more than two or three hours' walk.

"Shall we skip the map and just walk it?" Erik suggested. Andrion considered for a moment, then shook his head.

"Once we have those books, we're going to need to take them back to Mhyrzon." Andrion looked to Berni, who was at his shoulder. "I assume you're okay with us going back to the Academy and finishing this out?" he asked. As much as he loved her, his

41

protectiveness was modulated by respect. She might be ten years his junior, but he considered her an equal in most ways and if she said they should go questing and leave her behind alone, he didn't think he should try to argue her out of it.

She grinned at him. "Here's the deal. I can manage fine here by myself, but I need a little time to make some arrangements. And I'd like it if you and Erik could come back here one more time before you venture into this 'Portal of Doom'. I'm really sorry to be missing this, and I insist that you give me all the gory details. Plus, of course, I expect you guys to be going out there armed and armored to the teeth, with as many healing potions as you can carry..." Her smile told him she wasn't *entirely* serious, yet Andrion didn't doubt she meant every word of it.

Andrion threw an arm around Berni and gave her a squeeze. "I faithfully promise to return at regular intervals with exciting reports... and not to get killed." She squeezed him back.

"See that you do... don't..." On Andrion's other side, Erik grinned at the two of them then got back to the washing-up before the water should get too cold. The dypalfar metal their sink was crafted from was impervious to corrosion, but it did conduct heat rather a lot. Perhaps stone or ceramic would have been a better choice.

Bernadette awoke from a delicious sleep, lying between Erik and Andrion in their enormous bed. Their session last night had required a little educational work on her part, as both of them were unsure whether it was all right to make love to a pregnant lady with their usual vigor. She assured them that it would be months yet before her condition would impact her ability to have sex, and urged them on to extra effort. It might, after all, be awhile before she got the opportunity again.

Now she stirred and tried to slip past Andrion without waking him. He always presented himself as the likeliest of the two for this attempt, yet it rarely worked – and this time was no exception. However, he contented himself with enfolding her to him as she tried to climb across him, his stiff cock pressing into her belly; then he let her go, rolled over, and went back to sleep.

Bernadette headed for the bathroom, carrying a robe, but not bothering to put it on yet since it was fairly warm in the house. She slipped into the hot tub, loving the sensation as the waters closed around her, and sinking down until they came up to her chin. Her breasts floated on the surface of the water, nipples more pronounced than usual when sitting in warm water. They felt a bit sore and achy, which had actually had something of an impact on their lovemaking the night before. She expected that would pass with the morning sickness, though. Were they already bigger? She'd been generously endowed since the age of fifteen, but now her boobs seemed to overflow her hands more than they used to. Oh, she thought. They'll probably be as big as the baby's head by the time I'm nursing…

In a while she got out and toweled off, slipped on the robe and went to the kitchen. She built up the fire and put on a kettle of water for tea, then set about slicing the remains of yesterday's stale bread for toast. Sigh. With an effort, Bernadette stifled the urge to picture a cheese omelet, or some steaming hot sweet rolls. They'd only set her off.

While the water heated, Bernadette returned to the bedroom. Erik was up, putting on a robe and heading for a bath of his own. Andrion had had one before they went to bed last night, so likely wouldn't be taking one this morning. If he ever got up, the lazybones. He remained stubbornly asleep, but she didn't really need him awake for anything at the moment so she let him doze on.

Bernadette put on a comfortable skirt, blouse, knee boots, and one of the several semi-ornamental cuirasses she'd made for herself. It offered good protection for the body's most important organs, while being decorative enough that it was not unseemly with a lady's fancy garb. She'd started a bit of a trend here in Waterdon with these, and had sold several of them (by private arrangement, but with Alessia and Wolaf receiving a cut) to the ladies at Wyrmshalla.

For a weapon, she took her most lethally enchanted dagger. It wouldn't turn a shri into green slime or boot it into the next march, but it would cause it to regret (for the rest of its life, a very short while) attacking her. Thus arrayed, she left her somnolent love still snoozing and went to the kitchen to make the tea. Erik was just

43

coming back out of the bathroom wrapped in his robe, having kept his bath a short one.

"Are you heading for town?" he rumbled, embracing her briefly as they passed in the hallway.

"In a few minutes," she said. "I'm going up to talk with Lifa." Their friend, Bernadette's former body servant, was well along in her own pregnancy and beginning to show. Anja was very excited about the whole business, eager to greet the baby brother or sister who'd be joining their family before the year was out.

Bernadette toasted her bread slices over the fire, a few at a time. The dryer the better, as far as her morning stomach was concerned; though the tea seemed to help. Experimentally, she had begun adding milk to the tea and it seemed to stay down all right. She was going to need to add milk to all her meals, she realized. The calcium in the milk would be needed to build her baby's bones, and hopefully prevent that calcium from being stolen from her teeth.

Her minimalistic breakfast concluded, Bernadette left the kitchen just as Erik was coming down the hall, dressed. "I thought I'd walk down to the Maiden and get some sweet rolls," he said. "Want to come?" She thought about it for a moment. No, there wasn't really any need for her to go down there.

"I'd better wake up Andrion," she said. "I'm heading straight for Waterdon but I don't want to leave him wondering where everybody went."

Bernadette slipped into the bedroom. There he sprawled, a little mote in the ocean that was their communal bed. She had to crawl up onto it to reach him, as he'd worked his way in toward the center when his bedmates had left. All unconsciously, she was sure. She'd come to understand that Andrion really couldn't help it, it was just the way he was made. But she wished he'd make more of an effort to overcome the tendency, sometimes.

She crawled up to his ear and stuck her tongue into it. Then, as he stirred, she said "Andrion, rise and shine! I'm leaving…" His eyes flickered open and he turned to gaze at her. Oh. He threw his arms around her neck.

"I'm sorry, love," he apologized. "I think I must be map-lagged." She knew well what he meant. Fast-travelling took far less time than walking, to most destinations. But it still took time, and it seemed that your body was aware of that time even if your mind wasn't.

Bernadette backed off the bed and stood beside it, now Andrion was stirring. "Erik went over to the Maiden to get some sweet rolls, so there'll probably be some breakfast for you soon. There's hot water on the fire for tea, and cold milk if you want. I'm going in to Waterdon to talk with Lifa, then I'll be back probably by lunchtime. I suppose you guys can leave for Sindrendell then…" He smiled at her sleepily.

"I love you, Berni. Come back soon." Disarmed, she returned to the bed to give him a kiss before leaving. Then she exited the house and set off down the road to town.

Chapter 9: Waterdon, Year One

Bernadette arrived inside the gates of Waterdon after an uneventful and pleasant ten-minute walk. She was soon knocking at the door of Brightsgate Cottage. The door was opened almost immediately by Bjorn, who smiled down at her and gave her a little hug. "Bernadette! Come in. I was just on my way to work." Bjorn had picked up the building trade quickly during his time working with Hegmar on the project at Drakespring Farm, and he was now a full-time employee. His facility with architectural drawings had made him one of Hegmar's most valued workers, and his income was now more than enough to cover all of the Steadfast family's needs.

Even so, the Drakespring family often brought them little gifts from the Maiden. On this occasion though Bernadette was empty-handed, having brought nothing with her but her news. Lifa was washing up the breakfast things as she came in, accompanied by Anja. Both were wearing aprons, and the little one (now around six, Bernadette judged, though nobody knew when her birthday was) was drying as her mother washed. Lifa was about five months pregnant, and her already-enormous breasts had swelled to mammoth proportions. In her modest housewife's garb, she looked like almost globular – but still beautiful.

Bernadette came alongside and hugged her, then moved to her other side to hug Anja as well. "How's my sweetie doing?" she asked. The girl, who looked from her coloring as though she might be Bernadette and Andrion's daughter, threw her slightly damp arms around her "Aunt Berni" and returned the hug with interest. Bernadette bent to plant a kiss on the girl's head. It was her and Andrion's discovery of Anja, only survivor of a dragon attack that had killed her parents and destroyed her family's farm, that had brought about Bernadette's change in attitude about commitment and eventually led to her marriage.

Anja had a new mother and father now, and soon she would have a baby sibling as well. Though Lifa had explained that she would not be able to play with the new baby for a good long while after it was born, she was still very eager for its arrival. "I've got a new book to read," Anja chirped. In the last few months she'd gone

46

from learning her alphabet to really reading, and her papa Bjorn had been making her little storybooks with lots of pretty pictures in them. Though literacy was widespread in Iscandia, picture books for beginning readers were hard to find.

Lifa finished the washing, and carried the dishpan out through the back door to dump in the dooryard. Bjorn had installed this door to gain access to the little workshop he'd set up in the cottage's back yard, but he and Lifa were now planning a major expansion in that direction. As an employee of Hegmar's, he could get the services of the entire team at a deep discount. Lifa was envious of the piped hot water system at Bernadette's farm, but it was unlikely they'd be able to set something like that up here. There wasn't enough space for a cistern, for one thing. They hauled their water from the well in Waterdon's central plaza, up at the other end of the road.

Returning inside, wiping her hands on her apron, Lifa approached with a serene smile on her lips. She was a much happier person now than the reserved, hard-bitten body servant she had been when Bernadette first acquired her services after discovering her Fireblood status. "Can I read you my book, Aunt Berni?" Anja wanted to know.

"Certainly," Bernadette replied, "but first I have some news to share with you." She subsided, and stood looking at Lifa and Anja with an expression of simmering joy, about to explode.

Lifa looked her up and down critically, then burst into a grin. "You're pregnant!" she exclaimed.

"Wow," Bernadette said. "you're good."

"What else could it be?" Lifa said dismissively, but still smiling. "I know you and your guys have been hoping for a baby soon, and you look like the cat that got the cream."

Bernadette sighed. "Exactly right. I'm thinking that if everything goes well, our baby will be born early next year. I just missed my period a couple of weeks ago. But that means no questing, no potions, and… for a while yet, I'm afraid, no hearty breakfasts."

Lifa laughed. She'd encountered the same problem, but morning sickness for her had been less pronounced and she'd been able to delay telling anyone about her condition until she was already a couple of months along. At this point Anja, who felt she had been quite patient enough (not that she wasn't pleased to learn that she'd be getting a new little "cousin" in addition to her sibling, soon), demanded to read the book.

Bernadette was amused at the tone of the book Bjorn had made for his little daughter. It was beautifully illustrated, the simple tale of a beautiful woman known as "The Fireblood" who embarks on a quest with her two brave knights to slay the fierce dragon Tarragin. Well, what did she expect from a man who, until recently, had spent his entire adult life as a fierce warrior – bunnies and kittens? It did only have small words in it, and the story was quite stirring. Plus the pictures really carried it.

When Anja had finished the tale Bernadette said, "Thank you, Anja! That was wonderful." Well pleased, Anja ran off to amuse herself with more books from her growing library, leaving Lifa and Bernadette to talk quietly about issues of motherhood. Though Lifa had been acting as a mother to Anja for several months and was further along in her pregnancy, Bernadette's experience with her two younger siblings had given her a better idea of what to expect with a baby on the way.

Not counting banditry or some other line of work where you were liable to end up permanently on the wrong end of a sword, motherhood was Iscandia's most hazardous occupation for young women. Unless you were killed outright before you could take a potion, you could come back from most injuries or diseases with no lasting effects. But if you cared about the life of your child and your future prospects for motherhood, you needed to stay away from such things when pregnant. Healing spells, as well, might well draw life force from your unborn baby to feed the recovery process. So early pregnancy was a perilous time. Another reason people usually kept their families small.

Eventually the topic of conversation worked around to Andrion and Erik, and their reactions to the news. Which led to Bernadette revealing that both her husbands were in the middle of an exciting quest, and were likely going to be spending quite a bit of time away from home for a few days at least. Bernadette's extensive questing experience had shown how one thing could lead to another, and from

Andrion's description this one seemed open-ended. Who could say what they would find, when they entered that mysterious portal?

Lifa's brow furrowed in concern. "Leaving you all by yourself? With all that farm to take care of? Why don't Anja and I come down and stay with you for a while, until they're finished with their quest?" Bernadette felt relief. She'd been hoping Lifa would volunteer, but hadn't been going to ask her.

"What about Bjorn?" she asked, concerned. Lifa thought about it for a moment.

"It's not as if he wasn't used to doing for himself when he was in Alfenstein," she mused. "But maybe all three of us could move in with you for a while? We can just shut up Brightsgate Cottage for a few days."

"That's a fine idea!" Bernadette exclaimed. "I'll put some clean bedding on the master bed and you three can take that. I'll just bunk in Erik's or Andrion's room." In the past couple of months the Drakesprings had acquired extra sets of bedding for all their beds, making sheet changes easier during the long process of washing them. A clothesline threaded through a couple of dypalfar pulleys now ran between the house's southwest corner and the cistern tower, enabling them to dry laundry.

"All right," Lifa smiled, "I'll start gathering up the things we'll need to bring with us. Bjorn can borrow a cart from work after he gets home, and we'll all come down this evening."

"I'll feed you all supper, then," Bernadette promised. "Well, I need to be getting back home. I promised Andrion I'd return and see them off on their quest."

"See you in a few hours, then," Lifa said, hugging her. Bernadette got a hug and kiss from Anja as well, then went on her way.

As long as she was in town, Bernadette decided to pay a visit to The Potent Potion. It was now midmorning, and she needed some more of the herbs used in her tea plus a few other items. As she'd hoped, Adele also knew the name and location of the town's foremost midwife, one Inge Fordorsson. In her conversation with Lifa, she'd learned that she hadn't yet been to see a midwife and didn't know whom to contact.

Bernadette popped in at Valkyrie before leaving town, collecting some money from Wolaf and promising him and Alessia some more arms and armor in the near future. She'd made a few pieces yesterday, but hadn't felt like hauling them in with her this morning. She decided to withhold the news of her pregnancy from them for a while yet. The Steadfasts were like a second family to her; but though Wolaf and Alessia were her business partners and close friends, she'd prefer not to spread the news far and wide until it was certain she would really be having a baby.

After she got home again Bernadette borrowed a wheelbarrow from the cistern tower (which they used as a sort of garden shed), then went to the Maiden and got Fenris' help loading up the items she'd crafted yesterday. Next she wheeled them home, returning them to the shed and locking the door. She might perhaps get Bjorn's help taking the wheelbarrow and its contents into town tomorrow.

By the time she'd finished all this, it was midday and Bernadette's stomach was growling. A few slices of dry toast and a little tea were all very well for her delicate condition first thing in the morning, but she was ready to eat a whole ox by lunchtime. She was delighted, therefore, to find Erik putting together some sandwiches for their lunch, as Andrion sat at the dining table drawing in his sketchbook. He'd obtained a bound book of blank pages from somewhere, and was gradually filling it with plans and drawings for devices he wanted to make.

"Good news," Bernadette caroled as she came in the door. She sidled up to Erik to give him a squeeze, and filched one of the plates he was preparing. Seating herself at the table she wolfed down a couple of bites, saying "Mmf! Thish ish good!" Then, clearing her mouth, she added "Erik, could I have a mug of milk please?" Erik grinned at her. This morning's output from their cow was in dypalfar metal flasks chilling in their cold storage chest, except for the one he'd already gotten out in anticipation of her request.

Washing down a swallow of sandwich with a big gulp of milk, Bernadette realized both her husbands were watching her expectantly. "You had news?..." Andrion prompted.

"Oh! That's right, excuse me. Apparently I'm ravenous. Give me another minute?" She hastily devoured the remainder of her sandwich, following it with another big gulp of milk, then looked around and said "Are there any potato chips?"

They all enjoyed the crispy chips and delicious "Dragon fries" Lev made down at the Maiden. Lifa cooked them at home, but Bernadette had found it rather a mess and a nuisance keeping a big pot of tallow around for frying; so they usually got such things down the road at the Maiden and carried them home to eat, if they didn't feel like eating out. Bernadette and Erik had crafted a couple of fry baskets for the inn's kitchen that made cooking the greasy treats a much quicker and simpler task.

Now, Lev had found another use for the fry baskets – a way of cooking chicken that was bringing even more customers to the Maiden, many of them locals who just wanted a meal away from home. The plucked and cleaned bird was cut up and dredged in flour, then dipped in a mixture of egg and milk, before being rolled in a mixture of flour, dry bread crumbs, and powdered herbs. Then it was placed in a fry basket and cooked in the hot fat until golden brown. Once again, Bernadette was happy to let that happen in the Maiden's kitchen, not trying to recreate the dish at home.

Erik had brought a linen sack of potato chips back with him along with the sweet rolls this morning, and Bernadette was soon munching some and finishing her glass of milk, beginning to feel much better and, finally, ready to relieve her men's suspense. "The Steadfasts are going to come and stay with me while you guys are gone," she told them. "I won't be by myself all day, I'll have some help around the farm from Lifa and Anja, and I'll likely be eating better if it's not just me I'm cooking for."

They both looked pleased. Bernadette having good friends staying over while they ran off and left her helped to relieve the guilt they were both feeling. Now, this trip might very well turn out to be fun!

Chapter 10: Sindrendell, Year One

In the end, they walked it anyhow. Andrion had the magic map tucked inside the undershirt he wore beneath his armor, but there was nowhere they could fast-travel to that was any closer than home was to their destination. Whatever had inspired Mindhal to flee here, carrying books stolen from the Academy's library, it was clear to Andrion and Erik as soon as they approached the keep that the mages here were hostile – renegades.

The Academy stood as an example of employing magic in the cause of good – giving its students not only a grounding in magical essentials, but a moral code to be applied in the use of what they'd learned. But the basics of spellcraft could be learned by anyone with a bit of magical aptitude; and in wild and nearly-lawless Iscandia, the empire's northern frontier, there were many enclaves where mages who wanted to use their powers only for personal gain or monstrous, illegal research could gather.

The place was largely ruinous, one substantial tower built into the mountainside and two or three smaller towers scattered around the remains of the walls. They immediately came under fire from a couple of figures in black mage robes. From the corpses' youth and the contents of their pockets, they had been apprentices. They'd never see journey level now.

The prominent door in the front of the main tower proved to be locked, nor would it yield to Andrion's attempts with a lockpick. It seemed to be magically warded against Erik's axe blows, as well; so they started looking around for another entrance. Down a flight of steps off to the west of the main gate, they discovered a small wooden door leading into what appeared to be the dungeons.

The doorway led to a dark, dank stone corridor. Beyond that they waded through water to another corridor, giving out onto a large room that was under two to three feet of water. Andrion spotted a mage standing motionless on a balcony overlooking the room – and that mage failed to spot him. In another second their adversary was lying on his back with a smoking hole in the center of his chest.

Evidently the dead man had been harboring some pet chillmarrow spiders, however. Two good-sized ones suddenly appeared at the top of the steps leading down from the balcony to the floor where Andrion and Erik were standing. Stone pillars then blocked the men's view until the creatures were a lot closer, but as soon as the spiders appeared again Erik put an arrow into one while Andrion fried the other. He was really beginning to appreciate this new approach to battle magic. Too bad he hadn't had it a few years ago, when he was fighting for his life against various dungeon denizens on a regular basis.

The two comrades climbed the stairs and explored the area, searching the corpse of the mage. Andrion was hoping they might find a key to that door they'd been unable to open. Heading down a corridor, he spotted a pressure plate trap on the floor ahead of them. You'd have to be walking blind to miss it. Motioning to Erik, Andrion squeezed past it on the left, observing the line of holes that would fire arrows at anyone foolish enough to trigger the trap.

A passageway opened up on that side and he took it. This shortly led into a room with a hostile mage in it, accompanied by a spirit demon. Andrion might lack much in the way of artistic talent (certainly when compared with his friend Bjorn Steadfast) but he had an artist's appreciation of beauty. It was one of the things that had drawn him to Berni. The glimmering creature from the planes of the Netherworld, looking like a fierce and beautiful woman who was only partly there, tore his heart as he sent it (her?) back where it had come from.

Erik, never one to hang back from a fight, had charged in and decapitated the mage that had summoned the demon in a matter of moments – but not without cost. "Ouch," he remarked, as they approached the corpse.

"You've got plenty of healing potions?" Andrion asked.

"It'll be all right in a few minutes," Erik assured him. In his middle 20's and strong as an ox, Erik seldom worried about things as trivial as a little battle damage.

Now that they were unopposed, the two took a good look at the room they had entered. It was ringed in cells, and each cage held a vampire. The vampires sat there sullenly, refusing to engage in conversation with their possible rescuers. After their recent association with the Daywatch Brigade, during which they had destroyed a nest of vampires while befriending an ancient vampire woman, the pair opted for a middle ground – neither killing the captives nor freeing them. They continued on their way hunting for Mindhal, or perhaps an area with books in it.

They continued along a series of corridors, occasionally leading to stairways up or down and barred by simple wooden doors. In a while they came to a room that appeared to have been set up as a sort of target range for battle magic – something Andrion was intimately familiar with. Two mages were using it. He sent a bolt of white-hot energy through the man nearest to him, who appeared to be the instructor. The mage fell to the floor dead. Then, as the apprentice approached in confusion, he killed her as well.

They entered the room and explored both it and the corpses of the two mages Andrion had killed. Still no keys to be found. Continuing up a flight of steps, they rounded a bend before climbing higher. Suddenly the two found themselves in a pitched battle with a horde of reanimated skeletons that had arisen from their coffins after Andrion had sent their necromancer to join his familiars.

Onward they journeyed, climbing steadily now. They must be approaching that main tower's top, Andrion judged. They encountered a few more hostile mages, but Andrion blasted them with narrow bars of raw destructive power. Any he missed were either skewered with arrows from Erik's bow, or hacked into small bits by Erik's axe. Andrion was very glad that Erik was his closest friend, whenever he got a chance to observe the young giant in action with *that* weapon.

At last one more set of double wooden doors blocked their passage. Andrion pushed open the doors to be confronted by a well-lit chamber, stone-floored. At last, some books! The room was lined with shelves, a very complete-looking library. At the very center was a stone lectern, behind which a young Norseman stood. He was clad in mage robes, and was looking at them coldly – an expression that seemed out of place on his youthful features.

"You're Mindhal?" Andrion asked.

"And you're the one who's invaded my home, killing my followers and destroying my projects?" the man replied. What projects? Those gruesome experiments?

"Mhyrzon sent me here for the books you stole," Andrion said grimly, "and your 'followers' got in the way. Hand them over, and I'll leave you to your 'work'."

"After the damage you've caused, I don't think I'll be giving you anything," Mindhal replied. "You have no idea what you've walked into, here." He stepped back and raised both hands, thumb and index finger tips touching as if framing a triangular shape in the air. At his feet, a small portal appeared. Rising up out of it, as if emerging from beneath the sea, came the head and shoulders of a monstrous-looking creature.

There was a strangled "Urkh!" from Mindhal as an arrow appeared in his throat, shot from Erik's bow. The young mage collapsed to the floor choking on his own blood, and the portal suddenly winked out of existence. Lying on the stone floor twitching, the upper half of the demon's body had apparently been severed by the sudden closing of the portal through which it had been coming.

"Thanks, Erik," Andrion said, as casually as if his brother had just passed the potatoes. Then he walked over to take a look at the thing on the floor. It was roughly manlike in shape, but cold and slimy to the touch. It had skin that was deep green shading to a sickly yellow, with a frog-like face and enormous red eyes, fringed ears far larger than an elf's standing up above the crown of the head. One ugly sucker.

"He actually created a portal to one of the planes of the Netherworld!" Andrion said excitedly. No way this thing was a native of Terris. Creatures from the Netherworld appeared here often enough, either arriving under their own power like the daimonic "lords" who claimed to be gods, or conjured like the flame, frost, tempest, and spirit demons who could be brought here and forced to fight on the behalf of the conjurer for a short period of time.

"Maybe that's not one of the critters you can conjure," Erik suggested. He had fought enough demons to be aware of the way in which certain magic users could bring them here from other dimensions, but had no deep understanding of the subject.

"You could be right, Erik," Andrion replied. "I've studied conjuring enough to know there's no spell for conjuring a frog demon. But I sure wish I knew where this kid got the portal spell. Depending on how it's configured, that could be really useful."

"Sorry," Erik grinned ruefully. "If I'd known you wanted to interrogate him, I could have shot him someplace less fatal." Andrion brushed it off.

"Maybe we'll find something in these books," he said hopefully. "Why don't you start checking the titles on this bookcase, and I'll take the one over there?"

Erik shrugged. Scholarship was not his thing, but he could read as well as anyone in Iscandia and he wasn't an idiot. Andrion handed him a scrawled list of the titles Mhyrzon said had been stolen, and added "Just read the titles. If you see any of these, or any title that mentions portals, the Netherworld, or Gryndhaal, pull it out and give me a holler."

After a couple of hours of this activity (fascinating for Andrion, stultifying for Erik) the two took seats at the room's table and broke out some trail rations and water. Six hours later, they had searched the entire room. Andrion's hope of finding a spellbook on the subject of creating portals was dashed, and he now deeply regretted that they'd had to kill everyone here. True, there were still some vampires alive down there in the cells; but he doubted whether the test subjects would have had access to any of their captors' arcane knowledge. If any of them knew the portal spell, they'd have used it to escape.

They had at least found the three titles that had been stolen from the library at the Academy. *Day of Dread* told of the elven invasion of Gryndhaal, when combined dypalfar, nachtalfar and leukalfar forces had broken past the outer defenses and killed everyone in the upper city. Gryndhaal as it existed today was only the basement, as it were, of that once-proud city founded by Iscandia's earliest Norse inhabitants.

Another of the titles, *Lost Arts*, proved to be only an overview of magic spells known to the ancients, spells that had already been lost to modern man by the time the book was written – which, from its condition, was probably several centuries ago. It described how, using immense amounts of magical energy, permanent portals could be created linking one place with another. They could be configured to be two-way or one-way, and could even be keyed (as Duraenis had done, with the portal to the Eparchy) to admit only those carrying certain enchanted tokens. Fascinating, and Andrion really wished he could just make off with this one for the collection he was building at Drakespring Farm.

But while he could easily claim not to have found the book when he reported to Mhyrzon, he couldn't deal so falsely with the old uruk. He was hoping they could genuinely become friends in the future, and that wasn't how you treated with friends. Likewise, the book about Gryndhaal was long and was going to require more study. But they really should be going.

The third book, *High King of the Eldalfar,* was interesting but had nothing to do with the subject matter at hand. They loaded up their packs with other non-apropos volumes Andrion intended to take home for his personal library, and let themselves out through a trap door. They'd found the key to it in the late Mindhal's pocket. Emerging into Sindrendell's ruinous bailey through the door that had been barred against them on their arrival, Andrion and Erik soon found themselves shivering in the courtyard at the Academy. It appeared to be dawn, and heavy snow was falling.

Chapter 11: Drakespring Farm, Year One

Bernadette woke with the dawn. Little slivers of daylight were coming through the shutters of the windows in Erik's bedroom. She rolled over onto her stomach, a sleeping position her golden giant favored, and inhaled his scent from the bed's sheets. The three of them tended to spend most nights sleeping together in the farmhouse's master bed, frequently after a three-way sexual liaison that would have raised eyebrows all over the march; but Erik and Andrion also made use of the beds designated just for each of them. This bed smelled of Erik, and she loved it.

She sighed. Sometimes, life didn't work out quite like you'd wanted. She'd expected to have her loves with her, at this happy time. But, Bernadette was coming to find, times like this only made the times when everything was as you wanted it all the sweeter. And having the Steadfast family living with her wasn't without its compensations. She slipped out of bed and into the robe she'd tossed atop Erik's chest of drawers the previous night. Another sigh escaped her lips as she considered how much more fun it would have been to have spent the night with him beside her.

Oh, get over it! Bernadette told herself sharply, as she made her way across the hall to the bathroom. Their houseguests were already stirring, and while soaking in the hot tub she greeted Bjorn as he made his way to the privy. He seemed a little embarrassed. She was no longer his warden, the arbiter of his life's course; but she was still an attractive young woman and she was currently in the nude, all her lush charms on display. Bjorn's upbringing had failed to prepare him for such eventualities; but he was doing his best. For her part, Bernadette tried to put him at his ease by acting as if there were nothing out of the ordinary.

Lifa and Anja seemed less constrained, and they appeared, wearing robes, just as Bernadette was thinking it was about time to get out and dressed. "Good morning!" she chirped. Her former body servant and the girl who was now her daughter had stayed here before, and had come to love Drakespring Farm's bathing tub. The fact that it was a private pool, not likely to be inhabited – or viewed – by random strangers, was a plus.

Though she'd been about to get out, Bernadette lingered for a while to spend some time with Lifa and Anja. Lifa's lush figure was in some ways a preview of what she had to look forward to – not that Bernadette's hips and breasts would ever reach those proportions. At five months' pregnancy, Lifa resembled one of those stone-carved fertility goddesses from the dawn of human pre-history, her belly swelling in a high curve below her enormous breasts. Those now floated splendidly on the surface of the bathing tub, like moons in an evening sky.

Ignoring their nudity, the three females chatted quietly and amiably for a while. Then Bernadette excused herself and got out, toweling off before putting on her robe again and going to the master bedroom to get some clothing out of her closet. By now, Bjorn was dressed and had made his way to the kitchen, where he'd built up the fire and was heating water for tea. Bernadette had dressed and slipped out just as Lifa and Anja were leaving the bathroom. She joined Bjorn in the kitchen. "You have to leave for work soon?" She asked.

"Time for some breakfast first," he rumbled. He was nearly as big as her Erik, though older and considerably less sunny. "We'll be starting on *your* job pretty soon," Bjorn added.

Bernadette initially drew a blank, then she remembered: after several months of ever-increasing inn business, she had agreed with Lev that it made sense for the tent he'd borrowed (for the purpose of temporarily expanding the Maiden's sleeping capacity) to be replaced with a permanent structure. Hegmar and his crew had been booked up, so they'd had to wait until he was free before the work could begin. This project was going to cause an interruption in the Maiden's ability to accommodate the usual number of overnight guests, but they were ready to re-pitch the big tent in the area to the south. And in any case, a growing percentage of the Maiden's business was from sales of food and drink to locals.

Bernadette smiled at Bjorn. "Good, I'm glad that'll be going forward. I can't believe how much this area has grown in the last few months." Bjorn smiled back at her. Now that she was clothed, he felt capable of interacting with her as a friend. She considered the resources on hand. Now that they had their own, growing flock of chickens, eggs were always in good supply. She'd begun trying her hand at cheese-making, now they also had their own milk cow; but this was still in the development stage and she got most of the cheese their household needed from Lev.

What they were out of was bread. While Bernadette now had the capability to bake bread, the desire to arise at four in the morning in order to begin kneading and rising dough so that fresh loaves would be available at breakfast time had as yet eluded her. "Bjorn, would you mind walking over to the Maiden and getting us some bread?" Lev now had a couple of employees who were being *paid* to get up at four, with the result that fresh hot bread and delicious warm pastries were all to be had there at this hour.

"No problem," Bjorn said. "I'll be back in about fifteen to twenty minutes." Bernadette judged that would be just about the right amount of time. She broke a dozen eggs into a bowl, added a little cream, and shaved a wedge of crumbly white cheese into slivers. Chopped young onions with the tops, along with some chopped herbs, went into the bowl. Lifa and Anja came down the hall, now clean and dressed, and accepted cups of tea.

"Bjorn is fetching us some bread," Bernadette told them. "There'll be omelets in a while."

Bjorn soon returned with a fragrant cloth-covered basket of fresh bread. There were a few sweet rolls in there too, Bernadette noticed; and wondered how many he'd eaten on the walk back. She doubted it would have much impact on his appetite – Erik had given her a pretty good idea of how much a man of that size needed to eat, just to keep from wasting way to nothing.

The basket sat on the table steaming, a bowl of fresh butter beside it, and Lifa put plates and cutlery around as Bernadette began making omelets. Preferring the flavor of a small, fast omelet to one made to feed a crowd, she quickly put out a series of individual ones. The fire hot, she ran a bit of butter into her long-handled omelet pan and as soon as it was bubbling, she used a tankard to feed an appropriate amount of the egg mixture into the hot pan. During its few seconds in the pan she sprinkled a little of the shredded cheese over it, then folded it over with a deft twist of the wrist. Moments later, the omelet went onto a plate.

In only a few minutes everyone had their own omelet, along with as much fresh bread (or sweet roll, in Anja's case) as they wanted. Silence reigned at the table, broken only by the sounds of eating. When all had finished, Lifa volunteered to do the washing-up – as usual, with Anja's help. The girl had come to accept this chore as a part of everyday life. But from Lifa's perspective, it was a breeze. With a double sink and hot and cold running water, doing dishes at Drakespring Farm was very nearly a joy.

After cleaning his teeth and combing his hair back, Bjorn kissed his wife and daughter and thanked Bernadette before leaving for work. Bernadette sat relaxing, drinking her tea. She'd actually eaten a small amount of omelet and a roll of fresh bread, lightly buttered, without feeling the urge to run off and puke. This was a victory.

Later on in the morning, Anja asked "Aunt Berni, are you really The Fireblood?" Ah. Bernadette hadn't gotten the sense after yesterday's reading of the picture book, that Anja realized her aunt was the same person killing dragons in the book. "Yes Anja," Bernadette replied thoughtfully. She wanted to strike a balance between preserving Anja's enjoyment of the story and letting her understand that reality wasn't quite like what you read in books.

Bernadette spent some time regaling Anja, and Lifa as well, with the true tale of their adventures fighting Tarragin. She left out all the sex, of course, and most of the graphic details of violence as well; but when all was said and done Anja was enthralled. "I want to be just like you when I grow up," Anja announced positively.

"And just like your mama too," Bernadette pointed out. "Your mama and papa are both powerful warriors. Did you know that?" Anja nodded.

After considering briefly, she added "I need some armor and weapons if I'm going to be a warrior."

Huh, well *this* was a change from Little Miss Frills and Lace. Bernadette supposed that possibly all little girls went through that stage (though she could not recall doing so herself), and eventually most of them came to something else. She had an inspiration. "Anja, I think it may be time that you *had* some weapons and armor." Anja's eyes were wide. Was speaking one's wishes all it took for them to be fulfilled? Perhaps, if you were spoiled enough…

Bernadette fetched a tape measure and took a few measurements of Anja. Then she led the girl and her mother out into the farm yard. She gave Anja a bucket of grain with which to feed the chickens, and tasked her with collecting their eggs in the same bucket after it had been emptied. Lifa had already demonstrated the ability to milk the cow, having apparently learned this skill prior to being orphaned. Those tasks underway, Bernadette told them she'd be back by lunchtime and headed for the Maiden and its basement crafting facilities.

At lunchtime the three of them regrouped. After the livestock had been dealt with, Lifa and Anja had amused themselves weeding the wheat field and the cabbage patch, and thinning out the onion and tomato seedlings. At this season, everything was growing like weeds – including and especially the weeds themselves. Having once been instructed in the difference between a weed and the desired cultivar, Anja pursued the death of the former with inimical intent.

Bernadette was carrying a muslin bag, which Lifa immediately identified as similar to the one in which her wedding gown had arrived. Anja had been so distracted by the farm chores that she had not made a connection, and the three of them tucked into lunch without arousing her curiosity about the bag's contents. It was only after they'd eaten that Anja picked up on the meaningful looks passing between her mama and her auntie.

Anja now recalled that Aunt Berni had said she would have weapons and armor. Could it be possible that they were here so soon? "What's in the bag, Aunt Berni?" she asked shrewdly.

"This?" Bernadette replied with a shrug. "Oh, nothing." Why don't we all go out to the yard?" she went on. Anja was far sharper than most people realized, and she smiled in anticipation. Something good was coming.

The three of them, led by Bernadette, walked over toward the archery butt that had been set up in the yard. "I think you should take off your shoes, Anja," Bernadette directed. "And pull your dress off over your head." Anja was taken aback. There was no one around, but this was still broad daylight and in full view of anybody with eyes to see. Observing Anja's hesitation, Bernadette said "Don't worry about it. If you're going to be a warrior, you need to be unafraid of anything. That includes people looking at you in your underwear."

Anja nodded, stuck out her chin, and stripped to her underwear. Above all, she was a survivor. Bernadette now began pulling items from the bag. She'd crafted a tailored set of leather armor in Anja's size, neatly fitted to the girl's childish contours. In addition there was a pair of leather boots, a little roomy so that that thick woolen socks could take up the slack. Anja donned them eagerly, and Lifa too was exclaiming at the beauty and utility of the armor. She'd enjoyed dressing Anja in ribbons and lace, but at heart she was a warrior and it delighted her to see her daughter wanting to follow in her footsteps.

Two more items emerged from the muslin sack: a child-size longbow, and a quiver of half-size arrows tipped with smooth, blunt steel caps. They would penetrate a target, barely, but would be unlikely to do much harm to a living being that was accidentally struck. Anja's eyes lit at the sight. "My own bow?! Thank you, Aunt Berni!" She wanted to take it and start shooting immediately, but Bernadette had become quite serious.

"This is a deadly weapon, Anja," The Fireblood said. "You must always respect it and use it with care. Do you understand?" Owl-eyed, Anja nodded. "First, I am going to show you how to string the bow. Bowstrings will stretch, and bows will lose their power over time while they are strung. So you only string your bow when you're going to use it soon. Here, hold it like this..."

Chapter 12: The Library, Year One

The library looked the same as it always had. Andrion felt sure that Mhyrzon must have a life outside this place, or at least must occasionally spend time in the stacks, rearranging the books, looking things up, *something*. But every time he'd seen the uruk, he'd been sitting either behind the desk or in a chair up against a nearby pillar. The latter, in this case.

The old librarian looked up as they came in, anticipation showing. "Andrion, you're back!" he said. "Did you find Mindhal and the books?"

Andrion dug them out of his pack and set them on the desk. "I'm afraid we had to kill him," he admitted. "He seemed to be leading a whole pack of renegade mages there. They had vampires locked in the dungeons and were doing some kind of experimentation on them."

"That kid always was interested in vampirism and the Netherworld," Mhyrzon said with a shrug. "We don't allow students to remove books from the library, as I'm sure you know. He was in here every day or two, studying what we had on those subjects."

Andrion considered that. "There is a connection, you know," he said. "The daimonic lord Haemion was the originator of the vampire contagion, according to my friend Nerissa. You remember her, from when we were here looking for books on religion?"

Again that fearsome smile. "She was quite a looker, as I recall," Mhyrzon remarked. Hmm, Andrion wondered. You'd think anybody without tusks and green skin wouldn't appeal to an uruk. But he supposed it took all kinds...

"She took the cure later," Andrion supplied. "Now she's not a vampire anymore, she's back with the Daywatch Brigade helping them in their fight against vampirism."

"All to the good, I suppose," the librarian replied; but Andrion sensed a hint of disappointment. Another elf with a thing for vampires?

"So what's the word on Gryndhaal?" Andrion asked. "I don't suppose Dalandrin just wandered back through the portal while I was gone?"

"Sorry, no," Mhyrzon said seriously. "Faramund has returned, and is acting as magister in Dalandrin's absence. They've got guards posted on the portal and the whole dig site locked down. But he's anxious for you to report back."

"I haven't had a chance to study these books yet," Andrion told him. "I'm thinking the one about Gryndhaal is likeliest to tell me what I'm trying to find out. But I'm anxious to spend some time with the other one too, once we get Dalandrin back. Don't let it get away again!"

He'd intended the comment in jest, but Mhyrzon glared at him and snatched the other two books off the desk top. "Erik, maybe you could see if you can find Faramund and tell him I'm here and working on the project. He's a really old Norseman, a little taller than Berni, with shoulder length gray hair and a short beard. Likely he'll be wearing mage robes."

"Sure, brother," the big man said with a grin. He went across the room and trotted down the stairs, and Andrion carried the massive book over to his favorite research table and pulled up a chair.

An hour later he was interrupted at his studies by Erik, the old mage in tow. "Ah, Andrion!" Faramund said. "Your young friend found me, and I had to speak with you. Have you found what you sought?" He gestured for the old man to take a seat.

"This book isn't as specific as I'd hoped," Andrion admitted. "But there is something here in *Day of Dread* that gives a hint about the portal."

He put his finger around halfway down the page and began to read, "*Then when ye alfarre had overrun the citadel, and ye defenders were driven down into ye catacoombes, dyd ye sorcerer Durendyn declare that he wode a mighty working make. And he dyd shut himself within ye lowest chambre, for a day and a night as ye alfarre battered at ye door. Yet they could not come through, for their bloode was not ye bloode of men.*"

"The language and spellings are so archaic, I believe this must be a contemporary account that's been accurately transcribed over the millennia," Andrion put in.

"The blood lock!" Faramund exclaimed. "It opened for you, but it might not have done so for Dalandrin!"

"Indeed," Andrion agreed. "I think that's also why the invading dypalfar were not able to get into the laboratory in Faastenberg."

He continued reading. "*Then came forth Durendyn from ye tombe, and with him came an army of daimons, who did set upon the foes. Ye invaders were driven from our city, but they had left it in ruins. We few who survived were too few to rebuild, and we fled west. But Durendyn came not with us. He and his daimonic allies returned to ye tombe, and as instructed we dyd lock ye doors behind them.*"

"The portal must lead to a plane of the Netherworld, then!" Faramund exclaimed in amazement. Andrion nodded.

"Yet Dalandrin seemed to think it would take him to someplace familiar," he said. "Did the magister have dealings with the Netherworld in the past?" The old man shook his head.

"Dalandrin is far older than I am," he said. "He has been magister of our Academy for more than a century, and it is said that once he was a student here. But this place has been operating for more than two thousand years. He appeared to be as old as he is now when I first came here as a young man."

Andrion noticed Faramund didn't say exactly when *that* had been, but it was undeniably true that the alfar had lifespans far longer than those of the races of men. Had he himself not met and spoken with some who had been around for more than a millennium? Come to think of it, if it had been four thousand years since the dypalfar had poisoned the leukalfar, Duraenis and his Apoldrian brethren must be still older than that. He shook his head in wonder.

"If Dalandrin visited this plane of the Netherworld before, he must have found the experience a pleasant one," Andrion reasoned aloud. Erik was leaning up against a bookcase with an air of relaxed contentment, his usual state when he was not in the midst of battle.

"It's true, he seemed if anything like he was anticipating a visit," Faramund replied. "I know little about the planes of the Netherworld, but I gather that not all of them are unpleasant."

"My readings have suggested that there are many planes, and that we refer to them collectively as 'The Netherworld' only because they are discontiguous from the plane in which our own universe resides," Andrion said. "But these other places are not necessarily in the same universe as each other. Some of them may just be little pocket universes of their own, encompassing only a small area, while others may be as large as our own. I believe that Tarragin's 'Ekelvelt,' as it was called, was an entire planet spinning around a sun in one such universe."

Faramund eyed the younger man thoughtfully, but had no comment. "In any case," Andrion went on, "whatever the nature of this other plane the portal leads to, we can assume that there was some good reason why Dalandrin failed to return from it. In that other book Mhyrzon had me retrieve, it mentioned that portals can be set to be one way only, or to be keyed so only one bearing an enchanted token can pass through."

"But we know this portal worked both ways," Faramund pointed out. "This ancient sorcerer, Durendyn, used it to bring forth daimonic allies. And as we didn't find their skeletons within the chamber, they must have gone back through it."

"You're right," Andrion replied. "But something might well have changed since Durendyn's day. Perhaps a daimon sorcerer on the far side of the portal changed the nature of it so it could not be used for transport back to our universe."

"It could be as simple as setting guards on the portal," Erik pointed out. Just when you thought it was all going over his head, the gigantic Norse warrior would surprise you. "Maybe old Dalandrin pops out, looks around, and the first native that sees him kills him on the spot." The other two men looked at him in consternation. "Aww, probably not," Erik said with a grin. "The guy's a powerful, ancient elf mage, right? Maybe they just barricaded the entrance."

"I think we need to go have another look at the portal," Andrion said. "But first, maybe a nap – and some breakfast?" The day was young, but neither of them had slept since night before last – nor had anything to eat in what seemed like a long, long time.

"There's some food in the student residence hall," Faramund said. "And you could bunk in your wife's room. As for your friend, I..." The beds in the dorm had never been intended for anyone the size of Erik. As a Norse mage, Faramund was an exception to the rule. Most of his race had relatively little talent for magic.

"I brought a bedroll," Erik told him cheerfully. "I can just toss it down on the floor next to the bed in Berni's room. But I *am* starving. Where's this food?" Faramund walked them over to the residence hall and showed them the dining room. The table was heaped with the kinds of foods young students like – fresh fruit, crackers, hard cheese – things that didn't need any preparation or cleanup. As the two young men sat to make a meal of this fare, washed down with some bottled ale, the old mage took his leave.

"Come see me," he said, "when you're ready to go to Gryndhaal."

Chapter 13: Gryndhaal, Year One

They entered the lower levels of the dig site after passing a pair of armed guards lent to the Academy by the Eorl of Icemarch. Another pair were on guard inside the portal's chamber, and one at the top of the stairs behind the door to the shortcut – which was once again locked from the inside.

Faramund hammered on the door. "Who is it? What do you want?" came a faint voice through the heavy stone panel.

"It's me, Faramund – acting magister of the Academy. Let me in!" There came a rumbling and creaking, and the door vanished up into the wall above it in response to the guard having pulled the chain suspended from the ceiling on the inside.

The guard, wearing a helmet that obscured his eyes and nose, looked to be barely old enough to shave. "Anything to report?" Faramund asked him.

"There's been nothing," the lad assured him. The three of them made their way down into the bowels of the tomb and a second door leading into the chamber. That one had been left open.

Two more faceless guards were seated at the room's small table, rolling dice. They hastily put their game away when the important-looking mage and his two well-armed companions came into the room. The portal looked exactly as it had when Andrion had first beheld it – probably the same way it had looked eight thousand years ago when Durendyn had created it.

The awesome power of the ancients' magic amazed Andrion, when he thought of it. For some reason – maybe the same one that had lured Dalandrin to go there – the mage had gone back into the portal with his daimonic allies, leaving this world for good. He had left that aptrgangr, which must have been created using his powers of necromancy, to guard it. And then Andrion, along with old Faramund, had blithely stumbled in and killed off the guardian – thus bringing an ancient peril back to life. Real smart.

"We need to do some experimentation on this thing, try to find out what's on the other side without just sending more people into it to become trapped," Andrion said.

"I could hold one of those guards by the feet and he could look around, then I could pull him out again," Erik suggested with an evil grin. The guards looked up at him anxiously.

Andrion quirked a half-smile. You needed to know Erik for a while before you could tell when he was kidding. And even then, it was still a good idea to be on his good side. "Why don't we try it with something inanimate first?" Faramund suggested hastily. He'd assembled a pack with whatever useful items he could think of bringing while his two volunteers had been catching some sleep.

He now set the pack on the floor and pulled out a coil of silken rope. Then he tied one end of it to a steel dagger, and swung it out over the portal. The dagger and the length of rope attached to it vanished, the rope severed at the spot where it crossed the portal's border. The cut was perfectly clean – just like it had been on the torso of that demon Andrion and Erik had seen in Sindrendell. The thought of that caused Andrion's stomach to turn upside down, and he was glad their meal had been a few hours ago.

"I think it's safe to say holding one of the guards upside down would be a bad idea," he said.

"Okay…" Erik said. And then he stepped onto the portal and vanished. Shit!

"Erik, you idiot! Come back!" Andrion shouted. Oh no, oh no. What was he going to tell Berni? What…

"It's kind of dark in there," Erik reported, stepping back into the room."

Andrion seized the larger man in both arms, crushing him to his chest – despite the fact they were both wearing armor. "You big ox, I thought I was never going to see you again!" he gasped. Then he held him out at arm's length, making sure they were well away from the portal. "Well, what's over there?" he asked.

"It's a kind of small room," Erik said. "I think that sometime in the last few thousand years the people over there in the Netherworld have built a protective housing around the portal. There's no light, but the portal casts a pretty good glow. The walls are black, and featureless, and there's a heavy iron door in one wall with some kind of big lock on it. I didn't have any lockpicks with me, and I didn't want to get my axe all dinged up chopping through the walls.

Besides, I didn't want you to worry…" he brushed Andrion's chin with one ham-like fist in a gesture of affection, smiling into his eyes.

Andrion grinned back at him. "I think we can guess why Dalandrin hasn't returned," he said to Faramund. "I'm assuming a mage of his caliber wouldn't have had any trouble at all unlocking that door. Then he steps out, and somebody sees to it he can't return. But at least we know that the portal still works from that side. Erik and I are going to have to go in there, but first we need to pick up a few things. Do you have any spellbooks I can borrow?"

Back at the Academy, Faramund ushered them into the Magister's Quarters. If Dalandrin had been magister here since Faramund was a youth, this apartment must reflect his own personality even if the apartment *was* the property of the Academy and a perk offered to its head wizard. The furnishings were comfortable if spare, and the place was very clean and uncluttered.

There was, Andrion saw with pleasure, a very large bookcase. Some of the books were histories of magic or biographies of famous mages, and there were even a few of the sorts of book people read for entertainment. But there was also the largest collection of spellbooks he had ever seen together in one place.

These books were rare and valuable, items enchanted to magically teach a spell to anyone who read them – provided they had any magical ability at all. An experienced mage like Andrion could usually learn a spell just by being close by as another mage was casting it – though he'd been unable to do that with the spell Mindhal had been casting when Erik had killed him. But learning in this way was a matter of fine skill, whereas almost anyone could be taught a spell by a spellbook. Once the book had been enchanted, the knowing of the spell would burrow its way into the mind of any who opened the book. The book's power would wear out over time and repeated uses, but could be recharged with magical essences at need.

Andrion's early training had seen him in good stead for years, as the spells he'd learned from his master in Auverne were honed and practiced. But except for his recent acquisition of the same minor healing spell Berni had, he had not picked up any new spells in a long time. Now, he was like a kid in a candy store – the way Berni had been, he realized, when they had camped overnight in the laboratory in Faastenberg and she had learned every dragon spell the Edelmied could provide.

He learned unlock, explosive burst, short sleep, a fire spell that burned black and consumed without creating heat, a faster healing spell, a spell that would let him draw objects to him from a distance, and one that silenced his footsteps. Soon his mind was reeling, and he felt more tired than he had been since that day they'd spent searching for the fourth shrine in the Eparchy. It was a good thing he'd been sitting down.

"Oof," Andrion said, leaning back in the chair with his arms dropped on either side. "I think that had probably better be it for today."

"Take a stamina potion," Erik suggested, handing him one from his pack. Andrion did, and immediately felt a lot better. But though he no longer felt as if he were ready to faint, he could tell that he needed a meal and a good night's sleep before he was going to be back to normal again. And he knew where he wanted to get it.

Andrion got to his feet. To Faramund, he said "Erik and I will gear up and be ready for a rescue expedition beyond the portal when we get back. But we promised our wife we would check in with her. We need to go home first." The old man eyed him questioningly.

"Did you say 'our' wife?" he asked, eyebrows raised.

"It's a long story," Erik replied. "We'll tell you after we get back."

Chapter 14: Drakespring Farm, Year One

This morning, Bernadette awoke in Andrion's bed. Just as she often went back and forth between her two lovers' beds before they'd married, she'd moved from Erik's bed to this one – wanting the chance to be close with Andrion in his absence, inhaling his scent from the sheets and soaking up the ambience of the room he'd made uniquely his. Already the built-in bookshelves were beginning to fill with books, on a wide range of subjects.

Yawning and stretching, Bernadette slipped out of bed and put on a robe, taking a moment to straighten up the bedclothes before padding down the hall to the bathroom. The wooden hall floor was mostly covered with a series of tanned furs and area rugs, the latter bought from Gatti traders while the former were her own manufacture. She used the privy then slipped into the hot tub, taking only a brief bath before getting out. She'd brought some clothes with her to Andrion's room to put on this morning, not wanting to disturb the Steadfasts in the master bedroom.

She'd become completely caught up in the project of outfitting Anja as a warrior maiden yesterday, and had forgotten all about her intent to take that wheelbarrow-load of arms and armor into Waterdon. Now Bernadette was anxious to be up and ready to go early, so she could get Bjorn's help in pushing it into town (read: have him push it while she walked along beside him).

Bernadette brought the cookfire back to life and put a kettle on, preparing two pots – one with her special tea for morning sickness and the other a popular flavored tea with aromatic spices and dried flowers in it. Bjorn soon joined her in the kitchen, dressed in his workman's garb. His job with Hegmar's construction company was more supervisory, drawing plans and making sure they were followed on site; but he was large and strong and was often called on to lend a hand with the actual construction.

Bernadette toasted some thin slices of stale bread for herself to munch with the tea, meanwhile starting a good-sized kettle of whole-grain porridge with dried apples and sweet spices in it. She was thinking about going down to the Maiden sometime today to confer with Lev, and maybe arranging for some of the Maiden's baked goods to be delivered to them tomorrow morning. She didn't mind cooking most times, but was finding it hard to get into the spirit of it first thing in the morning when her stomach was in rebellion.

As Bjorn was sitting down to a hearty bowl of porridge, and Bernadette spotted Lifa and Anja now up and heading for the bathroom, she sat sipping her tea and said "Bjorn, you're working up in town today, right?" He looked up at her, his one eye inquiring. "I was wondering if you'd mind helping me take some things up to Valkyrie," Bernadette continued. "I don't want to strain myself pushing the wheelbarrow up that hill in my… delicate condition."

Bjorn's face broke into a grin. He wasn't in the least bit fooled. The day The Fireblood turned into a delicate flower was the day he'd start going around in pink dresses. But she was their benefactress, the person who had made his new life with his loved ones possible, and he was more than happy to do anything in his power to help her. "Sure, I'll be your beast of burden," he rumbled. "A wheelbarrow, did you say?" She nodded, smiling back.

Bernadette took care of feeding the cow and milking her before time to leave. Lifa and Anja joined them for tea and porridge just as Bernadette and Bjorn were getting ready to leave. She'd offered to pack him a lunch, but he now made more than enough money to afford patronizing The Flying Horseman at noontime, usually in company with some of his colleagues. "Ladies, I'll be back probably early this afternoon," Bernadette told them. "Anja, could I get you to help feed the chickens and collect eggs?"

Anja's eyes lit up. This was a favorite chore of hers. She loved the way the excited, slightly musty-smelling birds clustered around eagerly when she tossed them grain; and plucking warm eggs from the nests (while the hens were elsewhere, of course – broody hens were left alone to incubate their clutches) was almost like finding hidden treasure. "Sure!" she said. "Can I practice my archery, too?"

Bernadette exchanged glances with Lifa. "Be sure you're wearing your leathers," Bernadette told Anja. "If you don't have protection on your arms you'll get very sore. But I'm sure your mama can show you how to shoot just as well as I can." Lifa had preferred using sword and shield during her time as a warrior, but she was no stranger to the bow.

Hugs and kisses were exchanged at the door, then Bjorn fetched the barrow from the cistern tower and the two of them set off up the road toward Waterdon. The morning was cool for this time of year, and Bernadette was comfortable in the light leather armor she'd chosen to wear today. It didn't provide all that much protection, but it was comfortable and form-fitting and not at all bad-looking. She enjoyed looking feminine and lovely on occasion, but in this outfit she felt… competent. Fortunately, her form could still fit into it. It occurred to her that soon she was going to have to get Gerde to sew her some maternity clothes.

Bernadette had strung her bow and carried it with her, ready in case they were attacked. Shria were the most frequent threat, but she had seen wolves here occasionally and once a misguided smilodon had mistaken her for lunch. Today, the hostile wildlife was on holiday and the pair made it up through the gates of the city without incident. Bjorn was hardly even breathing hard as he pushed the wheelbarrow up the hill.

He dropped her and the barrow-load of arms and armor off near the front door of Valkyrie, and she hugged him in thanks; then he continued on his way up the hill. Hegmar's crew was involved in adding another story to one of the homes in the upper city, their last job in town before they started on the new wing for the Maiden.

It was early yet, not yet business hours, but Bernadette knew Wolaf and Alessia would be up. She pounded on the locked door, calling "Alessia!" until it rattled and her friend stood there on the other side, wearing her smithing gear and drinking a cup of tea.

She smiled wryly. "Oh, it's just you. I thought maybe there was a vampire attack."

"Brought the stuff as promised," Bernadette said – grunting slightly as she lifted the wheelbarrow up off its legs and pushed it into the shop. Alessia's eyes lit at the sight. Going into partnership with The Fireblood had proven to be a very profitable move for them, to the point where she and Wolaf were now thinking of trying to start a family. They'd been married for years, but she'd been working so much she'd been afraid they'd go broke if she took time off for childbearing. Now, though…

Exercise and fresh air had eased Bernadette's nausea, so she took Alessia up on the offer to share their breakfast. The couple lived in small quarters on the second floor above the shop. They chatted for a while, Bernadette once again avoiding mention of her pregnancy. Then Wolaf got out the books and recorded the items she'd brought in. "Be sure to let me know if you come into any daimon blood," Bernadette asked him. She was going to run out of her supply soon, faster if she spent more time at home crafting and none out questing.

Bernadette bid her friends good day and went on a few errands around town, selling some items at Bernard's and picking up some more of the tea herbs at Adele's. She put in a request for daimon blood there, as well. Adele would be delighted to turn over such a high-ticket item if she got the chance. The stuff was hard to come by.

She walked up to the Snowhairs' clan house and consulted with Gerde, swearing her to secrecy. Alas, she feared the news might soon be all over Waterdon. After that she returned down the hill, collecting her wheelbarrow on the way. She dropped the barrow off at Drakespring Farm but then continued on to the Maiden. Lev (or rather, his kitchen help) had started baking bread at two-hour intervals from four in the morning until six in the evening each day, and she picked up a basket of fresh loaves.

They discussed the new wing, and the preparations being made for it. The field to the south of the Maiden was being mown and leveled (fortunately there'd been no need to drive off or kill any triceratops, this time) and tomorrow a crew would arrive to take down the tent and relocate it. That should leave the land on which the new wing would rise ready for construction to begin. Andrion had suggested using a sewage system similar to that at their farm, but it seemed impractical for such a large establishment. They'd be going with the usual outdoor privies, and chamberpots in the rooms.

There were plans, however, for another hot pool identical to the one in the Maiden's main building. Messages had been sent to Diane, who had announced that she was nearing completion on a hot pool for Daywatch, and when construction was further along she'd be coming to visit and work on the water system. Andrion would help, as well.

At Lev's insistence the new wing, like the annex at Drakespring Farm, would have a full stone-lined cellar. Within that cellar it would also have a series of specially-constructed cold rooms for storing food and hanging meat. The inn's food business had grown enormously despite its out-of-the-way location. Since Waterdon's population was on the rise and the only other places to get food away from home were the Horseman and the Pickled Eel, it was not surprising.

After arranging a delivery of fresh-baked sweet rolls for the morning (sure to be a hit with Anja, she thought), Bernadette took her basket of bread and headed for home. She was there in plenty of time to prepare lunch for the three of them, the warm loaves forming a major component of the meal. They passed the rest of the afternoon pleasantly, playing games and performing small tasks.

Lifa took over the cooking for the evening meal, and it wasn't until an hour or more after they'd finished eating and Anja had been tucked into bed, that they heard a step at the door. Bjorn and Lifa were sitting across from one another at the dining table, talking quietly, and Bernadette was reading by lamplight at the room's other small table.

The door was locked for the evening, and when Bernadette heard a key turn her heart soared with joy. They were back! She jumped to her feet and nearly bowled Andrion over (despite that he was eight inches taller than she was, and considerably heavier) as he came in the door. The men were both armored and she'd changed into a comfortable skirt and blouse before supper, so she couldn't really hug them all that well; but she tried.

Lifa and Bjorn stood and greeted the masters of the house, put slightly ill at ease by the realization that they and their daughter were occupying the trio's bed. "Oh!" Bjorn said, "We didn't know you'd be getting back tonight. Anja's already asleep in there." Erik considered. They could scarcely boot their friends back to Waterdon in the middle of the night, besides which he expected he and Andrion would be leaving again soon. The Steadfasts might as well continue to occupy the master bedroom for a while longer.

"We've both got our own beds, and Berni can sleep with one of us," Erik told Bjorn. "You and Lifa and Anja should just stay where you are. I suppose we'll be going back to Gryndhaal pretty soon?" he added, looking to Andrion for confirmation.

"We're committed now," his brother said with a hint of regret. He was beginning to wish he had never gotten them into this mess. Sure, he and Erik together were nigh-on unstoppable. But what if the unthinkable happened, and their pregnant bride was left without them? He tried not to think about it.

The Steadfasts were all looking at Andrion and Erik in puzzlement, though Bernadette knew what they were talking about. "I think Erik and I need to get out of this armor and take a bath," Andrion said. "Then we'll explain the whole story." Bjorn and Lifa nodded, and resumed their seats at the table. But Bernadette chased them down the hall. She peeled off at Erik's room, it being the nearer, while Andrion continued on past the master bedroom to his own space.

Erik was pleased to see Berni had followed him inside. But he was tired, hungry, and grungy. They hadn't had a real meal, a bath, or more than a brief rest since leaving home – however many days ago that was in real time. He suspected she could smell him from across the room, as he peeled off his armor. It didn't seem to deter her any. Shortly he was naked. And, no surprises, his cock was on the rise.

Sometimes Erik felt like he was fifteen again, when he was around this enchanting woman he had stood up with and promised to spend the rest of his life loving. Even after the better part of a year, when they were together his libido seemed to have a mind of its own – despite a lack of sleep and food. He grinned. He had no idea what it was, but he had to admit he enjoyed it.

Bernadette grinned back at him. Erik never failed to delight her. But despite his enormous physical resources, she could sense that he was in need of some things. Besides her cunt, that is, though he appeared as if he might be ready to give her, right now, what she so very much wanted. "I really just wanted the opportunity to hug you properly," she said, stepping close and pressing herself against him.

They stood clasped together for a moment, a shot of passion running through Erik that caused him to seize her with unusual force and run his tongue into her mouth. His cock stiffened more. Oh yes, tired he might be – but not *that* tired. After a few moments of the embrace they pulled apart slightly, panting. "Oh, Erik!" Bernadette breathed. That near-magical lust connection between them ebbed and flowed, but it had definitely not gone away despite months of marriage.

Bernadette got a grip on herself. She was horny, and Erik was right here and naked… and rampant. But she could see that he was also tired and hungry, and smell that he was, truly, in need of a bath. "Love, I think you'd better take that bath and then have some food. We'll have time together later – I promise." Erik just held her to him. How incredibly lucky he was, he thought, to have stumbled into a life with this woman beside him! And with Andrion as a friend and brother, as well.

"I love you," he murmured gruffly. Then he broke from the embrace and grabbed his robe from the hook where it usually hung.

"I think I'm going to join you two in the tub," Bernadette said. As at the Maiden, there were robes scattered all over the place in the Drakespring household. Bernadette pulled one from another hook, and in moments had shed her clothing and put it on. Erik, whose cock had been subsiding, got another boost as she undressed. Was it his imagination, or were her breasts getting bigger?

They met Andrion in the hall, and the three of them went quietly to the bathroom. They didn't want to wake Anja, presumably now fast asleep in their enormous bed. Hanging their robes on hooks, the three of them slipped into the hot water. Bernadette sat beside Andrion and put her arms around him, sighing pleasurably.

"I'm so glad you decided to stop in for a visit," she said. He turned and kissed her, having missed out a bit earlier. "And I'm glad you and Diane were able to create this tub!" Bernadette added. The work her two lovers had done to create their dream home as a surprise for her on their wedding night still amazed her. And to think she'd been oblivious to their activities, so wrapped up in plans for her own and Lifa's weddings that she'd never noticed their skullduggery!

After Bernadette and Andrion had had a chance to embrace properly and kiss, they sat back and just enjoyed the hot water for a little while. "I'm saving my tale of terror for after the bath," Andrion reminded her, "so tell me what you've been up to while we were gone."

"Oh, nothing much," Bernadette replied smiling. "Barfed a few times, sold a bunch of arms and armor. Let's see… Looks like Hegmar and his crew are almost ready to start on the Maiden addition… and Anja has become a warrior princess."

Andrion and Erik both looked at her questioningly. "You know that Bjorn and Lifa have been telling Anja about their adventures as warriors all along, right? Well, he made her a picture book featuring the adventures of The Fireblood and her valiant knights. So now instead of frills and lace she wants to wear armor and kill bad guys."

"Valiant knights, huh?" Erik rumbled, smiling. "Aren't knights supposed to be mounted on horses?"

Bernadette considered. "I believe you're right. But in Bjorn's picture book you two are just armed and armored. No horses in it. It's pretty accurate, actually. I wish we could get it published – it's closer to the truth than some of the stories I've been hearing." The three sat soaking and musing for a little while. "Anyhow," Bernadette went on, "I crafted a set of leather armor in her size and a little bow with some blunt arrows so she can practice archery. She's really getting into it."

The three lapsed into silence again, then Andrion said "Our little girl is growing up. Well, I'm starving! I hope there's something to eat?" Bernadette smiled.

"There's plenty of somewhat-fresh bread, and there's some cooked meat in the cooler. Lots of cheese, and some greens too. I think we can come up with something. Shall we?"

The three of them climbed out and toweled off, then slipped on their robes. They'd brought along soft slippers as well, so they didn't need to go get dressed. Lifa and Bjorn made way for Andrion and Erik at the table, as Bernadette (still robed) pulled some bottles of ale out of the cooler and passed them to her hungry husbands. With a frost staff on hand, they could have cold drinks without a mage around, in a pinch.

Erik and Andrion attacked the ales with enthusiasm, chatting with the Steadfasts, as Bernadette bustled around the clean kitchen putting together plates of sandwiches with cold meat and cheese, and some salads on the side. There were even a few potato chips to be had. For a while, conversation ground almost to a halt as the two adventurers tucked into their meals. Andrion could not actually recall when they'd last eaten – was it breakfast yesterday? They'd been fast-traveling so much they'd lost count.

Finally, the gnawing hunger satisfied, the two began telling their wife and friends about the quest: the hostile mages and their eerily powerful leader at Sindrendell, with their evil experimentation; Andrion's discoveries in the books they'd found. And finally, learning that the portal went both ways but had been contained by some kind of a structure on the far side – in one of the planes of the Netherworld.

The five of them discussed the situation. Both Lifa and Bjorn wished they could help, as did Bernadette. But they all had other responsibilities that held them back. Finally, they decided they'd all better get to bed. Bernadette walked with her two men down the hall. She locked Andrion in an embrace and kissed him deeply. "I'm going to sleep with Erik tonight," she told him. "But I'll see you in the morning!" He smiled tiredly and kissed her back most thoroughly. Falling into a deep and dreamless sleep right now seemed like a really good idea.

He continued down the hall with Lifa and Bjorn, who turned off at the master bedroom. Meanwhile Bernadette and Erik entered Erik's space. There were no books here, but the bed had acquired a plush coverlet and shelves were dotted with little handicrafts he had made. Plus, over in one corner, there was a fencing dummy. He used it to get a workout for a few minutes most days, when he was home.

Chapter 15: Erik's Room, Year One

They turned to face one another, so glad in one another's presence that for a moment all they could do was smile into each other's eyes. The fact that Erik had taken it upon himself to test his personal theory about the portal by stepping into it had not come up in their discussion, otherwise he would likely have now been getting the ass-chewing of his life.

Bernadette dropped her robe to the floor and held out her arms. Erik did the same, and he stepped to enfold her in his. His cock was rigid, pressed up against her midsection as he hugged her close. Kissing the top of her head, he spoke into her hair: "I was worried about leaving you alone. How stupid is that?"

She lifted her face up to kiss him. "It's not stupid, Erik, it's sweet. Well, maybe a little premature. Promise you won't leave me when I start walking like a duck, okay?" He smiled at the mental picture of his lithe young wife waddling around, looking like she was smuggling a lute under her dress. "Don't worry," she went on, "it'll be months yet. And in the meantime, I'm more or less myself. Sure wish I could eat a hearty breakfast, though. Most mornings I can hardly choke down the toast, and then I'm starving before lunchtime."

Breaking from the clinch Erik took Berni's hand and led her over to the bed. They sat down on the end of it. This was a bit bigger than the average Iscandia double bed, to accommodate Erik's unusual height. But it was still miniscule compared with the one in the room next door, which the Steadfast clan were sharing at the moment. "C'mere," Erik said, and gently pulled Berni up into his lap, her legs crossing his. This raised her up to a height where they could kiss and fondle each other without either of them getting a crick in the neck.

They sat there necking for a few minutes, lost in the pleasure of each other's bodies. Erik's member was beginning to throb, though, and he really wanted to sheath it. Bernadette, attuned to him after nearly a year of being his lover, sensed his growing urgency and rotated around so she was now straddling him, face to face. Her crotch pinned that hungry cock between them, and she began sliding up and down slowly, slicking the shaft with juices from her slit. Then he grasped her buttocks and lifted her a little higher, so she could slip right down over him. Aaah!

Bernadette's eyes closed and she moaned as Erik filled her. So big! He helped her move up and down on him, and in moments she felt that familiar sensation growing where the two of them were joined. Yes! Pumping faster and faster, she gave a muffled scream as her orgasm swept over her. Erik held her firmly as she vibrated and spasmed, then with an effort of his powerful muscles he stood, still clasping her by the buttocks, and rotated around so she now had her back to the bed. He leaned forward enough to lay her down on it without pulling out, kneeling and scooting them both along toward the head of the bed so he could make love to her in this new position.

The bath, the meal, and the chance to have Berni in his bed, all to himself, had energized Erik. The sexual tension created by their triad relationship kept him always hungry for just a little more. But as she wrapped her legs around his hips and he began thrusting into her, he realized that he was running on borrowed stamina. He decided to let himself ride the sensations to a quick climax, much as he would have liked to prolong it. All he had to do, really, was disconnect his mind and let his body, and his passion, take him away. In moments they were both exploding in mutual ecstasy; then gasping and panting, hearts pounding, they lay flat on the bed.

Erik quickly rolled them over onto their sides, Berni's bottom leg dropping down while the top one remained wrapped around his body as she continued to clench him inside her. He realized that, in months to come, they'd be needing to use some positions that wouldn't put any of his weight on her. Well, he knew one she liked a lot that should be good for right up to delivery day. He wrapped his arms around her and squeezed her close. "My love," he rumbled softly.

Bernadette lay in Erik's arms in a state of bliss. Being with him brought her such joy, and the longer she knew him the more she discovered to love about him – even after their wedding. She hoped Andrion wasn't feeling too lonely all by himself down the hall; but she felt as if this quest that had taken them away just as she learned of her pregnancy had been generated by a need *he* had for something beyond the love they shared – some public recognition.

For the most part, Bernadette enjoyed her fame and the perks it brought her. But it wasn't something she would necessarily have sought. When she'd left Auverne seeking her fortune, it had been more for gold, adventure, and the opportunities for hot sex with men like Erik and Andrion. The world-shaking destiny and special powers of The Fireblood were just a side benefit, as far as she was concerned. But she could understand how Andrion, a serious and smart man a decade older than she was, might feel the need to be accorded respect of his own instead of riding on his wife's coattails.

In any case, she wasn't punishing Andrion for running off on her by choosing to spend the night with Erik. She just figured that the quest he was embarked on might provide him with a little compensation for not being the one chosen. Erik didn't (at least at this stage of his life, in his mid-20s) seem to be hankering after personal fame. He'd accompanied Andrion because Andrion asked for his help, because they were brothers, and because he enjoyed that sort of thing.

Erik softened and slipped out. Reaching for one of the small towels they kept around the place to blot up the mess, Bernadette was surprised to find that he had dozed off. Poor baby, she'd had no idea he was so tired. She roused him gently with kisses on his face and suggested they might want to crawl between the sheets. Moments after they did, they were both asleep.

Chapter 16: Drakespring Farm, Year One

Bernadette woke at what, judging from the lack of any sunlight coming through the cracks in the shutters, must be a little before dawn. She needed to pee. Oh, she thought. Was this going to be something else she had to look forward to – getting up in the middle of the night to empty a shrinking bladder? Probably. How wonderful they had that flush privy right across the hall.

After urinating Bernadette returned to the bed and Erik's arms, but her mind had awakened and she couldn't go back to sleep. Erik stirred a bit and snuggled her to him, kissing her forehead. "Sweetheart?" she murmured. "I think I'm going to wake Andrion up. You two are going to want an early start, aren't you?" Erik had now come awake enough to consider this. She had a point – Andrion was notoriously hard to shift, most mornings. And no doubt Berni wanted to get in a few licks with him as well before he escaped her grasp again.

Putting on her robe, Bernadette moved silently down the corridor and let herself into Andrion's room. After she'd gone Erik lay there for a few minutes under the covers, looking up at the ceiling. What would it be like with a mirror up there, he wondered idly? Then, grinning to himself, he got up and began getting dressed. It looked like today would be another day for armor.

Dropping her robe, Bernadette slipped into bed with Andrion. She was pleased that he had, for the most part, adopted her habit of sleeping in the nude even when she was not sleeping with him. It made things so much more… convenient. He could be fun to play with in the mornings, sometimes. That fine mind of his took quite a while to wake up, and in the meantime you could convince him of almost anything.

Snuggling into his shoulder where he slept on his back, snoring softly, Bernadette stroked one hand down his firmly muscled torso and murmured close to his ear, "Did you sleep well, darling?" That got his attention. He opened one eye blearily. "Berni?" he asked hesitantly. He was pretty sure he'd been sleeping alone, last time he looked. Had he missed something?

Her proximity and the fact it was morning both had him on the rise. Bernadette's stroking hand went lower and gripped him where he lay stiffening. "Ooh," she purred, "are you ready for some more already?" Andrion woke up a little more. Oho, he was onto her little tricks. They hadn't made love in days. He could tell by the pressure in his groin, even if his memory wasn't reliable. But he decided to play along.

"After all the sex we had last night?" he asked, stroking her body. "Well, I suppose I *might* be able to go another round…" Bernadette gave him a discerning look. She loved it when Andrion, who could be so overly serious at times, got playful or even whimsical. She felt sure it was going to make him a good father. But she, too, played along.

"Wait a minute, mister," she said sternly, gripping his cock a little harder. "I just got here. So *who* did you have 'all that sex' with, huh?"

Andrion looked at her in wide-eyed innocence. "That wasn't you?" he asked as if horrified. "But she looked just *like* you… well, of course it *was* dark…" he trailed off. They both grinned like idiots and began laughing, rolling around in the bed and engaging in a tickle fight. At some point this went from hilarity to passion, and as they lay on their sides facing one another Andrion kissed Bernadette fiercely, even as she threw a leg up over his hip and guided his throbbing cock into her depths.

Andrion moaned, loving the sensation of being engulfed by her warm wetness. Preparing to thrust deeper, he squeezed her breasts as he had done a hundred times before – and Bernadette flinched and said "Ouch!" He released her immediately, his cock still deeply embedded in her cunt, and looked into her face with concern.

"Berni? Are you all right?"

Thrusting her pelvis toward him, beginning to work in and out, Bernadette had to recall that both her husbands were neophytes when it came to pregnant ladies. "I forgot to mention it to you, love, but right now my breasts are a little achy and extra sensitive," she told him. Oh.

"Can I still touch them?" Andrion asked hopefully.

"Very gently, please, and no firm squeezing, okay?" He grinned at her. A miracle was happening before his eyes, and perhaps he was the cause of it. High time he learned a little more.

After making love to Berni in this on-the-side position for a while, Andrion pulled out. His cock was quivering, glistening with her juices and pink from the friction. Berni looked a little disappointed to see it leave. He sat up, pushing the covers to the foot of the bed, and smiled down at her lovingly. "Just lie back for a moment, dear," he said. "I want to do some experimentation."

That was Andrion. She half expected him to be jotting down information in his notebook. Bernadette obediently lay flat on her back atop the bed, her legs slightly spread, as Andrion knelt to caress her breasts very gently. He cupped them in his hands, then ran his tongue around each nipple until it rose, before suckling gently. A jolt of unbelievable sensation ran through Bernadette at this. It might hurt to have her breasts squeezed right now, but this felt… amazing!

While lightly sucking on one nipple and running his tongue around it, Andrion reached down between her legs with his other hand and inserted a couple of fingers. "Oh! Oh yes!" she cried (trying to keep it down a bit), bucking beneath his hand. Andrion felt a warm gush of fluids surround his fingers as she shuddered. His cock was beginning to feel really lonely hanging out there by itself, so he released Berni's breast and lifted her gently by a shoulder, rolling her over on her side so she was facing away from him. Then he lay down beside her and reinserted his cock into her from behind.

Ah, back in the saddle! He thrust into her like this for a while, then they rolled over another quarter turn so she was face down on the bed. She got her knees under her and he knelt behind her, fucking her like a stallion with a mare. Yes! Berni's vaginal walls clamped down on him with each thrust as he pounded into her harder and faster, until his quivering cock erupted in a gush of semen – filling her as she spasmed again, coming one more time.

More towels were employed, and they lay there atop the bottom sheet in the afterglow for a couple of minutes. "What are you going to do when you get to the other side of the portal?" Berni murmured quietly.

"Unlock the door and do some reconnaissance, for starters," Andrion explained as quietly. "We suspect that Dalandrin was taken prisoner when he came through, but he was going in without any precautions. I think he expected to be visiting a familiar, non-threatening place. We'll be on the alert, so we should be all right."

Bernadette sat up in the bed, throwing an arm across her forehead to wipe away perspiration. "You two had damn well *better* be all right," she said with suppressed ferocity. "If you're not back in a week, I'll be coming after you. Even if I have to walk all the way to Gryndhaal. Even if it means I lose this baby. I refuse to lose you, and I refuse to lose Erik. Do you hear me?"

Stricken, Andrion came up into a sitting position and took her face in his hands. "Berni, don't even say that. We will be fine, I swear it. But if we're delayed for some reason, don't do anything foolish. You have Lifa and Bjorn for support, and you're safe here." She threw her arms around his neck and buried her face in his shoulder, tears running down her face as she gasped and sobbed. Then as quickly, she pulled herself together again.

Sitting back and wiping her eyes, Bernadette smiled ruefully. "Don't mind me," she choked out. "It's the hormones. Pregnant ladies just have a hard time getting a grip on their emotions." Andrion reached for her again and hugged her, kissed her forehead.

"You'll be all right, and so will we," he promised. As he swung out of bed he thought to himself please gods, let it be true.

"I'm going to take a bath," Bernadette announced next. She was feeling more than a little sticky. "But Andrion, here's the thing… You and Erik take as long as you need to fulfill your quest. But will you for Marmira's sake remember to eat, drink, and sleep while you're doing it?" He looked at her shamefaced. He had been driving Erik and himself a little hard there, but one thing just led to another and there hadn't been that many opportunities for sleep.

"We'll bring along bedrolls and plenty of trail food and water – don't worry, love," he said.

Giving him a kiss and hug, Bernadette went on her way to the bathroom and had a short bath. When she emerged and had put on her leathers again (she found this outfit not a bad one for doing farm chores in, as well as for any situation where light fighting might become a possibility), a marvelous smell was coming from the direction of the kitchen. She entered to find Andrion and the entire Steadfast clan at the table, eating warm sweet rolls from a large basket of them. Erik was standing at the cookfire, cooking bacon in a large frypan to the accompaniment of loud sizzling noises and a smoky, savory smell. He turned around to greet her as she walked in. "Care package from the Maiden," he called cheerfully.

Bernadette surveyed the feast. "I asked Lev to send down some sweet rolls this morning, but what's all this other stuff?" she asked. There were fresh bread loaves, fresh fruit, a couple of apple pies, flaky pastries… and that heavenly bacon. Drakespring farm didn't keep hogs, in fact there were few enough of them in the Waterdon area – and no smokehouses that she knew about.

Bernadette was dying to have some, it smelled so wonderful – but she was also afraid that a bite of the rich, unfamiliar food might send her running to the privy. At least there was fresh bread this morning, which was nice. Erik pulled the frypan off the cooking rack and set it on a carved wooden hot pad on the counter, forking the pieces of cooked bacon out onto a folded, clean towel. It was a little fatty, and there was a bit of fat residue in the pan; but it wasn't too bad. Maybe she'd just try a nibble. Erik soon put another few slices of the bacon into the pan and stuck it back on the fire, before putting a plate of cooked slices on the table.

Everyone was digging in with enthusiasm, and exclaiming about the treat. Bernadette was in agony. Finally she decided that she'd proceed judiciously. She quartered an apple and peeled it with a small kitchen knife, and put one of the quarters on her plate. She took a bread roll and halved it, lightly glazing the halves with a small amount of butter. She had her cup of "special tea" and had already begun sipping it, and she really seemed to be feeling all right this morning. Maybe all that exercise last night and again this morning had had some effect on whatever chemicals her body was producing.

Finally, she broke one of the crispy slices in half and put it to her mouth, nibbling carefully. It was amazing: crispy, meaty, a little bit sweet, a little bit salty, somewhat smoky. It tasted like More. But first she had another sip of tea and nibbled her apple quarter, had a few bites of the bread. So far, her tummy was raising no complaints. Eventually she ate the entire bread roll, the rest of the apple, and two full slices of the bacon. And felt quite happy afterward. A victory almost as heartwarming as the defeat of Tarragin!

Bernadette was feeling so delighted at having had a delicious, satisfying breakfast with no ill effects that she amused herself by wondering whether Erik and Andrion would mind if she also married Lev. He was a pretty good-looking guy under that frumpy innkeeper garb, and though Drelos and Larissa were now an item Lev had remained firmly single. Possibly too busy for romance, with all that he got done every day. His talents were beyond price, and she really wanted some way to make sure he didn't get away from them.

She smiled inwardly and decided she would not broach the subject with the guys. Erik might laugh, but she was uncertain whether Andrion would appreciate such teasing. After the bacon had all been cooked and devoured Erik drained the fat into a bowl. It would be good for sautéing veggies in, or as a flavoring ingredient. The pan he scrubbed out with hot water, no soap, then set it back on the fire to dry. That was all the cooking that had been done this morning, so all that remained was for them to gather up the uneaten items (of which there were quite a few – what, had Lev thought she was feeding an army?) and wash the plates.

"I'll take care of the rest of the breakfast things," Lifa told Erik firmly. "Thank you for cooking for us." Erik had cooked supper for the Steadfasts at Brightsgate Cottage, before they had become the Steadfasts, on several occasions. He stepped close and kissed Lifa, who was several inches taller than Bernadette, on the cheek. He got in a little rub on her protruding belly while he was at it. Lifa blushed, smiled, and slapped Erik's hand. "Fresh!" Turning to Bernadette as she gathered plates for the trip to the sink, the voluptuous woman added "Just wait until you're out to here. Everybody and their uncle will want to rub your belly."

Bernadette grinned at her, saying "I think it's supposed to be good luck."

The two Valiant Knights, now well fed and rested, began gathering their gear. "Berni, do you mind if we take along some of this surplus food?" Andrion asked.

"No please, take all of it if you want," she replied. "I can get more by walking down to the Maiden, and the gods know where you're going to find anything to eat walking around in the Netherworld."

They both made sure their magical weapons were fully charged from the assortment of filled vials of magical essence in the craft room. Thoroughly armed and armored, well stocked with food and water, bedrolls in their packs, they determined they were ready to leave. In the meantime, Bjorn had taken his leave of them and gone to work. "We should be finished up in town by day after tomorrow," he said. "So I'll be reporting for work at the Maiden site in three days' time. That project will likely take us months, but at least we're going into summer so we'll have lots of daylight to work in."

When they were fully ready to leave, Andrion and Erik were in no condition to be giving any full body hugs. But slight hugs and kisses were duly handed around to the three females remaining behind. Erik scooped Anja up and lifted her high, then brought her in for a kiss as if he were performing a snatch and curl. She giggled. "Be careful with that bow, now," he warned her with uncharacteristic sternness.

Bernadette, Lifa, and Anja went outside into the early morning sunshine and stood watching as the men walked to the road, then shimmered into nonexistence. Bernadette sighed. Then Lifa said "Come on, Anja, you can dry" and the two of them went back into the house.

Drakespring Farm's cow, which Erik had named Bloody Stupid Animal (Bloody for short), was making plenty of noise to show Bernadette what she thought of the delay in milking occasioned by their leisurely breakfast – even if they *had* all gotten up at the crack of dawn. Her last year's offspring, a bull calf named Beefsteak (lest they go all gooey over the cute little creature and forget his intended fate) had been converted to a bullock and would likely be gracing one of the new cold rooms at the Maiden in a few months' time. He was penned separately in another area of the farm, and after the milking was done she'd need to fork some hay into both enclosures.

Both cattle pens were overdue for mucking-out, as well, the manure to be composted and used as fertilizer in the wheat field, vegetable patches, and as a mulch around the farm's two apple trees. The chickens roamed loose during the day but spent the night in a snug coop, proof against foxes and wildcats. They needed to be let out and fed, and the coop was overdue for a mucking-out as well.

Despite her decent night's sleep and relatively hearty breakfast, thinking about it all made Bernadette feel tired again. Maybe they *did* need to take on a permanent hand.

Chapter 17: Gryndhaal, Year One

Andrion's jaw was clenched tight as he stepped forward into the portal, Erik at his side. He prayed to all the gods, Aderos especially, that they had not forgotten anything. If they found themselves enmired here and Berni came after them, he would never forgive himself. But did the gods of Terris have any power in other universes? Time would tell.

A single step found them standing in the close, hot confines of the small building Erik had described, its dark walls dimly lit by the blue glow from the portal that – soon, Andrion hoped – would carry them home again. He made his way to the door and applied the unlock spell to it. This spell was a variation on the one that allowed him to manipulate objects over distances, sort of a magical version of a lockpick. He had not yet become completely adept at it, but had practiced it enough times at the Academy before setting out for Gryndhaal once again that it was not more than a minute before the lock's tumblers turned and a click told him the door was now ready to be opened.

Andrion did not, however, throw it open and stride boldly out into whatever world awaited them. Instead, he opened it a crack and looked out through it. Oh good, it was daylight. Perhaps arriving in darkness might be more useful for escaping notice, but the two invaders needed to at least get a look at what they were walking into before they ventured forth.

"What do you see?" Erik murmured, anxious to get moving.

"Not much," Andrion replied. "We seem to be up on a rise with some columns set around it, like a shrine. Then everywhere else I can see looks like jungle. And do you feel that air?" The air coming in through the door's slight crack was warm and steamy, fragrant with greenness and exotic flowers. Neither man had ever actually seen a jungle, but Andrion at least had read about them and seen illustrations in books. The southern tip of Zahar, beyond the Great Desert, was said to be such a land.

"Any people… or demons?" Erik asked.

"Nothing stirring that I can see," Andrion responded.

"Let's go, then!" his brother suggested. "I'm so sweaty I'm about ready to slip out of my armor!" It wasn't a lot cooler outside the building, but at least there was a little bit of a breeze. They turned to look at it, Andrion locking the door behind them, and saw that it appeared to be made all of black stone except for the iron door they'd come through. It had a peaked roof, and small columns flanking the doorway; but otherwise lacked architectural detail.

The area on which the building sat was circular, surrounded by tall white stone columns that were joined at the top by a narrow ring. The resemblance to an ancient eldalfar shrine was remarkable. Erik gazed around them in wonder. "Are you sure this is the Netherworld?" he asked. The vegetation looked perfectly normal, green and leafy. No bizarre plants or strange animals roaming around... yet.

"The book said daimonic creatures came out of the portal," Andrion said. "I suppose it's possible they might have come here from someplace else first. We'll just have to see." A beaten path ran away from the front of the building, leading off down the hill into the distance, and it seemed as good a direction as any. Given that the missing magister was not conveniently hanging in a cage from nearest tree, they had no idea in what direction to search.

The two soon picked up a broad road, which seemed to be paved in a hard-baked tan substance on which nothing would grow. They had been walking on it for only a few minutes when the trees opened out and they discovered a large field off to their left. Neat rows of small leafy trees filled the field, bright red berries visible among the foliage – and little brown figures clad in loincloths were at work harvesting the crop!

"They look just like people," Erik said in surprise.

"About the same color as Afrans, but a lot smaller," Andrion mused. "At least they don't appear to be armed. Let's go down and find out if we can communicate with them." They stepped off the road and into the nearby field, approaching a small man who stood maybe five feet high. His hair was straight and glossy black, his features smooth and blunt, with black eyes that looked almost elven in a round, brown face. Aside from the loincloth, which appeared to have been hand-woven from plant fibers, he wore nothing but a thin silvery metal band around his neck.

A look of fear came over the man's face as he became aware of the two gigantic armed warriors approaching him. He carefully set down the hand-woven basket in which he was gathering the berries, and then threw himself to the ground at their feet. "Please, great masters, do not harm me!" he cried. "I am picking as fast as I can!"

He spoke in slightly accented Common. Andrion and Erik exchanged a glance. Could it be they were truly standing somewhere on Terris, rather than in a plane of the Netherworld? "We mean you no harm," Andrion told him, reaching to help the man back onto his feet. As he bent to do so, a bolt of lightning shot through the area where his head had been a second before.

"You there! Intruders! Throw down your weapons or you will be killed!" came a grating voice. Erik already had his bow drawn, and as the armed and armored figures making their way hastily along the path between plantation rows drew closer, one of them dropped to the ground in a spray of blue-green blood. Andrion crouched, firing an entwined, tight-beam blast of lightning and fire at the second figure. The energy bolt splashed on the figure's breastplate, sending hot globules of molten metal flying into its eyes. Then it burned through, and the second attacker fell beside his companion.

When all was silent, the cowering worker got to his feet. He gazed in awe at the strangers, then back at the two downed guards. Then a big grin split his face, revealing teeth that were stained a bright red. "Nice work!" he said, and there was a ragged cheer from other workers around the field.

Andrion and Erik trailed the worker as he made his way over to their fallen foes. Others were also converging on the spot, and in moments the two dead guards had been stripped naked. And the visitors were beginning to re-think the idea that they were still on Terris.

The two figures, which seemed to have stood around seven feet tall, were both male and generally humanoid. But their complexion was a deep blue, their arms disproportionately long, their genitals relatively tiny. And instead of anything resembling a human nose, they had a muzzle like that of a dog, with sharp teeth showing where the mouths hung open. They were also completely hairless, and had only three fingers and a thumb on each hand, four toes on each foot.

The other workers, each of whom had claimed an article of the dead guards' equipment, melted into the rows of trees like ants vanishing into their underground nest. The one Andrion and Erik had first approached remained. He gave each of the corpses a vigorous kick with a callused (and five-toed) foot, then spat on them for good measure. After which he turned around again and grinned up at the newcomers.

He held out his hands palm up, but down around hip level, in what Andrion took to be a gesture of greeting. "I am Dinka," he said, "and I am to be thanking you for ridding us of the *Grzhankh* overseers. You are doing me and my people a very big favor, as these two be deserving of death many times over. Might I know the names of my saviors?"

Erik crouched down a little, his hands held in the same posture, and grinned back. "Pleased to meet you, Dinka, and happy we could help. I'm Erik Drakespring and my brother here is Andrion Drakespring. We just came here through a magic portal in that building up at the top of the hill. Do you know anything about that?"

Dinka reached out and touched Erik's palms, evidently a completion of the ritual; but he looked worried. "That is a very bad place," he said. "Forbidden. The overseers, they tell us the door leads to a world of demons. But you are not looking very much like demons, I think."

"That portal leads to Iscandia, a place on the planet of Terris," Andrion said. "Most of the people there look a lot like us – or like you and your friends, for that matter. We're not demons. I'm wondering, though, how it is that we are able to converse in the same language?"

Dinka fingered the silvery band around his neck. "It's this," he said. "The goddess gives it to some, those who are leaders, so that we can communicate. The *Grzhankh* do not speak the language of the Henta, nor do we understand their vile demon tongue. But with the speech bands, all is understood."

"The Henta? That's your people?" Andrion guessed. Dinka nodded, a familiar gesture.

"We are the natives here," he explained. "Our elders tell of the Time of Legends, when only the Henta and the other creatures created by our mother Ashtrit inhabited Gaia. All was at peace, and we lived in harmony with the land. But then Luthia came, with her servants, and Ashtrit ruled no more. The forests were cut down, the animals slaughtered or overrun by the demon beasts that came with her. Now all the Henta are bound to serve her, working the land that was once ours and giving up our harvests to the *Grzhankh*."

"You mentioned a goddess?" Andrion asked, and Dinka nodded.

"Luthia, she who came to end the rule of Ashtrit. She resides in a palace in the heavens, they say, but it is one to which her servants – the higher ones that is, never the Henta – can travel."

"Have you ever seen this Luthia?" he asked next. Ashtrit sounded like she was probably just the center of a creation myth, if she'd rolled over so easily for an invading daimon. But might Luthia be as fictional?"

"Oh, certainly," Dinka said. An expression of dreamlike awe had come over his face at the memory. "It was she who placed the speech band on my neck. It cannot be removed, and it is a mark of my position among the Henta." Wow, what luck to have approached a chief on the first try, Andrion thought.

"So what does she look like?" he asked. "Is she one of the *Grzhankh*?"

Dinka shook his head emphatically. "Her appearance is that of a woman of the Henta, though far taller. As tall as you, maybe, Andrion. Young and beautiful, with silky black hair flowing down to her waist and luminous black eyes. The most beautiful woman I have ever seen." He sighed. "I do not understand why she does not do something to stop the *Grzhankh* from abusing her people."

"Thank you for the information, Dinka," Andrion told the little man. "There is one more thing I hope you can help me with. We would not have intruded on your world save that a friend of ours came here a few days ago and has not returned. We are searching for him. Have there been other strangers, recently?"

"An old man around your height, dark of skin, and wearing robes?" Dinka asked.

"That's the man!" Andrion exclaimed. Dinka looked sad.

"I'm sorry to tell you that he was shot by the overseers you killed. I don't think he even noticed they were there before they put a bolt into him. He is probably not dead, but the *Grzhankh* took him away. I heard one say he would carry him to the station, and have him sent to the palace."

"Station?" Andrion pounced.

"It's up the road around six hours by foot," the little man replied. Six hours for him, probably only five for the taller men. "It is there that the harvests are taken. I have been there once, and there are many circles on the ground with glowing lights. If a man steps on the circle he vanishes. It is all part of the goddess' magic, I believe."

Chapter 18: Gaia, Year One

Andrion and Erik continued down the road in the direction Dinka had indicated, trying to make as much speed as they could in the crippling heat and humidity. The likelihood that they would encounter more of the *Grzhankh* overseers, armed with magic staffs and apparently something resembling crossbows, kept them from stripping off their armor and going native. But it was abundantly clear that the loincloths worn by the Henta were much more appropriate garb for this climate.

Andrion was pretty sure the natives' "goddess" was anything but divine. Clearly this Luthia must be a daimon, or perhaps even a Terrian sorceress – able to use the arts of illusion to appear in whatever way she wanted. She had essentially taken over this planet, or pocket universe or whatever it was – even the speech band had failed to make clear what Dinka meant by "Gaia" – and was exploiting the natives to grow crops which she would then sell – probably in other universes, through a series of portals. Who knew how many different planes of existence this little place might link to?

They were going through the water they'd brought at a good clip – drinking it down to replace the fluids that were lost in perspiration. And that perspiration wasn't doing all that much to cool them, either. Fortunately, it seemed there was much water in this land. They were drenched, and somewhat cooled, by a brief downpour. And able to refill their skins from rainwater caught in the enormous, cup-like leaves of some jungle plant.

They came to another plantation, this one of some herbaceous plants with bushy, palmate leaves and a skunky, resinous odor to the foliage. Approaching stealthily, they found another pair of the blue-skinned overseers watching over the workers and took them out quickly and quietly.

Before the elated Henta could rush in and strip the corpses Andrion and Erik reached them. They waved the natives away, smilingly. None who'd approached were wearing speech bands, and they spoke in a lilting babble that made no sense at all to the two visitors.

Andrion searched one body while Erik took the other. "I didn't recall seeing one of these bands on either of those two other overseers," Andrion remarked. The blue-skinned man he was searching, his head nearly obliterated by the blast of magical energy he'd been hit with, was wearing one of the silvery speech bands.

"But we heard the guy speak, and understood him, remember?" Erik pointed out.

"And Dinka said the band couldn't be removed. Maybe it only comes off if the wearer is dead," Andrion mused. They hadn't really gotten a good look at the first two overseers before the dead guards' former underlings had swarmed over the corpses.

Their armor seemed to be made of a lightweight metal similar in appearance to sablium, but it felt cool to the touch. Perhaps, in this climate, it had been enchanted to both protect and cool the wearer? Andrion noticed that both of the dead *Grzhankh* had penises and scrotums, but neither had any sign of nipples. These daimons must not be mammalian.

They pocketed anything they thought might be useful: a magical staff that shot lightning bolts; a sort of oversized crossbow made of that same dark metal, and a sack of ammunition for it; a handful of what looked like it might be local currency; and, from each overseer, a black metal disk about an inch in diameter with an inner circle of glowing blue light.

"That looks just like a miniature portal," Erik remarked.

"I'll bet it's connected," Andrion agreed. He handed one to his brother and tucked the other into a pocket of the shirt he wore beneath his armor. One item yet remained: the silvery speech band. It appeared to be a single piece of gleaming metal, yet was flexible like chain. And it was too small to come off over the dead overseer's head. There had to be a way to remove it – one of the previous two must surely have worn one, yet it had been gone by the time they got a look at the bodies.

Andrion crouched beside the body, running the band around the corpse's neck as he sought for any seam, any connection point. He found none. How had a half-naked native managed to do something he, a trained mage, could not? He took the band in both hands, closed his eyes, and tried to extend his senses – analyzing the gizmo's magical signature. A mental picture of the band formed in his mind, perfectly circular and glowing blue-white in a field of darkness. Where...? There!

Without opening his eyes, Andrion sought the connection point and willed it to part. "You got it!" Erik said jovially. "Good work!" Andrion opened his eyes and held up the band, now draped over his right hand and hanging down like a dead silver snake. He had sensed no magic in Dinka or any of his fellows – how had they been able to remove one of these from the dead overseer?

Eh, perhaps they and their ancestors had had thousands of years of practice. Dinka had seemed friendly enough, but Andrion didn't doubt there'd been a secret or two the Henta headman had not blabbed to his new friends. "You going to wear that?" Erik asked, a hint of trepidation in his voice. Caution was not the big man's strong suit, and this uncharacteristic reserve gave Andrion extra pause.

He held the band up, the two ends together, and with an audible click they fused once again. Then he held out his left wrist and looped the band twice about it. "Just in case it does something besides translate – like maybe let 'the goddess' know where you are and what you're doing – I'd like to be able to get it off again," he said. Erik gave him a thumbs-up, and they walked on.

The area on either side of the road leading to the station was not as heavily cultivated as the two visitors had expected. This region looked capable of producing six times the crops per acre a farm in Iscandia (like theirs, for instance) could do. But for every heavily-planted field, there seemed to be another four that were currently fallow. Maybe the Henta weren't all that numerous, or the markets this Luthia had organized for the fruits of their labors not that extensive? There was little that passed for agricultural science in Iscandia, and neither of them really knew what they were seeing.

During their twenty-mile journey, along a road that was so perfectly paved it didn't look real, they managed to slip past several fields under cultivation without seeing – or being seen by –any of the blue-skinned overseers. The crops were myriad – short, waving clumps of some long-leafed plant that bore no discernible fruit, shrubs around ten feet in height sprouting clusters of oblong green and yellow fruits half a foot in length, more shrubs no more than four feet high that appeared to be grown for their leaves.

If no overseers were in sight, the Henta workers mostly glanced their way and then ignored them – probably assuming them to be servants of the "goddess." Or at least, none of their business. Hours had gone by, yet the sun seemed only to have crept a little way up from what Andrion and Erik had decided to call the eastern horizon. Days must be longer than 24 hours here, Andrion realized. It was, literally, going to be a long day.

They broke when they were tired and hungry, moving a little way into the jungle to sit and eat from their provisions and drink more water. Erik was tempted to sample the fruit hanging from nearby trees, but Andrion warned him away. "Just because the Henta look human, doesn't mean they have the same body chemistry we do. There might be some poisonous substances here that even a panacea potion couldn't handle."

"Right," Erik said, and took another bite of pemmican.

Twice more, they came upon cultivated fields where the *Grzhankh* overseers were close enough that they could not pass by unseen. They began to see a pattern, wherein the guard wearing the speech band also carried a lightning staff – while his partner had the crossbow. Each carried what Andrion was coming to think of as "portal tokens," too. And every one of them was male.

At last, some three hours after their lunch break, Andrion and Erik found themselves approaching the station. As soon as it came into view, without any discussion, the two of them ducked into the jungle that grew right up to the edge of the road but seemed unable to gain a foothold on its surface.

They'd been rained on twice more since setting out from the portal, and were beginning to get the idea that between the frequent rains and the long hours of daylight, maintaining those cultivated fields they'd seen must be a full-time job for every laborer that could be found. Here in Gaia, "sitting around watching the grass grow" was *not* a metaphor for boredom.

From the sanctuary of their hiding place in a tangle of rampant jungle growth, the two intruders surveyed the terminus point of the road. It had been laid out geometrically, with roads coming in from the east and west, north, and – the road they'd taken – south. The sun had finally climbed to its apex and was now, oh so slowly, on its way to the western horizon on their left. The land all around was flat and featureless, except for the rampant jungle growth; but ahead, far to the north, it rose to what looked like a volcanic peak higher than any that existed in Agena.

The four roads connected with a circular road twice the breadth of the others, and the inner edge of that circle was studded with what had to be portals. Lacking any elevation from their vantage point, it was hard to count how many there were. But Andrion guessed there were twelve, as he could see three in the quadrant of the circle that was nearest at hand.

Inside the ring of portals was a circular building, perhaps forty feet in diameter but only a single story tall. The columnar theme had been picked up here, as the outside was ringed with short columns similar to those on the building that had walled off the portal they'd come through. A door stood in the side nearest them, in line with the road they'd come in on, and Andrion was willing to bet there'd turn out to be four of them: one for each road.

This whole installation seemed to be the product of a mind obsessed with symmetry. That could be a disadvantage, an opening for them. But they needed to bide their time and observe, before moving further. Andrion and Erik broke into their stores again for a snack, as they relaxed in their hideaway waiting to see what might be seen.

"Have you noticed there don't seem to be any bugs here?" Erik murmured, as he removed his helmet and brushed perspiration from his brow. Now that it had been mentioned, Andrion was astounded. How could a natural world not include the smallest of creatures? He wasn't sure how everything from microbes to behemoths fitted together in an ecosystem, this science having not as yet been developed on Terris; but he sensed that it was odd.

But Erik was right. Sitting still, surrounded by jungle, the two intruders should have been eaten alive by insects – or the local equivalent. But they had seen nothing living smaller than a songbird. The "demon creatures" Dinka had mentioned had not been in evidence, either. Something was very wrong here. But at the moment, Andrion couldn't complain.

As they sat watching, carts loaded with crops began arriving from the east and west. Andrion wondered whether the overseers they'd bypassed as they traveled up the road from the south would be missing their dead counterparts. Was there going to be a point at which the alarm was sounded? He was a little surprised that they'd managed to get this far without triggering some kind of alert.

Each of the carts seemed to be manned by a pair of Henta, not necessarily only males, and supervised by a lone *Grzhankh* overseer. The conveyances were enormous, larger than the standard wagons of Iscandia, and pulled by teams of creatures neither Andrion nor Erik had ever seen before. They were the size of mammoths, shaped roughly like bullocks, and had six limbs. Their scaly hides suggested they were probably not mammals.

These teams were met by pairs of *Grzhankh*, more heavily armed and armored than the overseers. The animals were unhitched and led away, then the wagons were pushed onto the portals – clearly, far larger than the one that had brought them here – and vanished. Very well organized. But at this point in Gaia's long, long afternoon, the traffic was not all that heavy.

Andrion stood up, stretching. He and Erik had been resting here for hours, and he ached from the inactivity. He was only 33 – what was it going to be like in another 20 years? Never mind. "I don't see any more coming," he said. "What do you say we take out all the *Grzhankh* around the outside, and then go see what's in the central building?" Erik's evil grin in response was everything he could have hoped for.

Chapter 19: The Station, Year One

Andrion and Erik swung into action, a perfectly coordinated team. They'd worked together on quests only a time or two in the years they'd known each other before Bernadette came along to upset their lives; but since then, it seemed, they had become a well-oiled killing machine.

There were four pairs of *Grzhankh* guards at the station, that symmetry thing again. And each pair's view of the others, if they stayed on station ready to direct shipments to the appropriate portal, was obscured by the central building. Without much discussion, the two took out the pair nearest to where they'd been hiding with ranged attacks – before the guards had even reacted to the threat.

They approached the bodies carefully. The central building didn't entirely hide them from the view of the east and west station guards, but the south station guards had fallen quickly and silently and it appeared no one had noticed. Andrion stood guard while Erik quickly searched to see if these enemies had anything different on them than they'd found on the overseers along the road.

"More of those portal tokens, and no speech bands," Erik reported.

"These guys must not need to communicate with the Henta," Andrion opined. So far, there'd been no sign that the teams stationed at the termini of the east and west roads had noticed anything. He and Erik were considerably shorter than the guards, and their armor was golden not black; yet no alarm had been triggered. Were the *Grzhankh* really semi-sentient demons, and not fully sentient daimons?

They turned their attention to the east, where a pair of the tall, blue-skinned guards could be seen lounging at their station. They certainly *looked* sentient. Maybe they just weren't all that bright, or that assiduous in their duties. Andrion had armed himself with one of their oversized crossbows. It was not a fast weapon, but it had the advantage of being far less noticeable than an actinic blast of fire and lightning combined.

The bow Bernadette had crafted for Erik was superb, and with his powerful arms it packed one hell of a punch. As soon as the two intruders had crept within range, skirting the building's outer edge, another pair of guards was down. And so it went. As they did away with the last pair of guards, the ones manning the terminus of the road coming in from the west, Andrion was suddenly seized with anxiety. The day was wearing on, and at any moment another cart might appear.

Erik picked up on what was bothering him. "I don't think hiding the bodies is going to help," he said. "Let's just get inside there and see what's going on." Nodding, Andrion took the lead as they approached the building's western portal. They found the door unlocked, and crept quietly inside.

There were a surprising lot of interior walls, mapping out what was presumably a suite of offices. But ahead of them, down a corridor leading directly from the door they'd come in, was a glowing pool of blue light. "I'll bet that's the portal to Luthia's palace," Andrion said in a murmur. "But let's see if we can find some corroboration for that theory."

They moved silently down the corridor to another central circle, which seemed to have offices off to its outer side and smaller rooms, maybe storage areas, opposite. The building was utterly quiet, as if no one was here. Andrion and Erik exchanged glances, then nodded and headed off to their left. They passed through one full quadrant, finding curiously-shaped rooms with desks and chairs in them but no occupants.

Before long they came to the straight corridor leading in from the north, and continued past it. Then, in the second of three offices between north and east, they found a small humanoid figure working at a desk. Ducking back around the partition, Andrion looked Erik in the eyes and put his finger to his lips. This person didn't appear to be a threat, and he was interested in getting more information.

He came around the corner again and cast the short sleep spell. As he'd hoped, the person at the desk slumped face down and began snoring. The sleep would last no more than a couple of minutes, but Andrion hoped it would be long enough for their purposes.

They'd brought along rope, and used some of it to tie the office worker to the chair. Not that it really seemed necessary – this was not one of the *Grzhankh,* or one of the Henta, but a smallish man who looked like he might be a Reman. When he awakened, sputtering, he found himself trussed up like a chicken for the spit – between a large and serious-looking Galise mage and an even-larger Norse warrior.

"What… what do you want?" he demanded. From the way Erik seemed to understand him, Andrion guessed that he was truly speaking Common and not just communicating through the speech band.

"Some information, sir," he said with a smile that fell a little short of friendly. "Where does yon portal go?"

A look of panic came into the small man's dark eyes. "Who are you, and how did you get here?" he demanded.

"That is of no consequence," Andrion replied. "Your job here, as I see it, is to keep breathing. And to maintain possession of all your body parts. My associate will be happy to relieve you of any you don't appear to value. Is my meaning clear?"

On cue, Erik drew himself up to his full height and pulled forth a glistening sablium dagger, testing the edge while grinning with evil intent. A wet spot appeared on the small man's trousers, and spread, as tears came to his eyes. "D-don't hurt me!" he stammered.

Andrion gave his brother an equally evil grin, and Erik brought the point of the dagger down to rest against the little clerk's throat. "This portal goes to Luthia's palace?" he asked.

"Yes, yes!" the small man responded. "B-but you can't go there without a token!"

"Like this?" Andrion asked, pulling forth one of the discs they'd gotten off the dead overseers.

The little man's eyes widened still further. "Y-yes!"

Andrion sighed. He felt like a colossal bully, and he was not taking any joy from it. Motioning Erik to pull the dagger away from the man's neck, he said "I'm sorry to have come at you like this. Might I have your name?" The little man, white as a sheet beneath his tan, looked from him to Erik and back again.

"Sentius Belaricus," he managed. What in heaven's name was this Luthia thinking, assigning a man of Sentius' caliber to a post that might require some personal courage, Andrion wondered? Perhaps she found it hard to get good help?

"Sentius, I am Andrion Drakespring and the large man with the dagger is my brother Erik. We would really prefer not to kill or maim you, but we are looking for a friend of ours and we need some information. Will you give it freely?"

"Y-you're from Terris?" Sentius asked, beginning to show signs that his panic was abating.

"That's right," Andrion assured him. "We don't want to interfere with this little world, just bring our friend back. If you help us with that, we won't harm you. All right?"

Relief flooded the little Reman's features. "No problem," he said. "I'll tell you whatever you want."

"A few days ago, an elderly night elf named Dalandrin entered the portal twenty miles south of here," Andrion said. "He said he would return shortly, but he did not. Did he come through here?"

"Yes," Sentius replied. "He was brought in, injured, by a pair of Our Lady's servants and taken through the portal to Mulfane. I saw them come through, but wasn't told anything about him."

"Mulfane?" Andrion asked. "Our Lady's palace, the seat of her government on this world," the little Reman explained.

Andrion sighed. It was as he'd feared. He and Erik were going to have to step through another portal. And what would they find on the other side? "How long have you been here, Sentius?" he asked. The small man seemed to have abandoned his fear that the intruders meant to kill him or start lopping off surplus body parts. He put his hands together and began mentally counting off on his fingers. Then he announced, "Two hundred and thirty, no – thirty-one, years!"

Andrion and Erik stared at the man. He looked to be no older than his late thirties, maybe six or seven years older than Andrion. "Uh, how old were you when you arrived here, then?"

"Forty, as far as I can remember," Sentius replied. His expression indicated a hint of pride. He looked at his inquisitors. "What, can you imagine there would be some other reason to stay?"

A long time later, Sentius had revealed much and more. Yet there were many questions he could not answer. He had no idea how old Luthia, aka Our Lady, actually was. No one he had spoken with, in all those two-plus centuries, was able to tell of a time before the woman had arrived here and established her fane – atop the mountain that dominated the island on which it stood.

Yes, Gaia was a large island, surrounded by seas. During Sentius' tenure here, there had been no contact with any other areas of the planet. He didn't know if there *were* any other areas of the planet. He had been born in one of Remus' provincial cities, and had been lured to a portal near Sendon by a mysterious person who had been sent to recruit someone with the clerical and organizational skills Sentius possessed. He had been offered a comfortable lifestyle and unending life, and so far his employer had made good on her promises.

Hours had passed, and Sentius was becoming anxious again. "What happened to the servants?" he asked. "They should have reported by now for the end-of-day tallies!" Andrion and Erik exchanged glances again.

"I don't think they'll be coming," Andrion said gently. "But it's probably time we were leaving. Where in Mulfane will the portal take us?"

"To the entry hall," the Reman said. "The servants are a vital part of Our Lady's organization, but she prefers to deal with them in person as little as possible. The entry hall is at the very bottom of the palace, and most who arrive there never climb higher."

Chapter 20: Mulfane, Year One

"How long do you think it will be before Sentius sells us out?" Erik asked amiably.

"Less than an hour, would be my guess," Andrion replied. "Get ready." They stepped forward onto the broad central portal, and instantly found themselves standing within an enormous room – far broader than the upper story of Wyrmshalla, designed to hold captive dragons.

The entry portal stood in the middle of a vast empty space. And the newcomers quickly found themselves the objects of attention from a group of five armored guards. From their size they were probably still more of the *Grzhankh,* evidently Luthia's favored minions. Could she herself be a member of this strange race?

There was not going to be an opportunity to bullshit their way inside. As the group approached the new arrivals, moving apart to contain them, Erik called "Spread out!" He and Andrion fanned out, making two smaller targets, and began attacking. Erik stopped moving long enough to draw a bead on one of the figures approaching them – then darted to the side as soon as the arrow had left his bow. As the shaft took one of the guards in his center mass, a bolt of lightning shot from his companion's staff – passing through empty air to splash against the far wall of the room containing the portal.

Meanwhile Andrion broadened his attack, striking the four remaining guards with a lightning spell that jumped from one to another. Each strike was painful but not lethal – and the guards cringed and dodged as they tried to avoid the attack. Erik took down another couple of them with his bow while they were distracted.

Now there were only two arrayed against them – and they could not possibly lose! Surging forward with his axe swinging, Erik dodged a desperate attack with a lightning staff. His extra-large blade clove the enemy's head from his neck, and the hapless guard fell in a welter of blue-green blood. To Erik's left, Andrion drew his sword and swung – slashing deeply into his opponent's shoulder and forcing the *Grzhankh* to drop his staff. He brought the blade around to rest its point against his adversary's chest.

"You will drop your weapons," the voice came echoing throughout the cavernous space. Erik and Andrion felt a presence at their backs, and looked over their shoulders to see a small army of the tall *Grzhankh* guards, weapons at the ready, behind them. They must have come in through the portal. Ahead, behind the last standing guard, they saw a troop of another ten guards flanking a tall woman. Other than her height, she bore a surprising resemblance to Bernadette.

"Oh, shit…" Andrion muttered, and dropped his sword to clatter on the stone floor. Erik took his cue and dropped the axe, then stood unresisting as he was swarmed by the blue-skinned guards. They were taller than him by half a foot, but probably no heavier. In moments they'd taken his pack, his bow and quiver, a couple of daggers, and his armor. He was left standing in a pair of abbreviated underdrawers and a linen under-tunic, as was Andrion beside him.

Luthia watched with growing satisfaction as the two intruders were stripped. Nice, oh so very nice! Her eyes were bright with anticipation of the fun she was going to have with these two. Odd, that both of them seemed to be fixated on the same small red-haired woman. Were they rivals for this woman's affections? Her power to delve minds could not produce details, only impressions and emotions.

But which of these magnificent specimens should she take as her new consort? Though it had been less than twenty years since she had taken Malcim, she was already tiring of him. The man was gorgeous to behold, as beautiful as a sunrise; but weak, needy, and increasingly unable to perform in bed. Surely, one of these would make a satisfactory replacement – and Malcim would make a lovely addition to her Hall of Memories, encased in crystal to be admired for all time.

Luthia sensed that the darker, older man was a powerful mage, something that excited her. Ah, the times she and Dalandrin had had, when their love was new! But look where that had led. She had shared her greatest arts with him, and he had fled – spurning her gift of eternal love and life to return to Terris, closing her portal behind him. The old man he had become would suffer for a long time for that slight, now that she had him in her power once again.

Perhaps the big blond would be the better choice. Not too bright, but a perfect physical specimen. He'd make love to her all night, and stay loyally by her side all day – not spend his idle hours plotting to betray her. Hmm, or perhaps she could arrange for the two of them to fight to the death for the chance to be with her! Luthia's heart beat faster at the thought.

"Take them to the tower cell," Luthia commanded in her mellifluous voice. Andrion and Erik, still being held at crossbow-point, were marched away. They found themselves hustled down stone corridors and up a series of broad, winding staircases to be shown into a spacious circular room. There were carpets on the floor and wall hangings softening the cold stone, a little light and air coming in through arrow-slit windows, and rich furnishings including an upholstered sofa and a pair of large beds. Not exactly a rat-infested dungeon, but it was a prison nonetheless.

Seemingly out of nowhere, the red-haired woman produced a pair of garments and handed one to Erik the other to Andrion. "There's a bathing pool over there," she said with a gesture to the side of the room beyond the beds. "Refresh yourselves, then don these. You will be joining me for the evening meal." Her voice was stern, no nonsense, yet her eyes spoke mischief – and promise. Andrion stifled a shudder.

She left them then, and the iron door clanged shut. No doubt half a dozen of the guards had taken up station on the other side of it. The two men sat side-by-side on the sofa, where they could talk quietly without being overheard. "That has to be Luthia," Erik said. "Do you think she can read our minds?"

"She has to have gotten into them enough to be able to make herself look like Berni," Andrion replied. "But she can't have known everything that was going through my mind, or she'd have killed me on the spot instead of inviting me to dinner."

Erik grinned. "It's fucking eerie, how much she looks like Berni," he said. "If she weren't the better part of a foot taller, and if she'd keep her mouth shut, I'd swear she *was*."

"I *wish* she was," Andrion sighed. "We'd just pack up Dalandrin, wherever he is, and go home. I'm really starting to think I shouldn't have gotten involved in this business."

Erik patted him on the shoulder, hard enough to jostle him where he sat. "Don't worry, brother," he said cheerfully. "Let's hit that bathing pool and get ready to dine with 'Our Lady.' I kind of think she likes us, and that's got to work in our favor."

The bathing pool proved to be a stone-lined circular affair eight feet across, three feet deep near the rim and deeper in the middle. The water inside it was crystal clear and the same temperature as the water in the bathing pool at home; but it had a faint, floral fragrance to it. There was no sign of a mechanical system for keeping the water clean and hot, so perhaps it was as illusory as Luthia's red hair and pale skin. Might she really be a member of the *Grzhankh* species?

The garments the "goddess" had given them proved to be gold-trimmed white kilts that barely covered any more skin than did their abbreviated underdrawers. The fabric was like nothing either of them had seen before, silky and shimmering. Quite comfortable, really. Each kilt fit its wearer exactly.

"Did you notice it's not hot and muggy inside the palace?" Erik remarked as he adjusted the hang of the kilt. There was a jeweled boss on the waistband, which he assumed was supposed to go in front.

"More of Luthia's magic?" Andrion guessed. He walked over to one of the walls and stuck his hand through an arrow slit. The walls were close to two feet thick, and he barely managed to reach the open air.

"It's not actually all that hot and muggy outside, either," he said. He withdrew his hand and peered through the slit. "We seem to be up in the mountains here. It stands to reason the 'goddess' would prefer to live where it's not so miserably hot. That would certainly reduce the amount of magical energy needed to maintain comfortable living conditions, too."

The two got no more time to talk privately, as the door was thrown open and a team of eight blue-skinned guards surrounded them and marched them back down the stairs. Andrion stayed alert, trying to commit the floor plan to memory as they were led through a series of stone passageways to a cavernous, high-ceilinged dining hall. The guards had earlier relieved him and Erik of the speech bands they'd scavenged, and none of their escort was wearing one.

What few words passed among the guards as they were hustled along were incomprehensible.

Though the room could have held enough tables to seat three or four hundred people, there was only one. It sat on a low dais, and appeared to have been carved from a single enormous log of hardwood – twenty feet long, six feet wide, and with eight legs formed like the limbs of some clawed creature.

The guards escorted Andrion and Erik along the rear of the table, and gestured for them to take seats on either side of Luthia. She was already seated, in a chair half again as large as a normal dining chair – also carved from that same hardwood.

The men gasped as they beheld their hostess close up. She seemed to have turned up the power on her illusion, making her look less like Berni than before. The little freckles and scars were gone, her hair longer and more glossy, her eyes slightly larger and more luminous. Berni's eyes could look anything from gray to blue to colors in between, but Luthia's now appeared almost purple. She was wearing a dress of that same soft, shimmering material, cut in a way that left little to the imagination.

And she was admiring them, as well. Oh yes, their torsos were magnificent! Especially the blond's… Luthia almost wished she'd just commanded them to appear naked, so that she could get a look at their cocks. But there'd be time for that, soon enough.

Across the table from them sat a young man, or perhaps he was an elf – or even maybe, a daimon? He was astonishingly handsome, perfectly chiseled features and big green eyes with long dark lashes. A luxuriant mane of waving dark hair cascaded to his broad shoulders. He was glaring at Andrion and Erik with an expression of poisonous hatred.

Luthia smiled across the table at him, then said smoothly to the men on either side of her, "I fear I have been remiss. We were not properly introduced when you arrived." She seemed to speak in flawless Common, but they noticed she had one of those speech bands around her ivory throat. "I am the mistress of this place, Luthia, and this is my current consort Malcim. What are your names, and what brings you to Mulfane?"

As was often the way when the two of them were together, Erik deferred to his older brother. "I am Andrion Drakespring, affiliated with the Mages' Academy of Eisenstag on Terris," he said coolly. "My brother Erik and I came here only because Magister Dalandrin had failed to return. We will happily leave your domain as soon as we are able to bring him back."

Luthia looked pained. "If you seek Dalandrin," she said, "you have found him. But I fear he will be unable to accompany you back to Terris. He and I have… unfinished business." She gestured across the room, and the Drakespring men were stunned to realize that what they had taken for a piece of sculpture, over on the far side of the huge chamber, was a man – Dalandrin!

The elderly nachtalfar mage was stripped naked, his withered black skin hanging in folds, and he was suspended by steel manacles from a sort of scaffold, so that he must stand on tiptoe in order not to suspend his entire weight from his wrists, arms, and shoulders. The old magister's eyes flickered open, and he stared across at them – his face a mask of misery and exhaustion.

Andrion's warm brown eyes blazed hot, and he started up from his chair. Across the room, eight *Grzhankh* guards brought crossbows to the ready. Luthia shot out a hand and dragged him back down into his chair, red-lacquered nails digging into his forearm.

"He is an old man! Why are you treating him so?" Andrion demanded. Luthia's eyes widened. She was not used to defiance, and she found it infinitely exciting.

"He deserves everything he has received, and there is much more to come," she said coldly. "I have robbed him off his magical powers, and soon I will take other… things. I will leave him his eyes until the last, though, so he will be reminded of what he threw away."

Get a grip, Andrion thought, reining in his fury with a will. They needed to cozen this powerful sorceress, not go toe-to-toe with her and her legions of oversized blue guardians! "Sorry," he said, reaching out and patting her arm. "I was unaware that Dalandrin had committed an offense against you. But he is very old. Do you not fear to kill him, with your… punishments?"

Luthia looked sideways at him, an amused expression on her lovely face. "Certainly he is old," she said. "Far older than you can imagine. For a thousand years he was my consort, my great love. I taught him all of my arts, and we ruled Gaia together in peace and prosperity." Erik and Andrion eyed her, trying to avoid showing shock.

"He could have continued to rule at my side, young and handsome forever," she went on bitterly. "But he spurned me, left me so that he could return to Terris and become… *that!*" she snarled, almost spitting in her revulsion. Clearly Luthia valued youth and beauty, and the idea that anyone she had gifted with eternal youth should throw it away to become a creaking old ruin was almost more than she could bear.

Their hostess seemed to pull herself together, then. "You need not fear I will kill Dalandrin," she said calmly. "My powers of healing assure that whatever I do to him, I can restore him once the pain has been fully savored." Erik and Andrion shuddered internally. "I have had many consorts over my time on Gaia," Luthia went on. "Every one of them still lives… in a way. After supper I will show you my Hall of Memories."

Chapter 21: The Hall of Memories, Year One

Dinner had been surprisingly delicious, though none of it was familiar. There were sweet, meltingly tender tidbits of a white flesh served in a sauce studded with tropical fruits; a grain dish with a nutty flavor; a salad of spicy greens mixed with little cubes of what they thought was probably cheese; and much, much more. It had been a long time since their impromptu lunch beside the road, and Erik and Andrion ate with good appetite despite the company.

Luthia was animated and cheerful, now that the distasteful subject of Dalandrin had been put aside, delighted to be entertaining two such dazzlingly attractive men. Erik sensed that she was lonely, and made an effort to be friendly. If they could win her to their side, might she not be talked into letting the poor old magister go? Surely, his having become old and decrepit was punishment enough for leaving her.

Malcim had little to contribute to the table conversation, drinking too much of the light-tasting but potent pale green wine and alternately sulking or glaring in open hostility at the visitors. Andrion tried to draw the man out, but soon concluded it was hopeless. Malcim saw that his consort was looking to replace him, and he didn't like the idea. After supper, they learned that the loss of his comfortable lifestyle and the perks it offered were not the only reason.

"You can go to your quarters, Malcim," Luthia said dismissively, as she took Erik and Andrion by the elbows and led them away from the table. She had barely acknowledged her consort's existence during the meal. He turned away, head down and eyes burning, and skulked off down a corridor on the far side of the dining hall.

The troop of eight armed guards followed Luthia and the two visitors at a respectful distance – but well within crossbow range – as she led them down a different corridor and into another large hall. This one was even larger than the dining hall, and configured as a trophy room. But instead of mounted bears, or mannequins wearing exotic armor, this room held a series of three-foot-tall plinths. On each was a block of gleaming crystal, and within each block was a man.

"My Hall of Memories," Luthia said with a happy sigh. "I have reigned here on Gaia for millennia, and have shared that reign with many consorts. Few lasted as long as Dalandrin, I fear. He was one of my greatest successes, and my greatest failure." The men stared in horrified fascination.

"Are they chronological?" Andrion asked, as if it were a matter of clinical curiosity.

"Indeed they are," she replied. She smiled sweetly at him, leading them down toward the far end of the hall. Each plinth, with its frozen inhabitant, occupied a space perhaps fifteen feet on a side. Running her fingers like a butterfly's kiss down Andrion's bare back and making his hair stand on end, Luthia removed her left hand from Erik's arm and gestured at the man on the plinth in the far corner.

"Mierklin," Luthia said dreamily. "My first. It was he who taught me the portal spell, who combined his magical essences with mine to give us the power to open the first portal from Gelzen, our home. We were so young then, so full of ambitions and plans. I sometimes think that Mierklin was, truly, the love of my life. But I've had so many loves."

Mierklin was tall, as tall as Erik perhaps, lean and muscular. He was dressed in a sort of draped sarong that left his torso bare. His skin was a dark coppery brown, wide eyes black, face with no sign of beard or mustache. He had a hawk nose, slightly pointed ears, and a queue of glossy black hair hanging down his back.

"You were with Mierklin a long time, then?" Andrion asked.

"Nearly three thousand years, the longest of them all," Luthia admitted. "It was he who helped me to open portals to the other worlds, to obtain the *Grzhankh* guards, to cow the Henta and replace their mother goddess with me. Had their religion worshiped a creator god, it might have been him who achieved divinity." She sighed.

"So what happened to him?" Erik asked casually. Here they were discussing what must be presumed to be a living man, as if he were a pickled laboratory specimen in a jar. Luthia smiled ruefully and strode to the next plinth. The man encased in crystal, standing there like a hero out of legends, looked to be a Norseman. His silver-blond hair fell halfway down his well-muscled back, his commanding blue eyes staring as if into the middle distance.

"Durendyn," Luthia said with a gesture, and lifted her head to gaze avidly. Andrion stifled a gasp. The ancient Norse sorcerer who had created the portal beneath Gryndhaal!

"He looks like a Terrian," he remarked.

"Yes," the sorceress replied. "The only one of my consorts after Mierklin who found his way here unaided. He had somehow learned the spell to create portals, and directed it to answer his immediate need. The portal opened many miles from here, in one of our plantation areas, as I and a large party of *Grzhankh* guards were on our way to administer punishment to a village of Henta who had failed to meet their tribute quotas. That was before we instituted the overseer system, of course…"

Andrion raised an eyebrow. "So this Durendyn just appeared at your feet? Then what happened?"

"I was… quite taken with him, I must admit," Luthia said coyly. "So beautiful, so fierce and warlike, and so exotic. I had never seen a Terrian before at that time. I was wearing my speech band of course, so I was able to understand his plea for aid. I lent him my guards, and they went back through the portal to rout his enemies. But in return, he came back here to stay. I had the portal walled off later, though he'd assured me no others of his kind would come through."

Andrion looked from Durendyn to Mierklin and back. "And Mierklin had no objections to this? I thought he was a mighty sorcerer." A secret smile appeared on Luthia's face, her eyes misty with remembrance.

"One of the mightiest I have ever known," she admitted. "Mightier than Durendyn, or your Dalandrin. But after I administered the magical-essence poison to Mierklin, as he lay sleeping in the bed we shared, he was helpless to resist me. I still cared for him, but our relationship had grown… stale. I could not just kill him and put him in an unmarked grave, so I converted this room of the palace to a place where I could visit my past loves, and look upon them as they were in life."

Could this "magical-essence poison" have been the same potion Andrion, Erik, and Bernadette had administered to the late Tarragin? Andrion had hoped never to encounter it again. And if that was what

Luthia had used on Dalandrin, rescuing him from captivity was not going to restore him as magister of the Academy.

"I thought you said that your former consorts were all still alive?" Andrion asked, keeping his tone casual. Luthia shrugged.

"They are not dead, and certainly they were alive when I cast the spell that froze them into the forms you see now. But though their eyes are open they do not see, they do not breathe."

"Ever thaw one out just for old times' sake?" Erik asked jovially, maintaining the pretense that Luthia did not make him want to run screaming from the room.

"Alas, no," their hostess replied, like a housewife who'd been asked if she was caught up on her mending. "The spell does not kill the subject, and I suppose if he were fully healthy when frozen and were reanimated within a week or so after being preserved, he might return to normal after a period of recovery. But, no..."

"You tried it?" Andrion guessed, and the beautiful woman made a moue of regret.

"Durendyn's successor proved less than satisfactory," she admitted. "After only about a century I was greatly regretting my earlier decisions, and I decided to bring Mierklin back to life. He had been encased in crystal for more than a thousand years. And though his body was as young and healthy as it had been when I enspelled him, his mind was gone. He was not the man I had once loved, just a drooling idiot. He could not even feed himself!" She made a dismissive gesture.

The tour continued, highlights of the predatory swath Luthia had cut through the better-looking male humanoids of the various planes of existence. She had sent her servants scouting on several occasions – not just for new consorts, if the current one had begun to pall, but for functionaries like Sentius with a particular skill set she felt she needed. Each was offered the chance at a comfortable life, free from all care, along with eternal youth and life unending for as long as they remained loyal to Our Lady and responsive to her needs.

"How come you don't have any female servants, Luthia?" Erik asked. They'd noticed that Our Lady seemed less likely to question the big, blond Norse warrior's motivations, and if his questions were a little too pointed she wrote it off mentally as naiveté. The brothers had become a team that was effective in situations that went beyond armed violence.

"Females only create friction," she replied haughtily. "I see no reason to have them around me, with their plots and intrigues, stirring up trouble."

"But don't your guards, and your other male servants, get frustrated with no women around?" Andrion put in – genuinely curious.

Luthia snorted a laugh. "Quite a few of them are happy to sate their lusts with each other," she said. "I have added the preference for sex with one's own gender to my list of desired qualities, when I go seeking through the dimensions for additional help. Most of the *Grzhankh* are heterosexual, of course, but their species breeds only seasonally and the males do not develop a sex drive except in the presence of a female who is heavy with eggs. It's the principal reason Mierklin and I chose their race for our guards."

The tour was concluded. "I hope that I have given you an idea of what wonders could await you as my new consort," Luthia said while looking first to Andrion, then to Erik. "I'm afraid only one of you will win the prize, but I intend to audition both of you. The loser will of course have to be killed, unless he has some skills that would commend him as an ordinary servant." She looked questioningly at each of them. "I'll have the guards escort you back to your quarters, then," she said dismissively. "Draw lots, and decide which of you will share my bed tonight. Guards will arrive to collect the winner in two hours' time."

Chapter 22: The Tower Cell, Year One

The iron door clanged shut, and the Drakespring men fell onto the sofa with a groan. "Gods save us, the woman is insane!" Andrion gasped.

"Kind of impressive though," Erik, replied. "Her confidence is so supreme, after ruling as a goddess for millennia, that she thinks her 'Hall of Memories' is some kind of recruiting tool!"

"I suppose that *is* kind of impressive," Andrion admitted.

Erik grinned at him. "I think she's attracted to your magical power but also afraid of it," he said. "She might try to slip you the same poison she gave to Dalandrin, just to be sure you don't enspell her." Andrion's brows knit.

"I'm afraid she might have poisoned him with the Destroyer of Magic or something like it," he said. "If Dalandrin's lost the ability to regenerate magical energy, he's not going to be able to continue as magister. But we have to rescue him anyway."

"We need to break him out of those shackles, first," Erik replied. "I think I had better win the 'draw' for tonight's trip to Luthia's bedchamber."

"You're not going to *fuck* her?!" Andrion gasped in horror.

"Gods forfend, no. I'll just lead her on and keep her distracted. Meanwhile you'll slip out, free Dalandrin, and make your way down to the portal room so we can get back to the station – right?"

"We're probably going to need tokens to use the portal," Andrion pointed out.

"Don't most of these guards have them?" Erik countered. "We'll just have to keep searching bodies until we find some. Or if you find three, leave one near the portal for me. As soon as I can, I'll leave Luthia incapacitated and make my way to the portal. But don't wait for me. We'll have a twenty-mile journey on foot from the station to the portal back to Gryndhaal, and that's where the guards are going to catch us if we don't keep moving. You and Dalandrin should just move as fast as you can up that road. I'll be unencumbered, so I'll catch you before you get there."

Andrion bent forward and put his head in his hands, elbows resting on his knees. He was considering Erik's plan, and though he didn't like it he couldn't think of a better one. "I wish to hell we had our weapons and armor back," he said. "All my magic, and I still feel naked without plate on my chest and a blade at my belt."

"I'll bet they stuck our packs somewhere not that far from where they confiscated them," Erik pointed out. "Maybe you'll get a chance to pick them up on your way out."

The two discussed strategy and tactics until the door clanged open. A small sea of blue-skinned guards resolved into a party of four tasked with escorting Erik – the "lucky winner of the draw" – to Our Lady's bedchamber. Four remained behind, guarding the landing at the top of the stairs and the door to the tower cell. Andrion lingered in the doorway, calling out "Knock 'er dead!" to his departing brother.

None of the four remaining guards were wearing a speech band, and none understood what he had said. Perhaps they might have found it odd, that these two strange beings from another dimension were urging each other on instead of fighting tooth and nail for the privilege of fertilizing the female's eggs. But they were caretakers over creatures so different from themselves that empathy was impossible. When Andrion's sleep spell came, as the senior guard was reaching for the door to swing it closed, the four dropped as one to the stones of the landing.

Oof, these guys were heavier than they looked. The *Grzhankh* appeared so lanky that it was hard to remember they stood seven feet tall. Having dragged the fourth guard into the tower cell, Andrion cast the sleep spell on the group once again. His recent practice with refining the breadth of his spellcasting had stood him in good stead.

Quickly, expertly, Andrion rifled the bodies. He removed armor, weapons, everything until the blue-skinned guards were as naked as they'd been the day they'd hatched from their mothers' eggs. One of them had held the key to the cell, as he'd hoped, but none of them had any of the portal tokens. These were palace servants, not expected to leave the confines of Mulfane, he guessed. He pulled the iron door shut, quietly, and made sure that it was locked. Then he crept down the stairs.

Chapter 23: Luthia's Bedchamber, Year One

Erik was dropped off at the door to "Our Lady's" bedchamber, taken inside by Luthia. The four guards were commanded to stay nearby, but on the far side of the room's shut door. As one might expect from the boudoir of an ancient temptress with delusions of grandeur, the place was lavish beyond belief.

"Wow," Erik said, playing up the "dumb blond hunk" thing as far as he thought it would go. "This place is amazing!" Luthia, who in the interim had changed into an outfit even more seductive than the number she'd worn at dinner, smiled. This was just what she needed, she thought. New men, different men, fantastically attractive men who would admire her and everything she had built over the past ten thousand years. Immortality had caught up with her, but she refused to acknowledge the problem.

Erik was given the tour of the suite, from the enormous bed hung with gauzy curtains – and a mirrored ceiling – to the bath chamber where a pool as large as the one in the tower cell gave off sweet, spicy scents. He had half expected Luthia to simply jump his bones on the spot, after that "draw lots" business. But she seemed genuinely committed to seducing him. He appreciated the thought.

And he had to admit, his body was responding. His mind screamed in outrage at the wrongness of this woman and her millennia-long campaign of exploitation, murder, and betrayal – but his cock was getting interested. Luthia looked enough like Berni, it seemed, to trigger whatever magic it was that sent his member surging to monolithic status whenever his beloved was near. Which creeped him out so much, it soon subsided again.

Erik needed to draw this out, but he was finding it increasingly difficult. He wasn't sure he was going to survive this, and he wanted to be sure Andrion had enough time to free Dalandrin and make his escape. He went for sincere, his native tongue – but corrupted by deception.

"Luthia, you are the most beautiful woman I've ever seen," Erik said – echoing the words of Dinka. "You've become a goddess. But how did you start? What was your early life in... Gelzen... like?" She was delighted that he had remembered. A sure sign that this blond godling was truly interested in *her* – not just in all she had to offer him.

"Come over to the bed, and we will talk," Luthia said, entranced. This early stage of a relationship always excited her, moved her. A pity it was so soon over – followed by years, decades, of staleness. It seemed to her as if the length of time during which her consorts could capture her attention, and her affection, was growing shorter and shorter. She drove the thought out of her mind.

"The world of Gelzen," Luthia began, "Is quite different from this one. The climate is cold and harsh, and though the people are not so different from the Terrians, or even from these little Henta, the system of government that was in place when I was born, and grew to young womanhood, denied any opportunities for those of us with superior skills and intellect to rise. My people were oppressed by another group, who ruled a kingdom to the south where conditions were not so harsh. All of my race were denied access to anything worthwhile."

"That sounds horrible," Erik said, and kissed her on the forehead. The gesture warmed Luthia to her core, and she continued her tale.

"Among my people, we of the north, the aptitude for magic is strong. I met Mierklin not long after I came of age, as I was struggling to learn the arts that were forbidden to us by our oppressors."

"He was older, then?" Erik asked, urging her on. If she cared to pour out her life story for another hour, that would serve his purposes well.

"Old enough to be my father," she admitted, and somehow the ancient woman managed to echo the teenage girl she had been in the impossibly distant past. "He taught me everything! All that I had been unable to learn on my own!"

Pity welled up in Erik's soul, as he empathized with that long-dead girl. Yet she had become a woman willing to cast aside the lover who had taught her all she knew, just because she'd grown bored with him. He hoped he, Andrion, and Bernadette didn't live long enough for that to become an issue.

125

Luthia's tale soon wound up with her and her now-frozen mentor coming to Gaia, and Erik found himself on the spot. "Would you like to hear about *my* life?" he suggested. And Our Lady was – apparently – eager to hear the short, 26-year tale of a young Norseman born a fisherman's son, raised in an icy outpost of the Reman empire and off to seek his fortune at the age of nineteen. He omitted any mention of his marriage.

Now Story Time was over, and romance was next on the agenda. Erik gazed into those dark blue-gray eyes, so like those of his beloved. As they were lying horizontal in the bed, the discrepancy between Luthia's 6'2" height and Berni's 5'6" was less noticeable and if he squinted his eyes and closed his ears, he could almost imagine it was Berni beside him in the bed. His cock began to rise.

"Shall we remove the rest of this clothing?" Luthia suggested, her breath coming in little gasps.

"Sure," Erik grinned lazily. There was another gasp from Luthia as she saw the full size of his erect member. Oh my, she had finally found a man to rival Durendyn!

Luthia's body was an exaggerated version of Berni's – breasts larger and rounder, waist smaller, hips and buttocks more pronounced. And where Berni's pale skin was spotted with freckles and little scars, Luthia's was eerily smooth and perfect. Erik locked his mouth on hers, tongue probing inside, hands massaging those enormous tits. Damn, they felt real! But he just couldn't quite make himself believe it.

Luthia was fully aroused, panting – and really annoyed, as she seized Erik's cock, to discover that his erection was subsiding. "Luthia," he moaned. "You have made yourself look like a woman I once desired. But I want you, the real you. Your story has moved me, and I don't want any deception between us. Show me who you truly are, and I will make love to Luthia alone!"

Erik's appeal struck home like a thunderbolt. Luthia's arousal grew still more – this magnificent man wanted her as she truly was, and oh how she wanted him! In a moment she changed, becoming a tall, lithe and muscular woman with deep red-bronze skin, small firm breasts, and long black hair framing a face with luminous black eyes. She was still beautiful, still desirable, and now –for the first time –

126

real. Erik gazed into those eyes – and then tightened his powerful hands around her throat.

Chapter 24: Mulfane, Year One

Damn, Andrion thought, as he crept down the stairs to the palace below. I wish to hell I had some of Berni's invisibility potions with me! He felt astonishingly naked as he moved through the palace, following the remembered path to the dining hall – where he *hoped* he would find Dalandrin still held captive. The *Grzhankhs'* armor seemed quite useful, but it had all been fashioned for men who were nine inches taller than he was, yet weighed little more. So he was still wearing the kilt provided by Luthia. Well, he did own a decent ward spell or two…

He met none of the guards before reaching the dining hall, and found none when he got there. So far, so good! Poor old Dalandrin still dangled from his manacles, where they had last seen him at suppertime. Andrion thought Luthia's assumption that the elderly elf would not just expire from the abuse she was giving him was awfully optimistic. But when he reached the scaffold, he found the old mage breathing.

In moments the unlock spell had opened the manacles, and Andrion gathered the captive in his arms as he collapsed, unconscious. Wishing he'd spent more time with the healing spell before coming on this trip, Andrion gave Dalandrin everything he had. The magister stirred in his arms, and in moments he was fully conscious and looking around.

"Sir, we need to get out of here," Andrion told him. "Can you walk?"

"Yes, certainly," the old elf said.

"Do you know the way to the portal room?" his rescuer then asked. Andrion had been from the portal to the tower cell, and from the tower cell to here – but there must be a more direct route. Of course Dalandrin's memories were probably at least a few centuries old – would he remember?

The old mage's mental faculties seemed unimpaired, to Andrion's great relief. "This way," he said curtly, and began moving off to yet another of the many corridors that led to the dining hall. He had not been moving long, though, when his stamina seemed to have left him and he began limping and stopping for breath.

"What is it?" Andrion asked.

"Luthia… did something to me," he said. "I ought to have known it was insane for me to come back here."

"You lived with her for over a thousand years and didn't pick up that she was poison?" the (much) younger mage asked in disbelief. Dalandrin looked him in the eyes.

"Of course I did," he said tiredly. "But you've seen her… haven't you?"

Andrion shook his head, and gave Dalandrin an arm to lean on as they hurried down the corridor. Night had fallen hours before, and things were eerily quiet as they made their way along. Considering how few threats Mulfane had to face, here on this mountaintop, it was surprising that Luthia maintained as large a staff as she did. This palace was not a place where human life went on, just a cold sterile bastion where one immortal woman tried – unsuccessfully – to find joy in an existence that had become futile thousands of years ago.

"The portal room is right around that next bend," Dalandrin croaked. What was the matter with him? Luthia had said she'd stolen his magic, but why had not Andrion's healing restored his physical abilities?

"Luthia said she had robbed you of your magic, magister," Andrion said. "Is this true?" He wasn't sure he was up to the task of taking them all the way back to the portal into Gryndhaal unaided.

"Not entirely," the old elf croaked. "She poisoned me with something… something lingering," he breathed. "My strength, my health, my magical energy, seem to be running out of me like ale from a leaky barrel. I continue to regenerate, but if I try to do anything, to move or use magic, the outgo swiftly exceeds the inflow. My magical energies are actually stronger now than they were an hour ago… but if I should attempt to cast a spell, I would soon be undone."

Dalandrin looked awful, worse than he had when chained on that scaffold in the dining hall hours before. Andrion gave the old mage another prolonged shot of healing, feeling his own magical energy plunge as the unaccustomed spell drained him of all he had. If only Berni were here!

At least his own magical energies were rebounding normally, quickly surging back to the high level he usually maintained. Taking a deep breath and holding it, Andrion motioned the revived magister to stay there while he peeked around the corner to see what awaited them in the portal room. He hoped it was going to include some tokens. And prayed it would also include his and Erik's packs, armor, and weapons.

To his left, just inside the huge portal room, was a relatively small room caved out of the larger space. Andrion had identified it as a guard station when he and Erik had arrived. It was from inside this room that an additional two guards had come, augmenting the force of three who'd been on station watching the portal. Now, late in the evening, he saw nobody in the larger room. Was the guard force reduced, overnight? Considering how rare incursions must be, he couldn't see why that wouldn't be the case.

"Stay here and rest," Andrion ordered Dalandrin. The old mage nodded, and sank to the floor with his back against the wall.

"I've got enough magical energy now to paralyze anybody that shows up," he promised his rescuer. "Go get 'em!" As anxious as he was, Andrion couldn't stop a tight grin from forming as he crept silently, carefully, toward the guard station.

Chapter 25: Elsewhere in the Palace, Year One

As soon as Luthia's struggles ceased, Erik released his grip. This woman under his hands undoubtedly deserved death many times over, for the lives she had ruined and the things she had done. But was it not more fitting that she be sentenced to an eternity of her sad, barren existence? Luthia could have come here and devoted her life to bettering the lot of the Henta, but nothing could have been further from her intentions. She whiled away centuries, millennia, playing with her never-ending parade of "consorts."

He stood, and began a desperate search of Our Lady's personal suite. Presumably there were four seven-foot blue guardians outside the door, and Erik wasn't entirely sure he would be able to get past them – given they were armed and armored, and he was completely unarmed and dressed in nothing but a short kilt. Putting that back on, hiding his treacherous cock (how could it possibly have risen for this horror?), had been his first act after choking Luthia into unconsciousness.

The rooms were full of furniture – wardrobes, cabinets full of drawers, simple chests like one might find in Iscandia. Erik began rifling them. On the bed Luthia moaned and stirred, and he returned to place his thumbs on her carotid arteries – cutting off the flow of blood to her brain and plunging her back into unconsciousness.

The wardrobes were full of silky clothing. The drawers were full of colorful, scented underwear and items like perfumes and cosmetics. Ah, but the chest! It seemed to contain what Erik could only assume were trophies, items confiscated from visitors who had wandered here from one or another of the worlds Luthia's portals had linked to this one. Here were bits of armor, interesting and unusual clothing, and a few remarkable weapons.

A grin spreading across his face, Erik liberated a breastplate that was a little snug but still offered some protection for his vital areas, a curious-looking green metal dagger sharp enough to cut a thought, and a four-foot-long warhammer that appeared to be made out of solid gold. He hoped it was going to be strong enough to do the trick.

Erik tied a sash from the wardrobe around his middle below the breastplate, and used it as a belt to hold the dagger. He checked on Luthia to make sure she was still out cold, then hefted the warhammer in both hands and pushed the door open slightly. Then he jumped back into the dimly-lit room, bumping against the walls and emitting little grunts and screams.

"Oyra damet! Da gomega?" came the voice of one of the guards. None of them were wearing a speech band, and neither was Erik. Pitching his voice as high as possible, he gave a little squeak of anguish. As the first guard came in through the door, he brought the hammer down hard.

The other three guards rushed into the room, to find themselves in the midst of a vicious whirlwind of destruction. In short order all four of them were down, bent double over blows to the abdomen or nursing broken limbs from the strokes of that devastating hammer. It might *look* like gold, but it appeared to be a lot harder.

Erik bore the *Grzhankh* no personal malice, but he didn't want them coming after him or raising the alarm. By now, he hoped, Andrion had freed Dalandrin and carried him through the portal to the hinterlands. With a sigh of regret, he pulled the extremely sharp dagger and dispatched them one by one. Their blood was blue-green, not red, which somehow made the procedure less upsetting.

What was happening to him? Two years ago he'd have happily killed anyone who stood in his way without worrying about it in the least; and now he was feeling regret over slaughtering some helpless daimons? Berni seemed to have more magic to her than the ability to stiffen his dick from a dozen paces…

Erik dragged the guards' bodies deeper into the room, out of immediate sight from the door. There was nothing to be done about the pools of blood, but he let it pass. He needed to get moving! As he put his hand to the door, it was suddenly thrust open and he found himself confronting… Malcim!

The man's eyes were wild. He stared at Erik in his strange getup, at the blue blotches on the floor, at the naked Luthia lying on the bed. She was wearing her original semblance, something Malcim had only seen once before. Before the arrival of the interlopers, Luthia had almost always been a pale maiden with short dark hair and eyes of the deepest blue – like Serenla, she whom he had not seen in more than twenty years.

"Wh-what have you done to her, you monster?" he cried, brandishing a short sword. Erik stepped back and hefted his warhammer in a meaningful manner. He'd added one of those crossbows and some bolts for it to his arsenal, but he was beginning to form an attachment to this gleaming two-handed weapon.

"Relax, Malcim," Erik rumbled soothingly. "Luthia is unhurt, and she's all yours. Andrion and I are leaving, and we're not coming back. Just let me through that door and I'm gone." The smaller man stepped aside, and Erik surged past him into the corridor. It was empty, thank the gods.

Shaking, Malcim stepped into the room and looked down at her. His love, his goddess, the woman for whom he had happily given up everything he had known before – coming to this miserable hellhole of a planet. No friends, no diversions, nothing but the promise of eternal youth – and an eternity in this charming, opulent palace where nothing ever happened.

Even the joys to be found between Luthia's legs had begun to pall, and this had not gone unnoticed by Herself. She had been ready to take one of those strange intruders for a replacement, and encase Malcim in crystal to join the others in that beyond-creepy "Hall of Memories" of hers. These visitors had made their escape, but it wouldn't be long before she found another to take his place.

Luthia took a long, shuddering breath, her lovely dark eyes fluttering open. "Malcim…" she moaned. In an instant she had gone from copper brown to pale, her dark hair suddenly short, the black eyes gone blue. "Malcim, you must call the guards!" she cried, trying to rise. He said not a word as he plunged his short sword into her breast.

Chapter 26: The Portal Chamber, Year One

Andrion crept silently into the deserted portal chamber, approaching the doorless entry to the guard station. His magical energy was fully recharged, and he was feeling surprisingly buoyed by the knowledge that old Dalandrin was watching his back. Paralysis, huh? That would be a useful spell to learn…

Inside the guard station, he spotted two of the *Grzhankh* seated in chairs before a long counter. Beyond that counter was a long window, apparently filled with glass. It looked out on the portal from the station, and Andrion had the feeling that at this time of night the pair's duty must qualify as Most Boring in Mulfane. Did they give out awards for staying awake?

If so, these two weren't going to win them. A second later both of them slumped back in their oversized chairs, snoring. They would only be asleep for a couple of minutes though, so he had to move fast! Besides the counter with its row of chairs overlooking the portal, the room had a couple of small tables with additional chairs. Up to twelve guards might be stationed here, it seemed – though it was hard to imagine why anyone would bother having so many on duty at one time.

The wall opposite the door Andrion had come in by was clad in metal, and seemed to consist of a dozen lockers – one row across the top, the other across the bottom. If his and Erik's confiscated gear was not here, he had no idea where to look for it.

Andrion stood for a moment staring at the wall, trying to put himself in the place of a blue-skinned guard the better part of a foot taller than he was. Which locker would he choose, to stash what had to be a highly unusual cache of surplus gear? He doubted any of Luthia's staff had seen this much action in decades.

He started with the upper left, quickly unlocking it with his spell. The spell took relatively little magical energy, and was faster than searching the room – or the sleeping guards – for the keys. Empty. Next he tried the upper right, and came up empty again. Damn! How much time was left?

Going for the most sheltered, most emotionally "secure" location, Andrion next opened the locker on the lower left – tucked up against the rear corner. There was Erik's pack, along with his armor and weapons! Yes! He hauled it all out, checking over his shoulder that the guards still slept.

The locker next to it, second from the left on the bottom, held Andrion's own belongings. His underwear had been left behind, up in the tower cell. But he put the armor on over the kilt. After strapping on the sword and shouldering his pack he began to feel as if he were ready for action. But what about the guards? He couldn't leave them for Erik to deal with.

They began to stir, and Andrion sent them off to dreamland again. Then he went around the corner to reclaim Dalandrin. The old elf was alert, his dark eyes searching the area for signs of movement. That, at least, was something he could do without tiring himself out. "It's time to leave," Andrion told him. "I put the guards out with 'short sleep,' but I don't want them waking up in two minutes and sounding the alarm. Do you have something more permanent we can use?"

"I have just the thing," Dalandrin said with a slight, rather grim smile. He stepped into the office and placed a hand on the head of each guard. Andrion could see the effort it cost him, as his small fund of magical energy was exhausted. There was no obvious effect on the guards, though.

"What did you do?" he asked. "Oh, I just stopped their hearts," the old mage said. "Do you have something I can wear?"

Distracted, Andrion dug a spare mage robe out of his pack and handed it over. It hung on the wiry old elf, but wasn't a bad fit – and it offered some boost to the wearer's magical energy. Now he turned his attention to the guards. He had watched Dalandrin cast the spell, and he knew in his heart that he would now be able to cast the same spell at need. He prayed the need would not arise. Killing an enemy in the heat of battle was one thing – killing him when he was helpless and unconscious was another. Well, it was too late. The two guards were dead, and Andrion could only hope they had portal tokens on them. He hadn't found the ones he and Erik had been carrying in the locker with their packs.

The guards' armor fit them snugly and it was not easy getting into the pockets. But he did eventually manage it, and came up with a single portal token from each guard. Then he realized that there was a drawer hung under the counter, hidden in the shadows. It proved to be full of the things. One of the portal guards' responsibilities must be handing these out to anyone who needed them. Andrion raked out a handful and stuffed them into a side pocket of his pack.

"Do you want a weapon?" Andrion asked Dalandrin as they approached the portal. Quite a few guards from the far side of that portal had shown up to help take him and Erik into custody, but it seemed likely they would have returned to their usual posts afterward. And where *were* those posts?

Andrion was also considering weight, and logistics. Getting Dalandrin twenty miles up the road from the station was going to be a difficult task, and he was afraid it was going to involve carrying him – an old elf nearly his height, if thirty or forty pounds lighter. He had better not try to carry Erik's pack with him, then.

He set the pack down on the floor near the portal and began going through it, taking all of the stamina and magical energy potions he could find but leaving some of the healing ones. Erik might need them more than Dalandrin did, since at least the elderly mage was accompanied by someone who could perform a healing spell. Erik's weapons, the pack, and a handful of the portal tokens he left sitting on the floor. Come and get them soon, brother, Andrion thought to himself. Then he took Dalandrin by the arm and, sword at the ready, stepped through the portal.

Erik was lost. I had only been a matter of hours since he and Andrion had been escorted from the portal chamber to the tower chamber. But since then they had been marched down a dizzying confusion of corridors, and somewhere along the line he'd lost track. How the hell long had it been since they'd slept, anyway? Shaking his head to clear it, he turned to the right and found himself in the dining hall.

All right! The cavernous space was deserted, and he was hugely pleased to see that the scaffold where Dalandrin had been chained was now uninhabited – the unlocked manacles left behind. He closed his eyes for a moment, retracing steps in his mind, and set out for the tower chamber.

At the iron door, there were shouts and poundings from inside. Andrion had locked the guards into the very prison they'd been guarding! Excellent! Mentally blocking out the noise, Erik closed his eyes again and fixed the pathway between here and the portal chamber in his mind. Then he set out once again. The palace corridors seemed to be deserted.

Erik wondered why the guards had not been called out. He'd expected Luthia to awaken mad as a smilodon with a sore paw, and have her entire guard force out combing the palace for him. Yet he'd managed to wander across half the palace corridors in finding his way here, and there'd been no sign of an alarm. Had Malcim managed to sweet-talk her out of her wrath? Or perhaps, he'd restrained her so his rivals could escape. Erik put it out of his mind, and made the best time he could as he sought out the portal chamber.

With only a single wrong turn, quickly corrected, Erik reached his goal in around twenty minutes. Everywhere wall-mounted lamps glowed, warmer than the dypalfar ones he was used to but similar in their constant, unwavering light. He approached the portal chamber cautiously, but saw no one moving. A hundred feet ahead, at the edge of the portal, he spotted a lump that he guessed – hoped! – was his pack.

First, though, a check of the guard station. A pair of the *Grzhankh* sat slumped in chairs that looked out on the portal. There were no marks on them, but Erik didn't have to feel for a pulse to know they were dead. A couple of open locker doors on the far wall had their own tale to tell, and he hurried on his way.

Yes, everything was here – and Andrion had even left him a handful of those odd-looking portal tokens. Bless you, brother! Erik got into his armor as quickly as possible, shoving all of the tokens into a pocket of his pack, and stepped into the portal.

Chapter 27: Gaia, Year One

Andrion and his charge stepped into the station from the central portal, finding the building in darkness. Only the gently swirling blue glow of the portal lit the room that housed it. "Looks like Sentius must have gone home for the evening," he murmured. Dalandrin looked at him questioningly. "A little Reman clerk we met on the way in," Andrion explained. "He seemed anxious to be of assistance, but I have to assume it was him who raised the alarm and sent all those guards through the portal after us. He claimed to have been here for a couple of hundred years, though he didn't look a day past forty."

"Luthia and her first consort put an enchantment on the palace, and another on this building as well as on some of the residences for their servants," the old elf explained. "Those who remain within the walls will not age at all, nor will they suffer from diseases."

"What about the blue guys out in the fields with the workers?" Andrion asked, curious.

"They rotate in and out," Dalandrin replied tiredly. "The *Grzhankh* are a long-lived species, in any case, but eventually they age to the point where their usefulness as guards is ended."

"So then what, Luthia kills them?" Andrion asked with a touch of bitterness. He wondered how Erik had fared with the bitch queen in her boudoir. Would he have had to kill her?

"Not exactly," the old mage said with a trace of wry humor. "She just sends them back through a portal to their own world, with no token to return. They can live out their days among their own people. It's a hot world, not unlike this one in many ways."

Andrion was still having trouble wrapping his mind around that idea that Dalandrin had actually spent a thousand years living here with Luthia at his side. Certainly she could be beautiful – on the outside. But she was a complete psychopath, which led him to wondering about the magister's own state of mental health. On the other hand, he *had* eventually left her.

"How long ago did you leave here?" Andrion asked.

"A little more than three hundred years ago," Dalandrin replied sadly.

"And why the hell did you come back?" his rescuer demanded. The old elf slumped, an expression of bitter regret on his lined features.

"I destroyed the portal to Terris through which I'd come when I made my escape," he said. "I had believed that the only open route between Gaia and Terris. All of the portals between Gaia and the other worlds had been created by Luthia working together with Mierklin, and I had hopes that she would not have the power to create one on her own. The spell is immensely complicated and requires a huge fund of magical energy to power it."

"And then you saw the portal below Gryndhaal, and realized where it went?" Dalandrin nodded in the dim light, his face still a mask of woe.

"I am old, and it appears I am an idiot. The magical signature of Gaia brought back all those memories of my youth – the power, Luthia's intoxicating beauty, the unending days of strength and glory. I knew that she would kill me if she ever got her hands on me again, but I guessed that this must be the portal Durendyn had created – that opened far out among the plantations. I was just going to go through for a quick look, a sight of the world where I once ruled as a god, a scent of the air…"

Come on, Erik, what's keeping you? Andrion thought anxiously. He had wanted them to go together on the twenty-mile journey up the road to the portal. Dalandrin went on, "I opened the door and stepped out – and almost immediately I was spotted by a pair of Luthia's overseers. They had been warned to shoot anyone seen around the building housing the portal, and the crossbow bolt they hit me with had some kind of lingering poison on it. I was unable to heal myself, was lucky not have died in the hours it took for them to return me to the palace. Later, I wished I had."

"I guess it's never too late to learn from your mistakes," Andrion said sardonically. He was feeling a bit annoyed at all he and Erik had been put through, because of one old elf's nostalgic foolishness. "Come on, we'd better go." He stepped through the gap, heading for one of the doors to the outside, and as he did so every light in the place blazed to life. Oh shit, he had triggered some kind of alarm!

"We need to move, now!" Andrion said sharply. So far as he could tell, the building was deserted. But how long would *that* situation last?

"I'll do my best," Dalandrin said. "But I fear my strength will soon be exhausted." Andrion dug out every health, stamina, and magical energy potion he had and handed them over to the old magister.

"I'll leave it to you to dose yourself when you need it," he said, "but this is all we have, so you'd better make them last. Let's get out of here!"

Some twenty minutes later Erik stepped out of the portal into glaring light. It had been dark out for hours – surely that little Reman clerk would have long since gone to his bed, wherever that was? He looked around to make sure no one was in the building, axe in hand and his bow strung ready for use. Then he moved quietly toward the door that opened on the building's south side. Seemingly his innate sense of direction worked even in an alien universe.

Lights blazed around the outside of the station as well, from fixtures on the building itself and mounted on the columns that were spaced around the perimeter of the circle road. "Da! Schuz ihm!" A barked command roared out, and Erik rolled to the side and came up with his bow drawn as four crossbow bolts slammed into the side of the station building.

The guards were keeping their distance, and Erik would be willing to believe that the other three doors were being guarded as well. If he could get past these, he might have a chance to escape into the dense vegetation beside the road before the ones on the other sides could reach him.

He got off two shots while the guards were re-cocking their crossbows. These, it appeared, were of an inferior design to the ones Diane was making for the Daywatch Brigade. Cries of pain told him he'd hit his targets. Outside the circles of light cast by the lamps, all was in darkness. Erik dodged again as the remaining two crossbowmen shot their bolts, then slung his bow behind his back and rushed them with his gigantic axe swinging, roaring a battle cry. Though the guards were taller than him, his ferocity took them by surprise and they fell back before him in panic. The axe blade sank deep into the shoulder of the guard on his right as he passed their line, the one on the left escaping unscathed. In another moment Erik was down the road – heading south as quickly as his long, powerful legs could carry him.

As soon as he could no longer see his shadow on the road ahead, cast by the lights surrounding the station building, Erik dodged into the shelter of a clump of some kind of tropical shrubbery and drew his bow again. He could hear the *Grzhankh* guards pounding down the road behind him. With their long legs and lanky builds, they should easily be able to run him down. But not if they were afraid to follow.

Either Gaia had no moons, or it/they were not currently in the sky. Only stars lit the road, which glowed faintly light tan against a backdrop of black-looking vegetation. The shapes of approaching guards stood out like shadows against the smooth road surface, and Erik took the first one in the neck. His companion halted, peering anxiously around him in the darkness, and a second arrow penetrated his breastplate at close range. Not a killing blow, but certainly a discouragement. The wounded guard turned and shouted to his cohorts, who were close on the heels of the leaders.

"Aktan! Der mander zint!" he called, and they gathered around him. Erik bided his time, moving ever so carefully a little further south through the undergrowth. The foliage was so dense it was nearly impossible for someone his size to move silently, but he hoped his foes would be too focused on their wounded comrade to mark his movement.

Erik crept another thirty yards down the road, staying hidden in the vegetation, and waited again. Soon he heard the clatter of boots as the party of guards came up the road again. They were moving cautiously, peering from side to side for any sign of their quarry in the dimness. *Grzhankh*, he guessed, must have night vision no better than that of men. Thank the gods for small favors!

They were spread out, and there appeared to be six or seven of them – so far as he could tell in the darkness. He waited until all of them had gone past, then crept out into the road behind them. Rising to his feet, he shot quickly at the dark figures obscuring his view of the pale road ahead. One, two, three! The last three in line were struck and fell. He may have killed one of them, but the other two were screaming bloody murder.

Wishing his skin were not so pale, Erik crossed the road and plunged into the vegetation on the far side. A hail of crossbow bolts came crashing in, striking tree trunks and deflecting from leaves. One of them hit his elven bracer, but zinged off harmlessly. Its force must already have been dissipated by its passage through the dense growth. He popped up and sent a couple of arrows flying in the direction of the road without aiming, then hurried south again beside the road as the guards saw to their wounded.

Another thirty yards down the road, Erik came back out of the undergrowth and peered north. The guards were a dimly-seen cluster of darkness where he'd left them, and he doubted any of them had spotted him. He stalked silently backwards, keeping the guards in view, until he could no longer see them around a slight curve in the road. As he was doing so, it occurred to him for the first time to wonder what *other* denizens of Gaia might be out an about at this hour. Was there a local equivalent to smilodons, bears, or something nastier? He really, really hoped not. Turning tail, he began running at his best sustainable speed, heading south.

Andrion stopped again, waiting for Dalandrin to swallow another potion. Whatever Luthia had poisoned the old mage with, any pace above a crawl seemed to exhaust his energy. Periodically Andrion added a jolt of healing, which seemed to help somewhat. But even as long as the days and nights here were, he was beginning to wonder if they'd still be staggering down the road, halfway to the portal building, by the time the sun came up and exposed them to the view of every overseer left in this area of plantations.

"The natives' belief in Luthia as a goddess wasn't enough to ensure full production," the old magister had told him. "After Durendyn took over as her consort, they built enchanted residence compounds for the *Grzhankh*, centrally located houses where squads of guards could act as overseers, riding herd on the Henta in the fields, while others in their units would be resting in the houses. It minimized their aging, while making sure the workers applied themselves to their duties."

That accounted for all the extra guards who'd shown up when they were caught at the palace – even though Andrion and Erik had killed six of them as they made their way from the portal building to the station, and another eight around the station itself. The ones they'd seen in the fields would have been only half the local complement. None had come running to the station when they'd set off that alarm, though. He had his fingers crossed that he and Dalandrin would make it all the way to the portal without running into any. And that Erik would catch up with them before too long.

Erik rested at the side of the road, hidden by the shadows of a grove of densely-growing tropical trees, and rifled through his pack. He kept his dagger, his axe, his bow and what arrows remained in his quiver, but threw out the two extra water skins (after taking a big, deep drink from one of them first), extra food, extra clothing and anything else he didn't think he was going to need between here and Gryndhaal. By the time he'd finished lightening the load he'd recovered his breath, and set off at a lope once again. Might Andrion and Dalandrin have already reached the portal?

An hour later, Erik was just thinking of stopping to rest again when a sharp blow hit him in the back, knocking him face down on the smooth road surface. That was a crossbow bolt! It had hurt, but it didn't feel as if it had penetrated his armor. He stayed flat on the ground and crawled hastily off to his left, toward the dubious shelter of the black vegetation growing densely along the road edge.

Suddenly there was a sizzling crack, and the vegetation in front of Erik's face went white for an instant as he felt the soles of his feet tingling. Shit, one of the guards had a lightning staff! He kept crawling, burrowing beneath bushes and trying to put as much distance as possible between him and the road. By the time he'd gotten far enough away that the staff's bolts could not reach him, the vegetation at the side of the road had caught briefly on fire. His night vision was shot, and he had no view of the road or its inhabitants. Would they try to follow him in? At least he could hope that use of the staff had destroyed his foes' night vision, as well.

The plantations formed a checkerboard pattern on either side of the road through this stretch of country, with perhaps two-thirds of the land remaining a fallow jungle while another third was under cultivation. That was probably as much land as they could manage to plant with the available labor. Erik, continuing south at a distance of around thirty feet east of the road, stumbled out of the jungle to find himself walking the furrows of a field planted in herbaceous shrubs maybe ten feet high. His night vision was beginning to return, and he made his way cautiously back toward the road.

The group of five guards were barely visible as a dark patch in the road sixty feet away. It seemed that three, including the one with the lightning staff, were standing in the road while the other two ventured into the jungle looking for their quarry. Erik drew his bow, taking aim on the center of the dark patch. He could only *hope* to hit anything, in this light.

Then suddenly the road was lit up bright as day, as a coruscating swarm of lightning bolts fell upon the guards from overhead. Erik took a bead on the staff-wielding guard and dropped him, then held his shot as the men he was aiming at hit the ground. The lightning had vanished again, and he turned his head. Andrion!

"Saw the light and thought you might need some help, buddy," he said with a grin. Dalandrin was standing a few paces away, huddled in a mage robe a little too big for him.

"I told you that was a good one, son!" he said cheerfully. To Erik he added, "Your friend here is a quick study!"

There was no sign of the two guards who had gone into the jungle, but the two on the road were starting to stir again. Another flurry of lightning bolts crashed around them, and they lay still. Blue and red afterimages were flashing in Erik's eyes as he turned toward his brother. "New spell, huh?" Andrion grinned like a kid showing off his new toy, barely visible in Erik's compromised vision.

"The magister has the ability to teach a spell without actually casting it, like he's a walking spellbook," he said. "I really need to learn how to do that."

"Andrion, I think what we *really* need to do is get a move on," Erik replied. "There are two more men out in the jungle there, and I don't know how many more might be coming down the road from the station."

"There's kind of a problem with that," Andrion said. "Luthia poisoned Dalandrin with something that is constantly bleeding away his health, stamina, and magical energy. If he does anything more strenuous than move at a snail's pace, he becomes exhausted in about two minutes."

"Can you take my pack?" Erik asked, holding it out. "Uh, I suppose…" It was lighter than he'd expected, and he slung it over one shoulder while moving his own pack to the other. It was a bit of a strain, but he should be able to manage. The bigger man walked over to the old magister and said "Up we go, sir" – slinging the old elf across his shoulders. Then he set off at a jog.

Goggling at Erik's strength and endurance, Andrion took up the rear. He was keeping his eyes open for any signs of movement. Would those two other guards turn back to help their comrades, or try to ambush the escaping prisoners as they ran up the road?

They were moving at a pace that permitted some conversation, and after Andrion was convinced that the guards had all been left behind he closed the distance to trot beside Erik. "What happened with Luthia?" he asked. "Did you…?" Erik grinned, though it was hard to see in the darkness.

"Last time I saw her she was unconscious, sexually frustrated, and under the guardianship of Malcim," he replied. "There was no alarm put out while I was wandering around lost for twenty minutes after that, so I have to assume our Malcim was more than willing to see us get away."

Andrion could think of another reason Malcim might not have sounded an alarm, but he decided not to voice it. "Sorry you had to deal with all those guards," was all he said. "When Dalandrin and I came through the portal we waited for you a little while, but then decided we'd better leave. And when we stepped out of the area immediately around the portal, it set off some kind of alarm."

"Oh, that explains all the blue guys who were waiting for me when I came out!" Erik said jovially. "I killed a few of them, but the rest have been chasing me since I left the station. Except I killed a few of those, too. Not sure how many are left."

"There may be lot out here in the plantations," Andrion warned. "I'm just hoping they haven't gotten the word about us yet." They ran on.

Even Erik could not long maintain that pace while carrying a human being over six feet tall, who weighed more than 170 pounds. After three-quarters of an hour they rested, Andrion on the alert for signs of pursuit. Dalandrin was quite glad to be set on his feet for a few minutes. The jostling of being carried along across Erik's shoulders had exhausted him almost as much as walking. "That was the last stamina potion," he said, throwing away the empty vial.

"Do you need healing?" Andrion asked anxiously. A pity there wasn't a spell to grant stamina, or magical energy, to another.

"I feel all right now," Dalandrin replied. "We'd better get moving again."

As they jogged along the road moving south, they began to see a glow in the eastern sky. Was dawn approaching? Then a huge silvery crescent, horns up, appeared above the eastern horizon. It was a moon, and what a moon! When full it might have lighted up the landscape as bright as the sort of daylight one usually got in Eisenstag in the winter. Now in its first quarter, it provided enough light that they could make out details of the fields they were passing on either side of the road.

"I think we're almost there!" Andrion said excitedly, as they came past a broad orchard of medium-sized green trees bearing red berries. "Yes! There's the portal building!" He pointed ahead and Erik put on an extra burst of strength, carrying his burden up the slight rise to where the squat black stone building sat surrounded by white columns.

Erik set Dalandrin down again, and the old mage slumped to a sitting position beside the front door. He pulled out a potion and drank it, then gradually regained his strength. "There are two more magical essence potions," he said, "And this robe helps somewhat. I can use my own magic to give myself more strength."

Meanwhile Andrion had cast a white glow from his left palm and was examining the lock. "This has been tampered with," he said with a frown. "It looks as though something has been forced into the keyhole." Dalandrin put his hand over the lock, delving it.

"Molten lead," he said. "We will need a hot, finely focused fire spell to melt it again, then a spell of unlocking to turn the tumblers before it cools."

"I have a faster way," Andrion said. "Stand back." He hit the lock with a concentrated, intertwined tight beam of fire and lightning, and in a few seconds the lock melted away leaving a gaping hole in the door. It swung open. "Watch out, it's hot," he warned, as he led his companions inside.

"That was very impressive, young man," Dalandrin said thoughtfully. "But I had hoped we would be able to lock it behind us."

"Can't we just close the portal, or destroy it, once we get through to the other side?" Andrion asked. "You said you did that with the one you escaped through."

The old mage shook his head. "I was in the prime of my strength then. Now I am old, and this poison is bleeding my mana away with every breath I take. There is not a chance I will have enough strength to perform the spell."

"Could you teach it to me?" Andrion asked. "I believe so," Dalandrin replied, "But I doubt that you have the strength to perform it either. You are what, thirty years old?"

"Thirty-three," Andrion replied. "I've been practicing magic, and building my strength, for a little over fifteen years."

The old elf gave him a wan smile and patted his hand. "I think we had better get on our way before more of those guards show up," he said. "When I closed the portal near Alfenstein, I had been practicing magic for well over a millennium."

Chapter 28: Gryndhaal, Year One

The three of them found themselves standing on the floor beside the portal in the lowest chamber of the ancient Norse stronghold – Andrion and Erik's departure point of however many hours ago. It felt as if it had been way more than a day since either of them had slept.

But their tiredness was nothing compared to Dalandrin's. The old man seemed dead on his feet. Two Icemarch guards, who'd been nodding in chairs at the table that had been brought in, started up at the arrival of the newcomers. "Where's Faramund?" Andrion demanded. "We need him, and anybody else with magical ability."

"I'm here, I'm here," the old man's voice chimed in. The noise had roused him from where he'd been sleeping on a bedroll thrown down on the stone floor at the other end of the chamber. He stood there barefoot, wearing a nightshirt that came only part of the way down his pale, skinny shanks.

Faramund surged forward to where Dalandrin stood swaying. "Magister, they have found you!" he cried. "But what has happened?" He motioned to the guards to assist the old mage to one of the chairs, and Dalandrin sank down into it as if exhausted.

"Do you have any potions on you?" Andrion asked, startling the old man.

"I, no, I don't… I wasn't expecting…"

To the guards, Andrion said "Draw a bead on the spot where we came through the portal, and shoot anything that appears! We've got hostiles on our trail!" They, and Erik, took up station as Andrion applied healing to the magister. He revived, becoming more alert. Now that he was not walking, or being hauled along like a sack of potatoes, his regenerative ability could keep up with the outlay.

Just then there was a "thwack" and a stifled scream, and a blue-skinned guard in black armor fell back into the portal and vanished from sight. "They're coming," Erik reported unnecessarily and nocked another arrow to his bow.

"Magister, teach the portal closing spell to both me and Faramund!" Andrion urged, holding the old elf's withered hands.

Whatever you might say about the *Grzhankh*, it was clear that they didn't lack courage. Faced with a mysterious portal and unseen death waiting beyond it, they leapt right into the breach. Erik's next arrow took the next guard in the throat, as he'd moved around to the side where the portal let out and motioned the two Icemarch guards to do the same. They all needed to be shooting in the same direction.

Andrion found he could not simultaneously learn the spell to close the portal, and also learn – by observing – whatever spell it was that enabled Dalandrin to teach it to him. Soon both he and Faramund had the spell, but now what? "If all three of us cast the spell together, will the effect be cumulative and do the job?" Andrion asked. This was magic he had not even read about, in all his studies over the past fifteen years.

"If you lack the magical energy to cast the spell by yourself, nothing will happen," Dalandrin explained. "I must link with you two so I can draw on your magical energy as well as my own. Only then do we have a chance of closing the portal!" In front of them, a hail of crossbow bolts came through the portal and rattled off the wall beyond where Erik and the two guards were standing. By the greatest good luck, none of them was hit.

Erik pulled out his axe, causing the eyes of the Icemarch guards to go wide. The next blue-skinned guard to appear before them was nearly cloven in two before he could get his bearings, falling with a splash of blue-green blood as he vanished back into the portal. Maybe that would get the wind up the rest of them.

"We must act soon," Dalandrin said firmly. There was nothing wrong with *his* courage, either. "Take my hands, and hold the spell in your minds as I channel our combined energies. Do not let go, and do not falter!" Andrion took the old magister's left hand as Faramund reached across the table to take his right.

It was a convention of the magic taught in Agena, especially with battle spells, that the action of the spell, the channeled magic, emanated from the hands of the spell caster. But it need not. As he drew in the shaped magical energy of Andrion and Faramund through his hands, the spell exploded from Dalandrin's forehead to the portal in the floor.

The flat pool of swirling light suddenly rose up in jagged peaks, as if a storm had struck a calm sea. Streamers of light exploded from the surface, spun in the air, and then sank back as the color went from a cool blue to white. Dalandrin's dark eyes flared white, beams from them joining the one connecting his forehead to the portal. As the spell went on, Andrion felt as if every last particle of energy was being drained from him.

The portal had gone from a flat blue pool to a vertical column of white light, fraying at the top edge as if it were beginning to dissolve. Was the spell faltering? Would it not be enough? As Faramund seemed to sag, still clinging to Dalandrin's hand but on the verge of collapse, Andrion dug deep for still more strength to add to the meld. Suddenly he felt his left hand being seized, held tight in a warm grip of steel. Erik was a pure Norseman with very little magical ability. But what he had to offer, he gave.

Abruptly there was a cold white explosion as the light from the portal reached its maximum intensity and then winked out. The room's occupants blinked, afterimages making it hard to see in the dimly-lit chamber. But they had done it! Where the portal had stood, there was only a gray stone floor.

Erik released Andrion's left hand, and Andrion turned to the right. The hand in his was cool and limp. Across the table, Faramund had dropped the magister's hand and was slumped in his chair, unconscious. Dalandrin's head had fallen to his chest, his eyes closed. Releasing his hand, Andrion reached out to feel for a pulse. The magister was dead.

Chapter 29: The Mages' Academy at Eisenstag, Year One

No potions had been available, but in a few minutes Andrion's magical energy had regenerated to the point where he was able to cast healing on Faramund and bring the old man around. He felt all right himself, yet more tired than he could ever recall being in his life.

He fast-traveled himself, Erik, and Faramund back to the Academy, arriving in the middle of the night. The old man went off to his bed in the instructors' residence hall on the far side of the quad, while the two younger men sacked out in Berni's student dorm room – scarcely bothering to remove their armor before falling into a deep sleep.

Erik's dreams were troubled by images of making love to Luthia, strangling her while she screamed at him "Fuck me! Fuck me!" He awoke before Andrion did and went off looking for something to eat. It seemed to be morning, from the dim light coming in through the residence tower's bottle glass windows.

Feeling a lot better after a bit of breakfast, Erik went back to the room and woke Andrion. "Rise and shine, buddy!" he said cheerfully. "It's over! Luthia and her minions can't come through to menace Iscandia, and we're free to go home to our pregnant wife. Doesn't that sound like a good idea?"

Andrion sat up yawning, and stretched. His mana was fully restored, and he felt as though the overall level of it had increased somewhat. He grinned at his brother. "I'm sorry I dragged you into this, Erik. It certainly wasn't any of *your* business. But I know I couldn't have done it without you." Erik clapped him heartily on the back, nearly knocking him over.

"Forget about it," he said. "What are brothers for?"

As Andrion sat breaking his fast with some apples, pears, crackers and hard cheese, Erik discovered a little more room and joined him. "Damn, I just wish we hadn't lost Dalandrin," Andrion said. Everything they'd gone through to rescue the magister, and it hadn't done any good at all. But at least they'd closed the portal once and for all.

"So I guess Faramund will be the new magister, huh?" Erik mused around a mouthful of cheese.

"Stands to reason," Andrion said. "He's been acting in that capacity since Dalandrin disappeared." Finishing their meal and gathering their belongings, they left the residence tower and walked across the quad to the central building. They'd just say their goodbyes, and be on their way home.

The large circular room beyond the front doors seemed to be full of people, and they spotted Faramund among the crowd. The old man was standing near the center of the room, with a dozen men and women gathered around him. "Here he is!" Faramund said, beaming as Andrion and Erik came forward to join them. There was a smattering of applause.

Andrion gave a shy grin. He wasn't used to much in the way of acclaim. "I'm sorry for your loss," he said, addressing all of them. He didn't see anyone here who looked old enough, not even the two elves, to remember a time when Dalandrin had not been their leader. To lose a fixture like that must be like having a limb amputated.

"Dalandrin bravely gave his all to save us from invasion," Faramund declared. "It was a fitting end to his long, long tenure as the Academy's magister, and we will deeply feel the loss of his guidance, his knowledge, and his experience. But life must go on. We are gathered here to elect a new magister for the Academy, and were just waiting for you to arrive."

Andrion looked at him blankly, then said "I don't think I'm supposed to get a vote, but you can have mine. You seem to be the most senior person here." Faramund twinkled at him, a slight smile wreathing his lips.

"Seniority is not everything," he said. "Wisdom, bravery, selflessness and vision are also important qualities for the one who will lead the Academy into the future. And you, Mister Drakespring, have *my* vote!"

Andrion stared at him, too astounded to speak. There was a prolonged burst of applause, and everyone was looking at him with smiles on their faces. "All in favor?" Faramund asked, and there was a roar that echoed off the walls and ceiling of the cavernous hall. "Any opposed?" There was not a sound.

Chapter 30: Drakespring Farm, Year One

It was a beautiful spring day, and the sun was getting hot. Bernadette, dressed in a light cotton shirt and trousers, downed her wood axe and stood, hip shot, wiping perspiration off her forehead with one arm. Phew! Chopping firewood was not something she often did if she could get out of it, but it needed to be done and she'd felt like getting a little exercise in the fresh air.

We really need to set up an outdoor forge here, she mused, panting slightly from the exertion. I could be making us money with another consignment for Valkyrie, but who wants to be down in the basement on a day like this? It was late morning, and she was alone on the farm. Bjorn was just down the road working with Hegmar's crew as the Maiden's new wing began construction, Lifa and Anja in town running errands.

The crops were sprouting well, as were the weeds; but Bernadette had found that Anja liked pulling the leafy interlopers out if they all worked together; so that was all done. She'd really been enjoying having the family here with her while her men were gone, snuggling with Anja and reading to her in the evenings. But she missed Andrion and Erik, a slow, deep aching that never quite left her though it was worst at night. Hurry back, you two, she sent the thought flying.

Well, this wood's not chopping itself I guess. Bernadette picked up the axe again and swung it over her head, ready to split another log. From the corner of her eye she spotted movement out on the road, as two figures shimmered into existence. She nearly dropped the axe on her foot, launching herself from the wood pile as she ran to meet them.

Andrion was dressed, not in the armor he'd been wearing when they left, but in a rather fancy-looking set of mage robes. Erik, standing a little behind him, was dressed as before. They were both grinning at her like maniacs as she barreled toward them, ruddy ponytail flying behind her. Since Andrion in his soft robes was more huggable, she latched onto him first, leaping up into his arms for a kiss. He held her close, so filled up with love, joy, and pride that he thought his heart might burst.

Her legs still locked around Andrion's middle, after kissing him thoroughly Bernadette pulled back, hands clasping his neck, so she could study his face. "*What* have you been up to?" she demanded. He looked extremely pleased with himself.

Andrion had been thinking about telling her the big news for some time, wondering how to slip it in for best effect; but faced with his beloved, he just blurted it right out: "You, my love, are in the arms of the new Magister of the Academy at Eisenstag."

Bernadette dropped to the ground. Her face was not the picture of delighted surprise he'd been hoping for. "You're *what*?!" she demanded, looking him up and down. He smiled down at her, pride at his achievement plain on his face.

"It's a long story, but these are the official robes. And I have the key to the Quarters, as well. I thought you'd be pleased…?"

The appeal on Andrion's face was so plangent that Bernadette stifled her misgivings. This was just what he'd wanted, she knew. She gave him a big smile and another warm kiss. "This is wonderful, Andrion!" she assured him. "I'm just surprised, you know – you and Erik were going off to help bring back Dalandrin, and the next I know you're the Academy's Magister? What happened?"

Erik had come up alongside and was looking for a little attention, too. "We rescued the old magister, but he didn't survive the ordeal," he said seriously. "Turns out the old guy had been into some not-so-good stuff a few centuries ago, and it came back to bite him on the ass."

"Oh, I'm sorry," Bernadette said. That Andrion's new status came as the result of the old elf's death was sad. But from what Erik had said, Dalandrin had sown the seeds of his own destruction.

Suddenly Erik pounced. He was wearing his armor, so she couldn't just climb up him as she had Andrion; but he scooped her up like a small child, holding her in his massive arms and bringing her in for a kiss. She threw her arms around his neck and kissed him deeply and hungrily. It had been too long since she last had him in her bed!

Bernadette suspected they both might be tired and hungry, and certainly in need of a bath. There were none to be had at the Academy, she knew well, nor at Eisenstag's little inn. And, no doubt,

Andrion would prefer to be telling her all about their adventure rather than standing there in their front yard watching her neck with Erik; so reluctantly, she broke it off. "Are you guys hungry?" she asked.

The question was directed to Erik, who still held her off the ground, but they answered as one: "Starved!"

"I was just going to put together some lunch after I finished chopping the wood," Bernadette said. "But why don't we walk on down to the Maiden? I'm sure Lev's got something tasty for us." This suggestion met with great approval. The dishes the Maiden's ever-expanding kitchen could turn out put home-cooked food to shame. Plus of course, the guys were eager to share their tale with their former colleagues.

The two of them had gone from fellow employees to bosses, a success story passed on to each new "Hospitality Specialist" recruit. They went inside the house long enough for Andrion and Erik to shed their packs, and Erik hastily dropped his armor off in his room and emerged wearing trousers, boots, and a shirt. Then the three of them went arm-in-arm down the road.

Chapter 31: The Bathing Maiden, Year One

As they walked down the road toward the Maiden, Andrion and Erik were surprised at the horde of construction workers swarming over the area to the north of the deck. The new wing's construction had begun, and in a couple of months they should be capable of handling a lot more business, reaping ever greater profits – most of which would go to Bernadette and her household.

The Drakespring trio were around the Maiden much less often these days, and everyone was glad to see them. Lev and his kitchen staff were ramping up for the lunch rush, which had not quite yet begun; so in minutes Bernadette, Andrion, and Erik were seated at the beautiful Owner's Table enjoying mouthwatering, freshly grilled sandwiches with minced beef, cheese, bacon, sliced tomato, spring lettuce, and some kind of savory sauce. A steaming mound of crispy, salty Dragon Fried potatoes filled out each plate, all of it washed down with chilled ale.

Bernadette had worked up a quite an appetite after her minimal breakfast, between the morning chores and her interrupted wood chopping; and neither Erik nor Andrion had eaten a decent hot meal in days. For a long while, there was only the sound of chewing. Bernadette was seated between her husbands, and from time to time would squeeze one or the other of them on the knee. The hunger in her stomach was not the only one she was feeling. Thankfully, the nausea she often felt in the mornings rarely troubled her past ten or so.

After the last crumbs had been devoured and their mugs were drained, the three got another round of ales. Bernadette had heard tales that drinking alcoholic beverages was a bad idea for pregnant women, but she didn't see how a couple of ales could hurt. The alcohol content was minimal, and the stuff was even sort of nutritious. It wasn't like drinking brandy.

Now that their mouths were free for talking, Andrion and Erik began relating their adventures on the far side of the Gryndhaal portal. Luthia's plans for the two of them, and Erik's dalliance with her in the interests of distracting her while Andrion made off with her captive were… downplayed. Berni certainly knew that they loved her and only her, but Erik still didn't think it would be a good idea to admit that he'd been naked in bed with a woman who looked like an idealized version of her.

Lev and his helpers were far too busy serving food and drink to a flood of locals, but various other members of the Maiden's crew, friends with the three of them, stopped by the table to hear of their latest exploits. None had yet been told of the forthcoming Drakespring heir.

After they had sat there for nearly ninety minutes, Andrion remarked "I could sure use a bath."

"Why don't we go home, then?" Bernadette suggested. They could, of course, strip off and go into the pool below them. It was not all that heavily populated during the lunch rush. But their own private bathing pool held a lot more appeal for them. Erik turned to the two Maiden employees who were currently sitting at the table with them, and smiled.

"Sorry," he said. "You'll have to get the rest of the story later."

They said "Awww," but knew they'd get caught up on the details before too long. The reason for Andrion's curious garb had not yet been revealed. Bernadette, Andrion, and Erik thanked Lev as they walked out and headed for home. They could eat at the Maiden whenever they wanted to for free; but often they preferred the intimacy of meals at the farm. All three of them were finding that having their own place was a big improvement over living in one as public as the Maiden.

Chapter 32: Drakespring Farm, Year One

Back inside, at now around one in the afternoon, they found Lifa and Anja having lunch at the dining table. Lifa looked up, surprised to see the men of the house returned. "You're back!" she exclaimed. "Everything went all right, then?" Andrion smiled at her jubilantly.

"I've been made Magister of the Academy at Eisenstag," he announced proudly. Bernadette felt a twist of emotion at the words. She was proud of Andrion and his accomplishment, but couldn't shake the feeling that he had, in some way, left them behind.

"So, you'll be back to stay?" Lifa was trying to marshal her plans. If the men of the house had finished their questing, she and her family could return to their home. And while they'd all enjoyed staying here, she was eager to be back under their own roof, with no one to worry about but themselves. Andrion considered, understanding the reason for her question.

"If you and your family want to go back to Brightsgate Cottage now, I think that'll be fine. We really appreciate your staying here with Berni while Erik and I were away."

Lifa smiled at him and bobbed her head. She'd need to gather up their things, and change the sheets on that enormous master bed. "We're going to go take a bath, now," Andrion continued.

"We'll get ready to go," Lifa told him, "then we'll stop by to talk with Bjorn before we go back to Waterdon." Though the two families were close friends, the imbalance of Lifa and Bjorn having once been in sworn service to Bernadette, and owing her so much, cast a certain shadow on the relationship.

Bernadette observed all this and was sorry, but didn't see any help for it but patience. After enough years of treating with the Steadfasts as equals, perhaps the taint of the servant-master relationship could be expunged. It was early days, yet. Lifa and Anja returned to eating their lunches, while the other three continued down the hall and went into the bathroom.

They locked the door. If the other occupants of the house wanted to use the privy, they might just have to wait. Bernadette had of course had a bath this morning on arising, as she did every morning unless unusual circumstances intervened; but there was no way she was foregoing the opportunity to get naked with these two. Their bathing pool was big enough for four adults, in a pinch.

She sat on the tiled floor, watching them strip. Neither needed any assistance. Two finer specimens of the male anatomy, in Bernadette's opinion, had never been seen on Terris. Andrion's deliciously smooth caramel-colored skin over rippling muscles, Erik's golden magnificence in a slightly larger scale; these sights filled her eyes with beauty and her mind with lust.

The two of them were mindful of their beloved and the fact that it had been several days without any loving; but they were also concerned about things like muscle aches, grime, and the desire to finally relax after many hours of nearly nonstop effort. So they plunged right into the water once they'd stripped off their clothing. Andrion took some care with the Magister's robes. Those were rare and valuable, and he hung them on one of the several hooks lining their bathroom's walls.

Bernadette, grinning down at her two adored men as they sank naked into the hot water, performed a little bit of a striptease as she removed her boots, shirt, trousers, and the underwear beneath. Her audience leered at her appreciatively. When she, too, was naked, she sat on the rim of the pool for a moment before slipping into the water with a sigh.

Bernadette gazed at her husbands, filled with joy to have them here with her at last. Erik sat opposite her, Andrion on her left. "I'm so glad you're home!" she exclaimed. "Lifa and her family have been great, but I've missed you two so much!" She turned to Andrion as he sat beside her, wriggled over and sat in his lap. She felt his cock begin to stiffen at once. Oh good, that hadn't changed. In her mind, she knew that Andrion's need for public recognition didn't have anything to do with his love for her or his commitment to their family; but she was pregnant, awash with hormones, and her emotions wanted to cast his new status with the Academy as an act of abandonment.

After a deep kiss with Andrion, Bernadette drew Erik in as well. She stretched out on the surface of the water, floating, to throw her arms around his neck and kiss him. Andrion, feeling both commanding as the new Magister of the Academy and incidentally randy as hell, spread her legs as she drifted near the surface before him, and entered her from behind. Oh!

Their three-way romp in the hot pool continued for some time, with one then the other of Bernadette's husbands taking turns to sheath himself in her eager cunt, while the other kissed and fondled her or got his cock sucked. The reduced gravity of making love in water came into delightful play. And eventually she had come several times, each of them had come once, everybody was clean and glowing, and they'd managed not to pollute the bathing pool. Very much.

By the time they emerged from the bathroom, clean and dressed and relaxed, Lifa had put clean bedding on the master bed and gathered her family's belongings. "We'll go down and tell Bjorn to come home to Brightsgate Cottage this evening," Lifa said. "You're all set in the master bedroom." She hugged each of them, as did Anja.

"See you soon, and thanks for everything!" Bernadette said as they departed.

Alone together, the three sat at the dining table. "You haven't finished telling me about everything that happened," Bernadette reminded her men. The tale went on for some time, as the men sipped chilled ale and Bernadette switched to tea. There *were* limits. She was fascinated at the idea of this immortal sorceress, and her succession of lovers, taking over an entire land and treating its people as if they were farm animals. By going along with that, Dalandrin had truly forfeited any compassion she might have felt for him being tortured, poisoned, and eventually robbed of his life.

As evening came on, and the tale wound down, the men were feeling mellow from drinking ale all afternoon while Bernadette was quite sober. She didn't want to broach the subject, but she had to know. Looking her first love in his warm brown eyes, mentally biting her lip, she said "What does this mean for us, Andrion? Are we still a family?"

Andrion was shocked. Looking into her face and seeing her pain and anxiety, he folded Bernadette in his arms and hugged her to him, tears starting in his eyes. How could she imagine that he would ever leave her for some title, some exalted position? "Berni, it's all right," he told her urgently. "You and Erik and our life together, the baby that's coming, are the most important things in the world to me." He released her from the hug to lock gazes with her. Tears were running down her cheeks, but her expression was hopeful.

"Really?" Bernadette said tremulously. "What about the Academy?"

"It's sort of a figurehead position," Andrion assured her. "There aren't even any duties you can put a finger on. I get the use of the Magister's quarters and all of the Academy's resources, and there's even a small stipend; but it's mostly just prestige. I don't even have to spend any time there unless I want to."

Bernadette looked surprised. She hadn't really spent all that much time at the Academy, and wasn't aware of what being the magister actually entailed. "Look," Andrion said, picking up the pack he'd dropped in a corner of the room when they'd arrived earlier today, "I brought back a big sack of books from the library. Mhyrzon just handed them over to me with a smile! He wouldn't even let me in the place when I first arrived a week or so ago. I can keep these as long as I need to, for my studies, and return them whenever I feel like it. This will be a huge plus for us! Wait'll you see what I can come up with, now that the Academy's archives are at my disposal!"

Bernadette was smiling now through the tears that made her eyes sparkle all the more. This was the man she loved, the man she'd married, the brilliant mind that was going to take all their problems and wad them up like so much scrap paper. She fell into his arms.

Chapter 33: Brightsgate Cottage – Sungold, Year One

Downstairs, the men waited with concealed anxiety. They were bantering in the manner of comrades-in-arms, and trying hard to ignore the sounds that were coming down to them from above. In the cottage's little master bedroom, Inge Fordorsson had her sleeves rolled up past her elbows. Bernadette stood near the head of the bed holding Lifa's right hand as, stripped from the waist down and knees up, she strained.

It had been suggested that Anja might like to wait downstairs with Papa and her uncles Erik and Andrion; but her new identity as a tough warrior woman seemed to be sticking, and she had demanded to be present. "Come on, Mama, you can do it!" she piped. "Push!" she echoed the midwife's commands. Through gritted teeth, Lifa eyed her daughter with a sidewise glance, and pushed.

"Here it comes!" Inge cried. A round red head, dark hair plastered to the skull, protruded from Lifa's swollen vulva. It was face up, eyes screwed tight shut, and looked as if it were concentrating as hard as the rest of them were. Then with a gush of fluids, the rest of the quite-large infant emerged from her as she cried out with the effort. Oh, the relief!

Inge cradled the baby in her arms, quickly wrapping it in a clean cloth after she had tied and cut the umbilical cord; then took it over to the room's small table for an inspection. "You have a son!" she proclaimed triumphantly. She cleared the baby boy's mouth and immediately he began screaming his lungs out. What was this rude awakening? He was a strapping boy, dark of hair and (for now, at least) blue of eye, and he had all his fingers and toes. Cleaned and swaddled, he was handed back to his mother as she lay panting and smiling in the bed.

"He's beautiful, Mama!" Anja exclaimed. She'd been excited about the baby since his advent had first been hinted at, and they could all see she was going to make a wonderful Big Sister. When the afterbirth had been expelled and Inge had cleaned Lifa up a bit, provided her with an absorbent pad, and pulled a sheet up over her lower body, the men were invited up to see.

Lifa's breasts had become gigantic during her pregnancy, far larger than the baby's head now. She pulled one free of her loose blouse and offered the nipple to her new son. He was a big boy and going to be a lot bigger – his parents were both well above average height – and he eagerly suckled, taking in the colostrum that would help his digestion and offer him protection from disease. As his mother beheld him there at her breast, an expression of utter peace and happiness suffused her lovely features.

Bjorn, Andrion, and Erik crowded into the room, the Drakespring men hanging back a bit with Bernadette (who was now, herself, swollen with child) to let Bjorn get close. He crouched on his heels at the head of the bed, one hand holding Lifa's while the other gently stroked the baby's head. He leaned over to kiss Lifa on the forehead. "A boy," he breathed, radiating joy. "You know what we decided, Lifi…"

She smiled at him, at the baby, at Anja on her other side, and finally at the three Drakesprings where they stood near the entrance to the room. "His name," she said, "is Fjurbund."

Chapter 34: Drakespring Farm, Year Two

Now it was Bernadette's turn. They'd covered the master bed with a waterproofed hide, topped by smilodon pelts for softness. Lifa and Anja had come, and were in the room with her and Inge – and Andrion and Erik as well. They didn't care if birthing was a woman's thing, this was their wife and their baby and nothing was going to keep them anxiously pacing around in the dining room while their beloved endured hours of pain. Bjorn had opted to hold down the fort in the kitchen – looking after Fjurbund, boiling water, and otherwise making himself useful.

The labor had gone on, in Bernadette's opinion, far too long already. She'd witnessed the births of her two younger siblings and little Fjurbund, so had some idea what to expect. But seeing somebody else in labor is not, it transpired, the same thing as doing it yourself. Erik had been giving her back rubs, Andrion freezing water for ice chips she could suck on. And every couple of minutes, her entire body went into a spasm over which she had absolutely no control.

She'd spent most of her young life in full control of that body, a marvelous instrument. Now it was swollen to ungainly proportions, she walked like a duck, and she was currently at the mercy of a process that was taking place without any conscious intent on her part. Bernadette couldn't wait for it to be over, to get to the prize.

The contractions came faster now. Lifa applied a damp hand towel to her forehead, soothing her somewhat, as Inge urged her to start pushing and Anja stood off to one side, eyes wide. Having been there for the birth of her baby brother she (now close to seven) imagined that she was an old hand at this sort of thing; but Aunt Berni was taking a lot longer than Mama had. Mama was a bigger woman.

Augh shit, it hurt! Bernadette felt like she was trying to pass a full-sized gourd through the vaginal opening that hitherto had never seen anything bigger than Erik's cock. She seemed to recall a conversation along these lines many months ago, but speculation had been light and jolly. This was real, and relentless, and more painful than anything she had ever experienced in her life. Yet somehow, she felt joyful.

"It's crowning," Inge advised after the last contraction had released its grip. Bernadette lay there panting, knees up. This is very likely the position I was in when this all started, she thought sardonically. In less than a full minute it started again, and Inge urged "Push! Come on, push it out!" With Andrion gripping one hand and Erik the other Bernadette bore down. I want this little bugger *out*, she thought, and gave it all she had. It helped to be in good physical shape, and she'd continued doing chores around the farm throughout her pregnancy.

The unbearable pressure suddenly released seconds before Inge, who was kneeling on the bed, bent to scoop the child up and proclaim "It's a boy!" Andrion and Erik, while not releasing Berni's hands, had their eyes glued to the little stranger who had just arrived in their midst. After dealing with the cord and cleaning the baby off, Inge returned him to Bernadette's arms.

He was perfect in every way, not crying that much, seeming comforted now that he'd been swaddled and put near his mother once again. He didn't have much hair, but what there was of it was drying quickly in the warm air of the bedroom. It was a light reddish brown, slightly waving. He opened his eyes and gazed up into Bernadette's face, that unfocused stare of the newborn that somehow penetrates straight to the bottom of your soul. Those eyes had the blue cast all new babies showed; but she could see already that they would be brown. Hugging her son to her, looking up at Andrion and then Erik in tired triumph, Bernadette said "This is Andreas."

Chapter 35: Drakespring Farm, Year Three

It was a partly cloudy day in late winter, and Bernadette was almost finished with her morning chores. Erik had taken care of the breakfast dishes and the milking, so all Bernadette had to do was weed the cabbage patch, pull carrots, feed the chickens, and collect their eggs. Andreas, who was now toddling pretty well, accompanied her on these rounds.

Her son was now almost fourteen months old, and Bernadette was already seeing signs that babyhood was slipping behind him. Such a sturdy, self-confident little guy! He was Andrion's son beyond a shadow of a doubt, but he seemed to be picking up traits from his other papa as well.

Until she had held her baby boy in her arms, she had never understood the depths, the overwhelming organic nature of mother love. He had grown inside her body for nine months, and then after he had come out he had spent another year and more obtaining sustenance from her body, maintaining the physical bond.

Bernadette loved Andrion and Erik, had been willing to give up her freewheeling lifestyle in order to forge a new life together with them; but Andreas had a lock on her soul. Sometimes when she gazed at his sleeping face as he nestled close to her breast, she thought her heart would burst with joy. Yet now she was thinking she should cut the strings a little bit, wean him and let him move on from baby to child. Though she hated to do so, she knew that it would have to be done sooner or later. And she wanted another baby, which would be likelier to happen if she stopped nursing.

All of these thoughts about motherhood had Bernadette thinking of her own mother, recently. She now understood what she had never done before: that her mother loved her more than she could know – and if they'd had conflicts while she was growing up, it was only because her mother wanted what was best for her and worried that her wayward, tomboy elder daughter would be hurt doing the things she did.

Bernadette hadn't left home until she was in her twenties, a woman grown. Indeed, something of an old maid in the environs of Pied de Puce. Her parents had not wanted to see her go, off to become a penniless wanderer at risk from a thousand perils; but they'd had no way of stopping her. The willful girl she'd been then wasn't taking advice from anyone. How she must have broken her mother's heart! And for all her family in Auverne knew of her since, she'd perished years ago at the hands of some bandit outlaws or a mountain bear.

I've got to think of some way to send word to them, to let them know that I'm all right and how successful I've been in life, she thought. But the distances were so great, and even the most skilled of messengers might have trouble locating Pied de Puce. She sighed. "Come on, Andi, time to go back to the house," Bernadette said, taking her little one by his chubby hand. A basket of warm brown eggs was slung over her arm.

Work was well underway on the construction of their outdoor forge, which would be floored in stone and with stone walls rising to a height of four feet before being continued in wood. A steel stovepipe would pass through the slate roof to carry smoke away, and enormous swinging doors could be opened wide to leave the entire eastern side of the building open to the air for working in nice weather.

That was the side that faced the road, so whoever was working in the forge could see anyone coming along it. When the forge was not in use, the doors could be shut and locked to keep thieves from making off with tools and supplies. They'd decided not to include a smelter. One was available nearby in the basement of the Maiden, if needed.

The work on this was being done by Erik, with assistance from Bjorn on his days off. Both of them had picked up some of the builders' skills during the construction on Drakespring Farm's annex; and in the years since then Bjorn had become a master of all such things. He guided Erik, training him in masonry work. Erik had a good eye for detail and the massive strength that made any such physical tasks easier. Bernadette looked forward to having the use of the forge soon, as spring was coming on.

Despite Andrion's initial assurances that his position as Magister of the Academy would not impact their family life, he was often away on Academy business or pursuing his various research projects for days at a time. He was there now, had been gone for the better part of a week. He'd told Bernadette and Erik that he was close to achieving a breakthrough on something that was going to revolutionize their lives, but he wanted it to be a surprise.

Bernadette supposed that without this work to occupy him Andrion might have hung around the place and driven them all crazy. His active mind needed new challenges, and there was only so much that studying books could tell him. Sometimes he needed to get out in the field and try things – and he wisely preferred to conduct experiments at the Academy, where he had other mages to assist him and his family was safe from anything that might go wrong. She'd decided she didn't mind, much. He was home more often than not, and he frequently brought them goodies when he returned from his excursions.

The family's income had remained fairly constant even though Bernadette had taken a long sabbatical from questing. Andrion still occasionally took Erik (or one of the Maiden guys, if Erik couldn't be spared) questing in dypalfar ruins, and along with the items of dypalfar tech he'd come for he picked up jewels, enchanted weapons, and valuable metals. Their income from the Maiden, now twice the inn it had once been, had greatly increased.

A couple of times over the past year, Bernadette had left Andrion at home with the baby so she and Erik could take a day trip up to the bandit lair across the river and clean it out. It was a service to the march, and good exercise as well. She kept herself in trim otherwise with chores, smithing, archery practice, and sparring, using practice swords, with either or both of her husbands. Her right arm was something to behold.

Inside the house, Bernadette set the basket of eggs on the kitchen counter. She'd put them in the cooler soon; but at the moment her nose told her the darling boy whose hand she still held was in need of a diaper change. Scooping him up carefully, she took him down the hall to the nursery. This room was now furnished with the baby's clothing and diaper storage, a small bed, a crib, a changing table, and an ever-growing collection of toys; though most nights he slept in a cot in the master bedroom with his parents.

Andreas' arrival had definitely put a damper on the active sex life the three of them had enjoyed before he was born. But they still managed to steal their moments. Sometimes Bernadette would spend the night sleeping with one or the other of her husbands in his personal bedroom while the other kept the baby company. This had only become possible once he had started sleeping through the night, of course – but Andreas had been a big baby and he grew fast.

After Andreas was sweet and clean once again, she turned him loose on the toys in the nursery while she sat in a chair and tried to read a book. As dearly as she loved her son, Bernadette was not the sort of adult who can really enjoy playing games with toddlers. Erik was the man for the job, but he was busy on the forge project now. Given that he was learning how to do it as he went along, and that Bjorn was only available one or two days a week to assist, the construction was dragging on for weeks.

Bernadette sighed. Maybe they really needed some help around the place, if only for a few hours a day to give her time to get a few important things done. She was about two years behind on her journal, for one thing – and the family relied in part on her forge income. She had become so good at producing weapons, especially enchanted ones, that she had created a maker's mark stamp patterned after her Fireblood signet. Those that were enchanted had an added mark indicating the enchantment. All of these had been carved in wax and cast in steel for her by Erik, working from her own designs. Genuine Fireblood arms fetched a premium.

As she sat with the book in her lap, eyes on her little one and her thoughts wandering, Bernadette heard Erik's booming voice calling from the far end of the hall. "Berni? Where are you?" "Down here!" she yelled back, and heard two sets of footsteps proceeding down the hall. Shortly Erik appeared in the doorway, nearly filling it. "Look who materialized on our doorstep," he said jovially – stepping aside to reveal Andrion behind him.

The book cast aside without another thought, Bernadette leapt to her feet and ran to enfold her prodigal husband in her arms. Andreas, too, had dropped what he was doing and was toddling to greet his "other daddy." "Papa Andin!" he called, the best pronunciation he could yet manage on the name that had given rise to his own. After giving Berni a fierce hug and a passionate kiss, Andrion bent to scoop his baby son up in his arms as the child ran toward him.

"How's my boy?" he asked, tickling his belly to make him giggle and then puckering up. "Give me a kiss!" Andreas was a sweet boy and he didn't mind giving kisses at all, though Lifa said Fjurbund preferred to avoid them.

After the youngster had been kissed and hugged, Andrion passed him over to Erik, who lifted him up to ride on his massive shoulders. They'd intentionally made the ceilings throughout the annex lofty, in consideration of Erik's 6'5" height. The little guy hugged Papa Erik's head, peering over the top of it to see what was going on.

Andrion had Bernadette's familiar magic map in his hand. He'd undoubtedly still been holding it when he arrived here after fast-traveling from the Academy. He must have left late in the evening, Eisenstag time, to be arriving home at this hour. It was around a 10-hour trip that appeared to take 20 seconds, to the person doing the traveling.

"This is what I was telling you about," Andrion said, addressing both Bernadette and Erik. Setting the map down on the changing table and opening it out (it was made of some magical substance that despite being folded and unfolded hundreds of times during years of use, never frayed nor wore out). Then he unslung his pack from his back and produced, out of the top of it, three smallish rolls of a material that resembled paper.

Andrion set two of the rolls to the side and unrolled the third one, remarking "They're all the same." It was a map! Now that they got a closer look at it, they could see that it was made of the same material as the original map. While the map never wore out, it had certainly picked up its share of smudges, fingerprints, and occasional bloodstains. It could be sponged clean, but nobody had done this in a while. The new map's background was a light cream color, unblemished.

Bernadette looked at Andrion in wonderment. "Are you saying this is…?" She could hardly believe it. Andrion smiled at both of them, radiating pride and pleasure.

"Yes, this is a new magic map, which I made! I finally figured out how it's done. The literature was spread all over the place and I had to fill in some missing information by trial and error, but look!" He pointed at Drakespring Farm, which was clearly marked. "It wasn't there when I left, using your map. You'll see that the major cities are marked, and you'll also notice this is a map of the whole continent of Agena including the major islands around the continent. I could have made it to cover all of Terris, but it would have had to be a lot bigger in order to show detail. Not to mention you'd spend the rest of your life filling it in with fast-travel points."

Erik and Bernadette were dumfounded. Andrion unrolled the other two maps to show that they were identical. "I tried them on Eisenstag first," he told them. "So I wouldn't have to go so far if it didn't work. There still doesn't seem to be any way to tell without trying whether a major point marked on the map is enabled for travel, yet. Just like with the other one, if you're in possession of a map and someone tells you about a place or gives you a quest, a marker will appear. But you'll still have to get there by mundane means, either with the map in your control or as a companion of the person working the map, before it will take you there."

Bernadette threw her arms around Andrion and gave him a deep kiss. "This is wonderful, Andrion!" she crowed. "Do you realize what this means? All we have to do is travel by coach to Auverne and visit our families, and then we'll be able to go straight home from there – and return whenever we feel like it!" Her longing to visit with her parents and younger siblings had suddenly spiked as she realized it might actually be possible.

Andrion had been gone from his boyhood home without any communication for a long time, and it hadn't even occurred to him that this was one use the maps might be put to. He'd been thinking more along the lines of visiting Remus, or bringing back dypalfar treasures from Darkreach. His immediate thought was that the three of them (once Andreas was weaned and could be left in the care of, perhaps, the Steadfast family) could use the original map, carrying the three new ones with them, and populate the new maps with all of the fast-travel points the original now had.

That project would take months, too long to leave their baby; but maybe they could do it a little at a time – a week here, another week there. Sort of a working vacation. They'd need someone to look after the farm, as well. Hmm… Andrion realized that he'd been so excited and enthusiastic about his success with the creation of new magic maps that he had not really given much thought at all to the practical implications. This was unlike him, and he felt he may have been playing too much with his new toys at the Academy and leaving most of the real-world concerns to Berni and Erik. Time to knuckle down.

"Would you really like to do that, Berni?" Andrion asked her. Her face was fixed in a big grin and her eyes were glowing with excitement. That looked like a "yes."

"Ever since Andi was born I've been thinking about taking him to visit my family," she told him. "There were issues that I had with my mom that I realize were completely ridiculous, now that I'm a mom myself. And I want to see what kind of people my baby brother and sister grew up to be. Even little old Pied de Puce is starting to seem attractive, after all these years away."

Both of Bernadette's husbands were looking at her with mixed feelings, but it seemed Andrion at least was ready to consider the idea seriously. "If we're going to take Andi with us it's probably best if we go while he's still nursing. That'll be less supplies to carry. We can acquire a coach and a couple of horses, and I'm pretty sure we can fast-travel *with* the coach over to Milburn. Then just shoot down the road to the Auverne border. Where exactly is Pied de Puce?"

"It's not on any map I've ever seen," Bernadette replied. "It's a little to the west and north of Arlise, though. If we go there we can ask around locally for the road. It's been so many years since I went that way…" Erik was beginning to take this all in with a certain amount of amusement. He had no reason to be travelling to Auverne, other than for the fun of it and to meet the families of his marriage mates.

"What about protection?" he threw into the discussion. "Stray arrows, that sort of thing? I wouldn't want anything happening to our boy…" He patted Andreas' chubby little leg, which was wrapped around his neck like a cloth-clad torc.

"I've got some mage robes with an armor enchantment on them. Berni can learn that and use it on a robe or cloak for Andi so that it'll stop anything short of a dragon from getting to him. And with us three riding the coach, what do we have to worry about?" Erik considered. True, he and his mates were more than a match for the average dozen bandits. Likely they would encounter some wildlife and monsters as well while traversing the wilds; but natural creatures rarely attacked coaches and monsters generally came one at a time.

"It sounds like a plan then," Erik said. "When do we leave?"

Bernadette and Andrion both looked at him, smiling. Good old Erik. He was their rock, the person in their marriage who was always ready for anything and always with a smile.

They spoke nearly at once, though, to say "We'll need someone to look after the farm…" Erik was unperturbed. He was friends with half the people in Waterdon, after living in the area for more than four years.

"I have a buddy in town who'll be happy to do it," he told them. "He grew up on a farm, so he knows what to do, and he needs a place to stay for a while anyhow. I'd be willing to bet he'll live here and do all the chores just for room and board."

Bernadette's eyes lit. She couldn't believe this was happening! But now she had to kick her mind into gear and think of everything that must be done before they could go. She hadn't put out such an effort since a couple of years ago, when she'd been planning Lifa's wedding and her own. "Erik, do you think you can acquire a coach and a couple of horses?" Coaches were rare in Iscandia, wagons being the usual means of transport for those who cared more about carrying capacity than speed.

"I'm thinking Arngeld could build us one. He'd probably use the wheels and chassis of a standard wagon and build up from there. That would give us the opportunity to have it built however we want it, maybe a little armor plating on the sides. Elvengild's pretty light… And if I put in an order with Skulvar at the Stables, he could have us a matched set of horses by the time Arngeld's finished with the coach."

Bernadette took a deep breath. "Okay, then. Erik, you're in charge of finding us a farm hand and getting the coach and horses ready to go. Let me know after you talk to Arngeld so I know how long we have before we can leave." It was a lot easier, organizing, when you weren't trying to keep the details secret from the participants! "Andrion, I'd like to get you to consult with Lev and lay in enough provisions to last most of the trip. We'll probably be able to restock, but it'll be better to have reserves. I'll get that enchantment going on a full wardrobe for Andi – you know how he goes through clothes – and start gathering up what else we're going to need to take."

Andrion and Erik snapped to attention and saluted, saying in unison "Yes, Ma'am!" Argh, could they be more annoying? Bernadette glared at them, then relented and smiled once again.

"If any of you would like to discuss rearranging this division of labor, feel free to do so," she said acerbically.

"Sounds fine to me," Andrion said, gathering up the collection of magic maps. "Erik?"

"I'm good," he replied with his usual cheerful nonchalance. "Berni, when was the last time you nursed this little fiend?" He gestured with his eyebrows to the tot still happily riding his shoulders. The view from up here was awesome!

She put a hand to her chest. Now that Andi was eating pretty much everything and occasionally drinking fruit juice, water, or cow's milk out of cups, her milk supply was on the decline. But she hadn't nursed him since right after getting up this morning, and her breasts were now taut, distended, and felt as if they might be glowing. In all the excitement, she'd let the usual nursing time slide right by. Odd Andi hadn't reminded her.

"I think it's about time," Bernadette told him. "What did you have in mind?"

"I thought after you nurse him, I might take him into Waterdon with me," Erik told her. With Andrion's frequent absences, Erik got the lion's share of Berni's sexual attentions and he knew his marriage mate would likely be hoping for some privacy. Besides, he needed to consult with Arngeld and Remy.

Bernadette exchanged glances, not with Erik but with Andrion. He gave her that little smile that had sent a thrill through her since the first time they'd met. Then she looked to Erik, who reached up over his head and handed Andreas down to her. "Want some boo-boo, baby?" she asked the tyke. This was the baby-talk term for breastfeeding that had developed between them. His eyes lit up and he reached for Mama eagerly.

"I'm going to get a little more done on the forge for now," Erik said. "I can probably get it finished before we're ready to leave for Auverne."

"I'll have to put in quite a few hours at the forge over at the Maiden," Bernadette said half to herself, only now recalling her obligations to Valkyrie. Her partnership with Alessia and Wolaf (who were soon expecting their first child, after years of marriage) didn't specify a number of pieces to be produced; but if she were leaving for weeks, she needed to get ahead of the demand.

"You're going to be staying here until we leave, Andrion?" Bernadette asked as she carried Andreas toward the master bedroom. It was a little cool today for her preferred nursing location, a rocking chair on their wonderful veranda overlooking the Brightwater. There was another such chair in the bedroom, and Andreas' cot was in there so he could go down for a nap after nursing, if he felt like it. More often than not these days, he eschewed naps in favor of nonstop activity followed by exhausted crankiness in the early evening.

"This project was all that was keeping me at the Academy recently," Andrion replied. "I think it's about time I stay home for a while." Bernadette smiled at him serenely. "I'm just going to get something to eat from the kitchen," he added. "Then I'll join you." In the master bedroom, she seated herself in the comfortable, padded rocker, snuggling her son in her lap, and he eagerly reached into her blouse to help her pull out one of her swollen breasts. Gazing into her eyes with adoration, he chomped down on the nipple.

"Hey, no biting!" she said firmly. A look of mischief passed across his sweet, innocent features so quickly one might easily have missed it. But after that he settled down to nurse, the intake of familiar nourishment in the arms of his mother soon sending him into a trance.

Andrion came in and sat on another chair at the room's corner table, just gazing at the two of them with love as he gnawed his way through a slightly stale bread roll layered with slices of cheese. He washed it down with some chilled cow's milk from this morning's milking. He would certainly have loved this child had he been blond and blue-eyed; but knowing that Andreas was the son of his body gave him a certain satisfaction he could not deny.

The boy seemed as if he might be drifting off to sleep for a while; but when Bernadette switched breasts he roused. By the time Bernadette's milk supply was exhausted Andreas seemed to have gotten his second wind and was looking around bright-eyed. He was wearing a moisture-resistant woolen garment over his absorbent cotton diaper, but she could tell from feeling his crotch that he was due for a change. With a smile and a look, she passed the damp tot off to his father. Andrion grimaced slightly, then smiled and reeled him in before heading down the hall toward the nursery changing table. He'd definitely escaped what some might consider his fair share of diapering duties, never mind the farm chores.

After Andreas was clean and dry once more Andrion and Bernadette carried him out to where Erik was working. He'd used up his supply of mortar and cleaned his tools, and was just tucking them away in the cistern tower shed. "There's my boy!" he cried, taking Andreas from Andrion's arms and hoisting him once again onto his shoulders. He had a dagger at his side, which should be adequate. The increase in the human population of the Waterdon area was gradually driving out both bandits and hostile wildlife, making the trip to town safer than ever.

Bernadette had brought along a bag with a couple of spare diapers, extra clothing, and some ointment, which she handed over. "We'll be back in about two hours, I expect," Erik said. "Probably pick up lunch in town. Say 'bye-bye', Andi!" This was one of Andreas' better tricks.

He waved his little hand, grinning from ear to ear atop his lofty perch, and piped "Bye-Bye!"

Andrion and Bernadette, standing each with an arm around the other, waved their free hands and echoed "Bye-Bye!"

They watched Erik and his small rider down the walk and up the road, then turned to one another. Ooh, it had been too long! Andrion briefly considered ravishing his wife right here in the farmyard, then decided against it. "What do you say," he asked her casually, "we go inside and mess up the bed?" She gave him a wicked grin, and took his hand. They walked back into the house.

In fact, it took a month before the Drakespring family were ready to leave on their map-marking expedition to Auverne. But Erik's friend Remy Caron, a young Galise, came to live with them no more than a few days after they'd put their plans into motion. He'd been staying with friends in Waterdon since being turned out of his previous lodgings when his landlady had needed the room for a newly-arrived cousin.

Remy's welcome there was wearing thin, so he was delighted to have the spare bedroom at Drakespring Farm and share the family's meals while he performed all the farm chores. He was a wiry young fellow, easy-going and not bad looking, a little on the small side. But he clearly knew his way around a farm, and after he'd been there a week Bernadette was glad indeed that they'd found him. She and Andreas still collected the eggs from the chickens sometimes just for fun; but no longer needing to be up at dawn to milk the cows (of which there were now two), let alone muck out their paddock, was a huge relief.

Bernadette, Andrion, and Erik took it in turns to keep an eye on Andreas while the other two worked. Andrion had carved out a section of their crafting room for his less-hazardous magical experiments, and was involved in two or three different lines of inquiry he was able to pursue from home. Erik, having ordered the building of their coach, put in as much time as he could spare on the smithy building, completing the stonemasonry and raising the wooden walls above it. He had Bjorn's and sometimes Andrion's assistance with the roof, which really required at least two people working at one time.

While Bjorn was there Lifa, Anja, and Fjurbund would come along. The Steadfast boy, some four months older than Andreas, was several inches taller and likely to be a man in the mold of his father Bjorn someday – though his coloring was more like that of his mother. Anja, now around eight, was far too old to play with the boys; but she was happy to keep an eye on them in the nursery while her mother and Aunt Berni chatted at the other end of the hall over cups of tea.

Bernadette put in quite a few hours per week at the Maiden's basement forge, turning out Fireblood blades and enchanted armor. It wasn't truly practical to enchant Andreas' entire wardrobe with the armored cloth spell – not even the Maiden had enough filled vials of magical essence for that. So she settled on applying the enchantment to a couple of sturdy outer garments for him, ones that would last for years and that he wouldn't immediately grow out of.

Finally the day arrived. The new Drakespring smithy was completed, forge ready for fuel, workbench, anvil, and grindstone in place. They already had an outdoor tanning rack. Valkyrie had a several-week backlog of arms and armor ready to put on sale while Bernadette was gone, and the family had a carefully gathered collection of clothing and armor, books, weapons, food supplies, water skins, and of course the maps.

Bernadette instructed Remy to go down to the Maiden for his meals while they were gone, something she'd arranged with Lev and Drelos earlier. If he wanted to cook for himself, they'd supply him with ingredients; but she wasn't surprised to learn that he was more than happy to have his meals cooked for him. Erik had said he was going to town to collect the horses and coach, and the rest of them were waiting anxiously for him to appear. He'd kept the details a surprise, and none of them knew what to expect.

Bernadette was arraying their packs, "helped" by Andreas, when a jingling of harness alerted her and she looked up. Coming down the road was the oddest conveyance she had ever seen in her life, drawn by a matched pair of Iscandia's sturdy, heavily built horses with Erik on the driver's seat. As she and her little one stood gaping, he pulled it off the road and up the drive toward the house, skirting the cabbage patch, and drew it to a halt. He was beaming with delight.

Pulling the brake lever, Erik used a step built into the front part of the coach to climb down into the farmyard. "Well," he said grinning, "What do you think?" Bernadette was at a loss for words.

"It's... it's simply astounding, Erik," she told him after a moment. "Was this your design?"

"I gave Arngeld a few specifications and some general ideas of what we wanted, but I think this is another case like the Owner's Table at the Maiden," Erik admitted. "You recall he's a big fan of yours, right?"

Bernadette had gathered Andreas into her arms, and was walking around the coach while both of them took it in through widened eyes. The running gear was approximately the same as that on a normal wagon, four enormous steel-shod wooden spoke wheels supporting a wooden framework. But the coach body itself was suspended above the frame on enormous steel leaf springs. Not that she knew what they were called…

The part of the coach they were to ride inside was shaped like a large box with a rounded bottom, and though seemingly made of wood it was plated all over the outside surfaces with elvengild, the metal used for elven armor. Her Fireblood crest had been worked into the plates covering the doors, embossed and gleaming. There were four small windows, two on each side, and a door on either side through which one could enter the coach. Each of these was served by a steel step mounted to the framework.

Erik was watching them with amusement. "You'll notice," he said, "that I got the horses to match your hair…" Bernadette blinked. They were light chestnuts, very close indeed to her own hair color. She smiled at him.

"That was so *sweet*, Erik. Go tell Andrion to come see. I think he's in the craft room." He nodded and disappeared into the house while his wife and son continued their explorations. Andreas was a lot more interested in the horses than he was in the coach. After making sure they were gentle beasts and were not going to bite him, she let him pat the nice horsey on the neck. He was thrilled.

"Come on, Andi, let's see what's inside," Bernadette told her son. The windows were too high up to look through when she was standing on the ground. Climbing the step with Andreas on her hip, she pulled the door latch and climbed inside. Oh, my! The ceiling was fairly high, not high enough for her (let alone Erik) to stand up in of course, but the interior seemed airy. There was a sheepskin rug on the floor and bench seats along the width of the coach at the front and rear. They were thickly cushioned and upholstered in dark red leather. Well-fitted shutters could be closed across the windows and barred, keeping out the weather and/or anything that might be attacking you.

179

The doors could be barred from the inside as well, so that in some ways the coach was like a little rolling fortress. Cabinets were built into the undersides of the seats, providing stowage, and there was a hatch in the ceiling. Placing Andreas on the rear seat, Bernadette unbarred the hatch and pushed it open. She could now stand up inside, and look around. The coach was armored up here, too, and had racks on either side to which you could tie more luggage.

Bernadette imagined that with those racks stacked high your view would be limited to the front and rear, unless you… hmm… Getting a grip on either side of the hatch with her strong arms, she boosted herself out the hole and made her way toward the rear. There were a couple of handholds, she saw, so theoretically someone could ride up here – perhaps with a bow.

She was now kneeling on top of the hatch, which opened toward the rear. Turning around, Bernadette poked her head back down inside the coach, where Andreas was looking around and beginning to get a little concerned. Where had Mama disappeared to? "Peek-a-boo!" she said, looking at him upside down. His eyes went wide, then he dissolved into a fit of giggles, bouncing up and down on the seat.

Bernadette pulled her head back out for a moment, then repeated the trick – provoking fresh gales of baby laughter. "Again, Mama!" he said with surprising clarity.

She did it a couple more times for him, then said "Stay right there, Andi. I'll be back in one minute." She stood on the top of coach, which shifted slightly on its springs. Likely this curious suspension would help to eliminate some of the worst bumps in the empire's dubious and neglected road system, but she doubted it would be a smooth ride.

Bernadette looked behind her. A quite large, metal-bound chest was mounted to the back, providing still more luggage space. Railings protruded from the rear of the coach on either side above it, making it possible for the top of the chest to be used as an extra seat for two people – assuming they were friendly with each other. At least they'd have something to hold onto. She stepped across the open hatch to the front, and down onto the driver's bench. There was more storage below it, and she realized that there was a rolled-up awning stowed up near the top of the coach. Sitting on the driver's seat, which was easily wide enough for two, she pulled a strap hanging from the awning and it rolled out to form a roof over the seat. Handy for hot sun or rain.

"Mama! Where ah you?" came Andreas' plaintive voice, reminding her she was taking too long.

"I'll be right there sweetie," she called back. Just then Erik and Andrion came out of the house, talking animatedly about something. Erik gestured at the coach, saying "ta-dah!" Andrion was as impressed as she was. Thought his background was both deeper and more sophisticated than hers, he too had never seen the like.

Realizing he had other resources, Andreas switched over to calling "Papa! Papa!" in a demanding voice. Andrion hopped up on the other side step and opened the door.

"Here I am, Andi!" he said, climbing inside and sitting on the bench opposite his son. Now that he was no longer bereft and alone, the tot was quite content to continue sitting on his comfy seat. "Erik, this upholstery is fantastic!" Andrion said, bouncing up and down slightly. It might actually be possible to ride in this for several hours without having one's backside blistered.

The family continued to explore the coach, Erik pointing out features Bernadette had missed, for some time. Then Andrion got a gleam in his eye. "This is perfect timing," he informed his marriage mates. "I have just finally solved a problem I've been working on for almost three years, and I think it's going to come in very handy on this trip." He walked a few paces away from them, facing away from them toward a fairly flat space not far from the front door of the farmhouse.

Andrion raised his hands in the familiar pose of a mage about to cast a spell. Erik and Bernadette had seen anything from fireballs to intense beams of white-hot energy capable of cutting through plate armor appear, when Andrion was standing like this. But neither of them was prepared for what came forth on this occasion, almost silently save for a faint "pumph" of displaced air.

On the flat space Andrion had been aiming at there was suddenly a sturdy wooden tub, around 3 feet in diameter and some 2 feet high. It appeared to be full of water, which was steaming even though the air on this early spring day was not in the least cold. After staring open-mouthed at it for a moment Bernadette and Erik turned to each other, each wanting to confirm that the other had seen what they had. Then they turned back to Andrion.

"By the gods!" Bernadette exclaimed, rushing to examine this prodigy in more detail. She felt the tub. It appeared to be a perfectly ordinary wooden tub, slightly worn as though it had been in use for some time. The water within it was sparkling clear, and of a temperature close to that delivered by the hot water units in their house. You'd need to wait awhile before bathing in this, assuming the water would cool in time.

Wiping her hand on her skirt, Bernadette turned to Andrion, her face radiating delight. "You did it!" she crowed. "I can hardly believe you really did it!" She enfolded him in her arms, then jumped up, skirt hiking up her legs, to reach him with a kiss. Her reaction was everything he'd hoped for. He'd been working on this project, whenever he had the chance, since she had first mentioned it – back before they were engaged. Initially he'd envisioned a sunken tub big enough for multiple occupants, like the one in their bathroom. But this was what he'd been able to produce, and it had uses beyond bathing.

Bernadette had pulled away from Andrion a little now and was looking at him with a mock glare. "You! You never gave me the slightest hint…" He smiled down at her. If anything, he loved her more when she was mad – even if, as in this instance he suspected, she was faking it.

"I didn't want to get your hopes up if it didn't work out," he told her. Erik was still standing there looking delighted and half-unbelieving. Andrion had not confided any details of this project to him, either.

Andrion beckoned toward the steaming tub of water. "This has its limitations," he explained. "The water will cool just as if it were a regular tub of water sitting out in the air anywhere. Whatever dirt gets into it doesn't have anywhere to go. And, after exactly one hour, it will completely vanish without a trace. Any water from the tub spilled outside it will be gone, too. But of course after an hour the

water's going to be lukewarm at best. So this isn't for long soaks."
Andrion gazed into Bernadette's eyes. She might not be a scholar as
he was, but she was the possessor of one of the sharpest minds he'd
ever encountered, in either sex. "You realize what this means?"

He watched the wheels turning, then her eyes lit up and the grin
that had only left her face briefly since his demonstration somehow
got wider. "We can wash diapers on the road!" she cried, excited.
This had been one of her biggest concerns, taking what might well be
a month-long trip with a baby.

"Got it in one," Andrion replied happily. He had known she'd
see it.

Bernadette continued thinking through the implications. "Uh,"
she said after a moment, "What happens to the dirt or... whatever...
when the tub disappears?"

"It ends up on the floor, or the ground, where the tub was,"
Andrion replied. "It'll be as dry as it was when it went into the water,
though. For diaper-washing I think it'd be best to put the tub
someplace we don't mind getting dirty, or that'll be easy to clean up
afterward."

Another question occurred to her. "Can you do this multiple
times in an hour?"

"Yes," Andrion assured her. "But it takes a hell of a lot of
magical energy. Unless I take a potion for a temporary magical
energy boost or quick replenishment, I can only materialize a tub of
hot water about once every ten minutes."

"Oh," Bernadette replied, "that should be fine! I assume we
won't normally be producing these when we're under attack. But I'll
get to work in the chemia lab and whip us up some more potions. I
think maybe we should postpone leaving and not go until tomorrow
morning."

Erik had been following the conversation closely, if not
contributing to it. "That's a good idea, Berni," he chimed in. "What
do you say Andrion and I start packing all of these provisions into
the coach's storage areas while you work on those potions. And then
maybe later we can go have dinner at the Maiden and say goodbye to
everybody?" Everyone was in agreement.

Hours later, the horses had been rubbed down and put into the paddock with the cows, and the coach was packed with what the family hoped would be all they needed for the journey ahead. Bernadette had gotten so engrossed in making potions, not to mention last-minute list checking, that she'd left nursing Andreas until much later than usual. All of the excitement had distracted him as well, wandering around in a wet diaper gnawing on a stale bread roll; and after being changed and nursed, he'd dropped right off to sleep. Bernadette had put him down in his crib in the nursery for a change.

By now it was past six. Remy had long since finished the day's farm chores and had a bite to eat, and was sitting in a chair on the veranda with his feet up on a footstool, admiring the warm late-afternoon light as it set the mountains to the east aglow. He was something of a poetic soul, not as odd in a farmer as you might think. Bernadette let herself out of the nursery through the veranda door, and took a seat beside him. She spoke quietly. "Remy, as you've no doubt guessed we're not leaving until tomorrow after all. Andi's asleep in his crib, and we're going to go down to the Maiden for supper and to say goodbye to everyone. Can you keep an ear out for him?"

Remy gave her his shy smile. He quite liked the little tyke. "No problem, Bernadette," he assured her. "I'll be out here until it gets dark, so just leave the door open a crack. Then when I go inside I'll leave the nursery door in the hall and the one to the front of the house open so I can hear him if he wakes up while I'm reading." That was another thing about their young farm hand that surprised Bernadette. He was a voracious reader, and spent most of his evenings with his nose in a book. Fortunately their house had books aplenty, if not all of them were what you could call entertaining.

Bernadette thanked him and went back into the house through the master bedroom, then across the hall to gather up the sack of potions she'd made. In her mind, she was envisioning these as a month's supply of hot baths, or perhaps clean diapers and underclothes. Sack in hand, she headed out the front to add this last item to the luggage stowed in the coach. She found Erik and Andrion there, making a last check that nothing had been forgotten.

Bernadette found a space for the sack under the coach's front seat, tucked in among extra weapons and armor. Then she climbed down and suggested, "Why don't we wash up and then walk on down to the Maiden? I'm hungry." Erik and Andrion agreed. They ran a little hot water in the dishwashing sink, and used some of the nicer soap Bernadette had gotten from Adele recently. It was not as caustic as the usual stuff, and had a pleasant herbal scent.

Thus fit to sit down for a meal, the three wended their way a quarter mile down the road, arm-in-arm with Bernadette in the middle. Both the men had to slow their pace to accommodate her, but they didn't mind in the least. Andrion was still simmering with elation at having finally perfected the hot bath spell, and Erik was quite pleased with the way the coach had come out; so happiness reigned.

Shouts of greeting echoed around them as they entered the common room and made their way to the Owner's Table. They smiled and waved. All the Maiden employees and local regular guests knew them well, after the years since Bernadette had first come on the scene. Drelos hurried over to take their order. "You're here without the nipper!" he remarked. It was rare for all three of them to come to the Maiden together, unless Andreas was along.

"Remy's watching him so we can have an evening out," Bernadette told him with a smile. "We're leaving tomorrow, don't forget." They placed their dinner orders, getting some baked salmon with mashed potatoes and wilted spring greens. This early in the spring, there often wasn't much in the way of fresh food – but salmon were there in the river for the taking year 'round. People mostly let them alone while they ate, but after their plates were cleared friends swarmed around, eager to hear about the exciting trip, see one of the new maps, and so forth. Andrion was required to produce a tub of hot water on the spot, to cheers from the onlookers.

The Maiden staff were proud of their Drakespring family. Bernadette was The Fireblood, of course, and now Andrion, once one of their own, was Magister of the Academy at Eisenstag and clearly (as demonstrated tonight) one of the most powerful mages in the world as well as being a decent guy. And Erik was... well, Erik. Everybody who'd ever met Erik liked him (discounting bandits, vampires, and hostile mages, of course), and most came to love him if they knew him for long.

They could happily have stayed there all evening socializing, singing, and drinking. But an early departure was planned for the morning, and Bernadette was getting anxious about leaving Andreas for so long. So they walked back down the road before ten. They came upon a surprising scene of domestic bliss as they walked in the front door: Remy had Andreas on his lap and was reading him a story. From the stack of books on the floor beside the chair, this was not the first one. He smiled up at all of them, but it was "Mama!" whom he greeted. From the feel of her breasts, it was time to feed him again.

Bernadette took him in her arms and kissed him, snuggling him close. He was a cuddly little fellow, not like some baby boys. "He woke up only about an hour after you left," Remy informed them. "But he wasn't cranky at all. We've been having a fine time."

"I think I'll take him down the hall and see if I can't get him back to bed," Bernadette said to the room in general. "Thanks, Remy, I really appreciate it. Erik, Andrion, I was thinking I might take a bath before bed if I can get this guy down," she added.

Erik and Andrion exchanged a glance and said in unison, "Sounds like a good idea." It was getting to the point where they could finish each other's sentences. Bernadette got a dry diaper and a stretchy woolen sleeper with built-in feet onto her son. Nights could be chilly, at this season. Then she sat down with him in the nursery's comfortable chair and nursed him until, once again, he dropped off to sleep. He looked so unbelievably precious lying there in her arms, long dark eyelashes brushing his light tan cheeks, that tears of joy glistened in her eyes at the sight.

Ever so gently, Bernadette laid Andreas down in his crib and put a light blanket over him. Then she tiptoed out of the room. Andrion and Erik weren't in the master bedroom, but she had a pretty good idea where to find them. After stripping down she put on a robe, taking a moment as she did so to check herself out in the mirror. She had a couple of stretch marks from the pregnancy, but for the most part her body had tightened up pretty well. Nothing like farm life to keep you in shape.

Sure enough, Andrion and Erik awaited her in the tub. Smiling broadly at them, she took her robe off with a little flourish and hung it on a hook beside theirs. Here in the privacy of their own bathroom erections in the pool were not a worry, indeed they were usually welcomed. And both men were rapidly acquiring them. It was likely they'd have very few opportunities for sex in the weeks to come, and the anticipated deprivation had them all eager for a slam-bang sendoff.

Nominally in the tub to get clean, Bernadette soon found herself getting lubricated, stroked, fondled, kissed, and eventually penetrated at both ends. But after some minutes of this play they decided to take their fun across the hall. Coming in the pool could possibly overstrain the sanitizing system. Better to just finish up in bed.

The three of them, wrapped in robes and glowing from the hot water and sexual excitement, were touching and panting a little as they nipped across the hall and into the master bedroom. Then they slipped their robes off and hurled them onto the floor, to be picked up later. Much later. Bernadette threw herself into the middle of the bed as if she were diving backwards into a swimming pool (some of which might be no larger), bouncing as she landed. She spread her arms wide and declared quietly, "Come and get me!"

Chapter 36: Far Western Iscandia, Year Three

When all was in readiness Erik took the reins while Andrion sat beside him, Bernadette's original magic map at the ready. Inside, Bernadette sat holding Andreas on her lap. Each of them were carrying one of the new maps on their person, and they expected to find their destination appearing on them after they arrived. As Remy stood watching, the entire coach with its horses and passengers shimmered, then winked out of existence. He shook his head wonderingly, then headed for the milking shed.

The Drakespring family, their coach, and its two surprised horses arrived on the east-west road outside Milburn – the nearest point to the Auverne border that Bernadette and Andrion had visited together. They'd been past the entrance to the small village, a few hours' walk from the border station, on their way to other – and more interesting – destinations. Andreas had fast-travelled before, and he accepted the sudden appearance of unfamiliar scenery outside the coach windows with equanimity.

They weren't surprised to find that it was now dark outside. Most likely, from the distances involved, it was now around ten in the evening. Andrion had prepared some cool-glowing dypalfar lamps for the coach, and Bernadette dug them out of the storage compartment and set one in a sconce on either side of the coach's interior. Then she unlatched the small hatch she had at first not noticed, running between the inside and the area where the driver was sitting. It wasn't big enough to crawl through, but you could see through it except for the fact that the two large men sitting on the seat blocked the view.

"Here's some lanterns," Bernadette told them. You could also communicate through the hatch and pass small items back and forth.

"Thanks, Berni," Erik replied. Before setting the horses into motion down the road leading south, he and Andrion took a minute to hang the lanterns in the spots designed for them: one at the front of each horse's yoke, illuminating the road ahead, and one on either side of the coach itself, so they could see each other. The lamps' light was dim, just enough to see by, and shouldn't completely destroy their night vision.

Now able to see at least somewhat, Erik shook up the reins and the horses set off. They were feeling a little uneasy, and he kept tight control on them. As Erik drove, Andrion (who, like his brother, was armored) sat scanning the darkened countryside on either side of the road, ready to let fly with battle magic if anything approached.

Inside the coach, Bernadette was thankful for the seat's thick padding. The steel-shod wheels, rolling along the sketchy road, were constantly jolting them despite the springy suspension. She was also glad of the convenient handholds placed on the sides. It was noisy, creaking and rattling along. She kept the hatch to the front open so she and the men could speak to one another, and the forward windows shuttered and barred. The rear windows were open, so that she and Andreas could look out. Not that they could see much of the nighttime landscape as it went past.

Meanwhile Andrion was making a mental list of some additional spells he'd like to research. He knew that Gatti had an inborn power called Night-Eye, and he'd heard there was a spell that would temporarily give a human this power; but he'd never seen a book for it. There had not even been one in the amazing library he'd inherited from the late Dalandrin. Of course, up until right now, it hadn't occurred to him to look for one. Ahead of them, the horses screamed and Erik hauled back on the reins as a trio of hungry wolves came galloping out of the darkness toward them.

Surely a mere three wolves didn't have a hope of bringing down a full-grown horse, but the horses were terrified anyway and they were rearing in their traces. If they didn't do something soon, there was going to be possibly irreparable damage to the harness. Erik and Andrion exchanged a glance. Neither bow nor spell would work in this situation, without the risk of hitting their horses. And without the horses, the coach was nothing but a very small cottage without any plumbing.

Each of them pulled a weapon and hopped down, one on either side of the coach, to deal with the wolves close-up. Andrion brained one with his war-hammer, while Erik sliced the other two into wolf steaks with his khopesh. This wicked looking curved blade with a hook in the tip, heavy and long, had been developed by the Afrans of southern Zahar as a sort of cross between a longsword and a battle axe. Bernadette had crafted one for Erik, and it had become his favorite edged weapon.

Bernadette, clutching Andreas to her, was peering out the front slot trying to see what was going on; but all she could make out was the horses rearing and occasional glimpses of the men as they came into the circles of light cast by the lanterns.

The threat was ended, but the smell of blood had the horses in a state of near panic. Their instinct was to run away, but they could not do that. Erik had set the brake before climbing down. Bernadette correctly assessed the situation and exited through the side door, Andreas in one arm. "Here," she said shortly, passing the frightened boy to Andrion. "Everybody stand back, I'm going to use a dragon spell on them." Erik dragged the wolf carcasses off the road and out of their way, then backed off.

Bernadette stood facing the horses, who were nearly quivering, and quietly but firmly said "Ruh-Trau-Stil-Rir," the Calm dragon spell. It would quiet an attacking bear, and for the horses it took away the panic and left them feeling unafraid and slightly dazed. The effect would wear off in about a minute, but she hoped that unless something else attacked them, they would have settled back down by then.

She gave each of the beasts a friendly pat and a few quiet words of encouragement, then reclaimed Andreas from his father. "We'd best get away from the smell of wolf before that wears off," Bernadette pointed out as she climbed back inside with the tot. "Thanks Berni," Erik said as he climbed back up, Andrion doing the same. Soon they were rolling again.

Fortunately they encountered no more hostiles as they traveled down the road toward Auverne. After around couple of hours underway they came to the border. Auverne, like Iscandia, was just another province of the empire now – though many kings had ruled it in its time. There was a perfunctory border checkpoint with a gate, manned at this hour by two sleepy guards. Impressed by the high-end conveyance and appreciating that Andrion was Galise, they let them pass after no more than a minute's conversation.

Inside the coach, Bernadette sat patiently holding her baby. After all the excitement he'd wanted comforting, and he'd dropped off to sleep in her arms. And now her arms were dropping off to sleep. Or perhaps, about to drop off. We need some way for Andreas to ride in safety while he's sleeping, she mused to herself, and spent the next couple of hours thinking of ways to make that possible, as much to take her mind off her discomfort as for any other reason.

Chapter 37: Northeastern Auverne, Year Three

Once they were in Auverne, the Drakespring family were traveling through more settled lands. Much of the area between the border and Raienne was similar to the area around Waterdon, with frequent farms, cattle grazing, and a relative dearth of bandits and hostile wildlife. They arrived at the outskirts of Raienne around five in the morning local time, and found the city gates closed. Erik pulled the coach off the road into a wide flat area, probably a seasonal camping ground for Gatti traders, and he and Andrion got down.

They climbed into the coach with Bernadette. It was a pretty tight fit through the door for Erik, but he had enough room once he was inside. Bernadette looked on them with relief. Erik, intuiting what her problem was, held out his arms and said "Gimme." Smiling gratefully, she handed the boy over. He was really out like a light, incredible considering that he'd arisen from a full night's sleep only a few subjective hours ago. None of them had much experience with the effects of fast-travel on young children, but it seemed likely he was feeling as if the nineteen hours that had really elapsed had passed for him as well as for the rest of the world.

Bernadette began shaking and rubbing her arms, trying to get some circulation back into them. She spoke quietly. "Thank the gods! I don't think I could have held out another hour. Is anyone besides me starving?" Andrion nodded, and rummaged in the storage compartment beneath the seat. He pulled out some slightly stale sandwiches and passed them around, along with a water skin.

After stuffing about half her sandwich into her mouth in hasty gulps, Bernadette remarked "I really need to pee, too!" Erik unbarred his window and looked out at the countryside visible through it, on the side of the coach away from the road. Dawn was well on the way.

"I think it's getting too light out there to just squat at the side of the road," he murmured, careful not to wake the sleeping child in his arms.

"The city gate should open at 6," Andrion said as quietly. "Can you hold it another half hour?"

Bernadette bit her lip. "I guess I'll have to," she said ruefully. Add that to the list of improvements she wanted to make. They finished their impromptu lunch, or was it breakfast, and by the time they had cleared away the mess Andreas had decided to rejoin the living and guards were opening the gates a few dozen yards ahead of them. Time to move.

"Tell you what," Bernadette said to Andrion. Now that they were in no danger of attack, and the morning was a fine one, she'd had enough of riding inside the coach. "I'll sit up with Erik and hold Andreas on my lap, and you can ride in the footman position at the back." He smiled, empathizing with her desire to be out in the open air.

"Sure thing love," he remarked shortly and climbed up onto the rear box. Bernadette climbed the front, Erik passing the tot to her after she was seated, then he gathered up the reins again and they headed into the city of Raienne.

The place had been a major hub, once, the seat of one of the eight ancient kingdoms of Auverne. Now, after the Norse invasion of 400 years before, it was much reduced from its former grandeur – about the size of Waterdon. The stables were located inside the gates, and it was there that the Drakespring family stopped first. It hadn't been much of a ride, Bernadette thought as she handed Andreas back down to Erik.

"I'd like to stay here today and tonight and leave in the morning," Bernadette told her husbands. "Now that we're actually traveling, I've started discovering what else we should have brought."

"I know what you mean," Andrion told her. "I think we need to come up with some better protection for the horses. And maybe if we have to drive at night in the future, I ought to stay inside with Andi while you sit the box with Erik so you can use your Calm spell on any attacking animals." Bernadette considered that. He certainly had a point.

They arranged with the stable for the horses to be unhitched, rubbed down, fed, watered, and stabled until tomorrow morning. The coach would be left parked in their locked yard. Just in case though, they left carrying as many of their valuables with them as they could. There were a couple of inns in town, and they chose the larger of the two. Even so, they had to rent two rooms in order to get enough bed space for the four of them. Likely Bernadette and Andreas would take one, while Erik and Andrion bunked together in the other.

It was still pretty early for regular stores to be open, so they hung around the inn for a while. Bernadette nursed Andreas upstairs and changed his diaper again, having done so once already while they were traveling. He hadn't pooped, so she rinsed the diapers in some water provided by the inn, wrung them out and hung them to dry. Likely she'd have worse to deal with as soon as he got some solid food into him.

She took him downstairs and rejoined the men in the common room, where they were drinking hot tea and eating from a bowl of fresh fruit that had been provided. The baby was eager for some of that, and she let him follow it with a small pastry. He, at least, seemed to be getting into synch with local time.

They talked about the trip so far. They'd certainly had more exciting adventures, but throwing a year-old toddler into the mix added an element of harrowing anxiety as well as a host of practical concerns. Toward eight they decided it was late enough to get moving on their plans. "Erik, can you come with me and be 'horsey' for the little guy?" He grinned at her. Walking around with Andi on his shoulders was one of his favorite activities.

"I need to go find a general store," Andrion said.

"We may run into you around town. It's not like Raienne is a major metropolis. But if not, we'll see you back here this afternoon," Bernadette replied. They split into two parties outside the door, kisses and hugs exchanged, and went their separate ways. "I need a carpenter," Bernadette told Erik as they walked up the street peering at the businesses on either side. She had spent the night here nearly four years ago on her way to Iscandia, but she hadn't had any time for exploring.

Bernadette and Erik wandered the town for some time, peeking into this store or that. This was fun, she realized. It had been a long time since she'd been anywhere completely new that wasn't some kind of aptrgangr-infested ancient ruin. New cities offered new surprises, and while she wasn't finding what she'd gone looking for she was enjoying herself immensely – as well as picking up quite a few small, incidental items. Erik appeared to be as equable as ever. It was rare to find him not having a good time, whether he was relaxing in a hot pool with a cold drink or fighting his way through a swarm of bandits.

Andreas, too, seemed to be quite enjoying the excursion. Some babies are born shy; but while their darling boy had his moments of serious calm, he seemed as happy as Erik was to meet new people and explore new places. After all, everyone he met loved him – right? They stumbled onto a glassblower's shop. Now there was something you wouldn't find in Iscandia. The wares on display out front were decorative and beautiful – vases, little glass sculptures of flowers or birds in flight.

Inspiration struck Bernadette as she looked at some of the flowers, and they went inside. Fragile objects of art were an unlikely purchase for them on this trip; but she had something else in mind. "May I speak with the person who is blowing the glass, please?" she asked of the young man at the counter. He stammered a bit, no more than a pimply-faced kid confronted with a young woman both attractive and commanding; but in due course he escorted her and her party through to the back where a graying woman in her mid-forties, likely his mother, was at work beside a blazing furnace. The room was as hot as dragon's breath.

The woman nodded to them politely and stuck the pipe in her hands, with a blob of semi-liquid glass on the end, back into the forge fire to keep hot. Bernadette's years of working a forge with metals gave her some understanding of what was going on.

She approached the woman and they began talking quietly. The kid returned to the front of the shop to greet any other customers that might come in, and Erik (Andreas on his shoulders, beginning to fidget a bit at the uncomfortable heat in the room) watched as Berni and the glassblower carried on a brief but animated conversation. Hand gestures were employed that he found strangely interesting. In a minute or two the woman smiled and nodded, and Bernadette handed over some gold. Then they returned the way they'd come.

Bernadette thanked the kid and said they'd see him later, then they exited the shop. "We'll have to come back here later today," she told Erik. "We ought to tell Andrion about this place," he responded. Going on three years now, and the windows at Drakespring Farm were still glassless. They opened the shutters so they could see out whenever the weather permitted, but Erik knew that a big part of the holdup was that Andrion had never had the opportunity to consult with someone who worked in glass. The architecture of Iscandia didn't go in for it much.

Bernadette grinned up at him. "How're you doing up there, big guy?" she asked her son, perched on Erik's shoulders and enjoying the view. Andreas smiled down at her with what was becoming a full set of teeth, if a little widely spaced as yet. He seemed to be developing his own version of that warm smile that his father regularly used to melt her heart. Bernadette leaned in close to Erik to give him a little hug, and reached up to squeeze Andreas' hand. Then they continued on their way.

Bernadette and Erik had nearly run out of mercantile district and had not yet found a carpentry shop. Surely the people of Raienne, just like the people of Waterdon, must have someone to manufacture their chairs, tables, chests of drawers, and other such items? The skills required to produce such things were not all that widespread, but every town or city needed them. They reached the last shop on the street before a residential district spread ahead of them, a leather goods shop, and decided it was time to ask.

Bernadette inhaled deeply through her nose as they walked in, enjoying the scent of tanned hides. The shop was hung about with various sorts of leather clothing – also saddles, bridles, and bits of harness. She'd made leather armor often, but had never delved into some of these other items. She approached the proprietor, a man of around Andrion's age. They exchanged a few pleasantries, then she asked "I was wondering if you could tell me where I'd find a carpentry shop? I'm in need of a special chair."

The man smiled at her. He wasn't too old to appreciate a pretty young woman, even if she *was* apparently there with her hulking giant of a husband and baby son. "You'll be wanting Bertrand, down near the gates," he told her. Oh. Bernadette hadn't considered that the business district forked near the gates, and there was an entire leg of it they hadn't yet explored. Likely they'd been no more than a few dozen paces away from this Bertrand's place when they started their excursion.

"Thank you," Bernadette told him with a smile. She may have been an old married woman for the past few years, but she wasn't immune to the attraction that was flowing between them. He was dark-haired, with deep blue eyes and dimples, and she'd have jumped into bed with him in a moment back before her relationship with Andrion and Erik had begun. A thought occurred to her. "Say," she said, "do you have some fairly wide, sturdy leather straps a few feet long?"

Narrow leather strips a foot or so in length were in use throughout Agena in improving arms and armor; but what she asked for was not a stock item. The handsome shop proprietor showed her his dimples. "I don't have anything like that on hand, but I can cut you some in a moment. I've got plenty of hides in the back." Damn, those teeth were white. "Come on through," he beckoned them, and they squeezed past the counter into the shop's back room. Hides were hanging everywhere, and a large cowhide was laid out on a work table.

"So," he said, "what would you like? I can go up to about 8 feet long on this hide." Bernadette considered.

"I think about an inch wide and four feet long will do me, and I want four of them," she told him. Her ruminations on the journey had not really covered so much detail, but she thought this ought to be enough to do what she wanted. "I'm assuming you've got some buckles, as well?" she asked. Shops like this bought buckles from smiths or jewelers and used them to create belts, bridles, and horse harness.

"For these straps?" he asked. "Sure. Would you like iron?"

"I don't suppose you've got dypalfar metal?" she inquired. Iron was OK, and certainly strong, but it stained and rusted. The proprietor, who was at work with a razor-sharp tool and a straightedge cutting her strips from the hide, smiled brilliantly. Bernadette could almost see the guilder signs lighting behind his eyes.

"As it happens," he said, "I have a supplier who produces a full range of dypalfar metal buckles. Of course they're more expensive than iron, but…"

The four straps cut, Bernadette had the proprietor (who, at last, revealed his name was Jacques) rivet one end of each of them to a handsome, gleaming dypalfar buckle. She haggled with him a bit just for form's sake, saying she'd cut the straps to final size and punch her own holes. The final use of these awaited her discussions with Bertrand.

The morning had slipped away. Bernadette's breasts were beginning to feel heavy, and Andreas was beginning to act up. Erik let him down, rubbing his neck, and handed the tot a bread roll he'd secreted about his person. "I think our boy is getting a little damp," he remarked. Uh oh.

"Erik, would you mind taking him back to the inn and changing him?" she asked. "I really need to nurse him, but I expect that the carpenter is going to need some time to create what I want. So I really ought to get it ordered first. Then I'll be right back before my boobs explode."

Erik eyed her lasciviously. "Mmm," he said. "I'm here to help if you need me…" He was teasing. Both he and Andrion had, of course, succumbed to their curiosity and drunk of her milk. Neither could remember being nursed by their own mothers, nor did either of them find the product much to their taste. She gave him a reproving glare.

"This is the proprietor's reserve stock, and it's just for my favorite customer," Bernadette informed him. He smiled.

"See you there," he said, scooping Andreas up carefully and carrying him back down the street.

Bernadette cut through an alley and struck the business district's other branch, which she traversed hurriedly. Even so, she took time to look and see what was there. With her new magic map, the shops of Raienne had just become part of her trading area. She'd pulled the map out to check after they got here, and Raienne was definitely now on it where it hadn't been before. Admittedly, such a journey by magic map would use up almost ¾ of a full day – not a trip to be undertaken lightly.

She was surprised to see there were two clothing stores along this section. Perhaps Raienne really was bigger than Waterdon, after all. But she was very happy with the work of Gerde Snowhair, who'd been sewing her clothes (and those of Andrion, Erik, and even Andreas) for her for years now. As long as she could afford bespoke clothing, it would be hard to go back to off-the-rack.

Sure enough, there was the carpentry shop off to the right. It appeared to sprawl for some distance off toward the city walls, no doubt similarly to the yard at Arngeld's. She'd visited that place once with Erik and been seriously impressed with the industry of the middle-aged Norseman, his wife, and his horde of children. All but the youngest, who'd been born a little while before Fjurbund, were actively employed in building furniture or weaving cloth. The Drakespring family's coach was just the latest new branch for Arngeld's family enterprise.

Bernadette went into the shop. There were chairs and tables on the porch outside, more furniture including wardrobes, chests of drawers, and other items scattered around the floor within. A rather stern and businesslike girl who could not have been more than fourteen greeted her. "How may I assist you, ma'am?" she asked politely. Bernadette cringed. "Ma'am"? Was she really getting that old?

Her breasts were beginning to take on a feeling as if they were water skins that had been overfilled with warm water. Were they glowing through her blouse? This youngster had an air of competence, so Bernadette decided to try talking with her before demanding to see someone more senior. She had the idea that Bertrand's, like Arngeld's, was a family business in which the kids started learning the trade shortly after they could walk.

"I'm looking for a child's chair," Bernadette began. The girl looked attentive, as if she were taking in every word and analyzing it. "Sized for a toddler," she held up her hands indicating Andreas' general size.

"For feeding?" the girl broke in. "We have just the thing!" She left her position behind the counter and led Bernadette into the rear of the shop, which went farther in from the street than had most of the shops she and Erik had visited today.

Oh, it was nearly perfect! Bernadette had never seen such a thing. It was built of some glossy hardwood, sized so that a child up to about three would be comfortable in it. The legs were long, so that a child sitting in it would have its head at about the same height as adults sitting around the table. And it had a tray fastened across the front! This was carved from a single slab of wood, curving around to encompass the chair occupant's belly and attached to the chair's arms somehow. It had a recess, so that spilled food or drink would stay on the tray instead of falling to the floor.

Seized with a violent lust that had until this moment never been approached by anything short of her reaction to Erik's naked body, Bernadette knew she *must* have this chair. Actually, she must have two of them. But the second one would have to wait. Probably, she'd have to fast-travel here just to get it. As if it needed any selling, the girl added "My mom uses one of these with my baby sister. She loves it."

Bernadette's breasts felt like they were going to burst through her blouse, or start leaking milk down the front of it. Her inborn sense of parsimoniousness fell by the wayside under this onslaught. "I want it!" she said. "How much is it?" Having utterly failed to bargain, she heard a figure that would have made her cringe a few years ago. Now, she laughed it off. "Just one thing," she added, handing over the money. "I need you to cut the legs off."

The girl looked stunned. "What?" she asked, her composure momentarily disrupted.

"I'm going to use it inside my carriage," Bernadette tried to explain without going into too much detail. She needed to go nurse Andreas *now*!

"Uh, OK…" the juvenile store clerk responded. "It should be ready in an hour or two. Do you need anything else?" One thing the chair lacked was any padding between the chair's occupant and the smooth, hard wood. A common failing of chairs throughout the empire, Bernadette suspected.

"Do you by any chance have some small cushions?" she asked, looking around hopefully. A few of the chairs on display did have some tailored pillows padding the seats.

The girl smiled, the first such expression Bernadette had seen cross her face. "We have these," she said almost shyly, producing an elongated wooly lozenge from a bottom shelf and demonstrating its use by tucking it behind the chair's tray. It covered the entire seating surface from the top of the chair back to the edge of the seat, and was held in place with cords that tied to the chair back on either side. "It's sheared lamb," she explained, "and it's washable. This is what Mom uses on ours." Bernadette's eyes lit. "Costs extra of course," the girl explained smoothly.

This child might never have met Bernard in Waterdon, but it seemed as though she might be a close relation. Come to think of it, Bernard was also Galise. It made you wonder… Bernadette paid the extra money and was assured that the chair – shorn of its legs and padded with the fuzzy sheepskin – would be ready for her to pick up sometime this afternoon. Finally! She nearly sprinted down past the gates and across to the inn, where she found Erik occupying a table with Andrion and Andreas.

"I hope you didn't spoil his appetite," she said. The aching was getting painful.

"He just had that bread and a glass of water," Erik assured her. The men resumed their conversation as Bernadette enfolded her baby boy in her arms and bolted up the stairs to the room. Ah, relief. Her aching breasts emptied at last and Andreas fairly brimming with milk, she carried him downstairs again.

"How about some lunch?" she asked her husbands.

The inn offered a choice of several hot dishes, and they ate well. Andreas somehow managed to find the appetite for a few bites of stew – he was a pretty good eater – and sure enough, filled his diaper with a contented sigh not long afterward. Bernadette and Erik looked at each other, and then at Andrion, and said in unison "It's your turn!" Andrion sighed, and scooped up the tot.

When father and son returned, they found Berni and Erik in conversation about their adventures of the morning, and the errands they needed to run this afternoon. Andrion handed Andreas back over to Bernadette to snuggle, as the boy was starting to show signs of dropping off to sleep now he was utterly full as well as clean and dry.

"Berni," Andrion said, reaching into his pack and hauling out a couple of large pieces of folded cloth. They seemed to have some leather straps and buckles on them. "Did you happen to bring any vials of magical essence with you?" She looked at him questioningly.

"I always carry a few with me for recharging weapons and so forth," she responded. "Why?" He gestured toward the cloth items.

"These are horse blankets," he explained. "I was hoping you could enchant them with the same armor spell you put on Andi's coat. We really can't afford to have either of the horses injured or killed."

Bernadette considered. If a horse was hurt, she *thought* she could heal it. But she'd never tried using healing on anything non-human. In a pinch, they could halt the trip and fast-travel the coach and an injured horse or horses back home for medical attention. But that would really punch a hole in their plans and was best avoided. "Any idea where there's an enchanting table I can borrow?" she asked. Andrion nodded.

"There's one, and a chemia station as well, at that big chemia shop up the left fork of the business district."

Oh that's right, she'd noticed there was one there on her walk down from the top. She hadn't gone in though, having stocked up on potions before they left. It might be good to see whether the shop here had any ingredients that were hard to find in Iscandia, though. "Sure," she told her husband. "Just set them on the table and I'll pick them up when I have an arm free and go enchant them." She had a few strong potions to enhance the power of her efforts with her, which should help.

Andreas had fallen asleep in her arms, and Bernadette wasn't sure what to do with him. She caught Andrion's eye and gestured with hers to the sleeping toddler. "Why don't I take him up to the room to nap on the bed while you run your errands?" Andrion asked quietly. "I've got some reading to do. I picked up a couple of books I've never seen before while I was out looking for the horse blankets."

Bernadette smiled and very carefully handed the boy over. He didn't stir. Once he went down, it would take a small earthquake to waken him most times. He got that from his father, no doubt. Andrion cuddled his son in his arms, nodded and smiled, and carried him up the stairs. Bernadette turned to Erik. "Care to be my porter again?" she asked hopefully. She was going to have quite a lot of stuff to carry.

Erik grinned, happy to be along. "Let me carry those blankets for you," he suggested, scooping them up in one enormous arm as if they were handkerchiefs. Bernadette stood on tiptoe to give him a brief kiss. Then they exited the inn, leaving some coin on the table for the server, and headed up the right fork of the road once again. Bernadette had her newly-acquired leather straps and some tools for cutting and punching leather in her pack.

Their first stop was the glass shop, where the youth from this morning was still manning the counter. He managed a passable smile and said that her order was now ready to pick up. "Mama said to tell you the special stoppers still need to cool some, so you should open up the box when you get home and let the air in." He pulled a wooden box around a foot wide, sixteen inches tall and half a foot deep from a shelf behind the counter and set it before her, unlatching a little door on the front of it.

The box was actually a little freestanding cabinet, lined inside with thick, soft wool to protect the contents from breakage. These contents consisted of a quart size, heavy duty glass bottle of the usual type for wine, a standard item available almost anywhere, with a tight-fitting cork stopper. Not so standard were what appeared to be two additional stoppers, one like a straight-sided funnel around four inches long and two inches in diameter at the top, the other similar but surmounted with an oval cup shape maybe 4 inches across on its long dimension. Each of these was designed to fit tightly into the neck of the bottle.

Bernadette smiled, picking up the stoppers and admiring them. They were still a little warm to the touch, but not hot enough to burn her hand or the thin layer of cork that provided their seal with the bottle. "Perfect," she said to the lad. She handed over some more coins. "Thank your mother for me." He nodded and thanked her for her patronage, and they packed the box's contents snugly back into the padded box. It even had a little metal handle on the top for easy carrying.

Erik was looking puzzled. "Are those some kind of chemial implements?" he asked.

"Good guess," Bernadette said with a grin, "but no." Handing the box to him for a moment so that she had both hands free, she mimed putting a stopper in the bottle and then holding it to his crotch. His eyes widened, and he snorted in surprised laughter.

"Really?! That's actually a pretty good idea."

She took the box back and smiled with satisfaction. "Why walk cross-legged when you've got a little private room on wheels right there?" Bernadette asked rhetorically. "Then after you've relieved yourself you can put the tight cork in and stow the bottle in its box until you have the opportunity to empty it and rinse it out. You'll probably need to wipe the stopper with a rag or something after use, though…"

From here it was easy enough to cut through the same alley she'd used earlier, and they emerged on the business district's other street. Bernadette quickly spotted the chemia shop, and after she had chatted with the proprietress for a while (a youngish Reman, who allowed that her Galise husband was the enchanter), she handed the box to Erik once again while she took the horse blankets and enchanted each of them with the spell that would permanently give them the same damage-stopping capability as steel plate armor. The horses certainly ought to appreciate it, if they had any more incidents on their journey.

While she was there in the shop Bernadette looked over their ingredients. This was the first shop she had ever visited that had multiple vials of daimon blood for sale. The rarity of this substance was the biggest obstacle to her regular production of the wonderful and fabulously valuable daimonic arms and armor that were so sought after by Valkyrie's wealthier customers. She bought all three, though the price was high. You might try every chemia shop in Iscandia without finding that many, and killing your own daimon to obtain the blood was even more work – not to mention perilous.

Bernadette handed the re-folded blankets back to Erik when they got to the carpentry shop. The teen girl was there, and set down the bread and cheese she was eating to greet them. The chair, its legs cut off flush with the seat bottom and the wooly pad tied in place, sat waiting for them on the floor behind the counter. "Isn't this adorable, Erik?" Bernadette enthused. Personally he thought she and Andreas were adorable, but furniture didn't do it for him all that much. He smiled and nodded anyway.

Bernadette threw in a few extra coins for the work of cutting the legs off and thanked the girl. Likely the shop would find some other use for those lathe-turned hardwood legs, perhaps on a shorter chair. It wasn't terribly heavy, just a little awkward to carry as they exited the shop. "Let's take all this stuff over to the stables, shall we?" she suggested. All of it needed to be in or near the coach when they left in the morning, so they might as well leave it there now.

The elderly hostler who'd taken them in when they arrived greeted them. "Thought you weren't leaving until tomorrow?" he asked.

"We're not," Bernadette informed him. "But we have some purchases we need to stow. Could you let us into the yard so we can get to our coach, please?"

"No problem, ma'am," he said, walking bowlegged in the direction of the sturdy gates to the stable's walled-in yard. The back wall was actually part of the walls of Raienne itself.

Now I've got grandfathers calling me "ma'am," Bernadette thought with regret. It made her want to cut loose, and recapture some of her wild youth. When they got into the yard and approached the coach she waved the cut-down child's chair at him. "I have to figure out how to install this, so we'll probably be awhile."

"That's okay," he said. "I'll be back in the office. Just come and let me know when you're finished, so I can lock up again."

They thanked the man, then set about getting themselves and their purchases into the coach. A minute or so of shuffling went on as burdens were handed back and forth and first Bernadette, then Erik, climbed up inside it. Bernadette set the folded blankets on the forward seat, easy to get at so they could be put onto the horses in the morning before harnessing them. The box with her portable urinal would fit nicely in the storage compartment beneath the rear seat, after sitting open overnight for the stoppers to cool completely.

Now, Bernadette just had to figure out how to attach the little chair to that rear seat. She wanted to put it over to one side, near the window, so Andi could look out at the scenery while he was riding. She envisioned snacks or small toys occupying the tray, which would help to keep him in the seat if the ride got bumpy. Perhaps these straps could help as well.

As Bernadette knelt on the carpeted floor, setting the chair in place and trying to figure out how best to attach it to the coach's bench seat, Erik sat on the front seat admiring her behind. She'd always had a nice ass, and childbearing had only added to its appeal. Its rounded contours were clearly visible through the soft, draping fabric of her skirt. Mmm.

Bernadette got out her tools and the straps, and considered what to do with them. The bench seat was about three-and-a-half feet wide, so she buckled one strap to another to get one more than double that length. The backs of the coach's seats were slanted backward slightly for comfort, which meant that everywhere except at the very top, where it came up against the inner wall of the coach, there was a gap. Okay, so feed it through the splat at the back of the chair then up around the chair back's side support, around the coach seat, then all the way across to the other side behind the seat back… What she needed, apparently, were arms about the same length as her body.

Still kneeling before the bench seat, her double-length strap in one hand, Bernadette craned her head around and said "Erik? Could you help me please?" In an instant he was on his knees behind her, pressing up against her body. Oh! And he was rock hard inside his trousers, from the feel of it. She was taken by surprise. Making love with Erik was still wonderfully exciting and satisfying, but over the years of their marriage, and with the complications of pregnancy and the baby, their sex life had become kind of… predictable.

This, on the other hand, made her feel like a teenager again. It had crossed Bernadette's mind to wonder what it would be like to have sex in the coach, its status as a portable private room suggesting possibilities; and here they were in the middle of the afternoon, in the stable's storage yard, with nothing to stop them from doing whatever they wanted in here since the shutters were all closed.

Bernadette dropped the strap. It wasn't going anywhere. She humped herself backwards a little, pressing into Erik's midsection and his throbbing erection, sighing softly as he brought his strong arms forward to squeeze her breasts through the fabric of her blouse. "Oh, Erik…" she moaned softly. He leaned over her, pushing aside her hair and kissing the back of her neck. Then he reached under her skirt.

Erik's strong hands stroked and squeezed her under the skirt, then he lifted it up over her back to expose her rump, clad in the comfortable but utterly non-sexy linen underdrawers that were Iscandia standard. They didn't stay there long. He soon pulled them down to her knees, bending to plant hot kisses on her exposed buttocks. He backed up a little, as much as he could in this enclosed space, and bent to lick her slit. Then two fingers slid between her legs to massage her clit a little before sliding backwards and inside. Ah!

"Yes, Erik, do it!" Bernadette urged quietly. "I want your cock inside me!" He didn't need telling twice. He opened his trousers and slid them halfway down his backside, enough to free his quivering member from its restraints. The unusual situation was exciting him as much as it did her. Holding onto Bernadette's hips, he poised the glistening tip of that huge cock at the entrance to her vulva, then pushed it in. All the way in, sheathing himself completely inside her. Bernadette squealed.

A considerable time later, the baby chair had been firmly strapped to the coach seat. It occurred to Bernadette that some extra strapping attached only to the chair might be appropriate, as another way to hold the baby in place besides the wooden tray; but that would have to wait until later. She and Erik emerged from the coach pink-faced, a little disheveled, and grinning slightly. All their burdens had been left behind.

They went to the stable's front office, where the old hostler sat behind the counter with his feet up. There were boys to handle tasks like mucking out the stalls and feeding the horses – he'd earned his desk job. "You done, then?" he asked, eyeing them pointedly. Bernadette blushed, turning even pinker.

"It was harder than I thought to get the chair installed," she said, "but we finally got it."

"Must've been," the old man replied. "The way that coach was shakin', I thought she might tip over."

"Just testing out the suspension," Erik said, in a tone that suggested any further comments might be unwelcome.

The old man looked a little abashed. "Well then, I'll get her locked up. See you tomorrow morning." With that he shuffled off to lock the gates, and the Drakesprings, still straightening their clothing and smoothing their hair, returned to the inn.

Chapter 38: West Central Auverne, Year Three

They were on their way not much more than an hour after sunup, eager to hit the road for their next stopping point. The horses seemed to appreciate the new blankets for their warmth and the protection they offered from sun, rain, and flies. Bernadette had irreverently dubbed the gelding Sigrandil, and the mare Reshiva. That ancient and long-dead witch queen, the return of whom she and Andrion had scotched (earning the gratitude of Eorl Bergen and all of Mountmarch) would be rolling in her grave to learn of it.

Andreas took to his little chair with good grace, for the most part, though occasionally he demanded to be let out of it. They were still afraid to be travelling through the countryside with him exposed outside the coach, despite the armor protection of his enchanted coat; so he and one or another of his parents were stuck inside with him, though the spring day was a pleasant one and they'd sooner have been enjoying the fresh air.

Andrion, taking a turn inside with Andreas while Erik drove and Bernadette rode crossbow, made an attempt to read but soon found himself in danger of losing his breakfast. The empire, he was beginning to suspect, did not possess any truly smooth roads. At least he hadn't seen any in Auverne or Iscandia – the two provinces of the empire he had so far visited. He wondered what things were like in Remus.

They pulled the coach off the road between Eaunuee and Dupree for a midday break, going so far as to unhitch the horses and hobble them to graze while they spread out a picnic lunch. Andreas ran around, loving the freedom of movement after hours of confinement. Bernadette, Erik, and Andrion ate cold chicken, pickled vegetables, and reasonably fresh bread – washed down with some ale that Andrion had managed to chill nicely by setting the bottles into a box of ice before they left.

Andreas explored a nearby rivulet, fascinated by shiny pebbles and some little insect larvae that lurked at the bottom of the stream, protected in casings built of tiny stones. He brought one to Bernadette to show her, and she removed it from its little fortress so he could see what was inside. He ate some of what they were having, and topped it off with a generous helping of breast milk.

The stop had taken nearly two hours by the time the horses had been hitched to the coach once more, and the boy was fading. He dropped off to sleep almost as soon as they tucked him into his chair, cushioned by a couple of folded towels set on the chair's tray. So, leaving the front hatch open, Bernadette and Erik took the driver's seat while Andrion, battle magic at the ready should it be needed, relaxed atop the coach's rear trunk. He'd brought a couple of cushions up there to put between his back and the armor plating, which went far to improve his comfort.

The lands on either side of the road were sparsely populated, nor were there many wild creatures this close to the road. Andrion spotted a pair of smilodons trailing them with ill intent, and lazily sent a couple of lightning bolts their way. For a change, the predators took the better part of valor and slunk off into the undergrowth instead of pursuing the matter.

They rolled right through Dupree without stopping. The village had little to recommend it. Beyond it, Karthgran offered little more. They were making great time, Andreas was still fast asleep, and they decided to skirt Eiveille, the city once famed for the Chevaliers gladiatorial team, pushing to make more distance before nightfall. At this rate, they might make it all the way to the village of Passage d'Aimont.

All of them had thought of dragons as an Iscandian problem. It was there that they had returned to life with Tarragin's coming, there that Bernadette, Andrion, and Erik had fought and killed them. But they were flying creatures, after all, not limited by the borders drawn by men. Not far past Eiveille, they became aware of one circling in the sky above them, roaring out its defiance to the world in general.

This was an almost daily sight in most regions of Iscandia, and Bernadette wasn't concerned. Their coach and horses were too big, if seen from above, to be an obvious target for one of the *drachen*. Then, abruptly, she heard a wail from inside the coach. Their sleeping boy had finally awakened. He'd been asleep for hours, and was probably in need of a diaper change and a nipple or two to settle him down again. Erik pulled up, setting the brake, and the horses stood stamping as she hopped down and went around to climb in through the side door.

The dragon was making the horses anxious, and Erik did his best to calm them. Andrion climbed up onto the roof and walked across it to join Erik on the driver's bench. "Do you want me to drive for a while?" he asked.

"You know how?" Erik asked.

"Yeah, I've done it before" Andrion replied somewhat reluctantly. Letting Erik take all the driving duties had been convenient, but he was beginning to feel a little guilty about it.

Inside the coach, Bernadette had calmed Andreas down and changed his diaper. Until they could do some laundry, dirty diapers were being stored in a good-sized ceramic jar with a tight lid. She held him on her lap and offered him a breast, which soon had him quiet once again. He wasn't all that hungry nor was she all that bursting with milk; but the comfort factor was what he needed. This trip was stressful, and the familiar experience of nursing helped to relax both of them.

"Are we good down there?" Andrion called through the front hatch. Bernadette smiled up at him from her perch on the rear seat, next to Andreas' chair.

"Everything's fine," she replied. "Are you driving now?"

"Uh huh. Hang on," he called back as he released the brake and shook up the reins. The coach lurched into motion again, the nervous horses happy to be moving once more.

The road ran around a couple of bends, moving through low hills. The dragon seemed to have disappeared, perhaps flying back to whatever aerie it called home or stooping on some hapless stag. Bernadette had removed her breastplate to nurse the boy, and now that he was content she snuggled him on her lap, shutters open on both sides of the coach, so they could admire the view.

As they rounded another bend Andrion pulled back hard on the reins just as both horses reared in panic. The dragon had indeed caught a stag – in the middle of the road ahead of them. Andrion set the brake as Erik leapt to the ground, his bow at the ready. "Berni!" he shouted through the front hatch, "the dragon is on us!"

Oh, shit. Bernadette tucked Andi into his seat, squeezing him in as tightly as she could with the towels and tray. He began screaming in protest even as she shrugged into her breastplate and helmet, and picked up her bow to string it. Where was that quiver of arrows? Oh right – front compartment, toward the back of it now as contents had gotten shuffled.

She came over to hold her screaming son on either side of his face and plant a kiss on his forehead. "Be good, sweetie, Mama will be right back!" she said. After double checking that all of the shutters were barred, she slipped out the side door just in time to be buffeted back against the side of the coach as the dragon flew low overhead, roaring. She could hear Andi inside shrieking, but his tone seemed to be more of outrage than of terror, so she wasn't worried. It was a rare day he got through without at least a minute or two of outrage.

Andrion was sending sizzling beams of battle magic skyward and Erik was methodically firing his bow, but it was nearly impossible to bring a dragon down and kill it without the Dragonfall spell. Bernadette's first concern was to get it away from the coach and her baby, as quickly as possible. Waving her arms and yelling, she ran off toward the slope of a nearby low hill, away from the road. She wished she knew some good insults in the language of the *drachen*.

The dragon wheeled and, spotting her movement, it followed. Yes! It halted in air for a moment, huge wings flapping, as it prepared to incinerate her with Holocaust. And she cried "Alt-Wach-Sterb-Tot!" before pulling her bow, ready to shoot as soon as it came down. The beast staggered back, reeling from the effects of the dragon spell. Few of its kindred had heard those words and lived to tell about it.

Andrion and Erik, too, were running toward the spot where Bernadette stood, bow drawn and heart racing. Andi's screams could still be heard faintly from the closed-up coach, but he was down there and the dragon was *here*. Unable to stay aloft, the beast soon came crashing heavily down on its four taloned feet a few yards from where the three adult Drakesprings stood, deadly in their intent.

Bernadette hit it with an arrow in that vulnerable spot where the wing joined the body as it was distracted, trying to snap at Andrion. It roared in agony, turning its head this way and that as it tried to identify the location of the threat. As it did so, Andrion wove a tight, actinic beam of flame and lightning combined, cutting right through the dragon's hide and muscle where its other wing met the body. This dragon would not be flying again. Bernadette's second shot, combined with four or five more arrows that Erik had poured into it, was enough to kill it at last. It threw its head heavenward as if in disbelief, then collapsed to the ground. At this close range, its flesh almost immediately vanished as she absorbed its mana and soul.

The three of them stood there for a moment panting in relief that they'd been able to defeat the monster without suffering any injuries. The horses were safe, too, though they were still whinnying in terror. And their son was not exactly a happy camper, either. Bernadette started into action. "Andi! I'm coming baby!" She ran to fetch their son while the men searched the corpse for valuables. Dragons swallowed many things, all of which became available once their flesh had gone. The bones and scales themselves were worth a small fortune at smithies.

Bernadette entered the coach's near door and pulled the screaming boy out of the chair. He was so upset his face had gone bright red, and he was breathing in shuddering gasps. The horses were starting to settle down a little now that the threat had gone, so she decided to put all of her attention on Andi and not try to use Calm on them.

Andreas was hugging onto his mama as tightly as he could, his crying having subsided into the occasional whooping half-sob. She held him close, patting his back and stroking his silky reddish brown hair, as she walked back toward the dragon corpse. Andrion and Erik had just finished their investigation. "I wasn't expecting to get attacked by dragons here in Auverne," Andrion admitted. "Of course there were no dragons here thirteen years ago when I left; but there were none in Iscandia either until not long before I met you, Berni." She nodded thoughtfully.

"I'd hoped that once we killed Tarragin that would put an end to the supply," Bernadette replied, "and that after a while the surviving dragons would take themselves off to the wilderness and stop putting themselves into conflict with men. But it seems they haven't learned yet. I really don't like killing them anymore." The *drachen* were ancient and sentient, and likely an endangered species. It would be better if they would just live and let live.

"Well, we'd better get on our way again," Erik said. The sun was well down now and they'd be better off camping near civilization even if staying at an inn wasn't possible. "How about I ride with Andi and you two can sit on the driver's seat." Bernadette smiled gratefully at him. Andi loved his Papa Erik, as did most small children, and Erik could keep him entertained perhaps better than she could.

They'd taken quite a few of the smaller-size bones from the dragon, and as the coach pulled away once more, Erik and Andi were sitting on the coach's carpeted floor playing with them. He thought it poetic justice that the son of The Fireblood should make toys of the bones of her adversaries. Riding down there was a bit bumpy, and their constructions kept falling apart; but Erik made it all part of the game and Andi was soon shrieking in laughter at each jounce.

Andrion had dragged the remains of the stag off the road before they got started, judging it too charred and mauled to be worth trying to salvage some meat. Well, they had plenty of food supplies with them even if there was no fresh meat. It wasn't as if the three of them hadn't gone questing on short rations plenty of times in the past, and Andi had his food right there at all times – even if admittedly that was only a part of his diet these days.

Their passage down the road to the southeast proved uneventful, allowing Bernadette and Andrion to converse quietly. She remained on the alert, and had not unstrung her bow; but she was able to give some attention to her spouse as they rattled along. "I'm beginning to wonder if this trip was such a good idea," she admitted. When the idea first came to her it had seemed so wonderful and exciting, but the reality of traveling with a toddler was beginning to creep up on her.

"Nonsense," Andrion told her, as he casually guided them along the road. "It's still a good idea. You didn't think it was going to be completely trouble-free, or you wouldn't have brought so much armor or so many potions. Your mother is going to be thrilled to death when we show up there with her grandson." Bernadette smiled a little at the thought. He was right: they hadn't met anything they couldn't handle and Andi was doing fine, really. With three competent adults to look after him, there was nothing to fear. She shuddered to imagine what it must be like in families where the young kids outnumbered the parents.

Digue Sinistre, probably named for some ancient battle, proved to be little more than a wide spot in the road with a couple of farmhouses. They decided to camp here, in a flat area a little way off the road where a few trees clustered around a spring. They'd brought plenty of water, but it was always best to live on whatever was around you if possible, saving your stores for emergencies. There didn't seem to be anyone in town wanting to come and discuss a fee for the night's camping.

After riding for hours, Bernadette was feeling stiff and in need of some movement. Andrion kept an eye on Andreas, preventing him from falling into the spring, and Erik set up their camp with bedrolls and a fireplace. Bernadette donned leathers and went off to a nearby wood, traversing the space between two hills, to try a little hunting. It was a lovely spring evening and it seemed unlikely they'd need any tents, though they'd brought some. Andreas could easily sleep in the coach and Bernadette might, if she curled into the fetal position; but were Erik and Andrion to sleep in there it would be sitting up on the bench seats – to be avoided if possible.

The wood was not that large, and this close to town likely sparse on game. The few inhabitants must hunt here often. Bernadette felt quite a sense of accomplishment, therefore, when she returned to camp as darkness was falling with a couple of fat rabbits hanging at her side. By then, camp was all set up and the fire was going. She handed her catch over to Erik, who made short work of gutting and skinning the carcasses and spitting them on a long iron rod they'd brought along, to sizzle over the flames.

In their years of living in a house with a kitchen superior to most of those in Iscandia, not to mention a short walk from the fabled Bathing Maiden and its ever-expanding menu, the Drakesprings had become used to meals that were complex, subtly seasoned, and delightfully savory – often accompanied by the best vintages the empire had to offer. Yet somehow, this dinner of utterly unseasoned wild rabbit, cooked over an open flame and served with some slightly stale bread and apples, washed down with water, seemed as delicious to them as any they could recall eating.

Andreas was fully restored to his usual *joie de vivre*, and was watching the spitted rabbits with the same degree of concentration as his elders. He ate quite a bit of the juice-dripping rabbit meat and a lot of the bread as well, lightly toasted by holding it over the fire on the end of a long stick. And he was ecstatic when it transpired that Mama had a secret stash of nut confections, acquired at the inn where they'd spent the previous night.

When all were happily fed they sat around the campfire in a ritual as old as humankind, staring into the flames. They talked quietly, told stories, and even sang a bit. A pity none of them knew how to play the lute, Bernadette thought. She changed Andreas' diaper and then nursed him on both sides after supper, letting him settle like thistledown into sleep. It had been a very long day for their very little boy.

Bernadette carried him off and tucked him into a double bedroll Erik had spread out, one on the bottom and another on the top like she and Andrion had slept in before going down into Alzhenten, all those years ago. Tonight, it would be occupied by her and Andreas while Andrion and Erik each had their own. After laying the sleeping child down carefully, she returned to the fire. "Andrion," she said quietly, "I wouldn't mind one of your hot tubs of water about now."

He smiled. This was his new trick, and one he was happy to perform for his beloved. He walked around the fire a bit, looking for a good flat spot. "Right about here all right?" he asked.

"Looks fine," she said, smiling back. In an instant or two the wooden tub of hot water stood there, only a few paces from the fire, steaming. It would be right ruddy hot now, but should have cooled to a comfortable temperature by the time she assembled her towel, robe, soap, bath brush, and other necessaries. That was a nice thing about traveling by coach – you weren't limited to what you could tuck into a pack.

Andrion and Erik sat on their bedrolls by the fire, watching in obvious appreciation as Bernadette stripped down and then climbed into the tub. "Oohhh," she sighed, submerged up past her navel, "this is wonderful! Thank you, love."

"I think you might need some help washing your back," Erik rumbled, getting up and approaching the tub.

"And there's scarcely any need for you to wash your own front," Andrion chimed in. Bernadette looked at them in surprise. This was supposed to be a pleasant hot soak and a chance to wash off the stickiness of the day before climbing into the bedroll, not an invitation to sex in the near-wilderness with their baby son sleeping a few paces away.

Still, she couldn't help being drawn by their desire, which inevitably sparked her own. Ah, she loved them so much, and lusted after them still despite years of familiarity. She allowed them to mob her front and back, washing and stroking and kissing for a while, before she finally had to admit that this was simply ridiculous. "You two are insane!" she gasped, as Andrion's fingers slipped inside her cunt while Erik's strong hands gripped her buttocks. Andrion looked into her eyes, a slightly hurt expression just visible in the flickering firelight. Augh! For a man in his middle thirties, Magister of Iscandia's famous Academy at Eisenstag, he could sometimes act like as much the little boy as his son did.

"Oh, for the gods' sake!" Bernadette exclaimed, rising suddenly to her feet. She tried to modulate her tones, fearful of waking the baby. "There could be smilodons, bears, bandits, even curious locals come to see who's camping at the spring. We can't just have a sex orgy out here in the middle of the village green." Andrion now looked abashed. Behind her, his expression unseen, Erik leaned in and cupped her dripping-wet buttocks in his hands, kissing her bare shoulder.

"Aw Mooommm," he said, "you never let us have any fun!" Bernadette turned her head to grin at him.

"You and your brother are both incorrigible," she said, pretending outrage. "Now let me get out of here before the tub vanishes." She stepped onto a towel she'd laid down on the close-cropped grass surrounding the spring. Likely the villagers grazed their herds here, which also likely meant there was plenty of shit in among the blades.

Andrion handed Bernadette a second towel so she could dry off. Should she have waited long enough, the water would have vanished when the tub did; but it was cool enough out here she was anxious to get dry and into some clothing – as opposed to, say, into a three-way with these two hot studs who were attending her. Sometimes men seemed to have no sense at all.

But now, of course, she was aroused. As were Andrion and Erik, clearly. At least Erik had gotten a little (well, more than a little) yesterday afternoon in the coach. Hmm, Bernadette thought. The coach. Hadn't considered that... Checking that Andreas was still down for the count, instead of putting on her clothes Bernadette wrapped the towel around her and approached the coach, stepping carefully across the grass. Sigrandil and Reshiva had been unhitched, rubbed down, and were now hobbled, happily grazing in the darkness a few yards away. Should anything come near their camp, the horses would be an early warning system.

"You know," Bernadette said softly, "I think I left something in the coach earlier. Would you guys like to come help me look for it?" They were there like a shot.

Chapter 39: Central Auverne, Year Three

Bernadette awoke near dawn when Andreas did, after he had slept for the better part of nine hours. The little guy must have been beat after the stresses of the previous day. Certainly he was well and truly soaked through, come morning. She'd slept in underwear, the possibility of attack in the night seeming somewhat higher than usual, and on getting up added light leather armor.

After changing Andreas and taking him into the coach so she could have a comfortable seat in which to nurse him, she let him run loose for a while. Erik had risen too, so he was able to keep toddler and spring separated while she dealt with some other issues. Bernadette strode over and nudged the sleeping Andrion with her foot. "Rise and shine, love," she said without rancor. "I need to do some laundry."

Andrion groaned, rolled over, and pulled the top part of the fur bedroll over his head. "It can't be morning already, I just went to bed!" he said, muffled. They hadn't been up all *that* late playing in the coach. Bernadette sighed.

"The sun is coming up, dear. Please. I need another tub of hot water, then you can go back to sleep for a while." Andrion raised the upper part of his body, looking around blearily. Holding himself up on one elbow he focused on the flat spot where her bath had been the night before, and with a gesture materialized an identical tub of steaming water. Then he lay down again and buried his face in the covers once more.

Bernadette exchanged glances with Erik. "Maybe you could start on breakfast?" she suggested. He nodded, and set about resurrecting their fire. Andreas was fascinated by the tub, and she got the chance to wash his face and hands at least. The entire boy needed a soak, but now was probably not the time. Gathering the collection of soiled diapers and the sack in which they were keeping other items that needed washing, she dipped out some of the water into a couple of their largest cooking pots before adding soap to the rest.

She washed their linens and other clothing first, rinsing them in one of the pots and then wringing them out and hanging them on a rope strung up between two trees. Boy, this was a lot of work. Not that it wasn't a lot of work at home, of course, but there she had a better setup – and occasionally, help. Erik had his hands full trying to cook breakfast and keep Andreas from drowning, and Andrion was… Andrion. Sigh.

After the diapers had been washed, rinsed in the second pot, and hung up to dry, Bernadette's patience had been exhausted. She went over and nudged Andrion again. "Get *up*, lazybones!" she said firmly. Andrion accepted the inevitable and dragged himself to consciousness. He really couldn't help it, he just seemed to need more sleep than Berni and Erik did. Over the years of their relationship, he'd begun rising much earlier than had been his wont in the past. But it just wasn't early enough for her. Sigh.

All conflicts smoothed over eventually, the family sat on their bedrolls to eat scrambled eggs and toasted bread with apple butter, washed down with some hot tea. Andrion was feeling a lot better and more energetic by the time they'd finished eating, and provided another tub of hot water for Bernadette and Erik to do the washing up while he collected the clean laundry from the line and put it away. As soon as the earlier conjured washtub had vanished, everything that had been wetted with its water was instantly dry as a bone.

No more than three hours after dawn, the family was on the road again. Oddly, no one had emerged from any of the village's houses to inquire about them though they could see people working in fields as they continued on their way. These people were too busy scratching a living to bother themselves with the business of others, Bernadette supposed.

Once again, they started with Andreas in his coach chair and Bernadette keeping him company. The ride was noisy and bumpy, but she found herself able to read picture books with him. Bjorn had made several little board books aimed at a toddler audience for Fjurbund, and she'd been able to borrow a few of them for the trip. They nibbled dried fruit, and she got him out of the chair for a while to nurse.

After a few hours, Bernadette called through the front hatch, "Erik, can we stop for a few minutes? The boy needs a change." He leaned down so he could call back,

"There's a stream up ahead. Why don't we take a lunch break?" She smiled at him, though he couldn't see her face.

"Great idea, love." There was a reasonably flat area beside the little river, and Erik steered the coach over to stop beneath the shade of some tall hardwood trees. Away to the south and east of the road, the snowy peaks of the Rocheblanc Mountains were faintly visible through a light haze.

They didn't want to take the time to unhitch the horses, but Erik fitted them with some feedbags containing grain – and later held a pot of river water in front of each animal so they could drink. While Bernadette was diapering Andreas, Andrion set to work laying out a picnic for them. Bernadette had also used her new urinal, and on climbing down from the coach she carried it over into the trees to empty, then rinsed it out in the stream.

Before long they were on their way again, this time Erik keeping Andreas company while Bernadette and Andrion rode the driver's box. So far the weather had been very favorable, so the awning was only needed to shade them from the sun. She crossed her fingers it would remain so. The rest of the day's journey passed in blissful quiet, with no attacks by foes human or otherwise.

They reached the village of Jenois near sunset, and pulled up beside the place's only inn. Many villages didn't even have that. Erik dealt with unhitching Sigrandil and Reshiva and seeing to their food and water after rubbing them down, as there was no stable in town. The horses could be turned out on the green, hobbled, to graze.

Meanwhile Andrion and Bernadette took Andreas and some of their luggage inside. As before, they rented two rooms and Bernadette shared a bed with Andreas. In her role as ambulatory milk bar, it made the most sense. In the morning they were on the way again, earlier this time without the need to cook or do laundry. Bernadette, riding the box with Erik this morning, had her map out and was studying it. "This next village we're coming to is where we should be able to pick up the road to Pied de Puce," she told him.

He smiled, pleased that they were nearing their destination. "You never told me," Erik remarked casually, "what does 'Pied de Puce' mean?" Bernadette colored.

"It's Old Galise for 'Flea's Foot,'" she said with a grimace. "Some old king back before the empire took over in Auverne came through when the place was little more than a couple of huts, and didn't think much of it. But the name stuck."

At the next village they stopped and asked directions at the smithy, and were directed to a reasonably broad but unpaved track heading east a little further along. They were now getting closer to Bernadette's familiar territory, and she needed to ride outside the coach to act as guide. Andrion had gotten out when they stopped for directions, Andreas in his arms. As they prepared to get under way again, he said "Berni, do you think we might be safe having Andi ride up on the box with you now?"

She considered it. Danger could be anywhere, but moving through the landscapes she'd known all her life it was hard to take the threat seriously. "Sure," she replied. "Let's leave the top hatch open in case we need to get inside in a hurry, and you can keep an eye on our rear." He smiled and saluted, handing her the baby and going back inside the coach to unbar the roof hatch before opening it and crawling out to sit at the rear.

Bernadette handed the nipper up to Erik, then climbed up herself. In another minute or so the promised road forked off to their left, and she directed him to follow it. "I remember this now," she said musingly. It'd been such a long time. "I used to help some of my farm friends' families with taking their produce to market when I was a kid."

The road ran through an area of lightly wooded hills interspersed with narrow valleys. Erik was occupied with driving, but admiring the view; and Bernadette was rapt at the childhood memories that view was provoking. Neither of them were paying much attention, when suddenly there was an inarticulate shout from Andrion and a bolt of battle magic shot past them, off to the side of the coach. At almost the same moment, Erik pulled up sharply on the reins as an arrow from some unseen source hit Sigrandil in the side – and bounced off of his enchanted horse blanket.

Shit, bandits?! "Whip them up, Erik!" Bernadette screamed, as she clutched Andreas to her and began climbing up over the top of the coach to lower him down inside. He'd likely be rolling around inside there for a minute or two until she could climb down to be with him; but he'd sustain less injury doing that than if he took an arrow in the neck. Angered as well as frightened, the toddler was screaming his head off before he even landed on the coach's carpeted floor.

Andrion was continuing his ranged attacks on the bandits but was having some difficulty hitting moving targets, made even trickier as Erik urged the team into a run. Every bandit they'd ever met in Iscandia was on foot, and it seemed likely they could simply run away from trouble. That is, until a man who must have been the bandit leader, dressed head to toe in steel plate armor, came galloping past them on a huge piebald stallion and gripped Reshiva's headstall, dragging her off to the side.

Before the coach could be taken off the road and tipped over, Erik hauled back hard on the reins, halting the obedient if frightened horses in their tracks. Then he set the brake and pulled out his bow. Bernadette had hers out too, perched atop the coach and scanning all around it. They were beset by half a dozen of the bandits, encircling the coach. But now that it had stopped moving and the bandits were almost upon them, they had stationary targets to fire at.

One was hit and killed instantly by a direct hit from a double-strength lightning spell that flung him through the air thirty feet to lie like a rag doll – before the bolt jumped to another of the foes, staggering him. Bernadette picked off the staggered one with a single shot from her bow, then looked for another target. She put three more arrows into another of the bandits who was circling around toward the front. Meanwhile the bandit chief had ridden over on his horse to attack Erik where he stood on the platform in front of the driver's box.

Erik had slung his bow behind his back and drawn his khopesh, face set in a rictus of fury. The chief was heavily armored, but his mount was not. Much as Erik disliked hurting animals, there was need in this case. Parrying a slash from the bandit's longsword, he continued his stroke on down and cut through the stallion's neck a few inches above the withers – severing the spine.

The horse screamed and collapsed in a welter of blood, throwing his rider. In a battle frenzy, Erik jumped down from the coach to close with him on the ground. He had several inches on the man in reach, and the power of his arm could take that enchanted sword right through steel plate. Up top, Bernadette continued firing her bow whenever a target presented itself. Then she heard Andrion say through clenched teeth, "Gods damn you!" An arrow was protruding from his left shoulder, having gone right through the thin leather armor.

He was still shooting his blasts of battle magic though, and one of the bandits who'd thought to clamber up and attack the wounded mage at close range found himself falling limply to the ground with a one-inch, smoking hole through the middle of his head. That tight-beam fire/lightning meld Andrion had developed was certainly useful.

The gang's archer seemed to be hanging back in the verge of the trees, and he was still firing at them with deadly accuracy as his companions' numbers dwindled. Erik left the bandit chieftain in a pool of blood beside his dead horse and pulled out his bow again. "Augh! Son of a bitch!" Bernadette shouted as an arrow nicked the outside of her thigh. She was wearing a breastplate, but her armor was fairly minimal. They hadn't been expecting a fight for their lives in this quiet corner of Auverne.

It didn't hurt too badly. She was more worried about Andrion. Taking careful aim, she put an arrow into the archer's midsection just as Erik loosed one that missed the heart and took him in the throat instead. The man fell dead, and all was quiet except for Andreas' frantic crying inside the coach. After scanning around and finding no more live enemies, Bernadette knelt over the hatch, about to jump down and comfort him.

Suddenly his wails rose to a shriek, there was a blur of motion, and the coach door slammed. The last bandit, a woman who looked more like an Insurgent in her tribal garb, had Andreas around the middle – and she was running off with him toward the nearby woods. When she'd gotten a few paces away she turned to face them. Erik, Bernadette, and Andrion all stopped when they saw that she had a dagger held to the baby's throat.

The woman's face was pale with fury, tears running down her cheeks and her lips drawn back in a snarl. She addressed Erik. "You! You killed my Karl!" She was sobbing and panting. "He never gave me a baby, and now he never will. So maybe I'll just take yours, eh? Or come any closer and I'll cut his little throat. You want that?"

The three were paralyzed with horror. There was nothing any of them could do quickly enough to stop her from killing their boy. Or so it seemed. Bernadette's mind fought with fear and incandescent rage to consider her resources, and in a moment she had it. Schooling her face to that of a chastened and terrified mother (not very hard, really), she dropped her bow on the ground and took a tentative step toward the woman where she stood holding Andreas hostage.

"Please," she said tremulously, tears starting from her eyes, "don't hurt my baby. We'll give you whatever you want. We've got gold…" she dug some coins from a pocket and held them out, still approaching cautiously. "Anything, just don't hurt him. All right?" The woman's grief and desperation seemed to be giving way to greed, Bernadette thought, as she lowered the hand holding the knife to point it at Bernadette.

"Don't come any closer!" the bandit warned.

Bernadette's next words were a dragon spell. "Waf-Ond-Nied-Lorn!" The woman's dagger flew from her hand to roll on the ground some twenty feet away. While she stood there in stunned disbelief trying to make sense of what had just happened, Bernadette closed the eight-foot distance between them in a couple of heartbeats and kicked her, hard, on her left kneecap.

Shouting in pain and barely keeping her feet, the bandit flung Andreas to the ground as she used both hands, instinctively, to reach for her damaged knee. The toddler hit the turf with a slight thud and a screech of rage. In another instant Bernadette had drawn her own dagger, a daimonic one enchanted to siphon life essence from a foe, and plunged it into the woman's heart. Bernadette snarled "Die, bitch!" and twisted the dagger. It was not necessary.

As Bernadette was killing their enemy, Erik and Andrion converged on Andreas and scooped him up. He was shaken and extremely pissed off, but had seemingly sustained only minor bruises and scrapes. Bernadette stood over the fallen bandit, watching the woman's life blood soak into the ground for a moment or two until the flow had stopped. Then she struggled to get a grip on herself, tears running freely from her eyes.

"Oh baby, are you all right?" Bernadette took in her son from top to bottom. He halted his screaming at her approach. That other woman had been really awful, but now Mama was here. Bernadette gave him a burst of healing and his slight abrasions faded. Andreas began to look positively happy. Nothing like a snort of healing magic to put things right with the world.

Cuddling her boy to her breast, her heart still racing, Bernadette now took the time to inspect Erik and Andrion. Erik was a little scraped up, but essentially uninjured. On the other hand Andrion still had an arrow protruding from his shoulder, and the wound was bleeding. Devastated, Bernadette kissed Andreas soundly and handed him to Erik, then turned her attention to Andrion. "We've got to get that arrow out so I can heal you!" she said urgently.

Andrion looked at her blankly for a moment. "Arrow?" he glanced down. Oh right, now he recalled. He'd been really annoyed at the time, but when that bandit bitch grabbed Andi it had left his mind. Now that she mentioned it, it was really starting to smart… Bernadette gripped him by the arms, her face a picture of anxiety and regret.

"Erik's going to have to push it the rest of the way through so we can break off the point and pull it out," she said. "I'm afraid it's going to hurt."

Andrion glanced down. Knowing that as soon as the arrow had been removed he would be healed, and all pain would cease, made it a lot easier for him to accept the temporary agony. Looking into his beloved's eyes, he told her "It's all right, Berni. Go ahead, Erik." Erik handed the baby, who was now accepting events with equanimity, back to his mother.

"This'll just hurt for a second," he promised his brother. He could see from the position of the shaft that there should not be any bone in the way. He gripped it and gave it a mighty shove, pushing it through the skin of Andrion's back and out the other side until the barbs and a little of the shaft were standing free.

Andrion drew in a sharp breath, one Bernadette shared with him. To see her love in such pain was torment for her, almost as bad as the sight of that knife against Andi's throat. Erik grasped the two ends of the arrow and twisted, pulling down slightly. A spasm of agony crossed Andrion's face as he did so, yet he still managed to remain silent. Tears were falling afresh from Bernadette's eyes.

Carefully yet swiftly, trying to cause no further pain, Erik drew the two halves of the arrow from within his brother's body. Andrion sighed, more from relief than from pain this time. As soon as Erik had dropped the bloody shards to the ground, Bernadette handed the baby back to him so that she could dual-wield healing, delivering the power of the spell twice as quickly.

In moments Andrion's wounds closed up, blood flow ceasing. This was barely visible through the rents in his armor. As he stood straighter, smiling at her, Bernadette took him in her arms, her eyes searching his for any lingering traces of pain. He kissed her. "Thank you, love. I feel a lot better," he said. She'd healed him countless times in the past. The three of them owed their lives to each other many times over.

Breaking from the embrace and getting a grip on her emotions, Bernadette returned to the practical. "Take your armor off," she commanded. "I want to make sure everything's all right." Andrion felt fine – but there was a great deal of sticky blood in between his armor and his skin, so he was happy to oblige. A couple of little splinters of the arrow shaft had remained in the wound track, and had been carried to the surface by the power of the healing spell.

Bernadette was smiling now, once again cuddling her son to her. "You're a mess," she said.

"Uh, Berni," Erik pointed out, "you're still bleeding…" She looked down at her left leg and realized that its outer side was coated in blood from ankle to the still-oozing wound in her thigh.

"Oh," she said faintly, the aftermath of the adrenaline rush beginning to catch up with her.

"Here," Erik said, handing her a healing potion.

Chapter 40: Pied de Puce, Auverne, Year Three

Estelle Bouchard was washing dishes, her daughter beside her drying, when a knock came at the door of their little house. Jean was away, off at one of the farms in the district where he made a small living for the family doing the books. He was the area's only bookkeeper, and sometimes had to travel far afield. "Marie," she said, "would you go see who's at the door?" Estelle could not imagine who it would be at this hour of the evening. The sun was nearly down, and it wasn't as if they had more than half a dozen friends in the village.

The door was opened by a young woman of perhaps sixteen. Bernadette stood on the doorstep, Andreas in her arms. "Marie?" she asked in astonishment. Behind her, Erik and Andrion goggled. Bernadette was a vibrantly attractive young woman, whose looks had drawn them to her even before her other personal attributes had captured their hearts; but the young creature standing in the doorway was a ravishing beauty!

This could only be the younger sister, a heartbreaker if they ever saw one. Where Bernadette's complexion was lightly bronzed and freckled by her outdoor lifestyle, this girl's skin was porcelain tinged with peach. Her large eyes sparkled a deep blue, auburn hair curling around her shoulders, perfectly shaped mouth open in an "O" of surprise.

"Bernadette?!" Even the voice was perfection. "I thought… I thought you were dead!" Bernadette was a little taken aback. More than three years without communication, but she'd hoped the family would have more faith than that. Repositioning Andreas so he was riding on her left hip, Bernadette embraced her baby sister with her right arm.

"Rumors of my death have been greatly exaggerated," she quoted from some unknown source. "I'm here!"

Recalling her manners, Marie stepped aside and ushered them in. "Maman!" she called, heading back toward the kitchen, "It's Bernadette! Bernadette is here!" Estelle dropped a plate back into the washtub, cracking it. Bernadette was here, alive? It was too much to hope. Could Marie be mistaken? Wiping her hands on her apron,

Estelle made her way into the house's small living room, and nearly fainted.

"Bernadette!" Her eyes filling with tears of joy, Estelle embraced her daughter. In the interim Andreas had been passed to Erik. His trauma of a few hours past long forgotten, the tot was looking around with interest. Who were these new people, and how would they express their love for him?

"Maman," Bernadette said, squeezing her mother tight. The two women were nearly the same height, the daughter only slightly taller than the mother. "It's so good to see you. And Marie! But where are Papa and Gerard?"

"Your father is up the valley at the Lamberts', doing their books. He'll be back tomorrow. As for your brother…" at this Estelle rolled her eyes. "He's likely over at the Poiriers', helping them with planting. Or possibly trying to get next to Michele Poirier." Bernadette gave her a knowing grin. She hadn't seen her brother since he was a gawky adolescent, but he'd be a man grown now. Likely there were few enough eligible maidens in the district, but she wasn't surprised to learn that Gerard was sniffing them out. She'd certainly cut a swath through the young men in the area, back when she was his age.

Estelle's attention went back to her eldest child, and she just stood there in her housedress and damp apron, taking her in. She could still hardly believe Bernadette was here, alive and very clearly well. Dressed in a curious mix of normal clothing and armor, but still glowing with health and seeming even more self-confident than she had, nearly four years ago, when they had last parted company.

In another few moments Estelle registered the presence of the other people in the room. Two tall, very good-looking young men, one of them clearly a Norseman, and an adorable baby boy of about a year in age. Could it be? "Bernadette, please introduce me to your companions," she said, reverting automatically to the motherly authority that had, in Bernadette's case, been so woefully unsuccessful. While she loved her first-born dearly, the two of them had been at odds as often as not since the girl had reached adolescence.

Bernadette took Andreas from Erik's arms, bringing him close. "Maman, this is your grandson Andreas." Estelle looked into those warm brown eyes and melted. A grandson! A beautiful boy…

"Andreas!" his grandmother squealed, reaching for him. Ah, here was someone who wanted to love him. He smiled at her and reached out his arms to her, welcoming her devotion. You'd have thought it was Erik who'd sired him.

Estelle snuggled the boy to her, joy overwhelming her as she held him close. Her wayward daughter, alive – and this beautiful baby here in her arms! Her babies had not come easily to her, and she treasured them no matter what problems they caused her later in life. Looking at the baby, and at the two men in the room, she quickly worked a few things out. Or so she thought.

Gesturing at Andrion and speaking to Bernadette, Estelle said "And this must be your husband? Bernadette nodded. All right, here came the crunch.

"Yes," she said, waxing formal. "My husband Andrion Drakespring, this is my mother Estelle Bouchard. Andrion is from Rocharde," she added. Then, turning toward Erik, Bernadette went on "And this is my other husband, Erik Drakespring."

A couple of hours later, Gerard Bouchard returned home. While the Poirier family appreciated his help, Mathieu Poirier was not stupid enough to let the lad stay the night under his roof with his daughter. Gerard was a lanky young man a little above average height, still just beginning to fill out. His hair was darker than his older sister's, but still showed hints of the reddish hue all the Bouchard children had gotten, to one degree or another, from their mother.

Gerard found his mother and younger sister sitting around the front room of the house with three strangers and a baby, which had him completely flummoxed until he realized that one of those strangers was his sister Bernadette. She'd vanished from their lives years ago, off to seek her fortune in Iscandia. And now she was back? He couldn't wrap his brain around it.

Bernadette had been like a second mother to Gerard and Marie when they were little, probably the reason she had stayed around as long as she had. She and Maman had not gotten along well, those last few years. It wasn't until Gerard got into adolescence himself that he began hearing stories about his big sister – what a slut she was, what a shame to the family, so unladylike. He'd gotten into quite a few fights over it until he'd finally had to admit that the stories were true.

Now she was here, and it seemed she hadn't changed much. She was married, at least, and had a baby. But she was married to two guys at once! Plus she was apparently now this famous person called The Fireblood. News of Terris' close call with Tarragin had not penetrated this far into rural Auverne, so Gerard didn't know what to make of that tale. But after he got a good look at the coach they'd come in, he began to think the story wasn't bullshit.

The Bouchard house didn't begin to have enough room to accommodate four overnight guests, so it was fortunate that the village had an inn with a couple of rooms available. The Drakespring family parked the coach in the inn's yard and stabled the horses there as well, as they settled in to spend a few days in the region where Bernadette had been born and raised.

The men found they didn't mind spending time with their in-laws. Marie, despite her astonishing beauty, proved to be shallow and lacked the bright spark they loved so much in her older sister. She had suitors galore, and was only biding her time until she'd selected the one most likely to provide her with a comfortable life in the environs of Pied-de-Puce. She had no desire to explore the world any further than a day's ride from her doorstep. Still, she was so decorative to look at they would happily just spend time gazing at her.

Estelle, on the other hand, was a joy. Very much like an older version of Bernadette, she was intelligent, animated, slim, and attractive for her years. She was probably not much more than a decade older than himself, Andrion realized, and if he'd never met Bernadette but had run into Estelle unattached, he might likely have pursued her.

Bernadette's father Jean, who arrived back in town around lunchtime of the day after their arrival, was a bit prickly at first. A bookish man, he'd disapproved strongly of Bernadette's wild ways but had lacked the authority to rein her in as she was growing up. Then when she'd abandoned them (admittedly, at an age when most local girls would long since have left home for marriage and motherhood), and they had heard nothing of her for years, they had all presumed she must be dead. Iscandia was a long way off, but otherwise she must surely have communicated with them somehow?

Now it turned out she was not only alive and well, but rich and famous to boot – a mother, and in a marriage that went against all custom. Jean was resentful of the hurt she had caused Estelle, whom he loved more than life; but in time he came to see that Estelle held no such grudge. What finally won him over was Andreas. His grandson! And what an adorable, loveable boy. And he had to admit that Bernadette's husbands, both of them, seemed to be good, solid, respectable men. Their past careers as "hospitality specialists" did not come up in their conversations.

Jean liked that Andrion, who was clearly Andreas' father, was a fellow Galise – and was suitably impressed by his title of Magister. In this part of the world it was the men who were supposed to impress while the women stayed home and took care of the children. So his daughter's status as The Fireblood, savior of the world, meant less to him than did her husband's status as an important person at the Academy that even they, in this remote backwater, had heard of. That Fireblood stuff, Jean thought, was just another regrettable example of Bernadette's stubborn refusal to be ladylike.

Bernadette stopped by the village smithy on their second day in town, and was pleased to find that her childhood friend Louis was working the forge. He was married now, with two children, and had taken over the business from his father. After thirty years, Reynard had been happy to retire. He and Louis' mother now lived in a small apartment above the smithy and spent their days visiting friends in town or just lazing around.

Boy, he had filled out a lot, Bernadette realized as she came in and found Louis, shirt off beneath his blacksmith's apron, hammering a bar of cooling iron on the anvil. He looked up, face sweaty, to see who had come in. Then he did a double-take. "Bernadette?!" he set the bar back into the forge fire, off to the side to keep warm, and laid down the hammer.

Grinning, she held out her arms to him saying "Come give me a hug!"

Louis approached gingerly. "But… I'm all dirty and sweaty. Your clothes…"

"Do you think I give a rat's ass about that?" Bernadette asked scornfully. The girl he knew wouldn't have cared, and the woman she'd become didn't either. She enfolded him in her arms and gave him a squeeze, then a peck on the lips. They'd been like brother and sister growing up together, but the years apart had given her a new perspective on him. Had things been different…

Now Louis was grinning as well. "Everyone thought you were dead, Bernadette," he said. "What have you been doing?"

"It's quite a tale," she told him. "Are you really busy right now?" He shook his head.

"I was just making an iron sword to sell. During slow times I like to build up some stock for when customers arrive, so I already have some things made and they don't have to wait."

"Why don't you put on a shirt, then," she suggested, "and we'll walk over to the inn and have a couple of ales while I tell you all about it."

A couple of hours later they returned to the forge together. She'd learned about his new family and times in Pied-de-Puce among their peers, even as he'd heard about Tarragin, Lord Karazin, her double wedding, and her baby son. They'd also discussed smithing quite a lot. Louis wasn't completely surprised to learn that she'd become a master at the craft. She'd had a knack for it even when first allowed near the forge, when the two of them had been no more than ten.

Selene, the village wise woman/chemiast who had been like a sort of grandmother to Bernadette when she was younger, was getting up there in years but still operated her little shop. Many of the mothers of the region relied on her to assure that they did not become mothers too many times over, putting themselves at risk for an early death. Even Estelle, after Marie had been born, had taken to wearing one of Selene's amulets. Bernadette visited with her for an afternoon and came away with the secret of making the amulets, a treasure indeed.

Another day Bernadette and Gerard borrowed tack from the inn's stables and rode out into the countryside on Sigrandil and Reshiva, visiting the farms of some of her other childhood friends.

233

Pied-de-Puce was the central town in a broad valley checkered with small farmsteads. Any of them was bigger than Drakespring Farm, but few were above fifty acres. Louis got as much work making plowshares and other agricultural implements as he did making arms and armor.

Bernadette visited with some of her former swains, those gormless farm boys she'd loved and left in droves during her teen years. Without exception they were married now, many of them fathers as well. They all greeted her with a mixture of pleased nostalgia and trepidation. She'd been too much for them a decade ago, and now she was a mile out of their league. Plus in most cases, they were anxious not to have their wives know anything about her.

The pair lunched at one of those farms, and arrived back in town in the evening tired and sweaty. Andrion wowed the family by producing a series of his hot tubs in the store room, so that Bernadette and whoever else wanted one could take a bath. Twenty minutes was more than enough time for him to recoup his magical energy, as he wasn't using it for anything else in the meantime.

Gerard had now concluded that his big sister and her family were the coolest people he had ever met, so interesting as to make everyone else in his life seem dull as yesterday's dishwater. When they announced that it was time for them to be moving on for Rocharde to visit with Andrion's parents, he begged to come with them.

"I suppose that would be all right," Bernadette said, unsure how this would impact the rest of the family. Jean's income (as what in another universe would be a C.P.A.) was adequate to cover the Bouchards' living expenses. They owned their small house outright, and Jean kept a horse stabled at the inn so that he could make his rounds of the farms in the valley. As far as she could tell, Gerard's only occupation was as a freelance farm hand, receiving minimal pay for working at area farms when extra help was needed.

"By all means, take him along," Estelle said. The boy was more of a nuisance than anything at this stage of his life, always chasing after the girls in the area and likely to catch one, one of these days. She wasn't aware that, like his big sister, he'd had the sense to enlist

Selene's aid and now wore an amulet just like the one his mother had acquired a few years after he was born.

"Once we've made it to Rocharde, we won't need to travel by the roads anymore," Bernadette pointed out. The map she was carrying now showed several of the local farms as well as Pied-de-Puce itself and all of the other points in Auverne they'd travelled through. "Fast-traveling has its drawbacks, but now we'll be able to come and go between here and our home in Iscandia whenever we want. You can all come and stay with us!"

"Me! I want to stay with you!" Gerard affirmed immediately. Estelle gave him a look. She wouldn't mind going for a visit to see the world her eldest child had built for herself, but she doubted whether Jean would want to leave his clients for any kind of extended trip. And she was pretty sure they'd need to take Marie along.

"If you want to go visit with Bernadette and her family in Iscandia that's all right with me," she told Gerard, "and I'm sure it'll be all right with your father, too." She eyed Bernadette meaningfully. "But no more of this four-years-without-a-word business, you hear?"

Bernadette looked abashed. "Maman, I'm so sorry. Really I am. Now that we have these maps and can travel freely, we'll be in constant contact – I promise." Fast-traveling between here and Drakespring Farm would still take the better part of a full day each way, but it was much safer than going overland. "We'll drop by here to say goodbye on our way home," she added. "I hope Papa will be here then." Jean was gone again, off spending a couple of days doing the books for another client.

There were hugs and kisses all around, and admonitions from Estelle to "take care of our boys" – Andreas and Gerard, Bernadette realized, though she was pretty sure Gerard could take care of himself. He'd admitted to having some skill with a bow and she'd made sure he was carrying a good one, along with a top quality dagger from the collection of weapons they'd brought with them, before they left. The road from here to Rocharde took them through a part of Auverne's major mountain range, and it was possible they'd find peril along the way.

Chapter 41: Southeastern Auverne, Year Three

Rocharde was near the northern coast of the Nether Sea, seventy miles wide and three hundred long. Beyond it sat Remus, seat of the empire. This stretch of coast contained Auverne's most important towns and cities, with Sommet near the northwestern end and Dansmere at the southeastern tip. Slightly inland from the sea, Rocharde was no more than two hours' travel from Sommet. So it only made sense for the Drakespring party to head from Pied-de-Puce to the east, the way they had come.

But what a difference fast travel made! With everyone aboard the coach and Andrion with his map unfurled, he wished them to Arlise, the village they had passed through the better part of a week ago on their way from Digue Sinistre. Bernadette for one was glad they had not had to retrace their journey along the road where the bandits had ambushed them. Likely scavengers had reduced the corpses of their attackers to nothing but bones and grisly shreds, by now – but it was not something she wanted to see.

They'd left early in the morning and arrived what appeared to be a couple of hours later, from the position of the sun. From Arlise they headed due south toward Sommet, near the estuary of the Rive du Nord that separated Auverne from Remus. The road took them along the foothills at the southwestern end of the Rocheblanc range, neatly avoiding the need to overtax the horses by making them pull the coach up over any mountain passes. The Rocheblancs formed a barrier that ran from northeast to southwest across Auverne, crossable at either end and by only one good pass in the middle. They restricted commerce far more than the region's ancient political boundaries did.

After their experience with the bandits, Bernadette was determined that Andreas would not be riding outside the coach again – or inside it without at least one armed adult for protection. They had almost lost their baby! As the trip began, she and Gerard were riding inside with Erik and Andrion on the driver's box in front of them. With two people on the box, the view through the front hatch was mostly of armored calves.

At least, Bernadette now had some adult (make that quasi-adult) company to help keep her entertained. For the most part, Gerard pumped her for stories of her adventures. He seemed to have built her up as some kind of romantic figure from a hero story, and it was kind of flattering. About the details of his own life, he was much less forthcoming; but she didn't fail to notice that he was wearing a familiar-looking amulet.

She certainly had enough tales, all of them true, to keep Gerard entertained for hours. And the telling of them proved entertaining to her, as well. Andreas was mostly as happy as a clam just being there together with them, enjoying the social interaction even if he wasn't exactly participating in it. Each of them cuddled him in turn, and Bernadette nursed him when it seemed appropriate. Gerard didn't blink. Mothers feeding their babies, in the culture of Auverne, were not considered to be anything out of the ordinary. It looked like he was going to make a pretty good uncle.

The sun had reached its peak and gone down the other side by the time they reached Sommet. Though subjectively it hadn't been all that long since breakfast, they all felt ready for a break. The city was the largest and most populous in Auverne, and it would be a shame to pass through there without stopping. But how much of a break did they want to take?

Andrion allowed as how it'd be fine if they were to stay here overnight and proceed on to Rocharde in the morning. Bernadette sensed that he was not as eager for a reunion with his parents as she had been to connect with hers. After all, he had not communicated with them for over a decade. There must be some estrangement there, one he was willing to try to heal; but after all this time he must be dreading it. She drew him close for a hug and kiss, and suggested that it would be jolly good fun to spend the rest of the day exploring this city.

They found an inn with a stableyard and pulled in. Gerard was treated to a vision of how the other half lived, as his sister and her husbands casually rented *three* rooms, one just for him, tipped the stableboy for taking care of the horses, and paid another employee of the place to haul their baggage inside. By the gods, hooking up with them was the biggest opportunity he had had in his life! He'd go with them to Iscandia, make his fortune, and come back via Berni's map in a few years for a visit, to lord it over his old friends from Pied-de-

Puce. Maman and Papa might miss him, but they surely wouldn't begrudge him the chance to do something with his life besides sink slowly into the landscape surrounding their tiny village.

Andrion had of course spent a lot of time here in the past. Sommet was the major trading center nearest to the town in which he'd been born and raised, and he'd traveled there many times with his father in childhood and again, alone, as a young adult for a few years of magical studies before heading north and beginning his journey to Iscandia. The place had changed a bit in the thirteen years since his last visit; but he was able to act as a tour guide for Berni, Erik, and the kid (as he thought of his brother-in-law Gerard, almost young enough to be his son).

They felt as if they were on holiday, taking this unscheduled stop. Andrion was glad to postpone the harrowing experience of returning home to meet his long-abandoned parents, if only for another day. He led them to a popular eatery for a late lunch, then through the extensive shopping district, and finally took them up onto the castle heights where the view of the sparkling blue sea and Remus beyond it was superb. Everywhere people were bustling about their business, the lifeblood of a vibrant city. It was old hat to him, but his companions were impressed.

As evening began to fall Andreas was asleep in Erik's arms, and more than a little damp. They made their way back to the inn where they were staying and Erik handed the boy over to his mother, who carried him upstairs to change his diaper and nurse him. Exhausted by the excitement of the day, the toddler dropped off again after she'd fed him; but she could not just leave him sleeping in the room, with no one to hear if he woke. Regretfully, she carried him downstairs again.

Andrion, Erik, and Gerard had occupied one of the inn's tables and were ordering food. Bernadette had brought down an oblong basket with her, one they sometimes used as a portable bed for Andreas. He was beginning to outgrow it, and was now far too heavy to be carried in it; but after setting it on an extra chair at their table she laid him down and he continued sleeping without interruption.

"I think we wore him out," Bernadette remarked quietly to her companions. Gerard looked down at the sleeping boy with affection.

238

He was at an age where the responsibilities associated with raising a child couldn't be further from his desires – hence the amulet – but he had to admit his little nephew was very endearing. He'd love to have a son like that someday, after he'd had his fun for a few more years.

The inn was a popular one, and at suppertime the noise level in the common room was high. But it didn't seem to disturb Andreas. Bernadette had noticed, when he was quite small, that a loud environment seemed to cause him to shut down and go to sleep. Evidently the phenomenon had not gone completely away. They enjoyed their supper, some excellently-prepared food in the Galise style (heavy on the cream, butter, and herbs), and the boy didn't stir an inch.

They'd washed their meal down with plenty of wine. Evidently the trick of using frost spells to produce ice for chilling beverages had also been discovered in Auverne. In Iscandia, the Drakesprings had never encountered this obvious technique outside of the Bathing Maiden, where they'd pioneered it. Bottles of a light, delicious and cold white wine had flowed and by supper's end they were all feeling pretty mellow. Bernadette, Andrion, and Erik were also feeling pretty horny. There'd been no real opportunities for them to get together during their week's stay in Pied-de-Puce.

Bernadette glanced at Gerard and saw him looking around the room. Of course, he was horny too. A healthy young man his age was probably permanently horny. She was experiencing a sort of mental disconnect, between this not-bad-looking young man and the infant, the toddler, the child she'd cared for when she was little more than a child herself. Her baby brother, all grown up while she was away and not paying attention.

She felt that they had begun to bond again as brother and sister, though that four-year gap while she was gone was hard to bridge coming as it did at the time of life when Gerard was moving from adolescence to manhood. Even bigger, of course, was the seven-year gap in their ages. Could she relate to him as a fellow adult, would he accept who she was and be a member of her team, so to speak? Bernadette feared there was only one way to find out.

"Gerard," she said quietly. The fact that he was sitting at her elbow was useful for her purposes. "We were wondering if you might be willing to stay here and keep an eye on Andi while we, uh, go upstairs for a while…" Gerard eyed Bernadette knowingly, one eyebrow cocked. Where had he learned *that* trick? He grinned. Nothing helped a guy along with chance-met women like the presence of a cute baby, something he'd discovered when he'd been babysitting the niece of a friend.

"Sure," he replied diffidently. "If he wakes up, I'll just give him some of the scraps." Quite a few tidbits still remained from their sumptuous supper.

Bernadette grinned back, and squeezed his hand. "Thanks, Gerard. I owe you one." She rose and beckoned to her husbands. "Gerard's minding the baby for a while," she said quietly. "Why don't we three go upstairs?" They looked at her like wolves perusing a lost lamb.

Chapter 42: Rocharde, Year Three

Postpone it as they might, in due course tomorrow came. Andrion and Erik, sleeping alone in their inn bed after a passionate session with Bernadette the night before, awakened to cold daylight and put on their clothes. Bernadette, sharing her bed with Andi, awoke to fussy crying as he began complaining about the twin ailments of wet diaper and empty stomach. Gerard, happily sharing his narrow bed with a pretty girl around his own age, one of the inn's serving maids, woke when she kissed him with fervor and exclaimed "Nearly dawn! I must go!"

All of them save Andreas had found their sexual urges well satisfied. Andreas had his own urges, but they did not yet involve his penis. After diapering him, Bernadette nursed him until her breasts were empty and he seemed well content. Then she began gathering up her clothing. She anticipated they'd be able to make the trip to Rocharde, such a relatively short distance away, without heavy armor.

The four of them (five, counting Andreas) met in the hallway that joined their rooms. Bernadette, hugging the boy to her as he looked around with bright interest, suggested "Breakfast, then I guess we'll get on the road?" The others nodded. Neither Andrion nor Gerard was really awake yet, merely ambulatory.

Hirelings readied their coach while they drank hot tea and ate elaborately-prepared eggs smothered in savory sauces. Gerard was convinced that he had hit the jackpot. High class inns, delicious meals, willing maids… what more could a guy his age want? The rest of the party seemed to be under something of a cloud, though, a circumstance Gerard only became aware of after they'd been traveling down the road for a while.

Erik was minding Andreas inside the coach while Andrion drove and Bernadette rode beside him, her bow near to hand. She'd dressed with the expectation of a safe and short journey, but that didn't mean she was abandoning all caution. Gerard, riding the back bench and also keeping a bow at his side, eavesdropped on their conversation.

"You seem more like a man approaching his execution than one riding toward a joyful reunion," Bernadette said quietly to her beloved. "Are you ready to tell me yet what went on between you and your parents?" Andrion shook the reins up, taking Sigrandil and Reshiva into a trot. The road along here was in better condition than those in most of the empire, and a little more speed was possible. Bernadette didn't think he was doing it to speed their passage, though.

Sitting on his right, Bernadette squeezed Andrion's right hand where it held the reins. "You can tell me," she said. "If you don't want to go, we don't have to. We can stop any time and fast-travel to Pied-de-Puce, then go home." Andrion slacked the reins, but the horses continued on at a fast walk. He got a grip on himself. This was an issue that had haunted him for most of his adult life, and he knew it was time to let it go. It was why he had agreed to this trip. But it was not easy.

"My father…" Andrion began, finding the words hard to speak. "My father threw me out, and told me never to come back," he finished. Bernadette looked at him in concern. She knew him deeply, and the man he'd become was one she could rely on, would trust with her life. What had he done, as a youngster, that would provoke such an action?

"I loved him," Andrion went on haltingly. "And I think he loved me… but we never saw eye to eye." He sat silent for a minute, minding the horses as they pulled the coach along the road. Then he seemed to shake off a thought and continued. "It's ironic – he's a scholar, a teacher, spent his whole life pursuing knowledge. Just like me. But he was opposed to my magic studies. He thought that seeking power was wrong, that I should just study lore for learning's sake."

Now that the floodgates had opened, Andrion found the whole story pouring out of him. It was an incredible relief. "I was defiant. I thought his attitude was crazy. When I was seventeen I told him that I was going to study magic, battle magic, and I didn't care what he had to say about it. My mother was caught between us, and it nearly killed her. I was her only child, her baby boy, and I was in a standoff with the man she loved. There wasn't really anything she could do about it. So he told me to go, and I left. I'd saved money, and I went to Sommet and sought out a master to teach me."

Bernadette pressed herself to Andrion's side, hugging him and planting a kiss on his shoulder. All the years they had known each other, and he'd never told her this story. In fact, he'd barely revealed any of his early life before now. It must have been too painful. She was somewhat in awe that he had found the courage to face it now, to go back home and confront the father who had rejected him – perhaps, she guessed, for the sake of the mother who had been torn apart by the conflict between them.

Listening from his perch behind the coach, Gerard was troubled. He'd thought Andrion was a pretty amazing guy, but these daddy issues were a surprise. He and his own father were at odds often enough – Jean didn't deal well with Wild Youth. Gerard had grown up listening to Papa's complaints about Bernadette and her general lack of respect for convention. Well, at least Andrion was facing up to it like a man. Gerard didn't think it was going to affect him, much, and set his concerns aside. From where he sat, the world was his oyster, and other people's problems only a passing cloud.

They pulled into the town of Rocharde a little past midday, and Andrion drew the coach into the yard of the inn. "Why don't you all go inside and have some lunch?" he said. "I'll walk over to the old family homestead and see if anybody's home." Erik hadn't been party to Andrion's revelations earlier, and he was puzzled.

"Don't you want us to come along?" he asked, seeming a little hurt. Bernadette gave Erik a Look, and he backed off.

"All right, dear," she said. "We'll be right here when you get back." She led the party – Erik, Andreas, and Gerard – into the inn and took a table near the fire. They ordered some food and drink, and Bernadette gave a very abbreviated explanation of the issues Andrion was having with his family reunion. Erik nodded. He'd mostly dropped out of touch with his own family, as they all seemed to love living in places where it snowed year 'round and he preferred the smiling clime of the Waterdon area.

Andrion walked up the block and took a right down a side street, memories flooding his mind. He had not been back here in nearly half his lifetime, but he had never forgotten the slightest detail. He'd billed himself to Berni as a city sophisticate, a man of the world, but that was a lie. This little town had given him birth, and it was here

243

he'd grown near to manhood. Only when his dreams were threatened by his father had he left it all behind.

There was the house, no more than a cottage – he now realized. The house he shared with Berni, Erik, and their growing family could have swallowed this place up without a ripple to mark its passage. It looked as if it had not had a coat of whitewash since he'd left. Were his parents even still living here, still living anywhere? Might they have died, their only child unaware of their passing?

Steeling himself, his heart full of pain and regret, Andrion put his hand to the door and knocked. Then he stood listening. There were faint sounds, but no one appeared. He was about to knock again when the door was opened by a tallish woman in her early sixties – gaunt, her brown hair heavily streaked with silver, her dress faded from many washings. Her eyes, in their wells of wrinkled skin… were his own.

She took him in, and he her, for an endless moment. Then they spoke at once. "Andrion… ?"

"Mother?" Her worn face lit with joy, and she stepped through the doorway to embrace him.

"Andi, my boy, my boy! You're alive!" Tears starting from his eyes, Andrion hugged his mother back. She, at least, had never stopped loving him though he'd left her half a lifetime ago and never gone back.

After a few moments they broke the embrace, looking into each other's eyes. "Mama," he said, reverting to the name by which he'd called her in happier days, "is Papa still…" Christine Lamonte looked up at her son, embedding the sight of him in her mind. He was fully a man now, not a rebellious boy. Laugh lines, a trace of silver at his temples – but as beautiful now as he had been when he'd left them. She had loved him so much, this only child she had been able to bring forth. Still loved him, though he was that child no longer.

What had he meant to say – was Papa still adamant that Andrion could never return? Was Papa still alive? Tears of joy and sorrow running down her cheeks, Christine got a grip on herself and put a hand on her tall son's arm. "Come inside, Andi," she said. "You need to see." She led him down the short hallway and into the sitting room, where a wizened figure sat, swathed in lap robes, before the fire.

Papa! But not the man he once was. Francois Lamonte had been a tall, well-built man in his middle forties when he had told his only son to leave and never return. He had never been as muscular as Andrion, spending most of his days at the lectern or with his nose buried in books; but he'd been energetic, alive, his fierce intellect infusing him with a vibrant spark. Now he was shrunken, the left side of his face sagging, left arm crabbed and stick-like where it rested on the arm of the chair. Which, Andrion saw as he approached, was on wheels.

He crouched before the chair and looked his father in the face. The bleary eyes blinked at him but there was no recognition there. A rush of pity stabbed him as he beheld the remnant of the man who had once dominated his world. Rising again, Andrion looked at his mother and spoke quietly. "How long...?" She grimaced, fresh tears flowing.

"It was an apoplexy," she said sadly, "a little over ten years ago now."

Andrion looked thoughtful. That would have been around four years after he arrived in Iscandia, while he was still acting as a freelance mage and adventurer. He knew something about this ailment from his omnivorous reading. It was produced by a rupture of a blood vessel in the brain, causing parts of the brain to die. The immediate application of a healing potion or spell as soon as the symptoms manifested would heal the break, stopping the damage. But once regions of the brain were dead, there was no bringing them back with magic. You could reanimate a dead body, but the subject was not really the person who had died, just their body being moved by the force of the spell until it wore off.

Christine watched her son's face, seeing that he understood. After Andrion had been driven away Francois' aversion to magic had become adamant, bordering on the psychotic. He would not allow any healing potions in the house, and if he became sick with an infection he refused to take a panacea potion. She herself had sneaked out to the chemiast's shop to obtain such a cure for herself a couple of times, risking her husband's wrath.

The son she loved was gone, possibly dead in some far-off land. The man she had loved so dearly had become a cold, bitter fanatic. And then the stroke. She could not simply leave him to die, even if her love for him had been poisoned by his growing insanity. So she held on, bathing him and helping him to use the chamber pot, feeding him, getting money to cover their living expenses by taking in washing and gradually selling off Francois' extensive collection of rare books.

At least with Francois little more than a vegetable Christine was able to live a more normal life. She kept a few healing potions in the house now, ready for emergencies. She had even used one on Francois, when he'd fallen from his chair and hurt his head on the corner of the table. There wasn't enough of him left inside there to raise an objection, nor did she suffer any abuse from him as she had in the last years before his illness.

Andrion embraced his mother, sympathy overflowing. What she must have endured! And he could have been here to help, if he had stayed in communication. "Mama, it's all right," he said. "I'm rich now, and you won't ever have to worry about anything again." She looked up at him, hope beginning to light her face. He smiled at her now, hoping to cheer her up. "And I'm married... you have a grandson!"

"Here? In Rocharde?" Christine asked, fresh tears (but of joy, now) sparkling on her lashes. Andrion nodded.

"They're over at the inn," he said. "I didn't want to overwhelm you with a crowd until I saw how things were, here. For all I knew Papa would take one look at me and pull out a crossbow..." he joked. It might be in bad taste, but it made her smile.

"Please," she said, "bring them here. I don't have much food in the house..." Looking around, Andrion could see that money was very tight indeed.

"They'll have already eaten," he assured her. "That was what they were going to do while I was visiting here. I'll pick up something for myself and you before I come back."

Christine ushered him out with another hug and kiss, then nearly fell into a chair. Across the room, Francois had drifted off to sleep and was snoring slightly. By the gods, she couldn't believe it! Andi here, now rich and with a family of his own. It was too much to take in. She half wished Francois were here to see it – though she knew in her heart, with the way things had been going, that if he had not fallen ill she would have left him in another couple of years. The anger and psychological abuse had been wearing her away to nothing.

Perhaps twenty minutes later a knock came at the door and she rushed to answer it. There stood her boy, and gathered around him was a troupe of adults. What??... Flustered, Christine beckoned them inside, where they milled around in the sitting room. The house scarcely had room in it for this many people at once. "This is my mother, Christine Lamonte," Andrion was saying. "We were granted the clan name Drakespring by the Eorl of Waterdon," he explained to her, "so our family are the Drakesprings. This is Bernadette, my wife." A pretty young woman of medium height, a few inches shorter than herself, came forward with a smile.

"So glad to meet you, Christine. Or may I call you 'Mother Lamonte'?"

"Um, Christine will be fine."

Next to be introduced was a tall young man who bore a striking resemblance to Bernadette. This could not possibly be the grandson Andi had spoken of. He might remotely have fathered a child this age if he'd gotten on the project as soon as he'd left home; but Bernadette was no more than a few years older. Practically a child bride! "This is Gerard Bouchard, my brother-in-law," Andrion went on. "He's traveling with us for a while and we're taking him home to Waterdon with us when we leave Auverne."

Towering above the rest was an enormous and cheerful-looking young man, blond of hair and blue of eye, who could only be a Norseman. You didn't see many of them in this part of the world, though some of them were sailors and could be found around the port in Sommet. He grinned at her and shifted the beaming baby in his arms to the crook of his left elbow so he could extend his right hand. "Pleased to meet you, Christine. I'm Erik Drakespring, Andrion and Bernadette's marriage partner."

Christine's eyebrows shot up and her mouth formed an O, momentarily at a loss for words. She shook Erik's hand dumbly, drawn as if by a lodestone to the child he was holding. "And this," he went on (blithely ignoring her confusion), "is our son Andreas – your grandson." What a beautiful boy! She was still trying to make sense of Erik's designation of himself as their "marriage partner," but Andreas was unmistakably the offspring of Bernadette and her Andi.

Entranced, Christine held out her arms. And the boy beamed at her and held out his own. Someone else to love me! Hooray! Erik handed him over to her, and she snuggled him to her breast and began cooing at him, totally besotted. Andreas often had that effect on people, when he was in the mood. Oh! He looked so much like Andrion as a baby, save for the reddish tint of his hair, that Christine felt as if she'd been transported back to that time.

She was not so young as all that but still relatively young and pretty, Francois handsome and commanding, and they'd been so much in love, so filled with joy at the beautiful baby boy who had finally arrived to share their lives after years of trying. Tears ran down her face yet again. What a day! At this rate, she was going to need to wash her dress to remove the encrusted salt.

With an effort, Christine got a grip on herself. Francois had not roused at the disturbance. He spent most of his time sleeping these days, and it was a blessing. She kissed Andreas on the cheek. "Please," she said, "come in and sit down…" realizing that there were only four chairs, not counting Francois' wheelchair. Erik picked up on this at once. He might not be the sharpest of the Drakespring clan, but his social IQ was off the charts. He swiftly dropped to the floor and sat cross-legged on the threadbare carpet, smiling up at her.

Before sitting, Bernadette produced a sack she'd been carrying at her side. "Andrion said you hadn't had lunch, so we brought a few things from the inn," she said.

Christine took the sack hesitantly, and with a smile said "I'll just put it in the kitchen," scurrying from the room. Many Auverne homes, even humble ones like this, had food storage, preparation, and cooking facilities in a room to themselves. The Galise placed a high value on sophisticated cookery, and you didn't get that with one pot on a hook over an open fire.

Christine opened the sack to see what it contained. Fresh bread, fruit, an entire wheel of cheese, and some bottles of ale came to light, along with some delicate crackers and a pot of soft cheese, intended for spreading. She put the last item into the kitchen's cool storage area. Cutting a slice of the firmer cheese, she gobbled it hastily before returning to the cottage's front room and more people than she'd seen in one place in the last fifteen years. And she'd been wondering how they were going to get any more food! Francois' library was almost gone now, and her income from washing didn't cover much. Surely the gods had smiled on her in her hour of need. She whispered a fervent prayer of thanks.

The extended family sat around the tiny room for the next two hours, talking quietly. Christine was alternately astounded, gratified, and confused to hear their tales. Over the past four years or so Andi had been involved in some truly astonishing adventures. And he was now Magister of the Academy at Eisenstag, an institution even people in Rocharde had heard of! Were Francois his old self again, no doubt he'd be chewing nails at the news. His antipathy toward magic was already established before they had met, but had grown exponentially over the years.

As for the issue of Andi's marriage! Christine couldn't quite grasp the concept of one woman marrying two men – it was against any tradition she'd ever heard of. But she had to admit the idea held a certain appeal. She'd been a virgin when she and Francois wed and had never had another man – nor any man at all, since a few years after Andi's departure. Imagine having a choice of two, whichever suited your mood at the moment. That both together was an option, did not even occur to her.

But Erik was such a sweet young man, and such a hunk too. It was clear that deep bonds of affection ran between him and Andi as well as between him and Bernadette. From Christine's point of view, Erik was sort of an adjunct, an accessory to her son's marriage. The fact that Andreas was Andi's son reinforced this notion.

While the conversation had mostly focused on the doings of the Drakespring clan, the subject of Francois' illness had been raised and discussed at some length. Bernadette was itching to see whether there was anything she could do, even though Andrion was firm on the idea (gotten from books) that once the cerebral hemorrhage had killed off regions of the brain, no healing was possible. When Francois awoke, roused by hunger and confused by the presence of strangers in the room (of whom he was peripherally aware), Christine hurried to prepare some food he could eat.

Francois lacked the ability to chew without hurting himself, as he had very little control over the left side of his body. Likewise it was nearly impossible for him to speak clearly enough to make himself understood. The bleeding in his brain had wiped out large areas of his personality, as well as motor functions. He had remembered who Christine was, at least, and she had become his entire world. A glimmer of his former intelligence remained, but it came and went in fits. He had his good days and his bad.

Bernadette went into the kitchen as Christine was preparing some warm broth into which she broke pieces of the bread they had brought her. "Would you mind if I look at your husband?" she asked. Christine looked at her with puzzlement. "Magically," Bernadette went on. "I don't know whether there's anything to be done for Francois, but I'm pretty good at healing magic and I'd like to try."

Christine nodded. She doubted anything could be done. There were no magic practitioners above the apprentice level in their village, but everyone she had spoken with had assured her that if healing were not applied within a day or so of the apoplexy there was no hope for recovery. Whether the patient lived or died depended entirely on the location of the hemorrhage, and the part of the brain that had been destroyed.

Bernadette returned to the little house's main room, where Andrion's father sat in his wheelchair, turning his head from side to side and seeming very agitated. He could have no idea what was going on, and she felt immense compassion for him. He may have been a stubborn fool who had permanently wounded his brilliant young son with his inflexible notions, but he was still the father of her beloved Andrion, and she ached to improve his situation somehow.

Much as Andrion had developed techniques for battle magic that went beyond the basic spells learned from tomes, over her several years of using healing magic Bernadette had begun to refine her techniques. Unlike potions, which simply went everywhere throughout the body healing anything that was wrong, a healing spell could be focused and directed. When she cast the spell she was able to visualize what was happening inside the body of her patient, seeing in her mind's eye what was wrong and directing the healing to repair it.

She approached Francois tentatively. The fact that she was a pretty young woman worked in her favor, as he was not afraid at her approach. She took his hands, the normal right one and the withered left one, in her own, and looked into his eyes. She too had read some of those books of Andrion's, and learned that it was the right side of the brain that controlled the left side of the body.

As Bernadette let the healing magic flow and closed her eyes, visualizing Francois' damaged brain, she saw it. The area of darkness, like a black cloud radiating out from an area on the upper right side, nearer to the front than the back. Truly, that part of the brain was dead and there was no healing what lived no more. But could she connect the parts that were still living together, bypassing the area that had been killed? Healing magic was capable of knitting torn tissues together in seconds. Would it work for the tissues of the brain? Brains were different, she had read – not like muscles. But she had mended broken spinal cords, and weren't those just an extension of the brain?

Feeling her magical energy begin to fail Bernadette reached into the pouch at her side and produced one of those long-lasting magical energy-boosting potions they'd brought along to fuel their supply of hot tubs. So far, they hadn't been needed for that. And wasn't this a better use? As the spell continued, in her mind's eye Bernadette saw tendrils of brain tissue burgeoning, growing, encapsulating the dark spot until it was nearly buried by a web of live matter. She downed two more potions, caught up in the effort now to the exclusion of everything else, until Francois' brain had completely bridged the gap.

Suddenly Bernadette sagged, gasping for breath, and fell to the floor in front of the fireplace. She hadn't even noticed that the effort was draining her stamina as well as her magical energy. Andrion and Erik jumped to their feet and were at her side in a heartbeat. "Berni!

Are you all right?" She opened her eyes and looked up at them with love.

"Oh," she said. "I think I fainted. Have either of you got a stamina potion?" One was swiftly produced, and in moments she was climbing to her feet again.

The three of them looked down at her patient. He was reeling in his chair, gasping as sensations he had not had in a decade were coursing through his body. He looked around him wildly, then he spoke. The words were still slurred, as of someone drunken or with a speech impediment, but they were clear enough to be understood – and there was a mind behind them.

The old man was staring in disbelief at Andrion now, ignoring the other two. "Andi?" he croaked. "Can it be…?" His face contorted into a grimace, and tears began pouring down his cheeks. "My son…?" Andrion stood as if dumbstruck, staring at the shell of his father.

"Papa?" he said hesitantly. He'd been willing to accept that the man he'd known, the man he'd loved and fought with, was dead. What had Berni done?

Francois' left arm twitched as he tried to move it, tried to rise from the chair. The neural pathways had been restored, but his brain was giving orders to muscles that had not tried to move in more than ten years. "Help me…" he pleaded, reaching out to Andrion. As if bespelled, Andrion bent and took his father's withered arms, lifting him to stand in front of the chair. He swayed, only able to support his weight on the right side – though even those muscles had been mostly inactive for all these years.

The old man threw his withered arms around his son. They had once been eye to eye but now Andrion was half a foot taller. He hugged him back, more out of concern for him falling than out of any burst of affection. The wounds were too deep; and if Francois Lamonte was now returning from the grave, he had a lot to answer for.

"Andi," Francois croaked, cutting deep into Andrion's emotions with the use of the pet name his parents had called him by when he was small. It had seemed the most natural thing in the world for him, Berni, and Erik to use it for their own son. "I'm sorry. I'm so sorry…" Pain and love and regret welled up in Andrion like a tide trying to sweep him off his feet. Tears streamed down his face unnoticed as he hugged the old man to him. It was no use. Whatever Francois had done, no matter how much hurt he had caused, he was Andrion's father and right down at his core he loved the man and always would.

At this moment Christine entered the room, the bowl of warm broth with bread in her hands, and stopped dead. Her face went white as a sheet as the bowl, unnoticed, fell from her hands and shattered on the floor. "Andrion!" she cried, trying to make sense of the scene before her. "What…?"

Everyone in the room had been riveted by the tableau, but Bernadette broke away from it to embrace Christine. "I think it worked," she said *sotto voce*, "I think his mind has been restored. And the part of his brain that moves the muscles is restored too, but his muscles are too weak yet for him to move around. He needs to spend some time recovering. There's nothing wrong with them but lack of use, and healing magic won't do anything about that…"

The scene was almost too much for Christine to bear. Had Francois been restored to her, so he could resume his bitter ranting and psychological abuse? Would she have to nurse him back to health so she could have the satisfaction of leaving him? Had she dreamed that Bernadette would be successful, she would never have granted permission. All these years, really, had she not just been waiting for the man she once loved to die?

But Francois was not exhibiting any of the attitudes that had driven Andrion away and made Christine's life a living hell. He was apologizing right and left, in fact. Before their eyes, his mental and physical abilities seemed to be coming back to him – and he appeared to be much more the person the Lamonte family had known and loved, before the split that had destroyed their lives.

More food was fetched, real food. And Francois successfully chewed it, washing down the bread and cheese with ale and declaring it the best thing he had ever tasted. He seemed to be in possession of most of his memories from the time before the stroke, but viewed them as if they had happened to someone else. Bernadette gave it some thought. "I think," she told Christine quietly, "that the tendency for a cerebral hemorrhage as massive as the one he had was not a chance thing. It's very likely that before the big one he had a series of little ones, and they blocked off the parts of his brain that made him who he was. So the personality changes you saw were the result of brain injury, not insanity. When I re-grew his brain around the dead parts, I think I reconnected him to who he was."

Christine took this in, still half-bemused. It appeared that Andi had found himself a woman after his father's heart, or the father Francois had been when they were all much younger. Could that man be sitting there before her, trapped in that withered shell of a body but ready to re-emerge? For the first time since her son had been driven from her life, she began to really have hope.

Chapter 43: Pied-de-Puce, Year Three

The Drakespring clan, plus Gerard (who was more than eager to be declared an honorary Drakespring if the chance arose), stayed at the inn in Rocharde for several more days. There wasn't a lot for a young man to do in these parts, as he wasn't involved in Francois Lamonte's physical therapy; but Gerard managed to keep himself busy pursuing (and often, catching) the entire young, single, female population of Rocharde – one at a time – with an admirable singularity of purpose. He was beginning to suspect that this sort of thing ran in the family, and wondered how Marie had managed to escape it. That girl seemed determined to be a virgin on her wedding night.

Christine and Francois declined the Drakesprings' offers of relocation to Waterdon. They'd lived here all their lives, and now that they had some financial support from their long-estranged son they saw no reason to leave. The Drakesprings had furnished them with enough gold to see them through the next half year, and a promise to return for a visit long before then. Francois was now walking with a cane, and bemoaning the loss of his library. Andrion promised to bring him more books, and soon.

While Francois' prejudice against magic was long-standing and deep-seated, he'd now conceded that it was useful enough and ought to be allowed in certain circumstances. He was enormously grateful to Bernadette for restoring him, to Christine for her patient care while he'd been incapacitated, and to Andrion and Erik for working with him every day to restore his muscles to usability. He rather discounted his son's exalted position at the Academy, preferring to focus on his academic accomplishments and the fact that he'd married well and produced a beautiful baby boy.

The family, all packed up and gathered together in the coach, waved a final goodbye and shimmered out of existence in the road outside the Lamontes' humble cottage. It was now boasting a fresh coat of whitewash, and both of them were wearing new clothes. They sighed in unison. "Now that," Francois said to his wife as they turned to go back inside the house, "is something. I really need to do some studying and find out how he did it."

The coach and its occupants reappeared at the outskirts of Pied-de-Puce, only a few hours later by local time. Erik shook up the reins and drove them to the Bouchard house, where they planned a short visit before leaving for home. It was late afternoon, and Marie soon came to the door to see what the disturbance was outside. The sudden arrival of the coach had provoked barking from half a dozen village dogs.

She smiled up at them, her face like an angel's. Erik and Andrion were still astonished at her beauty, even if both of them had to admit that she was no Berni. Perhaps with time and a little more maturity, she might gain some of the substance her older sister had. But given that the height of her ambition was to marry the wealthiest scion this fleabite village had to offer, they doubted it.

They were in luck, and Jean was home. The whole family gathered around as Sigrandil and Reshiva stood swishing flies, relieved that there had been no more sudden disruptions in the scenery after that first one a couple of minutes ago. They'd fast-traveled often enough now to regard these translocations as merely a confusing nuisance, and were no longer panicked by them.

Estelle insisted that they must all come inside and have dinner, though it was still early for it here in the village. They could hardly refuse. They all gathered around the table in the dining area, filling it to capacity, and Estelle passed around bottles of ale. Then she laid out a basket of bread and a wheel of cheese, while she worked to provide something more substantial. There'd been no way for them to let her know when they were coming, but she'd anticipated about a week's hiatus since their departure and had been in readiness every day. All she needed to do was heat the stew.

Jean, Estelle, and Marie were riveted at the tale of their visit to Rocharde and Bernadette's restoration of Francois Lamonte to some semblance of the man he had once been. Jean had been feeling a little guilty about his cool reception to Bernadette's return, and his lingering disapproval of her lifestyle. One might have thought him susceptible to the influence of her wealth, fame, and powers.

As Estelle served them all bowls of beef stew, rich with the flavors of mushrooms and red wine in the Galise style, Jean volunteered "Andrion, you know… Rocharde's not that far away from here on horseback. Five or six hours, maybe. If you want, I could… look in on your parents for you sometimes." The thought that he'd be passing through the exciting port of Sommet surely hadn't influenced his decision to make this generous offer.

Savoring a mouthful of the delicious stew, which took him back to his childhood with its complex flavors and delicious aroma, Andrion replied "That would be very kind of you, Jean. I think my parents are going to be all right now, though. We left them with plenty of money to get by on and I have the feeling that their friends in the area will be rallying around now that Papa's got his mind back. But I appreciate the thought." Jean nodded and took another bite of stew. Estelle's *boeuf bourguignon* was one of life's great pleasures.

After the meal they gathered up to go. Gerard was hugged and kissed and filled up with advice, even from his little sister. He was fairly astonished when her parting words to him were "Keep your amulet on, big brother." She knew?! Andreas was kissed and hugged so much that Bernadette was seriously considering dosing him with a panacea potion just as a prophylactic measure. They all climbed aboard, and then they were gone. Going home at last!

Chapter 44: Drakespring Farm, Year Three

The horses, the coach, and its occupants materialized in the road below Drakespring Farm. It appeared to be the middle of the night. "This is it?" Gerard asked, surprised at the bulk of the farmhouse that seemed to go on forever in the darkness. Over the weeks they'd spent together his big sister and her husbands had told him quite a lot about the farm and the additions they'd made to it (including the new forge, just completed before they'd left on their trip to Auverne). But he hadn't really gotten a sense of the size. It was easily twice as big as any farmhouse he'd ever seen, though all on one level.

They pulled up the drive, over near the cistern tower, and Erik unhitched the horses while the rest of the family set about unpacking, hauling possessions from the coach to the veranda. They figured to take it all inside in the morning, when there was more light to see by. Bernadette did less of the hauling, lumbered as she was by Andreas. She let herself into the nursery from the veranda with her key, and lit a couple of lamps. There was an adult-size cot in here as well as Andreas' little crib, and she guessed this would have to be where Gerard slept while he was visiting with them.

Bernadette changed the boy's diaper and sat in the rocking chair nursing him until he'd dozed off. She'd noticed that he seemed even more susceptible to the effects of fast-traveling than adults did. Their journey had likely taken eighteen hours, and would have taken more than a week without any fast-traveling at all. No wonder he was so willing to nurse greedily, then fall asleep only a subjective hour since they'd eaten dinner!

When the coach was emptied and the horses had been turned into the cows' paddock with some hay and grain, the family gathered on the veranda for a conference. They were speaking quietly, not wanting to wake up Remy – whom they assumed was sleeping in his room. "Gerard," Bernadette said, "there's a bed in the nursery for you."

"Why doesn't he take my room instead?" Erik offered. "I'm certainly planning on sleeping in the master bed for the next few days." Gerard had not yet revealed his intention to make Iscandia his permanent home.

Bernadette grinned at her enormous, lovable husband. It had been a few days since their last opportunity for sex. Andrion, too, was eyeing her with desire. "Thanks Erik," Gerard said, "that'd be great." He'd much rather have a comfy, extra-large real bed than a cot in the room where his baby nephew was sleeping. Especially as he hoped he'd soon be finding someone to share it with. If young Bernadette's appetites had been prodigious, her younger brother's were gigantic.

Gerard gathered up his spare clothing and other gear, and Erik let him into the bedroom through the veranda door. Then he, Bernadette, and Andrion went into the master bedroom. The place seemed forlorn, somehow, with nobody living here for nearly a month. They were all feeling the effects of the mammoth journey they'd just undertaken, even if it had lasted no more than a few seconds in subjective time; but the men and Bernadette were also eager for one another's bodies, here in their favorite place in all of Agena. It was a long while before they slept.

Utterly map-lagged, none of the travelers was up all that early the next morning. But unsurprisingly, Bernadette was the first to arise. She went across the hall for a delicious wake-up soak in their hot pool. After that, putting on a robe, she decided she'd get the fire started and put water on for tea before going to get dressed and see to Andi.

As Bernadette opened the door to the front part of the house she stood there in stunned surprise – confronting Remy, wearing pants but no shirt or shoes, and a pretty blonde teenager dressed in a robe. Remy had been in the act of putting the kettle on. The girl's eyes got round as saucers and she bolted, barefoot, for Remy's room. Meanwhile Remy nearly dropped the kettle into the fire, and his face turned a very interesting shade of red as he faced the mistress of the house.

"Bern... uh, Mistress Drakespring! When did you get here?" he stammered. "I didn't expect you for another few days..." Bernadette glared at him, but inside she was stifling laughter. Well what did she expect, leaving a young, single, and not-bad-looking young man alone in their house for weeks?

"Wasn't that Hildi from the Maiden?" she asked. Hildi was one of the young women Lev had hired as maids, waitresses, and/or kitchen help. Remy nodded, shamefaced.

"I've been going over there for all my meals, uh, and we sort of hit it off… I really love her."

Bernadette relented. "It's all right, Remy. I don't mind if you have company as long as you're willing to vouch for her. You just took me by surprise, is all."

"That makes two of us," he admitted with a winning smile. He really was awfully cute. She sighed.

"But shouldn't you have been out milking the cows by now? It's almost 10 and you don't appear to be dressed yet." He cringed.

"I'm sorry, I know I should. I've been doing it around seven every day just like before you left, but this was the first time Hildi agreed to come and spend the night with me. We've been sneaking around at the Maiden for a few weeks, but…" his explanation petered out, as he sensed he might be digging himself into a deeper hole.

"Tell you what," Bernadette said finally. "Why don't you get dressed and get those chores done, and send Hildi back to the Maiden. I'm sure she ought to be getting to work pretty soon."

"Not until eleven," Remy said, then ducked his head and added, "Yes ma'am." He scooted for the room. Hildi was already into her clothes by now and also ducked her head as she left.

"Good day, Mistress, um, thank you…" For not getting me fired from my job, Bernadette supplied mentally after the girl had gone. She was feeling a bit annoyed.

As Gerard emerged, dressed, she told Remy "We'll talk later, after you've finished with the chores and we've all had some breakfast."

Some hours later, breakfast had segued into lunch and the three adult Drakesprings plus their young live-in farm hand and their still-younger houseguest were gathered around the dining table for a conference. Andreas was playing quietly with some blocks on the carpet across the room, paying little attention to them. He seemed to be showing the beginnings of the acute intelligence that his father and grandfather shared.

"I do appreciate the opportunity you gave me," Remy was saying, "but I really want to be with Hildi. I hope to marry her someday. And Lev says he'll take me on as a sort of apprentice innkeeper – teach me about procuring, bookkeeping, time management. Maybe even teach me to cook." Bernadette should have known Remy wasn't cut out to be one of the Maiden's "hospitality specialists." He was cute but not up to the studly standard of the men Lev preferred to hire for that position. Besides, it seemed he was already deeply in love – not a good time to be getting into a job where sleeping with the customers might be part of the job description.

As the Maiden's owner, Bernadette of course had final say on any hiring and firing of staff. But Lev had been running the place long before she came along, and he was far too valuable as a general manager to cross him by getting in the way of whatever he wanted to do. Very rarely had she prevailed on him to institute a change that she wanted, or denied one of his own requests. "I suppose we'll be seeing you at the Maiden then," she told the young man. "Pay attention to Lev. He really knows his job."

Erik and Andrion would be sorry to see the lad go, as he'd been an apt worker. All of them had appreciated having someone else to do the drudge work around the place, freeing them for more creative projects. The three of them were surprised when Gerard chimed in at this juncture. "How about if *I* become your farm hand?" he suggested. "It's the only job I've had for the past few years, so I sure know how to do it."

Bernadette hadn't expected this, probably because she hadn't been paying close attention to the signs. Her younger brother was as eager to get out of their tiny home town as she had been, years earlier. It was mostly due to the presence of him and Marie in their home that she'd lingered as long as she had. "I thought you were going back to Auverne soon?" she asked him. Gerard just gave her a look, and gestured around him.

"Would you want to leave all this to go back to that, for the rest of your life?"

"You're right," she said resignedly. She hoped her parents wouldn't think she'd stolen their only son away with her cosmopolitan blandishments. "Erik, Andrion, are you okay with this?" They both smiled and nodded. Gerard reminded them in many ways of Berni, and they were happy to have him join the family – since he was, to some extent, already a member of it.

Bernadette smiled brilliantly at her baby brother. "That's it then," she said, "you've got the job. You do all the farm chores we don't want to, plus help out with whatever else needs doing. You'll get room and board and twenty guilders a week, and you'll have evenings off plus one full day a week to do whatever you want." She was ticking things off on her fingers, trying to remember what else needed mentioning. "Oh yes, we'd like to meet any girls you want to bring over before they spend the night, if you don't mind. I'm not comfortable with strangers staying here. I think that's about it. You can start this afternoon – by mucking out the paddock."

Chapter 45: Drakespring Farm, Year Four

Almost another year had passed since their return from Auverne, and Bernadette once again found herself propped up near the foot of their enormous bed, on a waterproof pad, with her knees in the air. Erik sat behind her, supporting her back and massaging her neck, and Andrion held her right hand while Estelle held the left. Inge stood at the foot of the bed, coaching her.

The Drakesprings went back and forth between home and Auverne several times a year now, and when they had come for Marie's wedding (to the son of the owner of Pied-de-Puce's inn among other local holdings, arguably the richest man in the district) and Bernadette had admitted to her mother that she was pregnant once again, Estelle had vowed to come and help her when her time got closer. She'd been here two months now, sleeping in the nursery and really getting to know her grandson. At two he was not as friendly to all the world as he'd been a year before; but he did love his "Mimi."

Bernadette was finding that the process of giving birth didn't seem to hurt quite as much as it had the first time. Perhaps it was just that it was a familiar experience now, or maybe she'd been loosened up a little down there? She'd not had any complaints from her men about a lack of tightness, but then both of them were quite well endowed. When Inge commanded her to push, she did so with a will. And with a gush of fluids, her water breaking only as the baby emerged, a new Drakespring was ushered into the world.

Inge surveyed the child with professionalism acquired in two decades of midwifery. She'd need some cleaning up, but she appeared to be all there and not looking too bad. She, yes, a girl – which is what she suspected Bernadette had been hoping for. Bigger even than her last baby – it was a wonder the woman hadn't been screaming her head off. She tied off the cord and cut it.

Certain supplies had been prepared on the room's small table and in due course Inge had the baby cleaned and dried, mucus removed from her mouth, and swaddled up for the inspection of her family. She'd been complaining lustily, but settled down to a fretful whimper as Inge brought her over and put her into Bernadette's arms.

Andreas was down the hall, hanging out in the kitchen with Uncle Gerard eating snacks and playing games. It was the middle of a rainy afternoon. Erik scooted out from behind Bernadette, kissing her face as he did so, and they arranged some pillows at the head of the bed so that she could sit up, as they all gathered 'round to see their new little one.

"Did you say it's a girl?" Bernadette asked. She'd been a little distracted there in the first few moments after the birth.

"That's right," Inge smiled. "You have a daughter." Bernadette's face cracked into a joyful grin. Exactly as she'd hoped! She was really enjoying Andreas, but she wanted a girl as well. And she didn't want to have another six kids to get one, either.

The girl's damp curls, plastered to her scalp, looked deep auburn at first. But as they dried, a golden halo sprang up around her head. She was a strawberry blonde, with true blue eyes that were only a shade darker than her father's. Bernadette had worked at this a little. She'd been willing to leave the paternity of her first child up to chance; but now it was Erik's turn. She'd been all but sure from the first that it was he who had put this baby in her womb, and she'd been right.

Andrion was aware of this, had even conspired with her on the project. He gazed lovingly at his new daughter, stroking her silky cheek, then exchanged a triumphant look with his wife. "We're calling her Erika," he announced with a smile.

Chapter 46: Drakespring Farm, Year Five

After Andrion had returned from his latest excursion to Eisenstag, he and Erik and Bernadette sat down for a serious discussion about their future. "You probably should wean her," Andrion opined. "She's already nursed for months longer than Andi did, and she's drinking from a cup now. And maybe you'd better put the amulet on for a while. It's not as if you can't take it off again if we decide we want more kids later." Erik and Bernadette both nodded. It seemed like the best plan.

"You two are going to have to be the ones to snuggle her in the evening and put her to bed for a week or two," she warned them. "If we're going to break the habit, I'll need to stay away from the situations where I would normally be nursing her." Andrion and Erik grinned at each other. "Flip you for it," they said in unison. After nearly five years as a family group, they could finish each other's sentences; and each was usually in tune with what the others were thinking. Riki was quite possibly the planet's most adorable toddler, and they'd only been letting Berni hog the enjoyment of cuddling her in the evenings because of the nursing.

A week later, Riki was happily weaned and Bernadette was free to go places and do things that had not been possible for her during most of the past five years. Her breasts had returned to their normal size, ample but not gigantic, and she was beginning to get back in fighting shape. Not that she planned to go off slaying bandits just yet. She'd not been getting nearly as much aerobic exercise as she needed the past couple of years.

Crack! Bernadette's wooden sword, sized and weighted like an Elven longsword, smacked Gerard on his armored shoulder. If it had had an edge, it might have taken his arm off. "You've got to keep your point up," she admonished him. "Now try it again!" They danced back and forth across the farmyard, wooden practice swords clashing. Gerard, now 21, was an ideal sparring partner for Bernadette. He was shorter and slighter than Andrion, so a better match for her size; and neither of them were exactly expert with edged weapons.

Bernadette's archery skills had increased so quickly, and become so deadly, that she'd stopped using swords and axes early in her career as an adventuress. She still kept her marksmanship polished with hunting and practice at the archery butt; but she needed a more well-rounded workout, something to use all her muscles and improve her grace and balance. And as Erik said, learning a skill is never a waste of time.

By mutual unspoken consent the two took a break, leaning on their weapons and breathing hard. Larissa was here with Sintra watching Andi and Riki this afternoon, giving the rest of them a break. Erik and Andrion were in town running a few errands, and Gerard was more than happy to develop his swordsmanship instead of hoeing weeds or any of the other innumerable farm chores that were his daily lot.

Actually, Gerard had worked out a lot better as a farm hand than Bernadette had expected. He might be one of the Waterdon area's foremost horndogs, and awfully successful at it too, but he was also a steady worker who put his responsibilities first. Plus he genuinely liked living in the bosom of his sister's family. Being a quarter mile down the road from Iscandia's best inn didn't hurt, either.

He'd almost become an unofficial hospitality specialist, at least in the evenings – though clearly, he wasn't free to go on quests with the customers. He didn't get paid either, though he did get a lot of free food and drink. He'd become popular with the Maiden's regular staff, who had welcomed him in as one of the family – coming close to breaking Erik's old record as the Maiden's most sexually active fixture. But that was a year ago. More recently, he seemed to be settling down.

Andreas, breaking free of Larissa's oversight (something he was doing with distressing regularity these days), came running over. "Mama, Uncle Geri, when can I play?" He thought that their sword practice was a particularly interesting game, one he was eager to try. There'd be no problem for her to knock together a set of elven armor in his size, and Erik could carve him a sword. Maybe instead of the ash these swords were made of, some pine might be more appropriate?

Oh, who was she kidding? Boys would be boys, and boys were going to get hurt playing – whatever kind of wood you made their swords out of. That's what healing spells and potions were for. The trick was to make sure they didn't get killed outright, so you could heal them. The pain of the injury would prove a salutary lesson to be more careful next time.

Come to think of it, they'd have to make two sets of swords and armor, one for Andi's most likely sparring partner. Fjurbund Steadfast was several months older and would likely be bigger their whole lives, but he and Andi were fast friends. Fjurbund's mother, Lifa, was expecting another child in the summer and might welcome the invitation for her son to come visit with the Drakesprings for a while. Likely Anja, now ten and beginning to get tall and coltish, would also like to visit. She'd maintained her enthusiasm for the martial arts and was now quite a competent archer.

"I've been thinking about that, Andi," Bernadette answered her son. "It'll take a while to set it up, but maybe in a couple of weeks I'll have some swords and armor for you and Fjuri, and he can stay here with us so you can learn swordsmanship together." Andi's eyes went wide with delight.

"Really?! Thank you, Mama!"

As they stood there talking in the farmyard a rabbit ran right between them, startling them all. Bernadette frowned. She enjoyed eating rabbit, but she also enjoyed eating her vegetables – and she didn't want any bunnies nibbling them down to the ground. It was unusual to see them coming this close to humans during the day. Then they turned in the direction from which the rabbit had come, and realized why it had run.

An enormous wolf, limping slightly, was galloping toward them. A wooden sword wasn't going to be enough to stop it, but at least it was alone. Bernadette jumped into its path and called "Kraf-Luft-Struung-Wund!" The Gale dragon spell sent the wolf flying, tumbling along the ground like a wagon wheel, to fetch up in a furry heap near the bottom of the yard.

Bernadette knew he'd be on his feet in another few seconds though, and she sprinted for the forge – where there were always a few sharp blades to hand. She didn't notice her son, who was looking not at her, or at the fallen wolf, but within as if some marvelous revelation had just swept over him. He had only witnessed her casting dragon spells one other time, when he was only a one-year-old baby and mostly pre-verbal.

As Bernadette pulled a short sword from the rack inside the forge (which was standing open now, it being a pleasant afternoon) she turned and saw the wolf getting to its feet, still a little dazed but snarling in rage. And her son was walking toward it. "Andi!" she screamed, running toward him. She was already closer to him than was Gerard, who was standing as if paralyzed. He hadn't had her experience with combat situations. But she wasn't going to make it in time.

The wolf, recovering its equilibrium, prepared to pounce on the child as Andreas, without showing a trace of fear, continued walking toward it. Before Bernadette could close the distance and snatch her son from the jaws of death Andreas took a deep breath and cried "Kraf-Luft-Struung-Wund!" in his boyish treble. The tone was childish, but the results were not. The hapless wolf was bowled over once again and sent tumbling across the turf.

Before it could recover a second time Bernadette reached it and ran the sharp sword in her hand into its side, just behind the shoulder. It coughed blood and died. She left the sword sticking into the animal, its ribs showing through its fur. Obviously, it must have been starving to have attacked a party of humans on their home ground in broad daylight.

Bernadette knelt before her son, hands on his shoulders as she looked into his eyes with wonder and concern. He smiled faintly at her, his father's smile. "Andi," she said softly. "Have you been playing with Mama's jewel box?" Along with chemial ingredients and vials of magical essence for enchanting, Bernadette kept a little cask of gems in the crafting room. She'd acquired many extra spell stones and hadn't bothered to sell them all. They were pretty, unique, and she'd been thinking she might use some of them to create jewelry."

He looked up into her eyes, assessing just how angry she was going to get. "They're so pretty!" he said. "I like to let them run through my hands and sparkle. But sometimes when I would hold a jewel it just disappeared! I thought I had done a magic trick, but I didn't tell you because I didn't want you to get mad at me. I'm sorry…" His expression was so woeful, Bernadette felt like laughing. Instead she just hugged him to her and stayed there a long time, holding him, wondering what the future was going to hold.

An hour or so later Bernadette had recovered from her shock and had already performed some experiments with Andreas. She taught him Calm and Terror, the only two dragon spells in her repertory that she felt were safe for a four-year-old to have. He had apparently also absorbed the spell stone for the former, but not the latter. Yet she had no doubt that once he had that stone, he would be able to cause attackers to flee. Once a person with the fireblood heard a spell, read its words in a book, or was given them by a Spell Wall, they would not be forgotten.

Bernadette didn't know whether to feel proud or burst into tears. Her baby, fireblood! Had there ever been two both manifesting the ability at the same time before? Since evidently the powers were passed down through the generations, surely each Fireblood must have had the next as his or her offspring. But there was no mention of it in the lore. Indeed, there was very little mention of The Fireblood in any of the lore she had seen, though Andrion was always searching for more. Most of what she knew about what she was came from Adalbert, Ehrgeizig, the Well of Truth, and personal experience.

It made her wonder what would happen if they were both present at the death of a dragon. Which of them would absorb its mana? Suppose Riki manifested the same talent when she was older? Surely that couldn't be right. If being fireblood was as easily passed to one's descendants as red hair, the place would be crawling with them.

By the time the men came home, Larissa and Sintra had returned to the Maiden. Riki was taking a nap, and Andreas and Bernadette were in the kitchen preparing supper. Gerard had begged off joining them, going up to town again. He had begun spending a lot of time at Arngeld the carpenter's place. Arngeld had a couple of sons close to Gerard's age and they'd become friends soon after his arrival. Now two of his daughters were of marriageable age and the younger, Gytha, seemed to be working some kind of magic on the auburn-haired Galise. For the first time since his arrival in Iscandia, his constant womanizing had tapered off to nearly nothing.

Instead, Gerard hurried through his farm chores some days so he could go up to Arngeld's and work alongside Arngeld and his older sons building furniture. He'd begun to develop some good skills in that area, and Bernadette had the feeling that her baby brother might be just about ripe for plucking. They'd be needing another farm hand soon, if she was any judge of the way the wind was blowing. Come to think of it, she'd been scarcely more than a year older than him herself when love had convinced her to settle down and abandon her wild ways.

Andrion came in the front door followed by Erik, both of them smiling. "There's my boy!" Andrion boomed, crouching down to hug Andreas and plant a kiss on his forehead. He slipped him a sweet, and mindful of the hour and his watchful wife on the other side of the room said, "Save that for after supper, now." Then he came across to give Bernadette an affectionate squeeze. "How was your day, love?" he asked nonchalantly, expecting something along the lines of "oh, fine…"

Meanwhile Erik lifted the boy up almost to the ceiling, then gave him a carefully calculated bear hug before setting him down, and handing him a wooden top. This one, unlike any the boy had ever seen before, had a shiny metal disc inset in the top of it – cunningly carved in a pattern that produced interesting optical illusions when the top was spun. Andreas was totally distracted from both dinner preparations and his Big News (which he'd been eagerly waiting to impart to his two papas for hours), allowing the adults a few moments of quiet discussion.

While Andreas was engaged playing with his new toy Bernadette, who had just gotten a stew of mutton, mushrooms, carrots, potatoes and various herbs on to simmer, motioned them to sit down at the table. They sat facing her across its width, wondering at the seriousness of her expression. Their wife had gotten into some very serious situations throughout their time together, but through it all she'd maintained her wry sense of humor and generally upbeat attitude. In some ways, she was a meeting point between Andrion's approach to life and Erik's. No wonder they loved her.

Her ability to beat around the bush had not noticeably improved with age. "Our son," she said quietly, addressing both of them, "is fireblood." They stared at her. What?! "Today while Gerard and I were at sword practice a starving wolf came into the yard," she went on. "I didn't have any useful weapons on me, so I fended it off with Gale. Then while I was running for a sword, our little warrior over there walked up to the wolf and kicked it across the road with the same dragon spell I'd just used."

Both their heads swiveled to take in the boy under discussion, where he sat absorbedly spinning his top to observe the spiraling patterns. This child had the power of the *furml*? Andrion was fascinated, wanting to ask all the questions Bernadette had already considered. She went on. "He admitted having gotten into the cask where I keep the spare spell stones. I suppose I'd better take inventory to see what else is missing. He got the one for Calm, too. Now that Tarragin's dead I'm not sure whether The Fireblood has any more significance, but clearly the bloodline continues."

Bernadette reached across the table and squeezed a hand of each of her men. They were all in this together. "I really don't know what to do," she concluded, "besides try to make him understand that the *furml* should not be used except in cases of extreme emergency. He's too young to handle this power. Can you imagine if he started blowing his playmates across the farmyard? When he's older and has some weapons training, I can start teaching him other dragon spells. But not now."

The three of them concluded that Bernadette's scheme was the best one, and that they should downplay the significance to Andreas. The last thing they needed was a boy thinking he was a superman. He'd stopped being a baby eager for love from everyone and was now a lot more serious and thoughtful, more like his biological father. But he was still a sweet kid, and an innocent. There was time enough for him to grow into his heritage.

Chapter 47: Drakespring Farm, Year Six

It was spring once again, and Bernadette was playing hooky from her responsibilities. She sat, feet up, in a comfortable chair on their veranda, admiring the view of the sun climbing higher over the mountains and river to the east; and closer to hand, her five-year-old son in mortal combat with his best friend, Fjurbund Steadfast. What a pair of handsome boys they were becoming!

Fjuri, half a head taller than Andi and with coloring like that of his mother Lifa, was approaching six and already beginning to fill out. His father Bjorn was a total hunk, and Bernadette mused that in time Fjuri, with his raven hair and deep blue eyes, would be slaying maidens with a glance all over Iscandia. There'd be plenty of maidens left over for Andi of course, with his auburn locks and warm brown eyes that could melt you with a smile.

The two of them had been at this pursuit off and on for the better part of a year, and they were getting better at it. Bernadette had already made each of them three sets of elven armor, the old being melted down for its elvengild when it grew too snug and new made in its place. Erik was their resident swordplay instructor, though Bjorn had also favored edged weapons before he'd become a family man and had started drawing pictures and building houses for a living.

As Bernadette sat there watching them, it occurred to her that their early start might lead to both of them becoming champion bladesmen – though she was beginning to wonder about Andi's future. His Galise heritage and innate abilities as the next Fireblood meant that magic might better be his weapon of choice. Whatever else he might choose to do in life, it seemed inevitable that he would also be able to fight.

But there were years and years in which to worry about that. Right now he and Fjuri were contending with wooden blades, playing out the roles of the Hero and the Enemy, which they switched off each time for the sake of fairness. They'd have loved to have a real enemy, or so they thought, so they could be legendary brothers in arms like Andi's two papas, shoulder to shoulder against the forces of evil. What they needed was another playmate willing to be ganged up on, but there were no other boys they knew of a suitable age.

Bernadette sighed, enjoying the warm morning and a world that, for the most part, seemed to be humming along smoothly. Her children were healthy, Iscandia was at peace, the Bathing Maiden was thriving and so were the Drakespring clan. Remy, now wed to his Hildi and the father of a little boy, often did duty as the Maiden's innkeeper now while Lev used the magic map Andrion had made for him to scour the continent for supplies and equipment – the better to provide for their customers. Though Riki was now three, no one had proposed that Bernadette should remove her amulet to increase the tribe; and she was fine with that. She'd even begun enjoying some questing again, enriching the family coffers with the plunder of ancient tombs.

At the moment Christine Lamonte was in residence at the farm, enjoying a burgeoning relationship with her granddaughter. Riki might technically be no relation of Christine's, but that didn't stop the two from forming a deep and loving bond. Meanwhile Andrion had fast-travelled his father Francois up to the Academy at Eisenstag.

Francois was now completely restored to his much-younger self, at least mentally. He had come to realize that while magic might still be something he regarded with distaste, its beneficial uses were unquestionable; and the college where his son had long been Magister held the most extensive library in Agena. An inveterate scholar, he'd been drawn to it like a moth to a flame.

Bernadette had taken to delving Francois a couple of times a year with her healing spell, assuring that any bleeding vessels in his brain were healed and that his return from near-vegetative status stayed strong. The man was now in his late sixties and fully recovered, both physically and mentally, from the effects of a series of strokes that had ripped Andrion's family apart.

At Andrion's behest Bernadette had written a book on the subject, which had now joined the volumes in the Academy's famous library. People needed to know that the brain held the key to many illnesses people had thought incurable, and that there were ways for magic to correct damage even years after an injury had occurred.

Erik was over at the forge, taking advantage of the warm weather to open its doors wide as he worked on another section of ornamental iron fence. He planned to completely surround the farm with this, more decorative than practical. It wouldn't keep out a determined antagonist, but it delineated the boundaries of their property and added a certain amount of class to the place. Erik was more of an artisan than an artist, unless you counted his skills in the bedroom. But he definitely had a creative spark and it often translated into objects of beauty and lasting value.

The peaceful scene dissolved into chaos in an instant. Wind swirled over the house as an enormous red dragon spiraled out of the sky and landed in the road in front of the farm. Bernadette was jolted from her reverie in an instant, and reached for a bow and arrows. They kept such weapons all around the place, children strictly forbidden to touch, as an emergency response system in case of attack. Despite the Waterdon area's increasing human population, danger was never completely absent.

The boys let their wooden swords fall point down, staring in disbelief at the dragon. Neither of them had ever seen a dragon close up, that they could recall. During their lifetimes the number of dragons interacting with humans in the area around Waterdon had grown ever smaller. Andreas looked up the slope to where his mother was stringing her bow, as across the farmyard Erik dropped his smithing tools and picked up a sword. "Mama?" he said. She had not yet taught him The Dragonfall spell, did not intend to teach him any more offensive dragon spells for another decade if she could help it.

"Andi, Fjuri, get into the house. Now!" The boys dropped their swords and fled, as Bernadette stalked, bow at the ready, slowly toward the monstrous creature sitting nearly motionless in the road below them while Erik advanced from her right, converging on the same spot with a blade in his hand. This dragon was not displaying any signs of aggression. Any other *drache* would have been flying around screaming defiance at them and hovering in midair to roast them with Holocaust. Though Drakespring Farm's house and outbuildings were roofed with slate and not thatch, likely the wooden walls would have been aflame by now.

It seemed familiar, somehow. The size, the color… "Sneyagflug?" Bernadette asked, disbelieving. She had not Called him since the time, more than six years ago, when he had offered to come to her aid after the defeat of Tarragin. Since then she had turned her back on dragonkind, killing as few of them as possible and not delving into her bond with them as she went about the very human pursuits of mating, home-building, and child-rearing.

The red dragon turned his head toward her, breath steaming even in the warm air, as he said "*Fjurblut,* it is long since I have seen you." Bernadette stared at Sneyagflug. She was relieved to learn that her home and family were not under dragon attack; but *why* had he sought her out? She had the feeling the answer would not be to her liking. Still, she replied formally. The *drachen,* above everything else, were a formal people – and when the person you're talking to could devour you in one short bite, it pays to be polite.

"Great Sneyagflug, it has indeed been long in my years since last we spoke. But surely this is but an eyeblink to one of the *drachen*?" The red dragon almost seemed to smile. Bernadette had long had the sense that he was amused by her presumption, or something like that. After all, he'd volunteered to fight at her side though she was nothing but a puny mortal. "*Einkliin,* our doom is upon us." There was an air of sadness about his speech – as of someone who had nearly resigned himself to death, but still held out a faint hope.

Bernadette lowered her bow, then slung it behind her back. "Your doom, Sneyagflug? The doom of the *drachen*?" He bowed his head. "We are dying," he said ponderously. "We, who were immortal. For thousands of years we flew the skies of *erte*, but while we were gone it has become a place of men. Every year more of us perish, and with Tarragin gone there is none to call us back to life."

Bernadette peered up at the red dragon, so big at this range that she could not take him all in without turning her head. Erik was standing near at hand, taking in the conversation and ready to fight in her defense if needed. "Men die all the time," she told Sneyagflug. "It is part of life. Without death, there could be no new people – or Terris would be drowned in our numbers. Why must it be any different for the *drachen*?"

"*Fjurblut,*" the enormous red dragon said sadly, "It is as you say for mortals. But there are no new *drachen* to take the place of those who die. The last *murte*, mother of our kind, has been killed. She left no clutch of eggs, had not bred since Tarragin returned her to life. Now there will be no more *drachenkinde*, no children for us. And in time, there will be no more *drachen.*"

Sneyagflug's words pierced Bernadette to the heart. Dragonkind was often in conflict with man and humans had to come first, but that did not mean she wanted to see this ancient sentient species exterminated from Terris. If they were dying, she had to take a lot of the blame. She had eliminated the one of their number with the ability to resurrect those who had died, had been gathering in the souls of those she killed so they could never return to life. She still felt as though her connection to the *drachen* was more psychic than physical; but she could not shrug off the responsibility, nor the bond that made her determined not to see them vanish from the planet.

"You are here talking to me, Sneyagflug," she told him, "so you must believe there is something I can do about it. What would you have me do?" Sneyagflug's enormous head swiveled toward her, those gigantic eyes piercing her with their gaze. She remembered the first time she had been this close to him, and how terrified she had been then. But she really had no reason to fear him, here and now.

He spoke in his deep rumble, a voice like the passing of glaciers. "Two things we need to create a new *murte* for our race. The first of these is a potion, the making of which has been lost for many lifetimes of men. The other is a *furml*, and I know where that may be learned, where its stone may be found. But first we must have the potion. The instructions for its making will be found in a book, *Alchimia Draconis*. You who have found the Edelmied may be able to find this book. But without it we are lost."

Bernadette brightened. If anybody in Iscandia could put his finger on the location of a rare book, it was likely Mhyrzon din-Tzrek, the Academy's old uruk librarian. He was as prickly as ever, but he would grant whatever request his Magister might make. Then, assuming he could point them to a copy of the book, they had only to go and get it. Or, for all she knew, perhaps one resided in the Academy's library as they spoke.

"My mate Andrion will surely be able to help me find this book, Sneyagflug," Bernadette said confidently. "When I have obtained it I will bring it here and Call you. Will you still come to my call?" The great red dragon seemed pleased.

"It is as I have said, *Fjurblut*. I will come to your call." With that he trod down the road a few paces and took heavily to the air, his enormous wings struggling for lift. It was a wonder, she thought watching as he flew out of sight, that anything that big could get airborne at all.

Turning to Erik, who had been standing a few paces away throughout her conversation with the dragon, she smiled in relief. "This sounds like a job for Andrion," she told him, "and it should be a snap. Can you and Christine manage for a couple of days without me?" He smiled at her, but she detected a faint aura of worry. Having the mother of the family go off on quests at the behest of a dragon isn't the sort of thing most fathers are comfortable with.

Erik walked back to the forge to pick up where he'd left off, and as Bernadette headed toward the house she saw the boys' faces pressed up against the glass of the window in the master bedroom. The challenge of producing large size, clear plate glass was one Andrion had finally surmounted after years of study and a visit to Remus. Bernadette let herself into the bedroom through the veranda door, only to be mobbed by her son and his friend. Andi's eyes were wide with excitement. "Mama, that was a *big* dragon! What did he say? Did you scare him away?" Fjuri was too reserved to besiege her with questions, letting Andi handle it.

"That *is* the biggest dragon I've ever seen except for Tarragin and Ehrgeizig," Bernadette confirmed. The boys of course knew the entire Tarragin story backward and forward. The Drakespring clan had approached a well-known author in Remus, where most books in the empire were produced, to write the official story. It omitted their personal details but delineated the facts and gave credit where credit was due. In the book Andrion and Erik were her "valiant companions," with no mention of the fact they'd also been her lovers and eventually her husbands. The book was a bestseller, and they had great hopes its existence would mean that their story stayed true to the facts and did not become just another unlikely legend.

Bernadette went on, "that was Sneyagflug, an old friend of mine. You remember him from the story, right?"

"Of course!" Andi exclaimed, thrilled. "You and my papas rode on his back to Todenstor before you went to Asengard and killed Tarragin!"

"That's right," she said. "He came to tell me some very sad news and now I need to help him as he did me. Without his help then, our world might not even exist. I think we need to do whatever we can for him and his people, now. So I'm going to go to the Academy to see if I can find a special book."

The boys looked solemn and impressed. Bernadette began gathering up some items she would need to take with her. They now used a portion of the crafts room as a sort of armory, storing their bulkier arms and armor there. Shooing the boys out of the master bedroom she stripped down, then put on some lightweight leather armor enchanted with the same spell she'd once used on Andreas' coat when he was little. It provided more than enough protection for chance-met situations when you were travelling. A good enchanted bow, a large quiver of arrows, an assortment of potions, some spare underwear, and she was nearly ready to go.

Thus kitted up, Bernadette went in search of her mother-in-law. She found Christine out back by the Drakespring Water, supervising Riki as she splashed in the tiny stream. No crackclaws had been seen here since last year, and likely never would be again. The tot was making a mess and getting her clothes all muddy, but "Nana" didn't mind. After looking after an invalid for more than a decade, dirty jobs fazed her not in the least. And with hot running water in the house, laundry was easy enough.

While Riki played happily, Bernadette quietly explained what was going on. Christine smiled, a smile reminiscent of her son's and grandson's. "Give Francois my regards," she said off-handedly. He'd offered to bring her along on the extended field trip to the Academy, but she was much happier here with the children and with Erik, whom she'd come to like a great deal.

"Riki, come give Mama a kiss!" Bernadette called to her daughter.

The angelic-looking little girl (truth to tell, usually more angelic in appearance than in actions) gave her mother a brilliant blue-eyed smile, rather marred by a smear of mud down one cheek, and arose from the puddle she'd been excavating to come and embrace her mother. A chagrined glance at the quantity of mud her precious daughter was bearing caused Bernadette to back up slightly and stop her before she came into too-close contact. She gave the girl a kiss on the lips, then said "Bye-bye sweetie. I'm going away for a couple of days." Riki was already accustomed to her mother's occasional absences.

She just smiled and waved, saying "Bye-bye." Then she went back to her mud.

Bernadette then swung by where the boys had resumed their sparring and gave Andi a hug and kiss goodbye, squeezing Fjuri's hand. "I'll be back in a couple of days," she promised. Lastly, she went to talk with Erik. Just recently, with Andrion away at the Academy accompanying his father, they'd had their enormous bed all to themselves and had been enjoying it a lot. Her hug and kiss for him was far from perfunctory.

Erik was now, Bernadette realized, the age Andrion had been when she had first arrived at the Maiden seven years past. He'd aged well, with perhaps a few more laugh lines than Andrion had had at that age – given his fair complexion and the fact that he was almost always laughing or smiling. He was still built like a god, and still a smilodon in bed. He looked utterly beautiful to her. "Hurry back, love," he told her. "We'll miss you."

Bernadette walked out to the road and pulled out her map, fast-traveling to the Academy at Eisenstag. She braced herself as she did so, knowing it would likely be snowing there or at least as cold as a vampire's heart.

Chapter 48: The Academy at Eisenstag, Year Six

It had been mid-morning when she'd left, and as Bernadette came in through the front doors leading to the Gathering Hall it had recently gotten dark. It was probably about seven in the evening, so likely she would find Andrion either in his quarters to the left, or in the library to the right. There seemed to be no one in the hall itself, as she could see through its openwork doors.

The door to the Magister's quarters was locked, so Bernadette tried the door to the library. Many of the students and instructors at the Academy kept odd hours, and it wasn't unusual to find someone (almost always, Mhyrzon) here at nearly any hour of the day or night. In fact, she found Mhyrzon resting in a chair behind his librarian's desk, studying an ancient tome that was resting on his lap. Around a corner, she came across Francois Lamonte poring over a book open on a table, several more stacked nearby, while his son Andrion Drakespring was searching the shelves for another volume.

Father and son, once estranged over the issue of magic (and also in part, they now believed, due to personality changes a series of small strokes had inflicted on Francois), had now become friends and study buddies. While the father had never been a man of action like his son, they were otherwise so similar that Bernadette felt a twinge of sympathy whenever she thought of how deeply their rift must have hurt her beloved Andrion.

Francois Lamonte's antipathy toward magic predated any of his symptoms, however – he had thought that magic was a misuse of knowledge and led to bad things happening – and considering how many dens of renegade mages Bernadette and her husbands had had to clean out, many of them filled with dungeons where the pathetic victims of gruesome experiments languished and died, he had a point.

But since magic had brought him back from near-vegetative status and given him a new lease on life and love, Francois was beginning to rethink his position. He now saw it as Andrion did: a means by which one could achieve ends, with the ends being subject to praise or condemnation but the means being neutral. Now here he was, in his late sixties, actually studying magic (among other subjects) at the Academy where his once-rejected son was Magister.

Both of the men looked up as she came in and Andrion exclaimed "Berni!" as Francois said "Bernadette!" They looked expectant, waiting for her to come up with some explanation for her presence.

"Oh good," she said, "I'm glad I found you here." Speaking quietly (there was something about the presence of all these books that made it seem natural to do so), she briefly informed them of Sneyagflug's surprise visit and his request.

"*Alchimia Draconis,*" Andrion mused. "Dragon Chemia. Who could have written such a book, let alone figured out how to create potions that work on dragons?"

"Ehrgeizig had a close association with humans for millennia," Bernadette pointed out. "He was the only one of the dragons of antiquity to survive from that day until Tarragin's return. Perhaps in addition to his connection with the Old Ones, there was some chemial researcher that he worked with. Or maybe told things to…" She had as much idea as he did, really, only knew that they needed the book.

"Papa, have you ever heard of that particular book?" Andrion asked his father. Francois had considered chemia to be only a branch of magic, and had refused to keep potions around the house – one of the reasons he had been stricken down, a near-vegetable, for more than a decade. But on the other hand he was a noted scholar, and while he might not have approved of such studies he could have come across the book during his researches in other areas.

But Francois shook his head, his eyes far away as he searched his prodigious memory. He had been in his early forties when his mind had begun to be affected by small brain injuries, but he'd already been a scholar for twenty years before that and was still in possession of most of his faculties when the major apoplexy had stricken him down a decade later. All those memories he retained, and none of them included such a book.

"I've not seen it here," Andrion said, "or anywhere else I've looked. But I'll bet Mhyrzon can tell us something." The elderly uruk was likely the greatest authority on books in Agena. Francois continued studying the book before him on the table, while Bernadette and Andrion walked over to talk with Mhyrzon.

"Mhyrzon," Andrion said, "I wonder if you can help us with the whereabouts of a book. It's not one I've come across before." The old uruk looked up from his reading, sticking a clawed thumb in to mark his place.

"I'll be happy to help, if I can," he replied modestly. Actually he almost always came through with something.

"The title is *Alchimia Draconis*," Bernadette told him.

Mhyrzon furrowed his brow, making him look even more fearsome. He was not particularly more prepossessing than any other uruk, but the facial characteristics of his race could turn a casual frown of concentration into a grimace. "Grogmar…" he said quietly. Then, homing in on the memory, he continued. "Grogmar din-Burzag, down at the High Leap mine, sent me a message that he had found a copy. I don't know where. I was negotiating to buy it from him, when he sent word that it had been stolen en route by bandits."

"Do you have one of those maps?" the old librarian asked. Andrion's breakthroughs with magic maps had become common knowledge around the Academy. The magister nodded and pulled out Bernadette's original map, which any member of the family took with them when traveling around, along with his or her own copy of the Agena map. Thus slowly, they were building up their maps' collections of fast-travel points.

He pointed a clawed finger at a point on the eastern border of the map, not far from High Leap. "I think it's likely the bandits that took the book may be the ones that are laired up here at this dypalfar ruin, Granzek. Or they may be at Robbers' Deep. But most likely one of those two places. Bandits will steal anything of value, but they don't really know what to do with rare books. Some of the library's best finds came from bandit lairs."

Bernadette saw Andrion's eyes light at the phrase "dypalfar ruin." He'd become second only to their friend Diane Baudin (*nee* leBois) in his enthusiasm for ancient dypalfar technology, though she was more interested in their weapons and he in their innovations to enhance everyday living – such as the system that kept their bathwater clean and hot at home. Bernadette could guess which of these possible locations would be their first stop, and smiled.

"Thanks, Mhyrzon," Andrion told him. "If we find any other books while we're searching, I'll be sure to bring them to you." The old uruk smiled, hardly a more reassuring sight than his frowns. "I think it'd be best if we wait until morning to leave," Andrion told Bernadette. "Are you hungry?" Bernadette consulted her innards. It was likely approaching lunchtime at home, but an additional ten hours had elapsed since her breakfast and she definitely felt like she could eat something. A small roasted goat, perhaps, or a half-dozen salmon. She nodded enthusiastically.

They returned to where Francois was studying. "We think we found what Berni was looking for," Andrion told him. "We're going up to my quarters for a bite to eat, then we'll sleep the night and get an early start looking for the book in the morning. Will you be all right?" Francois grinned, his teeth yellowed and the worse for wear. Bernadette's healing had restored his mind and his ability to move, but little could be done for teeth at this stage of his life.

"I've got a couple of loaves and some cheese in my sack," he said, gesturing to the knapsack at his feet. "You two youngsters get some rest, and then go find your book. No hurry getting back." Francois gestured around the library. "At this rate, I'll be happily dug in here until they come to haul away my corpse," he joked.

Andrion clapped him on the shoulder, and said "I'll tell Mama you've left her, then…" His father glared at him. "Just kidding," Andrion assured him. Then he and Bernadette went arm and arm out of the library, up to the second floor and in through the private door that connected it with the Magister's quarters. Andrion could let himself into the library whenever he wanted.

Bernadette had to smile to herself at Francois' characterization of her and Andrion as "youngsters" – she was nearly thirty, Andrion soon to be forty. She was getting laugh-lines of her own, and her breasts were not as firm as they'd once been though she kept her body in shape. Andrion now had streaks of silver amidst the brown hair on the temples, making him look (in her opinion) wise and distinguished. Not to mention, still very hot.

The Magister's quarters had no kitchen facilities, but none were really needed. Food supplies were dropped off on a daily basis, and various spells would provide heat if it were required. As it was, they shared a small table and supped on fresh bread, cheese, smoked salmon, grapes, and some room temperature red wine. Through the meal they caught each other up on what had been going on while they'd been apart, and discussed the dragon situation.

As tentatively as possible, Andrion expressed his concerns. Try as he might, he had killed too many dragons in his time with Berni to be completely willing to trust them. "Are you sure that you really want to commit to Sneyagflug's project, love?" Washing down her bite of salmon with a gulp of wine, Bernadette nodded.

"If Sneyagflug had not been true to his word, if he'd just flown off instead of carrying us to Todenstor, we would never have been able to defeat Tarragin," she said. "I know he always seems kind of amused, like we're children he's humoring; but I feel certain that he's sincere about the risk of dragons dying out. He didn't give me the details, but I assume that he's planning to perform a magical sex-change on one of the male dragons – maybe even himself – so that baby dragons can be born again. How could we refuse to help him?"

Chewing on a bite of cheese, it was Andrion's turn to nod. He could see from his beloved's expression that she was serious about this. More dragons in the world didn't necessarily seem like a good idea, but maybe the young ones could be taught to avoid humankind, thus eliminating the conflict between the two species. In Iscandia alone, there were thousands of square miles of wilderness with scarcely any people at all living in it – and plenty of deer, wild sheep, wild boars, bears, and goats for dragon chow.

After the meal they sat on a fur rug before a fireplace for a while, enjoying the warmth and their closeness. It was always snuggling weather in Eisenstag. But Andrion had been more than a week without Berni in his arms, and he had in mind a bit more than snuggling. She was gazing into the flames while her thoughts drifted. He put an arm around her shoulders and drew her close, planting warm kisses on her cheek, her ear, her neck.

Bernadette turned her head for a kiss, which started out as a warm, tender thing and quickly gathered heat. After a moment or two they broke from it, gasping slightly. "I've missed you, you know," Andrion murmured gently. He knew full well that anytime he was away at the Academy Erik had Berni's loving all to himself, and it made him a little envious. But though Berni and the children were the dearest things in the world to him, his other mistress – Knowledge – kept luring him away.

She leaned into him, running her hand down the front of his trousers. While mages traditionally wore the robes that were the mark of their profession on a daily basis, Andrion had never been a typical mage and he preferred clothing he could move in. Staying in great physical shape was important to him, and even when he was hot on the trail of some bit of forgotten lore he took the time for exercise. "Oh," his wife murmured in his ear as she felt the hot bulge there, "you *have* missed me…"

It was so warm and comfortable beside the fire, and the thick smilodon-pelt rug was cushy enough. They began undressing each other, bit by bit, kissing and stroking between times. Before long they were both naked, the ruddy glow of firelight limning their forms, as they knelt face to face in a tight embrace, Andrion's throbbing cock pressed between them.

"Ooh," Bernadette purred. "I want to eat you up. Lie down," she commanded and her bemused husband complied. He lay flat on the rug, his member protruding upright, as she knelt beside him, gently running her fingers over his smooth skin. He might have a few lines on his face now, but the skin of his body had rarely suffered much sun exposure and was still smooth and supple – delicious.

Bernadette ministered to Andrion with her fingers and tongue, working her way down from his mouth to his shoulders, his navel with teasing strokes until she finally seized his cock in her mouth. He gave a little shudder, then sighed with pleasure and relaxed to let her work her will on him. Augh, that felt good. When she had him throbbing and glowing with desire, she applied a little extra spit to her crotch with a couple of fingers and threw her leg up over his body, piercing herself as she settled in to ride him.

She slid up and down on him, loving the sensation as he filled her, and then leaned forward to press her breasts against his chest and drink his mouth with hers in a passionate kiss. He moaned and clasped her tight. Then he flipped them over, nearly rolling off the rug, and she spread her legs wide to receive him as he thrust within her.

They rolled around on the rug, fucking energetically, and finished off with her kneeling as he pumped into her from behind. Oh, yes… Then they rolled onto their sides facing the flickering fire, which was beginning to die down, and lay there savoring the feel of their joining, the soft fur on their skins, the heat within and without.

In the morning Bernadette rose early, her internal clock making up for an absence of windows to let in daylight and tell her it was time to be moving. She'd always liked these quarters, though she'd visited them seldom enough in the past few years. Last night was only the second time she had spent the night here with Andrion. Since his accession to the title of Magister she'd been either pregnant or the mother of a young child the entire time, and not doing much traveling.

Throwing on a robe, Bernadette explored the chemial herb garden. She could see no sign of natural light to support the growth of the plants, and guessed it must be magic that kept them flourishing. After wandering around thus for a few minutes, she found a chamberpot and used it. Then returned to the bed and embraced her husband. "Andrion, sweetie," she murmured in his ear, "could I have a hot bath please?"

He rolled over and held her to him affectionately, planting a kiss on her forehead. "You'll have to take it right here by the bed," Andrion said sleepily, casting the spell. Then he lay there and leered appreciatively at her as she dropped her robe and climbed into the tub.

Chapter 49: Eastern Iscandia, Year Six

Their closest available fast-travel point was the small mining village of Fendal's Crossing, where years past they had cleaned out a gang of bandits who had murdered the mine workers and taken over the mine. They continued along the main road, as Granzek was quite a few miles south as well as east of their current location. At some point over the past few years Andrion had assumed the lead position when they were traveling together – now Bernadette was watching *his* back while he chose their path. He spotted a dirt trail rising up into a pass between the mountains to the east, and led them up it.

Bernadette was enjoying the trip. She was appropriately dressed for questing in the mountains, and it was almost like old times being out here in the wilderness with Andrion by her side. Sure, they were both older now. But they were both still hale and strong, and she relished the clean, cold mountain air, the beautiful vistas on all sides. She even felt a sharp satisfaction at dispatching the occasional attacking shri or smilodon.

Bernadette couldn't get her loved ones left behind at home out of her mind, though. She was no longer the carefree adventuress who had first come to Iscandia some seven years ago. Now she had property, and love fourfold, and all the responsibilities that came with it. Well, she'd be back home soon enough. Wishful thinking had her willing to believe that Sneyagflug's needs would be satisfied with the delivery of the book he'd requested.

The trail wound up into a mountain pass and then south before climbing east again. Soon they were trekking up a steep, snowy slope, and catching glimpses of some dypalfar structures on the hillside above them. A series of staircases went off to the left, and through a series of stone arches.

At the top of the stairs was a massive dypalfar building, long and low with multiple squat towers domed in tile. There did not appear to be any entrances on this side, and Andrion led them along to the right looking for a way inside. Bernadette had her bow at the ready and her senses on high alert, and was the first to spot the snow troll standing on the path near the building's southeast corner.

She put a hand on Andrion's arm and when he looked at her, she held a finger to her lips. Silence, please. Then she gestured at the troll and nocked an arrow. Maintaining her skills at the archery butts all these years when she wasn't questing much had really paid off: she put an arrow in exactly the right spot to drop the huge beast in its tracks. They stopped at the corpse only long enough for her to retrieve her arrow, then continued around to the building's eastern side.

A doorway hung with massive icicles was set there, and they were soon inside. It was a relief to get in from the cold. They found themselves in a partially ruinous stone entryway, out of which a corridor led to another set of doors ahead. The hall was flanked by two of the ever-burning dypalfar lamps, and Andrion took a few minutes to salvage them before they continued.

This ruin was not to prove one of his more exciting dypalfar finds, however. Always when exploring a previously-unseen site Andrion hoped for new technology, books, anything that would deepen his understanding of the dypalfar. Thousands of years ago that vanished race had possessed abilities the men of today could hardly dream of. How did it all work – and why, despite these marvels, had the builders disappeared?

Instead of corridors leading down into a maze of rooms filled with throbbing dynamos and hostile mechs, however, Andrion and Bernadette found themselves entering a dimly lit circular room with a series of enormous stone pillars holding up a ceiling that nearly vanished in the darkness above them. The pillars were set in a circle, surrounding a broad stone disk with a much shorter pillar in the middle of it.

As Andrion peered into the room's recesses looking for any other salvageable items Bernadette, more focused on the book they were seeking, stepped onto the disk to examine a pair of bodies that were lying on it. Here were the bandits Mhyrzon had mentioned, or a couple of them at any rate. She searched the bodies carefully, hoping for clues. Then she studied the little pillar.

Oh, it had a glowing blue button on top of it. Perhaps it would cause a stairway to appear, or open some gate on the far side of the hall? Bernadette reached her gloved hand out to touch it, and immediately regretted it. Suddenly the entire floor on which she stood spun on a hidden axis to stand vertical – dumping her, the dead bandits, and a few urns into an abyss. Frantic, Andrion screamed "Berni!" as she plunged from his view. As soon as he had reached the opening, and without giving it a second thought, he leapt to follow her.

Bernadette hurtled through empty space for what seemed an unbelievably long time but was probably only a second or two. She had time to take a deep breath and hold it, figuring if she was about to smash into solid stone it wouldn't hurt to do so with some air in her lungs. But she was relieved to strike water, deep water, and found that she could see well enough to orient herself toward the surface.

Treading water and gasping for breath, Bernadette peered up at the hole through which she had fallen. It seemed tiny, so far overhead. Around the pool of water she was swimming in stood a huge cavern with streaks of blue-glowing stone illuminating it. "Andrion!" she called loudly, wanting to let him know that she was safe. "Right here," came his voice – much closer to her ears than she'd expected. He was perhaps twenty feet away, and swimming toward her.

"Oh good, you came…" Bernadette said. She was a little touched, actually, that he would just plunge into empty space after her without knowing if he were falling to his death. Gallant, but stupid. Andrion lifted one arm out of the water and pointed off to their left. "It looks like we can climb out over there…" Good idea. Swimming in armor can be very taxing.

A stone walkway led up out of the pool, and a glance around confirmed Bernadette's suspicions. This was a place of the leukalfar. Sometimes they camped amid the machines and stoneworks in dypalfar ruins, sometimes in villages above ground; but they seemed to have a particular liking for the mostly natural caverns that underlay many of the dypalfar ruins she'd seen. It didn't look like Andrion was going to find many dypalfar goodies here.

"I'm beginning to think those bandits aren't the ones who stole the book," Bernadette told her husband as she peeled off her armor and began wringing out her underwear. Fortunately her pack and its contents had remained mostly dry. Andrion nodded.

"But if they did, and the leukalfar killed them, we might very well find it in a chest somewhere in these caverns. We'd better keep our eyes open."

Andrion applied a finely-tuned fire spell to speed her leather armor to dryness. When they were both reasonably dry and had put their armor back on, Bernadette put a dry string onto her bow and shouldered the quiver of arrows. She spotted a chitinous leukalfar chest up a small rock slope to her right, and went over to investigate. As she was examining its contents, she heard a sizzle of battle magic behind her and found Andrion bending over the body of the leukalfar sentry he'd just killed.

A rocky path of sorts led steeply up into a branch of the cavern ahead of them, and they followed it with care. The chitinous "sentry posts" of the leukalfar could be seen attached to the cavern's walls here and there, looking a little like mud wasp nests only much bigger. Come to think of it, the adult form of the mandimants (those insectoid creatures from which the leukalfar got many of their building materials) quite resembled a gigantic wasp.

Here and there Bernadette spotted elvengild ore deposits. Elvengild was valuable, but she felt they didn't have time to do any prospecting. She was eager to find the book and return to her family. As they made their way along the corridor, which appeared to be natural but ran almost straight, they encountered more leukalfar. Andrion happily let her handle any single scouts they met, as her arrow shots were considerably quieter and less likely to attract attention than his fiery bolts of battle magic.

After many turnings the pair came to a stone ramp crossing a chasm, well-lit by a brazier at the juncture of its two arms. Bernadette took a look down and swallowed. That was a long fall. As she looked up again Andrion let fly with a lightning bolt – three leukalfar were running across the ramp toward them, weapons drawn. She quickly fired her bow, dropping one of them. Moments later, before she could draw a bead on the third attacker, a blast of magical force hurled it from the ramp into the chasm below. Unless leukalfar were a lot more resilient than other humans, she didn't think it would be coming back.

The ramp ahead led to a carved stone doorway, then more of what appeared to be natural caverns studded with leukalfar sentry posts. Bernadette sighed, and Andrion looked over and grinned at her. "Just like old times, isn't it?" he asked quietly. She smiled back. Sometimes, adventures were better in the telling than they were in the living.

They had been searching the bodies of all their fallen foes, in case one of them might just be wandering around with an ancient tome on dragon chemia tucked into his loincloth. No such luck, and there'd been no more chests. This was not the sort of dungeon that yielded much to the treasure-seeking adventurer, unless you were really big on leukalfar weaponry.

Around another bend, they came on another leukalfar chest. Could this be it? It proved to contain some items of value, but no books. They pushed on. Unless Andrion was going to come up with a spell that would let them walk up walls or fly, there was no going back the way they'd come. As they crept ahead, Bernadette took the lead and she shortly motioned to Andrion to be silent. On the path perhaps forty feet ahead of them were another two leukalfar.

Despite their quiet approach, the one in the rear position seemed to hear something and he turned, searching for danger. Bernadette's arrow caught him full in the chest, dropping him silently. Then she put an arrow into the back of the one that was still walking away from them, and it too fell to the stone floor. But not silently!

Bernadette was riveted, as the second leukalfar collapsed to the ground, to hear a peevish wailing coming from the corpse. In all her years of fighting leukalfar she had never heard one utter a sound, no matter how seriously wounded. She rushed to the still body and turned it over, then stood galvanized by horror. The dead leukalfar was female – and there was a baby strapped to her, cradled in an armored leather sling. Now that its mother's weight was no longer pressing on it, the infant took a deep breath and began shrieking at full volume.

Tears of pity and remorse running from her eyes, Bernadette set her bow aside and bent over the corpse, unfastening the straps of the carrier and pulling the child free. As she held it close, rocking it gently in her arms, it gasped and shuddered, its cries tailing off into whimpers as it sensed that help had arrived. Holding it in one arm, she applied healing to it just in case it had been injured in the fall. It looked all right, or at least there were no obvious hurts.

This was the first sub-adult leukalfar Bernadette had ever seen, and fascination was warring with her guilt at having killed the baby's parents. Surely this must have been a family group, but she'd had no way of knowing before she shot. Every member of their race she had seen in her life had attacked her on sight. Andrion was standing at her side, staring at the infant with the same fascination and a trace of regret. What had Berni just gotten them into?

Assuming the leukalfar had roughly the same stages of development as Iscandia's other humanoids, this baby must be about six months old. It was cute in an ugly sort of way – wrinkled skin where the eyes should be, tiny button nose, pointed ears, a little mouth with, Bernadette could see, just a few not-very-sharp teeth coming in. Compared with the adults, the baby had a head too big for its body and an overall appearance of slight plumpness.

Bernadette peeked under the cloth wrapped around the child's loins. "It's a girl!" she said, in tones of awe. Then she tucked the baby back into her carrier and held her up to her body. Bernadette had a lot more going on in the chest area than any leukalfar female, but she was close to the same size and shape. "Help me with these straps, Andrion," she asked quietly.

Andrion goggled at her. "Berni," he began, trying to pick his words carefully, "we can't... I mean, a baby leukalfar? How would we feed it? And what happens when it gets bigger and starts attacking our own children?" She glared at him.

"Don't be ridiculous, Andrion. She's a little baby girl, maybe half a year old. If she's raised with humans she will see us as her family. She'll learn to speak the Common tongue, and maybe someday she can become an ambassador to her kind from the rest of humanity. Maybe the other human races and leukalfar could trade and interact peacefully, instead of killing each other every time they meet."

Andrion swallowed whatever else he'd been going to say. She had a point, and he'd had enough years of experience with Berni to know when she'd made up her mind and was not going to be budged on an issue. He stepped up and buckled the straps for her. The baby, feeling the warmth of her body, snuggled close and fell asleep. For a deadly effective warrior, he thought, his beloved certainly had a pacifist streak a mile wide.

They found no more chests, and the trail abruptly merged with a streambed leading to a small waterfall ahead. The stream seemed to be feeding into another cavern, which was relatively well lit. They crouched at the top of the fall, about a 6-foot drop, and looked down at a large pool that had formed at the bottom of it. Over on the far side, in a cavern lit by torches, a man dressed in typical bandit garb was working an ore deposit. Bernadette hoped this was their way out.

"Hello," she called down to the miner. "Can you tell me where we are?" The guy dropped his pickaxe and grabbed a bow. Not a miner, then. Bernadette stepped back, the baby she was carrying making weapon use awkward, and let Andrion blast him with battle magic. Then Andrion hopped down, and gave her a hand climbing down so she wouldn't jostle the sleeping infant.

Bernadette searched the dead bandit and looked around the cavern. A chest over to one side contained nothing of much value. "I'll bet this stream comes out somewhere," she remarked, gesturing to where the little creek exited the pool to tumble down a rock-strewn bed beside a series of stone walkways. The tunnel through which it ran was narrow, no more than twenty feet across and ten high.

Andrion took the lead. Now that he understood how Berni felt about the leukalfar baby, he'd instinctively gone into protector mode. It might as well have been one of their own children she was carrying, and he'd defend them both with his life. Shortly, he had to. A pair of bandits, one of them a young woman, surprised them walking up the stream as Andrion and Bernadette were walking down.

The man, nearly as big as Erik, pulled a huge longsword and prepared to run the intruder through; but he dropped it with a scream a moment later as a bolt of lightning shot from Andrion's hand to the tip of the sword, heating it to a white glow and blistering his hands. The bolt shot through his body to his steel boots, electrocuting him – and he collapsed into the water, smoking slightly.

"Reljik!" the dead bandit's female companion cried, her face suffused with grief and rage. "You bastard!" she screamed at Andrion, rushing him with blade drawn. Perhaps she thought that after a blast like that last one the mage in front of her wouldn't have enough magical energy left to repeat his attack; perhaps the shock of seeing her lover killed before her eyes drove her beyond conscious thought; or perhaps she was just stupid. Whatever the case, she soon lay smoking beside Reljik, the stream's icy waters washing over her limp corpse.

The encounter had alerted Andrion and Bernadette to the danger of meeting more of the bandit gang, and they proceeded from there with redoubled stealth. Soon they came to a side tunnel, with a wooden ramp leading up from the stream and a platform above it, probably for a lookout. Bernadette found that she could draw her bow adequately even with the baby strapped to her front, and she put a silent arrow into the ugly-looking brute who was sitting on the platform, his feet up on the rail, cleaning his fingernails with a dagger. He never knew what hit him.

The pair did a quiet search of the fallen bandit and the area around him, finding nothing much of value. From the look of things, this gang might have been getting most of their income by the sweat of their brows, mining the ore deposits in the cavern. The side passage continued up beyond the lookout post, and Bernadette led Andrion in that direction. In a few paces another, even narrower passage opened to the left; and beyond it she could see a figure wearing fur armor, working at a chemial station.

Bernadette glanced at Andrion to make sure he knew what was going on; then she drew silently and fired an arrow into the man as he stood working, dropping him in his tracks. At this range she could hardly miss. They continued another few paces then spotted a tripwire across their paths. Andrion took the lead and, standing well off, poked at the wire with a magical staff he was carrying. A spiked iron ball the size of a man's head, suspended on a chain, fell down from the ceiling and swung toward them, then back and forth until its momentum was expended.

Bernadette grinned at Andrion and said quietly, "*That* would have hurt." He smiled back and nodded. The room seemed an odd one for a pack of bandits. In place of the caches of weapons and gold one usually saw, the room was littered with chemial ingredients and books. A large and impressive-looking chest stood against the wall to their left, and when Bernadette opened it she found some gold and weapons. Not the book she was seeking. Her heart sank.

Meanwhile Andrion was examining the contents of the late chemiast's workbench, and he suddenly cried "Got it!" In among a messy stack of books was one that looked ancient, the title almost worn away. But it was just possible to read the words: *Alchimia Draconis*. He handed the book to Bernadette and she opened it carefully. The interior pages were in better condition, not too brittle or yellowed, and despite the archaic title it was written in the familiar characters and words of the Common tongue.

Bernadette was fascinated. She'd been concocting potions for years now, and all of the ones she had prepared needed only two or possibly three ingredients. These formulae, with names like "Potion of Long Flight" and "Potion of Stone Scale" seemed to require as many as six. And while some of the ingredients were familiar to her, others she had never heard of. No doubt Sneyagflug would be able to cast more light on the subject, but she was beginning to get the idea that merely retrieving the book for him was not going to conclude her obligations.

Andrion took the book back and tucked it carefully into his pack, then led them back down the side tunnel to the main tunnel where the stream ran. They followed it downstream, encountering a dead bandit but no more live ones, and eventually had to wade through waist-deep water toward a crevice in the rock, to emerge at a small lake with a dock on it.

Bernadette felt chilled. There was no snow on the ground here, but they were still well up the mountainside and she was shivering in her wet armor. Andrion pulled out his Agena map for a look. "Huh," he remarked. "This is Robbers' Deep. I wonder if these bandits were just another part of the same gang who died in Granzek?" "C-c-can we p-p-please go home now, love?" Bernadette asked him.

"Oh, sorry," he said. She wasn't as able to retain body heat as he was, a fact he sometimes forgot. In moments they were on the road outside Drakespring Farm, at what appeared to be the crack of dawn.

The sun was only just gleaming above the mountains to the east. As they made their way into the house the leukalfar baby held to Bernadette's chest stirred and mewled peevishly. She was probably starving.

Bernadette lifted her out of the carrier and handed her to Andrion. Wet, as well. They had a good supply of diapers and other baby items in the nursery, though their youngest was now three and it had begun to seem likely they wouldn't need them anymore. Somehow, they hadn't gotten around to giving them away yet. They walked down the hall to the nursery, and were greeted at the door by Christine, Andi, and Riki. All three of them stared at the baby in wonder.

"What is it?" Andi asked. He seemed to have inherited a forthright approach from his mother.

Rummaging in a storage cabinet for some clean diapers, Bernadette said "It's a baby. A leukalfar baby." Andi's education so far had included all of the tales of his parents' many adventures, so he knew what leukalfar were. As much as anyone did, really. So little was known about them, though they were clearly people with an evolved culture and technology.

Christine had lived most of her long life in a small village in Auverne and had never seen a leukalfar. But, like grandmothers everywhere, she was drawn to babies. "Oh!" she exclaimed in horrified pity, "It's blind!" Bernadette had taken the baby from Andrion and was now diapering her.

"Her, not it," she said offhandedly as she bent to her work. "And leukalfar are not blind, though they have no eyes. They can see well enough to shoot you with a chitin bow from the other side of a darkened room – don't ask me how. Maybe when she learns how to talk, she can tell us."

They were out of a farm hand temporarily, Gerard having married his Gytha and become part of the ever-expanding Arngeld enterprise. That meant the farm chores mostly fell on Erik, until they hired someone again. "Is Erik up yet?" Bernadette asked, then realized likely no one in her audience knew the answer to that question. "Never mind," she said briskly. "Christine, will you please hold… um, I think we're going to need a name for this child. Kids? Any ideas?"

"How about Merelle?" Andi chimed in at once. A pretty name for an ugly baby girl. Riki, while verbal, didn't really have enough of a grasp of language to be able to make up names.

Andrion said, "I like Merelle. Why not?" Bernadette felt a surge of love and gratitude for Andrion at the way he was supporting her in this. All her talk of raising the child as an ambassador between humans and leukalfar was just a spur-of-the-moment excuse. She was responsible for this innocent baby's orphanhood, and she felt she must make up for that however possible.

"Merelle it is, then," Bernadette said, handing the baby to Christine. She was still crying fitfully, but seemed comforted by being wrapped in motherly arms. Had things worked out differently, Andrion might have been the fourth of the Lanyas' six children, instead of their one and only. But no healing potion or spell yet discovered could cure infertility. Was it any wonder, then, that Christine took Merelle to her breast as if she were her own?

Bernadette looked at the sweet picture with fondness. She'd come to love and respect her mother-in-law, and was happy that she was staying with them for a time. "I'm going to see about rustling up some milk for her," she said, turning to go back down the hall. "Andrion, could you find a clean ale bottle and a clean handkerchief please?"

He smiled and said "Yes'm." They walked down the hall together, but when Bernadette went into the master bedroom he continued to the kitchen.

No Erik here, and when she went through into Erik's own personal room he wasn't there either. Had they unknowingly crossed paths without seeing each other? She went out Erik's veranda door and headed toward the paddock where they kept their two milk cows. Sigrandil and Reshiva, their coach horses, were now boarded at the stables near Waterdon, whence they were occasionally ridden or rented out. They were getting fat.

Bernadette found Erik in the milking shed – just finished forking hay into the manger for Bloody Stupid Animal, the elder of the two cows. He looked up in surprise. "Berni! When did you get here?"

She was still in her armor, having come here straight from their quest after the book; but she managed to get in a hug and kiss anyhow. "We just got back from finding that book Sneyagflug wants," she explained, "and I've got a surprise for you."

He looked questioningly at her.

"Oh?..." She motioned to him to get on with what he was doing.

"Hurry up and get some milk, dear... we need it for our new daughter." This did nothing to speed the process of milk acquisition. Erik stood there, the stool in one hand and a pail in the other, waiting for Bernadette to say something that made sense.

She looked up at him hesitantly, her heart shining in her eyes. He was slightly more immune to this than Andrion was, but not by a lot. "I killed her mother and father, Erik. I didn't mean to... I mean I meant to kill them, they were enemies, but I didn't know they had a baby. Anyway I couldn't just leave her there to die, and I certainly couldn't kill a baby myself..."

Erik's puzzlement was growing. "Bandits?" he asked, doubting it. The bandit lifestyle didn't lend itself to raising children, and almost without exception women who plied the trade or took up with the men in the band would have amulets to ward off pregnancy.

Looking into his eyes, Bernadette said "She's a leukalfar, Erik. The only baby leukalfar I've ever seen. Andi's already named her Merelle. Say you're not mad at me?"

An expression of fond exasperation crossed Erik's face and he set the pail and stool down. Then he stepped forward and enfolded Bernadette in his arms, armor and all, kissing the top of her head. "You wouldn't be the woman I love if you'd leave a baby to die, Berni. You can bring home all the strays you want."

She smiled up at him, tears glistening in her eyes. "Good! Can I have some milk, please?"

He positioned the stool and pail and set to work at Bloody Stupid's flank. Over the years his relationship with the animal had mellowed, and she now knew what to expect and no longer tried to step out of his reach or kick the pail over as he pulled at her teats. He'd brought a pair of pails with him from the house, one for each of the animals; but as soon as he had enough in the first pail to fill a bottle for a baby he handed it to Bernadette and pulled the other one over to resume milking. "Bring it back when you're finished, will you?" he asked quietly.

She bent and planted a kiss on his cheek as she collected the pail. Marrying this man was one of the smartest moves she'd ever made. "Thank you, love," she said softly, then hurried back to the house. Andrion had retrieved an empty mead bottle from the box they kept in the kitchen, and had been sterilizing it with ultra-hot water while she'd gotten the milk; then cooled it to room temperature with a delicately applied frost spell. Every few days they added their collection of bottles to the wagon-load leaving the Maiden, headed for the nearby meadery to be filled anew.

Bernadette held a dypalfar metal funnel in the neck of the bottle while Andrion poured in the freshly "squeezed," warm cow's milk. Bernadette suspected that the milk of cows was not ideal nutrition for a human baby; but it would fill the gap. Merelle had some teeth, so perhaps they could mash up some regular food for her. Or might it be possible to find a wet nurse?

She was a little uneasy about that last prospect, indeed about the whole business of taking Merelle into their family. Was leukalfar hostility toward other human races inborn rather than cultural? Would the girl be treated as a monster by people she met? If only leukalfar weren't so frightening to behold, with their wrinkled, eyeless faces. Despite Erik's cheerful acceptance, Andrion's support, and Christine's almost instant adoption of the baby as another grandchild, Bernadette couldn't completely stifle the feeling that she had let them all in for trouble.

Over the years Bernadette's impulsiveness and "run with it and hope for the best" attitude had begun to give way to a more cautious approach. She had a lot more at stake now: two beloved husbands, a growing son and daughter, property and friends and a far-flung reputation as a hero. But what could she have done differently, and what was the point of worrying about it now? The bottle filled, she took the clean handkerchief from Andrion and wadded it tightly into the narrow opening.

Bernadette and Andrion returned to the nursery, where they found Andi and Riki playing with toys and Christine rocking Merelle in the room's rocking chair. The baby was becoming increasingly fussy. Bernadette handed the bottle to Christine and she tipped it, causing the milk inside to soak the tightly coiled cloth. Then she brought the tip of the cloth to Merelle's mouth. A few drops of the warm milk dribbled inside.

The feel of the cloth was odd, nothing like her mother's nipple; but there was sustenance there and the baby had had nothing to eat for a long time. She was becoming weak with hunger, so she sucked greedily at the cloth and more milk came out. Heaving a huge sigh, she relaxed in Christine's arms and began concentrating on drawing in as much of it as she could get to come out at one time.

Bernadette stood there transfixed, delighted that the little one was not going to starve to death on them. Then she recalled. "Oh!" she said, "I've got to take the pail back to Erik." Andrion continued standing there bemused, watching his mother as she fed the baby. Christine had filled out a lot since they'd reconnected some four years past. She and Francois had barely had enough to live on, after Francois' stroke had made him an invalid. In his childhood memories she was pretty, and now she was handsome in a way, though her face was lined and her hair going gray.

Andrion still felt a lot of guilt that he had never tried to make contact with his parents again until more than a decade after his father had thrown him out; but that guilt was ameliorated by the loving relationship he had now formed with both of them. Being adults together with your parents was a precious thing, he realized. Perhaps it was high time they bundled Erik up and fast-traveled north to Norcove, for a longer reunion with *his* folks.

Bernadette got the pail back to Erik just in time, and hauled off the full one as he switched over to milking Freydis, the younger of their two cows. Freydis produced more milk than Bloody Stupid did, but she was a little more skittish and harder to milk. Bernadette took the pail back to the kitchen herself, straining slightly at the weight.

Chapter 50: Drakespring Farm, Year Six

Bernadette decided to take a couple of days before calling Sneyagflug. She wanted time with her children, with her husbands, time to work out some details of Merelle's care. Despite her inhuman appearance the girl seemed very much like any other baby. Once she had food in her stomach and a dry bottom, with warm arms to cuddle her, she became happy as a clam. She was able to sit up on her own, confirming Bernadette's guess as to her age, and could be entertained for a while manipulating wooden blocks or other toys.

Andi and Riki regarded the baby as a curiosity. She was too different from them to trigger sibling rivalry, and they tended to look on her as a sort of exotic pet. They were willing to interact with her for short periods and had even begun to think of her as somewhat cute; but she couldn't really do much, and they would soon be off on their own pursuits.

Bernadette consulted with Inge on the issue of a wet nurse for the baby, and was soon introduced to Ekka – an exceedingly fat and cheerful woman in her middle thirties. She had been pregnant or nursing for most of her adult life, it seemed, and had not quite weaned her youngest yet. The prospect of nursing a leukalfar baby didn't faze her for a moment, and she volunteered to come and live with them and take over Merelle's care in exchange for room and board and a suitable stipend. Her oldest, a girl of seventeen, would be happy to take over care of Ekka's own brood until such time as Bernadette's newest daughter could be weaned. Well.

The couple of days had become a week, and Bernadette decided that she could not in good conscience put it off any longer. Surely the extinction of dragonkind was not all *that* imminent. It might well not even happen in her lifetime; but she still bore the responsibility. Andrion and Erik came to stand with her as she stood out on the road to call the dragon. It reminded her of the day, all those years ago, when they'd stood at her side as she called him from the Great Porch in Wyrmshalla, very nearly visible from where they now waited.

"SNE-YAG-FLUG!" Bernadette Called. Then they waited. She did not entirely understand the magic that was involved, that the huge red dragon could hear her from wherever he now roamed and get here in moments; but it certainly appeared to work. They had not been standing, scanning the skies, for more than a minute or two when they spotted him winging toward them. The rest of the family was watching from the veranda.

Wind ruffled Bernadette's hair as Sneyagflug came in for a landing. "*Kliin murte,* do you have the book?" he asked in his deep rumble. "Yes, great one, I have it." Bernadette proffered the chemial book. It was so tiny when compared with Sneyagflug's head – could dragons even read? "*Guut, Fjurblut.* I knew I could rely on you," the huge creature almost purred.

"The potion you must concoct is the one called 'Potion of Dragon Transformation,'" Sneyagflug went on. "Can you find it?" Bernadette flipped through the pages. What was I thinking, she wondered? Of course it would have to be me that created the potion. The mental image of a creature the size of Sneyagflug attempting to use a human-sized chemia station was ludicrous. Clearly this book must have been a human-*drache* collaboration.

Bernadette found the page, and looked down at the list of ingredients. "Sneyagflug," she said, "there is a bit of a problem. I have Drakestongue and powdered dragon bone available (she hoped he would not take that last one amiss), but I have never heard of any of these other ingredients, let alone seen them." The huge red dragon seemed to ponder, his enormous lungs producing a slight susurration as he stood there.

"I should not be surprised," he said after a while. "The formula is ancient, and you are young. I may need to take you to where you can get these things." Another quest? Oh, crap. But her sense of obligation was as strong as ever. "It calls for Troll's Ear, Desert Stone, Maiden's Tear, and Fire Moss. I suppose maybe you can get Troll's Ear from a troll, but I have no idea about the others."

Once again Sneyagflug stood quiet, searching his ancient memories. Finally he spoke. "Troll's Ear is a fungus, not the ears of a troll," he said. "The others are all plants, too. They do not grow here in *Norsk*. But I can carry you to where they can be gathered. I'm sure your hands will be well-suited to this task."

"I'll need a companion, if we go," Bernadette warned him. No way she was going on a long, drawn-out quest without backup. Preferably Erik, she decided on consideration. Andrion had less herb lore than she did herself, and Erik was an invincible fighter and good company as well.

"Carrying another of you tiny *sterbliim* is not a problem," Sneyagflug replied. "Do you need time to prepare before leaving?"

Certainly. Ten years ought to be about right... "Where are we going?" Bernadette asked.

"The Troll's Ear will be found in the forests of the area you call Auverne," the dragon replied. "Desert Stone we can find to the south in Zahar, Maiden's Tear in Remus, and Fire Moss should be found in Darkreach. It would make sense to go for either the first or the last, then move in a circle until we have all that you need."

"My companion and I can get to Auverne on our own," Bernadette told him. "After we find Troll's Ear we can call you, and you can carry us on to Zahar. Will that work?"

Sneyagflug considered, then told her "Troll's Ear is a small, rubbery, semicircular fungus, medium brown in color, and it is usually to be found growing on the undersides of fallen logs in well-watered forests. After you find it, call me and I will come."

"I will call you," Bernadette promised, and the enormous creature heaved himself off the ground and took to the air. In moments he was gone.

Another two days were needed before the chemial ingredient expedition was ready to leave. Andrion had no intention of taking up a new career milking cows and mucking out paddocks at the age of 39, but Remy came to the rescue. Acting as bartender at the Maiden, he talked with young men looking for work on an almost daily basis. Waterdon had become something of a major destination in Iscandia, a place to go if you were young and looking to get started doing something with your life. Within a few hours the Drakespring clan were introduced to Umberth, a young Norseman from the region north of Deepwald.

The kid was about eighteen, tall and muscular, with sandy hair thatching his head like a haystack and pale blue eyes that looked as innocent as a baby's. He'd grown up on a farm so he knew the job, but he appeared not to be the sharpest knife in the drawer. Still, with supervision, he should do all right. Andrion was content. They acquired another bed for the nursery, and Ekka bunked in there with Christine and the children. The room was really starting to fill up.

Erik caught Bernadette admiring Umberth as he took off his shirt before getting down to mucking out the cattle pen, and nudged her. She turned and smiled wickedly at him. "Reminds me of you, a bit, only not so magnificent," she said wryly. Her days of tumbling every good-looking guy that came her way were long in the past, but she could still look. He reached down and grabbed her butt cheek for a squeeze. He was looking forward to their quest. Not only a break from the drudgery of farm chores, but adventure and Berni all to himself! Could it get any better?

Chapter 51: Auverne, Year Six

It seemed a shame to be visiting Auverne without stopping by Pied de Puce. Bernadette had not yet seen her new nephew Giles (son of her young sister Marie and her husband). But they had a long journey ahead of them, and Bernadette wanted to find the ingredients Sneyagflug's potion called for and return home as soon as possible. So she and Erik fast-travelled to Arlise, near the eastern side of the Rocheblanc Mountains.

From there they struck out on foot along the road to Sommet until they had rounded the range. Then they cut to the northwest, along the seaward side of the mountains. The foothills on this side received much more rain, and were heavily forested. Bernadette and Erik were armed to the teeth, which proved to be a good thing. Wildlife in Auverne was not as suicidally hostile as that they'd encountered in Iscandia, but even so they were attacked by a small pack of wolves and later, by a prowling smilodon.

Smaller creatures, including little spotted wildcats and deer of a smaller species than that in Iscandia, fled when they saw them. Sneyagflug had clearly believed that his description of Troll's Ear was adequate for her to recognize it on sight; but Bernadette had decided to gather samples of anything she came across, familiar or not.

The weather was cloudy as they hiked along the lower slopes, on the lookout for downed wood. They collected a few types of mushroom and some wildflowers, tree bark, and a few insects but had not found anything matching the dragon's description by the time dusk was falling. By then they were fairly starving, so they pitched a tent in a woodland clearing and made a fire.

Erik was really enjoying himself. Being alone with Berni in the wilderness reminded him of the earliest days of their relationship, when they were in it for all the fun they could get. The red-hot lust she'd inspired in him then, and still did on occasion now, had drawn him closer and closer until he realized that he not only wanted her, he liked her a lot. And he didn't want to live without her. He wasn't one like Andrion for soulful gazes and mushy declarations of love, but by now no declarations were necessary. They showed their love for each other in a hundred ways each day of their lives.

Bernadette had made up some packages of travel rations for them, a mixture of dried meat, vegetables, and herbs that could be tossed into a pot of boiling water and come out as a reasonably tasty stew an hour or so later. She soon had a pot simmering over their fire, and sat on a pile of bedrolls drinking from a water skin. The rain had held off at least, for a wonder. No doubt it'd start pouring in the middle of the night.

Erik took off his armor, which he was wearing over some light clothing, and sat beside her. She'd already stripped to a tunic and breeches. Speaking of red-hot lust… He threw an arm around her and hugged her to his side, then bent to kiss the top of her head. Their height disparity was ever an issue. Bernadette was feeling a little tired after their long fast-travel and hours of hunting through the woods. But not too tired to respond to her golden godling.

Soon they were necking like teenagers, and the heat was rising. Abruptly Bernadette broke away and rose to her feet. "Take off those clothes, you," she commanded, as she stepped over to the fire and moved the pothook over so the pot was now sitting above a much cooler spot in the fire. It had been close to boiling over. Eagerly Erik stripped; and when she turned back from the fire he was standing there – smooth golden skin over bulging muscles, enormous cock standing at attention, sweet little smile on his big, gold-bearded face.

She just stood for a moment enjoying the sight. Then she hastened to step out of her own clothes. With the fire, she trusted they were safe enough here in the woods. She remembered another time, so many years ago, when she and Erik had made love for hours in a woodland bandit camp west of Sylvanian. His libido might have dimmed a notch or two since then, but he was still a fantastic fuck. Hell, she could come multiple times just looking at him.

As then, Bernadette stepped close to him and he bent to grip her buttocks and pull her up to where he could kiss her. She wrapped her legs around his waist, her sex pressed up against his stiff cock as she pinned it between them. The necking resumed, but more urgently. Erik could feel how wet Berni was getting as she rubbed against him, and he lifted her up high enough to slip her down over his throbbing cock. Oh yeah!

By the time Bernadette had recovered her mind to the point of paying attention to their supper again, it was perilously close to sticking to the bottom of the pot. She added a little more water, stirred it up, and took it off the fire. Erik ate ravenously. For some strange reason, his appetite seemed to be hugely increased.

In the morning they rose, breakfasted on cold bread and hot tea, then broke camp and continued their search. Bernadette was considering how convenient it would have been to have Andrion along on this expedition. Though she'd become quite good at healing, she lacked the degree of magical energy required for the instant hot bath spell. Choosing Erik over Andrion as a questing companion had been an emotional decision, not a practical one. He made her feel young again.

Rain had fallen during the night, but their tent had kept them dry. It had stopped before dawn but the woods were soaking wet and soon so were they, picking their way through the forest. At least armor shed most of the moisture, and elvengild was not subject to rust. They managed to avoid a threatening bear rather than confronting it, and in doing so they went down into a little ravine.

The gulley had a small stream of water tinkling over rocks at the bottom, probably runoff from last night's rain. It was choked with vegetation, and Bernadette gathered more unfamiliar items that might have some chemial uses. She had the dragon chemia book with her, and many of the spells called for ingredients she didn't know. What she really needed to find, now, was a field guide to chemial ingredients of Agena, with reference drawings.

They followed the rivulet downhill, away from the bear, and eventually it opened out into a swale where a great number of trees had fallen. Their rotting hulks lay scattered around, the ground soft and muddy. Erik nudged Bernadette's arm and pointed. There, on the underside of a well-rotted pine log, were a series of little shelf-like fungal projections.

Bernadette made a beeline for it. They were rubbery, not hard like some bracket fungus she'd seen, and a medium brown in color. They marched in a line along the bottom side of the trunk where it protruded above ground level, the tree having fallen atop a much smaller one. She broke one off. It parted easily from the rotting wood, pulling out little pieces of the trunk along with some root-like structures. It was smaller than her palm, and must surely be the Troll's Ear they sought.

Bernadette gathered as many as she could find, here in this marshy glade. Fungus, she knew, spread both by spores and also by the part of it that grew below the surface, which was why you tended to find mushrooms of the same kind all growing in the same area. When she had a goodly sack full, she put one to her lips and took a little nibble. A sensation of warmth briefly ran through her, and she got the sense that heat was one of this ingredient's properties.

It only occurred to her after she'd eaten it that this was supposed to be an ingredient in a potion for dragons, not humans. Suppose it had poisoned her? Eh, if the effects weren't too rapid she'd have had time to down a panacea potion. She'd come well supplied. "Well," she said to Erik, after determining that she felt all right, "I suppose we'd better get to some open ground so that we can call Sneyagflug for the next leg of our journey."

They set off down the hill, certain that if they kept heading in that direction they would eventually leave the woods behind. After walking for another couple of hours they came out into rolling pasturelands, probably somewhere to the northwest of Rocharde. A few cattle could be spotted grazing, but otherwise the area seemed to be deserted. Bernadette Called "SNE-YAG-FLUG!"

Chapter 52: Zahar, Year Six

Erik sat snugged up behind Bernadette's back where they rode on Sneyagflug's neck, just ahead of his shoulders. It was windy there, both from the speed of their passage through the air and the flapping of those enormous wings. Once the gigantic dragon had gotten some altitude though, he found a thermal and glided, carrying them high above the Nether Sea and far south to the Great Desert of northern Zahar.

The two humans atop the dragon's back stared in fascination at the landscape below them. In a world without human flight, few sentient creatures besides dragons had ever beheld the land they lived in from this perspective. They could have gazed at it forever, ignoring their discomfort; but as they crossed over into Zahar dusk was falling.

This suited Sneyagflug well. He was anxious not to be seen by humans who might attack him. It would be too cruel, were he to fall to the arrows of some ignorant villagers, before he could put his plan to save the dragon race into action. He landed with a jolt and Bernadette and Erik slid down, almost continuing all the way to the ground after sitting for so long. "Ugh!" Bernadette grunted, shaking her limbs and trying to restore circulation.

"Sneyagflug, that was an amazing ride," she continued. "But the seat could use some padding." "*Enshul*," he replied sardonically. "You and your companion must rest now. In the morning you should be able to collect the Desert Stone plants. You will probably find them in an area where there are some other plants, as this shows there is water below the surface. It looks like a small, round gray stone sitting on the surface, but yielding to the touch. You must dig out the entire plant, root and all. It goes down below the soil a measure like unto the length of your face from top to bottom. I need not warn you, beware of the *sterbliim* you meet here. They do not welcome strangers."

He took to the air once more and hovered before them, saying in parting, "I must hunt now, then rest. Call me when you have the plants and we will continue our journey." In moments he had vanished into the growing darkness. They'd been chilled during their flight from Auverne, and as darkness settled over the desert they found it growing colder and colder. Neither of them had ever been in a desert before, but they had read about them and expected heat, not cold. Probably the heat would come with the sun.

"I wonder where we are," Bernadette mused. She pulled out her map. Both she and Erik had brought their Agena maps, eager for the chance to add some new fast-travel points to their collection. A feature of Andrion's new and improved magic maps was a small colored arrow that stood on the map in the place you were standing, pointing in the direction you faced. You could actually hold out the map and walk forward, watching the arrow move. But you were likely to step into a hole or trip over a rock if you did so.

It appeared Sneyagflug had dropped them some miles to the east and south of Gambala, which lay a little inland from the Nether Sea. Bernadette hoped they'd be able to find what they were looking for soon. They had quite a bit of water with them, but she suspected it would be hard to replenish. Nor were their clothes appropriate for the desert. And what about the natives? She hadn't heard that the Afrans were so uncivilized as to string up intruders by their thumbs, but then she didn't really know that much about them. Once again she found herself wondering if Andrion mightn't have been a better choice as a companion on this trip. But then she looked at Erik, a massive warm presence in the dusk, and thought "no."

Bernadette used a light spell to provide a glowing globe that hovered above her for a minute at a time. It gave enough illumination for them to pitch a tent. There was certainly no firewood to be gathered hereabouts, and they hadn't thought to bring any with them. So they ate a cold meal of trail bread washed down with water, then bedded down. She and Erik were both so stiff from their journey on dragonback, they settled for giving each other massages without anything more exciting going on before they fell asleep.

The morning came early. By the time the dark sky had begun to pale, long before the sun was up, Bernadette and Erik had rolled up their bedrolls and were packing away their tent. Again, Bernadette thought, here was an area in which Erik excelled as a questing companion. She'd be kicking Andrion in the ribs to have a hope of him getting up before well past sunrise. She loved both her men and they loved her and each other; but there was no getting around the fact they each had their strengths and weaknesses.

They could already feel the day's heat whispering its promise (or was it a threat?), and they dressed lightly – putting up with a few shivers now in anticipation of sweltering to come. They made sure their heads were covered, though, and that each of them had plenty of skins of water to hand. Breakfast was that trail ration made of dried meat, suet, and dried fruit. Bernadette felt a certain satisfaction as she gnawed her portion, washed down with plenty of water. She had feared she'd grown soft over the past few years of easy living, but she could still rough it.

As daylight spread across the land, they saw before them an expanse of dun-colored ground that seemed to go on forever. It was very daunting. The two of them were utterly out of their element, and had no idea where to turn. Nothing for it, but to shoulder their packs and set off in some direction or other. "I think maybe we should head north," Bernadette said. "We're not that far from the coast here, so if any moisture comes inland from the Nether Sea it has a better chance of being here than further east." The desert opened up to the east of them, and continued north and south for hundreds of miles. They had maybe enough water to last three days.

"Keep an eye out for any signs of greenery," Bernadette warned Erik as they set off. He was used to taking direction from her, and he had to admit that her agile mind often grasped things that escaped him. Not that he was stupid, by any means. Their minds just worked differently. Before they had been walking an hour the sun's heat was an agony, and perspiration was running down their foreheads. At this rate, three days' water might be less than two. But though they constantly scanned the terrain, they saw no vegetation.

By the time the sun had crossed overhead and was moving toward the western horizon the heat was unbearable. Finally Bernadette could take no more. "Is Sneyagflug trying to kill us?" she asked, flinging her pack to the ground and sitting on it. "Why did he dump us in the middle of nowhere?" Sweat was pouring down her face in rivulets, and the water in her skins was as warm as tea. She looked up at Erik and she could tell that as strong as he was, he was close to the edge of collapse. Just as he and Andrion were better equipped to withstand the cold than she was, he had a harder time losing body heat than she did and was now suffering more. He looked close to heat exhaustion.

"Erik," Bernadette said urgently. "We need to pitch our tent and get under cover until it cools off a little. It's insane to be walking around here at this time of day." He nodded, dropping his pack to the ground and rummaging through it for the tent. The two of them got it put up and crawled inside. The drop in temperature was miniscule, but at least they'd pitched it running north-south so it now shaded them from the afternoon sun.

They drank some more of their water, then lay there in misery, drowsing, as the sun gradually moved toward the western horizon and the air began to cool a little. When they'd rested enough and the temperature had become bearable, they rose and took down the tent, drinking more warm water. "I think we'd better head for the coast," Bernadette said reluctantly. "We're not going to survive another day out here. I don't know how in all the hells Sneyagflug expected us to find something that can only be seen in daylight, when daylight here is deadly." Her attitude toward her draconic friend was cooling dramatically. Was he insane? Or perhaps, as a creature of fire, he had no idea of the limitations of the *sterbliim.*

As they set off, unfortunately facing the setting sun, Bernadette considered their options. They were not truly in danger of dying in the desert – they had only to fast-travel back home, or to some other location. Then they could Call Sneyagflug and rip him a new one for dropping them into this hellhole. But despite her rising anger, she could not yet let go of the task at hand. She wanted to find Desert Stone, she *would* find it, and she wouldn't Call the dragon until she had done so. After which she would, assuredly, rip him a new one.

As the sun came close to sinking below the horizon they stumbled over a crack in the ground. It seemed to be running north-south, bisecting their path toward the distant coast. They halted at the little ravine's edge and took another drink from their water skins, which were getting thin. But with the sun almost down, the air had cooled to a temperature that was nearly pleasant – raising their spirits.

"A wadi!" Bernadette declared. She'd read about these. In the desert, rains came rarely. But when they did, they came with a ferocity that tore into the parched and granular desert soil like a sword into flesh. They carved pathways for themselves, and ever afterward rains that fell would naturally seek these low spots – carving them deeper over the years. If there were to be plants growing here, this would be the place they would seek.

"Let's follow this and see where it goes," Bernadette said. Erik's throat was too dry to reply. He just nodded. "If we haven't found what we're looking for by this time tomorrow, I think we'll go home. Fuck Sneyagflug." Erik nodded again. He was beginning to doubt the dragon's good faith, dropping them in this wasteland without guidance.

The wadi bent east and west while continuing in a general northerly direction. The sand at the bottom of it was soft, and it was now too dark to see where they were going. And getting colder by the minute. After the heat of the day, the cold was almost a blessed relief. Bernadette found that she was able to cast her light spell repeatedly, her magical energy recovering by the time the spell ran out. So they had glaring light aplenty as they continued on their way. Then two of the moons rose, and they no longer needed sorcerous light. Bernadette was glad. The light spell destroyed your night vision, and she preferred moonlight for what they were doing.

They stopped for a while, nearly fainting from hunger now that heat stroke was no longer a threat, and ate some of their trail rations. Nearly half of their water still remained. Then they continued on, and in a while they heard a sound echoing across the desert. It sounded like… music? The wadi bent toward the west again, and they crept carefully down it. Ahead, above the walls of the crevice, they saw lights. The music was now louder, and they could hear singing.

Bernadette stopped. Before them the wadi rose again, petering out. Or perhaps this was its beginning, and the terminus was behind them? This must be an encampment of the people of the Great Desert, against whom they'd been warned by Sneyagflug. But his failure to warn them of the dangers of traversing the desert in the daytime suggested that his information wasn't reliable. Should they approach?

It was at this point that Bernadette heard a slightly accented voice say, "You will please put down your weapons." Shit, ambushed! They'd been focusing so much on the encampment ahead of them, with its light and music, that neither of them had considered the likelihood of sentries guarding the approach from the wadi.

Erik and Bernadette looked to the ground above the wadi, now only at about head height. Four Afran warriors surrounded them, two on either side, and they all had bows drawn. "I think maybe we should surrender," Erik murmured. Coming from him, this was earth-shaking! Likely he'd have fought four warriors with drawn bows by himself ten years previously, and lived to tell about it. But Bernadette wasn't willing to risk it. They had only the dragon's word that these people meant them harm.

"Oh, I'm so glad to see you!" Bernadette said, dropping her bow to the ground. She was still armed with a couple of lethal daggers and various battle spells of course, not that any of those was worth much at her level of expertise. "We got lost in the desert and we didn't think we would find anyone out here!" She hoped she sounded sincere. It was nothing but the truth, after all.

The four Afran sentries jumped down into the wadi and had soon removed Erik's bow, khopesh, two daggers, and a small war axe. Even after they'd taken all his weapons they seemed to regard the gigantic Norseman with a great deal of suspicion, and they kept their bows to hand. Bernadette they treated more gently. She was not a particularly imposing person, a smallish armored woman in her late twenties, and they found one of her daggers but not the other. Not that one dagger, or her novice abilities in battle magic, were likely to save them if these people proved to be hostile.

They were marched out of the wadi and toward the lights, which resolved into a sprawling collection of tents lighted here and there with torches and lanterns. In the center of the encampment was an open space with a campfire (burning what, she had to wonder), and it was from here that the music and singing arose.

As they were shoved roughly out into the firelight, disoriented, they saw people sitting on the ground around the circle while a group of musicians sat at the front of a tent on one side. Beside that tent, a much larger one was pitched; and in front of it there was a chair. It was a perfectly ordinary looking chair, but in this land of no trees no chair was "ordinary." This must be the seat of the band's leader.

The guards guided them roughly to stand before the man seated in the chair. "We found these two skulking in the wadi," the apparent lead guard said. "Norsemen!" the man said. "What are Norsemen doing here?" Invaders from Iscandia were not often on the minds of the people of the desert. They much preferred to fight among themselves, as ownership of this gods-forsaken stretch of wilderness was not something most would contest with them.

"They were just standing there looking, Yusuf," the sentries' leader continued. "She claimed they were lost in the desert. I can believe it!" His white teeth flashed in the firelight. Yusuf took a lantern from where it hung on one of his tent's uprights, and brought it up to light the captives' faces. As he did so his own face was lit, and Bernadette had a flash of recognition.

"Yusuf!" she said, "I know you. When you were in Normarsh looking for the fugitive Jamal, it was I who found him and brought him to you so that you could return him to Zahar and justice." The man's jaw dropped, his mind clearly struggling to recall the memories. It had been nearly seven years ago, back during the time after the defeat of Tarragin when Bernadette was questing throughout Iscandia for fun and profit. Andrion had been with her then, so he would not remember Erik. Anyone who had met Erik once would be unlikely to forget him.

"Bernadette... ? The Fireblood?" Yusuf said, as his memories sparked. She'd been an incredibly attractive young woman then, and she was still pretty hot. Looking a bit the worse for wear, though, at the moment. The people of the desert had, at best, tolerant amusement for outsiders who came here. "I remember," he went on. "You lured Jamal to the cave north of town so that we could take him into custody, and we paid you for your services. What are you doing in Zahar?"

Bernadette removed her helmet and let her long auburn hair fall loose around her shoulders. She was dressed in her abbreviated elven armor, so that ought to help. "We've been wandering lost in the desert this day," she said. "Might we beg some water from you, and the chance to sit down? Then I'll tell you the whole story."

The gigantic Norse warrior was a bit of a concern, but Yusuf had no fear of this rather lovely woman. And she'd done them a big favor, all those years ago. He'd also heard that she was responsible for defeating the legendary dragon Tarragin, thus supposedly (if tales were to be believed), preventing the destruction of all Terris. He wasn't inclined to swallow such nonsense, but he was now satisfied that she and her companion were not a threat.

Their weapons were returned to them, and the sentries were dismissed back to their posts in the desert. Yusuf beckoned them to sit on carpets beside him, and they were provided with food and drink. Bernadette regaled him and his companions with her tale, suitably embellished. She made it seem as if her quest on the behalf of the dragon were an obligation she could not avoid, instead of one she had taken on willingly. By bedtime Erik had worked his way into Yusuf's affections as well, and he was calling them both "friends" as he sent them off to sleep in a well-appointed tent. He promised them aid in the morning.

Bernadette woke awhile before dawn, enjoying the chill that lingered and the opportunity it gave her to snuggle up with Erik. He was certainly warm and cuddly, in a hard-muscled sort of way. If they'd had more privacy she'd have loved to jump his bones; but their tent was packed in among a throng of others even if they weren't actually sharing it with anyone else.

Day had barely begun to light the sky before the camp was astir. Anything you wanted to do in daylight, here, had best be done early. Bernadette and Erik got up and dressed, and made their way to the fire where they were given overly-sweet, honey-dripping pastries to eat and a thick, bitter drink the Afran people called kaf. Bernadette discovered that the bitterness of the kaf somehow helped to cut the cloying sweetness of the pastries, producing a balance of flavors that she liked.

Yusuf greeted them smilingly as they were eating. "Did you sleep well?" he asked politely. Erik and Bernadette assured him that they'd slept like rocks, which was not far from the truth. Their trek of the previous day had exhausted them. They continued to exchange pleasantries until the guests had finished their breakfast. Then Yusuf introduced them to a dark-skinned, sloe-eyed young woman of exotic beauty. "This is Ayesha, my eldest daughter," he told them. "She will guide you to where the Desert Stone may be found."

Bernadette and Erik gave Yusuf their profuse thanks. Without his intervention, they might have been killed out of hand. Or at best, forced to beat an ignominious retreat from their attempt to find the potion ingredient they needed. They exchanged ritual hand-squeezes, wrists crossed, then nodded and let Ayesha lead them back up the wadi they had come down in darkness the night before.

Before they had gone very far the walls began to rise on either side of them, and Bernadette now realized that near the very edges on either side small plants were growing. Their foliage was hard and gray, the stems thorny, but they were eking out a life here in the scant shade provided by the walls of the little ravine – and whatever water accumulated there after the infrequent rains.

Ayesha was walking with her head bent, eyes to the ground. Soon she stood erect, smiling, and pointed. "There it is, the Desert Stone." Bernadette and Erik followed her gesture but could see nothing. Ayesha drew closer, crouching to touch the plant with her fingers. "If there is no water to be found, you can pull the Desert Stone from the ground and suck on it," she said. "It has much moisture hidden in its tissues."

Bernadette crouched beside Ayesha and peered at the ground. It looked for all the world like a dully polished, smooth stone. Almost exactly like dozens of real stones that were scattered over the ground in this not-quite-streambed. She dug her fingers into the dry, grainy soil and tried to pluck it up, but it would not budge. Only after she had pulled the lesser of her daggers and dug around it to the depth of nearly a foot was she able to wrest it from the soil.

Brushing sand from what she'd captured, Bernadette examined it. The tap root, thick and tapering, had a few hair-like rootlets growing out of it. She'd broken it off, and the thin bottom end probably went much deeper still. The part of the plant exposed to the air and the sun looked like a smooth rock a couple of inches in diameter, with a faintly visible seam bisecting it.

"When the rains come, the Desert Stone splits," Ayesha explained. She mimed the emergence of a flower stalk, which would bloom and seed in a day. Then the plant would die. But in the meantime, it might survive for years – waiting for its chance to create the next generation. Bernadette was fascinated, and she knew Andrion would be too. She could hardly wait to tell him of their adventures! She thanked Ayesha, sending her back home. Then she and Erik, now knowing what to look for, continued up the wadi with eyes sharpened to find more of the fleshy plants.

By the time they had half a dozen of them the Afran encampment was lost in the twists and turns of the wadi, and the sun was climbing to a point where they were already thinking of seeking shelter from it. "Let's call Sneyagflug and get the hell out of here," Bernadette suggested. The wadi's walls were eroded and collapsed in many spots, and it wasn't hard for them to climb out of it. Bernadette walked a few paces away, then once again Called "SNE-YAG-FLUG!"

Chapter 53: Southeastern Remus, Year Six

In the end, Bernadette decided to hold her peace. Neither she nor Erik said anything to the dragon about the way in which they'd virtually been left to die in the desert. They'd survived the challenge, and had found the plant they'd sought. The sense any human got in interacting with the *drachen*, of being regarded as a foolish child, made Bernadette too proud to reproach him. But she vowed to extract more information from Sneyagflug before he next left them on their own.

The trip from the Great Desert to the eastern savannas of the imperial province was a long one, and they didn't do it in one flight. Even Sneyagflug, large and powerful as he was, had his limits. As darkness once again fell on the land, he came down in the foothills of the mountain range that cut across the center of Remus, far south of the imperial capital of Roma. "It is time to rest," he told them. And no sooner had they descended from his back than he had walked, with the thumping gait of the *drachen*, into a nearby hollow and curled into a ball for sleep, his wings wound round him like a bat's.

Bernadette and Erik stared, fascinated. They had killed dragons together many times over the years, and had often found them resting – perched atop stone arches or the towers of fortresses, most often. Never had they seen a dragon sleeping on the ground! "I imagine it's not very common for dragons to fly as far in one day as Sneyagflug did today, let alone carrying passengers," Bernadette told Erik quietly. "I suppose he feels it's safe enough here for him to sleep on the ground, and that likely means it's safe for us as well."

"I hope so," Erik replied. "It seems there might be a few things *he* wouldn't fear that *we* might have to worry about."

Bernadette sighed. He was right, of course. "Maybe we should snuggle up with him?" she suggested impishly. "Nice and warm…"

"Pass," Erik said shortly, with a grin that was barely visible in the dim evening light. The smell of dragon could be a little… overpowering, at close range. They'd gotten used to it during their long flights, but would just as soon not spend the night surrounded by that reek.

They sought out a sheltered hollow between two boulders, and pitched their tent. They might possibly have found firewood tonight, as there were trees around; but searching for it in the darkness, as stiff and sore as they were from their long ride on dragon back, seemed more trouble than it was worth. They dug into their trail rations again. At least Yusuf's band had let them refill their water skins before they left.

As the sky began to lighten once again, Bernadette snuggled up with Erik and gave him a hot kiss. The pace of their journey was really taking a toll on their sex life, not to mention the fact that neither of them was as young as they'd once been. The night's rest had restored her energy and enthusiasm, however, and she doubted the dragon, whether sleeping or awake, would care if they had a little quickie. Nobody else was around.

Erik was soon awake, and so was his cock. Mmm, morning sex. A rare treat, with this woman. They were both still a little sleepy and it didn't take as long as they might have liked; but as he plunged deeply into her and exploded she came along with him. And felt a lot happier about getting back on the dragon, afterward.

In his hollow, Sneyagflug was awake and heard them coupling. Dragon faces are not designed for smiling, but amusement tinged his thoughts. Sex for the *sterbliim* was very different than for the *drachen*. So urgent, yet they did it all the time! No wonder the land was overrun with them, even if they usually had only a single child at a time, and lived for only a few decades.

They breakfasted on more trail rations, and watched Sneyagflug take to the air. Probably getting his own breakfast, Bernadette guessed. When he returned there were traces of blood on his claws and muzzle. Deer, she fervently hoped. This time she kept out a couple of their fur bedrolls and laid them over the dragon's neck before sitting astride him. It seemed to help.

Soon they were airborne, the air much chillier up here than it had been on the far side of the mountains. Remus was a rich and well-populated province, home to many more people than either Auverne or Iscandia, and Sneyagflug flew high. He was doing everything he could to enable the humans to fulfill his quest while keeping out of conflict with the swarm of their fellows on the land below.

A few hours after they'd embarked, Bernadette and Erik felt the dragon's wingbeats change cadence and he began spiraling down, keeping an eagle eye on the ground below to be certain they were not observed. They came down on an unpeopled stretch of rolling prairie, waist-high grass interspersed with rocks, small trees, and herds of smallish hoofed animals Bernadette thought might be some kind of antelope. These scattered at their approach, and Sneyagflug eyed them with interest as he landed.

After his passengers had climbed down he told them, "You are doing well, *kiin sterblit*. I believe the flower you seek here, Maiden's Tear, should still be blooming at this season. The plant is about as high as your knees, the leaves small and gray-green. The flowers are borne in small clusters, each of them white and shaped like a teardrop hanging down. It is the flowers that you need. I think I will hunt now – call me when you have what we need."

"Hungry again so soon, Sneyagflug?" Bernadette asked. His rumbling tones sounded amused rather than offended.

"Do you think the *drachen* to be reptiles, like snakes?" he asked. "We may be scaly rather than covered in fur or feathers, but we are hot. Hotter than you humans by far. We must eat much, and often, to sustain our fires." With that he took to the air and had soon winged out of sight.

"Huh," Bernadette mused. "I guess that explains how he can fly hundreds of miles in cold conditions without just dropping out of the sky." Now that they were on the ground again, and the sun was heading into early afternoon, it was warm and getting warmer. Nowhere near as hot as the Great Desert, but still far too warm for the clothing that had protected them during their flight.

The two spent the next few minutes adjusting their clothing and shuffling the contents of their packs. Erik spotted a line of taller vegetation to the west of them, and suggested "Berni, it looks like there may be a river over there. Why don't we go check it out? I wouldn't mind a swim, if it's safe." She looked at him with love so intense it nearly knocked him back on his heels.

The stream was further away than they'd thought. They found a game trail through the grass that was moving in the right direction (no doubt the local animals used it to get to the water, just as they were trying to do), and were able to make much better speed along it. Bernadette had her bow strung and at the ready, Erik his khopesh to hand. Both of them had hunted enough to know that predators might regard the path they were on as the ideal place to seek their next meal.

Indeed, they had not been moving down the trail for long, and were still a good distance from the water, when Bernadette's sharp eyes spotted movement in the grass to their right. "Erik!" she hissed. He was walking in front of her, his eyes also scanning to either side. He turned back to look at her, then followed her gesture to the grass stems rustling a few feet from the trail. He backed off a few steps to stand at her side, his sword drawn and ready. Bernadette nocked an arrow to her bow.

She also readied the Gale dragon spell. It was the first she had learned, and one of the most useful. It didn't do much damage to an enemy, but bought you a few seconds of time in which to gather your defense when you found yourself suddenly attacked. Dragon spells took a moment of mental preparation, fixing the words in one's mind; and after using them, as much as a minute might be required before its stone would be recharged and you could use that spell again.

The movement had stopped. Bernadette, looking down at the ground, found a medium-sized stone embedded in the pathway and prised it from the ground. Her years of work at the forge had given her a mean right arm, and she hurled the stone like a crossbow bolt at the spot where the grasses had been moving moments before.

With a yowl of fury and frustration, a creature much like a smilodon came boiling up out of the grass toward them. Bernadette immediately drew her bow and fired, slowing it down in its charge, then stepped in front of Erik and knocked the creature down with Gale. She might be able to heal the damage such a cat could do in a few seconds, but that didn't mean she intended to let it do that damage to her or her beloved if there was a way to avoid it. It tumbled several yards down the trail in the direction of the stream. Then she put another arrow into it. Erik was already closing the distance, and finished the cat with a powerful blow from his khopesh that split its skull like a ripe melon. Ugh.

The two approached the corpse for a closer examination. Neither of them had visited Remus before, nor were they familiar with all of its creatures. The dead animal was about the same size as smilodons of Iscandia, and very similar in shape. Rather than pale and spotted, it was tawny all over with only the faintest signs of spotting in the coat. Its fangs were shorter, as well, and it had ruff of longer fur around its head and neck. Bernadette relieved it of its fangs and eyes, useful chemial ingredients, but left the hide as being too bulky to carry.

The dead cat was likely the top predator in these parts, and they had some hope that its presence would have sent lesser ones packing. At any rate, they made it the rest of the way to the riverbank without being attacked. The river proved to be a fairly large one. Not as big as the river above which Iscandia's city of Sylvanian sat; but bigger than the Brightwater in their own front yard at home. Where the trail opened out onto the rocks and gravel of the bank, the stream took a slight bend and a deep pool nestled in the crook of it. Perfect!

Both Erik and Bernadette were beginning to feel as if they were ready for a break. The fate of dragonkind was not going to be altered if they took a little time off. Looking around, assuring themselves that no razormouths lurked in the shallows or wolves in the underbrush alongside the water, they laid their packs down and began to strip. There was a cool breeze along the water, which felt delightful on their sweaty skin. The fight with the cat had left them even ranker than before, and it had been days since they'd bathed.

They soon ventured into the pool. The current was slight here in this eddy, and the waters were as crystalline as those they were used to in Iscandia. Bernadette dove to the bottom, some ten feet down, then chased some large fish around as she rose to the surface. After dunking his head, Erik floated on his back with his big cock hanging to one side like a quiescent snake. She was a more agile swimmer than he was, as there'd been little opportunity for swimming where he'd grown up – the frigid waters around Norcove would kill a man in a minute or two.

After they'd cleaned and refreshed themselves, they waded ashore and pulled bedrolls out of their packs for something to lie on. The warm sun soon dried them. Erik's ability to tan was much greater than Bernadette's – she would freckle and burn in minutes. Luckily there was a potion for that – one you rubbed on your skin, rather than ingesting it. They'd both been using it in the desert, and she had Erik slather some all over her back for her as she lay prone on the bedroll. At this rate, they were going to run out before long.

The little beach, no more than a few feet deep, also offered quite a bit of driftwood. Erik gathered some and laid a fire, which Bernadette set burning with her minor fire spell. It wouldn't do more than inconvenience an enemy, but it was plenty good enough for these purposes. As Erik got the fire going Bernadette waded back into the pool and caught a couple of those fish, which she tossed to him on the bank.

By the time she was dried off again, the potion continuing its work for an hour after application despite her dip, Erik had cleaned the two fish and spitted them on sticks, suspended on pairs of forked sticks over the crackling fire. They were not salmon, but looked as though they would be as edible. The flesh was white and firm. After trail rations for the past few meals, this was haute cuisine! Breakfast had been many hours ago, and though they'd spent most of those hours sitting on dragon back they had still worked up an appetite. Waiting for the fish to cook, which fortunately didn't take all that long, they nibbled on dried fruit.

Bernadette found a bottle of white wine in the bottom of her pack. Sometimes, when packing for an expedition, she threw in whatever caught her eye – and regretted it, later, when the weight of the thing seemed to grow with each mile walked. Now might be a good time to lighten the load, and she had an idea. In the still water along the shore by the pool, she set the bottle in water up to its neck. Then she applied a carefully focused frost spell.

Bernadette had nowhere near Andrion's expertise with such things, but she was able to form a block of ice around the bottle without freezing the bottle itself and cracking it. Then she lifted the bottle and its ice block, dripping, from the stream and took it a few yards up the bank to the nearest patch of grass where she made a little nest for it. The ice immediately began melting; but by the time they were eating the succulent fish, the wine was considerably cooler than the air and refreshing.

They'd been hungrier than they realized, and devoured almost
every scrap of the fish – killing off the bottle of chilled wine as they
did so. After disposing of the bones they rinsed their hands in the
stream, then sat back on their bedrolls feeling satisfied and more than
a little somnolent. Time to renew the potion, Bernadette realized.
They'd eaten in the nude, the warm air like a caress on their clean,
naked skins. And she really didn't feel like getting dressed yet.

Hoping to wake up a bit, Bernadette went back into the pool for
a quick dip. Like every child she'd been warned about going in
swimming too soon after eating; but the theory hadn't really proven
itself. Besides, the pool was barely a dozen feet across and only deep
in the middle. She emerged refreshed and once again handed the
potion bottle to Erik. He'd been watching her lazily with a gleam in
his eye as she played in the water, admiring her taut belly and finely
shaped legs as she climbed out. In the year-plus since weaning Riki,
his wife had recovered her muscle tone in a way that he found more
than a little exciting.

Erik knelt beside Bernadette where she lay face down on the
bedroll, gently but firmly massaging the warm, slightly fragrant fluid
into her skin from the nape of her neck to the tips of her toes. He
lingered on her buttocks, squeezing and caressing, and she felt his
cock begin to stiffen, grazing her hip as he bent over her. She rolled
over onto her side and looked up at him, his golden hair backlit by
the afternoon sun, eyes the color of the sky. Ah, Erik…

"Perhaps," she said with a slight smile, "you might need a little
of this potion on some of your more tender parts." From the waist up
Erik had turned a golden bronze, but the parts of him that seldom
saw the sun were pale. She sat up, facing him, his rising member
almost in her face as he knelt there. Taking the bottle from him she
put a little in her hand and began rubbing it onto his crotch area, one
of the palest.

The potion was slightly slippery, and made a good massage oil.
In moments, as Bernadette stroked and squeezed, Erik's cock went
from rising to full-on rock hard, throbbing under her fingertips. His
blue eyes were alight with desire, and her face was turning pink – but
it had nothing to do with the sun. Their lovemaking this morning had
been brief and rather perfunctory. Now they were here in this lovely

wilderness on a perfect afternoon, and they had the time to do it right.

As Erik drew her to him for a passionate kiss Bernadette murmured, "I feel like we should be out there picking flowers…"

"Later," he growled. Afterward, they lay entwined for a while in a state of bliss, just gazing up at the puffy white clouds as they scudded across the sky. But they both knew they were asking for trouble. The wilderness held a thousand dangers – and besides, they were supposed to be working.

So, they sat up and kissed one more time, then set about getting back into their clothes. There was no more than another hour or two of daylight remaining, and their search for Maiden's Tear had so far involved scanning the grass on either side of the trail on their walk to the river, to see if any was growing there. Time to knuckle down!

They gathered their bedrolls and packs, and began walking along the shore of the river in a northerly direction. There was vegetation aplenty here, everything from grass and small shrubs to good-sized trees. Small birds flitted and called all around them, starting to find their roosts and get settled in for the night. There were wildflowers in among the other vegetation, and Bernadette gathered samples of all they found. Some looked familiar, probably the same plants she'd plucked in Iscandia; but others she hadn't seen before. She'd have to learn what they were before she figured out what, if anything, to do with them.

A quarter mile up from their beach they came to a small rivulet that joined the main stream from the east, winding down from a few low hills to the north and east of where they stood. They struck out along its course, and as they climbed into the hills they began seeing fewer shrubs and trees, and more wildflowers. There! Growing up around a good-sized boulder was a cluster of plants that exactly matched Sneyagflug's description.

Bernadette knelt to examine it more closely. The height of the stem, the small gray-green leaves, the clusters of white teardrop-shaped flowers hanging down in little sprays; this had to be it. She broke off every flower cluster she found, more than a dozen of them. The stems were surprisingly tender and snapped easily.

Erik was watching her work, fondness surging through him as he maintained a watch on the surrounding territory. By the time Bernadette had tucked the last of the flower clusters into her pack the sun had become an orange globe hanging just above the western horizon. "I vote we wait and call Sneyagflug in the morning," he said. She nodded.

"Good idea. I don't want to fly in darkness, and I'd just as soon not be having him for a bunkmate. Where can we shelter for the night?"

They had not come across any Remus landmarks, and as yet their maps had no fast-travel points in this province. That ruled out hopping home to sleep in their own bed, as appealing as that seemed. Bernadette smiled to herself at the thought. It would likely take more than two full days, had they been able to do it, to go home, sleep a few hours, and return here. Sneyagflug would have thought they'd been eaten by that cat, or its mate.

She looked up the slope, the golden rays of sunset bathing the hillside in fire. Was that some kind of a man-made structure at the top? "Let's go see what's up there," Bernadette suggested. They shouldered their packs and, weapons to hand, walked up what was clearly becoming a path of some sort. As the sun disappeared behind the mountains to the west, they reached the structure. It was a ruined tower such as those they'd seen in Iscandia many times, hollow inside and with a spiral staircase of weathered stone leading upward. Probably a wooden platform had stood atop it once; but if so, it had long since rotted away.

The floor inside the circle of stonework was packed dirt with wildflowers growing in it, and there was no sign of recent habitation. Bernadette imagined that the Reman legions, and the duchy guard forces, kept Remus much freer of bandits than was the case in Iscandia. Besides, bandits usually needed to camp in an area where a well-traveled road ran through, providing them with prey.

Erik walked the perimeter scanning for trouble, then returned inside. The doorway was around three feet wide and eight feet tall, and whatever door had once stood there had gone the way of the floor. Still, it was a defensible space. "I have an idea," Bernadette said. She went to work with some cord and various objects, rigging the sort of "intruder alarm" commonly seen at around waist height in areas where Insurgents made their homes. Carelessly brushing against the string would make enough of a rattle to alert them before an intruder could come inside.

Their lunch had been large and late. Bernadette and Erik nibbled on some trail rations washed down with water, then sat on their bedroll (they had spread two out so they could sleep together), shoulder to shoulder, talking quietly. Adventuring together was fun and exciting, and it was interesting to visit new places; but they both missed their home and the kids. Even ugly little Merelle had begun to worm her way into their hearts during the short time she had been with them. Eventually they lay down and slept.

Chapter 54: Central Darkreach, Year Six

When the travelers emerged from their night in the ruined tower, where they'd slept undisturbed, they were pleased to see that it now appeared on their maps. "Skywatch Tower," the marker read. It had been a long time since anyone had been able to watch the sky from here, and they wondered at the name. But the point was, they could now use their maps to return here whenever they liked – a starting point for a journey anywhere in the southern part of the province. Andrion already had Roma and some points north of there on his own map.

The dragon came at their call, his red color deeper and flesh seeming more filled out now. He must have been gorging himself on the four-footed inhabitants of the region in the interim, and he did not question them as to why it had taken so long for them to find the flowers. They mounted up, once again using the bedrolls as cushioning, and he headed north-northeast.

Below them, the land gave way to hills and low mountains. Then there were wetlands, gleaming in the midday sun and partially obscured as they flew above and amid low clouds. Bernadette and Erik's butts were getting sore and their bladders near bursting when Sneyagflug at last began his descent. The region they landed in was scrub, with streams crisscrossing it. The sky was completely hidden by clouds, but Bernadette thought it must be late afternoon from the amount of time that had passed since they had left Remus.

"I'll be right with you, Sneyagflug," Bernadette said as soon as she had steadied her legs after climbing down from the dragon's neck. Then she scurried behind a nearby bush and dropped her trousers to relieve herself. Ahhh! She thought as she did so that she was being ridiculous. She and Erik had been intimate throughout their seven-year relationship, and Sneyagflug wasn't even human. But somehow, she felt she wanted to preserve her dignity with him.

Soon, clothing adjusted, Bernadette turned back. "What can you tell us about Fire Moss?" she asked the dragon.

"It grows in damp forests," he rumbled, "hanging from the limbs of certain kinds of tree. Usually it will kill the tree in time, and when it does, and the source of its nourishment is cut off, it reacts by producing heat as it forms spores. The people of this region harvest it and use it to stuff their boots or gloves. Within a few minutes after being removed from the tree, if it is dry, it will begin to warm. The effect lasts a few hours."

Intriguing, and possibly useful! Much of Darkreach was on the same latitude as parts of Iscandia, and likely the winters here were cold. "So it's not fire red or something?"

"No," the *drache* replied seriously. "It is a very dull gray color, like mud. It hangs in long, fibrous strands. You will need to keep it moist until you make the potion, though. The potion must be made as the moss is heating. Just put it in a jar and pour some water on it."

"After we find this moss, Sneyagflug," Bernadette said, trying to phrase it just right, "we can go home by ourselves using our maps. I would like to rest there for at least a week. Will the potion keep, once it is made?"

"Put the potion in a sealed bottle," the dragon replied, "and it will keep indefinitely. I, too, could use a rest. I have flown longer and farther carrying you and your husband on this journey than at any time since I was reawakened. Call me when you have the potion, but make it soon."

With that he lumbered off to a nearby small stream and lowered his head for a drink. Steam rose from the water and there was a hissing and gurgling sound as he did so. Just how hot *were* dragons, Bernadette wondered? After his drink Sneyagflug lifted heavily into the air and had soon vanished above the clouds. This didn't look like good hunting territory for dragons, nor for humans either. The soil was mostly bare and blighted-looking, or covered in low-growing plants.

Erik was looking around them, assessing the threat level. There didn't seem to be much stirring, really. Nor was there any of that moss to be seen on the trees near to hand. The idea that they could be back home in a few seconds of subjective time as soon as they had their hands on that last ingredient filled Bernadette with happy excitement. She could hardly wait to be home, to hug her babies, to share their experiences with Andrion… to have a hot bath, and sleep in a bed!

Well, standing here wasn't finding them that moss. They'd munched trail rations and drunk water during the long flight, so hunger and thirst weren't much of an issue. Better start looking around. She strung her bow and readjusted the hang of the quiver, the better to get off fast shots if needed. She'd not studied the creatures of this region and had no idea what might show up to attack them, but she wanted to be prepared for anything. Erik, taking her cue, walked with his khopesh in hand.

The entire landscape looked dull under the leaden skies, the ground marshy in spots. It appeared as if the sparsely growing trees were a little more concentrated off to the north; so they headed that way. They had to ford a small stream, then came upon a narrow dirt road. It had the look of one that got a lot of traffic, at times. But this was apparently not one of those times. It was deserted in either direction as far as the eye could see. Just as well. It might be hard for them to explain to any native nachtalfar how they got here or what they were doing.

After a brief, quiet discussion Erik and Bernadette turned left, heading for denser woods in that direction. They proceeded in near silence, moving cautiously. The oppressive sky and bleak vegetation filled them with a sense of lingering dread, as if something awful was about to happen. Then it did. A very odd-looking light gray creature like a cross between a lizard and a beetle the size of a wolf suddenly charged from the woods to their right, attacking them with enormous mandibles.

Erik, on point, swung his sword and nearly cut it in two. Then they turned to see a whole pack of them coming, fanning out to surround them. Bernadette dropped a couple of them before they got close, but the creatures didn't have far to run and soon the two travelers were beset. Erik swung around him with his blade, and the monsters (whatever they were) were wary of it and jumped back out of the way. By whirling around he was able to keep them away for a moment, but they were fast and in a second or two would be back snapping at them with those jaws like enormous fangs.

Bernadette kicked one with her booted foot, knocking it back a few feet. She'd hit it square on the head and there'd been a crunching noise, suggesting she'd damaged its carapace. It seemed staggered, and she killed it with an arrow shot to the body before it could attack again. That gave her an idea, and she moved to the side where three of the monsters were trying to get at Erik. She put her hand on his arm to let him know she was there, then faced them and cried "Kraf-Luft-Struung-Wund!"

The dragon spells were awfully directional and therefore not all that useful against enemies that were spread out. But it bowled these three, spaced too closely for their own good, off their feet. Shooting with deadly accuracy and as quickly as she ever had, Bernadette put an arrow in each of them and they rose no more. She whirled to face the next foes and found Erik standing over two more corpses, wiping off the blade of his khopesh with a scrap of cloth. He tossed the cloth onto the bodies of his foes when he was finished.

Bernadette was fascinated. She'd never seen anything like these in Iscandia, even though that province too was full of unlikely monsters. They were not, she realized, exoskeletal; but they did have armor plating over much of their bodies. Their four limbs were spindly, each ending in three scaly toes that looked a lot like a chicken's – only many times larger. Their blood was dark red, and those insectoid-looking armored heads with the fang-like mandibles were the oddest thing about them. She pulled out her notebook and made a sketch, hoping Andrion might be able to tell her something about them when they got home.

Both of them were sporting a few scrapes and cuts from the attack, and Bernadette took a moment to heal these with magic. Who knew what infections might lurk in a place like this, eager for the opportunity to enter through a cut? She'd been careful not to touch the corpses with her hands, prodding them with a stick instead.

They drank some water from their skins, then continued their progress toward the forest that was gathered down the road a quarter of a mile to the west. The road ran through the middle of it, and it was a pale shadow of the forests in Iscandia; but it seemed to fit the definition here. The trees were twisted, not very tall, with scabrous-looking leaves. There was little enough undergrowth, so it was easy to make their way between the trees looking for any with moss on them. They kept a sharp eye out for any more of those pack predators.

The daylight was getting dimmer as they walked deeper into the woods, partly because of what shade the trees provided but mostly,

Bernadette feared, because up there above the clouds the sun was going down. Oh, she did not want to spend the night here! She pulled out her map and took a look. No such luck – the areas they had passed through today had not produced any fast-travel landmarks. The maps usually placed these at the sites of constructions of alfar or man, rarely at natural features such as mountain peaks or waterfalls.

Magic (other than the healing branch of it, in which she excelled) was not Bernadette's forte and Andrion had not gone into any details with her or Erik over the exact way in which the maps worked. Clearly he had penetrated their secrets to the point of being able to make new ones, though these started life virginal and only acquired fast-travel points as the map's owner passed through new places on foot. They'd flown over a couple of places that looked like cities on the trip from Zahar across Remus, and those had not shown up.

She made a mental note to quiz him when they got home. Could there be a way to force the map to place a fast-travel point wherever you happened to be standing? Maybe by holding the map and concentrating, which is pretty much how fast-traveling worked, or by writing on it with some special instrument, a… magical marker?

Such speculations aside, here they were essentially lost in an extremely unpleasant-looking forest as dusk was closing in. They'd left the road behind an hour or more ago. They should be able to find their way back to it – the map showed Bernadette an arrow, giving her location in an anonymous blank area north of the road. But it would be full dark long before they got there, and then what? The road was where they'd been attacked, so it wasn't necessarily any safer than where they were standing.

They came to a small clearing and sat down to eat some more trail rations and drink more water. By the time they'd finished this short break, it was getting too dark to see under the trees. "I think we should go on looking, Erik," Bernadette said as she put her water skin back in the pack. "At least for another couple of hours. As soon as we find that damned moss we can go home." She left her bow slung behind her back as she stood up and cast the light spell with her left hand.

The glowing globe, about the size of a small stewpot and with light both whiter and brighter than torchlight, rose to float a few feet above Bernadette's head. It would stay there, moving as she did, until it winked out of existence a minute later. The fact that the magic wash tub summoned by Andrion's spell stayed in existence for a full hour was prove of the strength of his magic. Provided she didn't use her magical energy for anything else, she could keep throwing up globes every minute until she dropped from physical exhaustion; so they had light with which to continue their search.

Erik's watchfulness became even more tense as they moved on their way. The magical light globe cast dark, flickering shadows that seemed as if they could hide anything. Bernadette mused that in many ways Erik reminded her of one of those big cats like the one they'd killed in Remus: huge, powerful, tawny, and usually as calm as a cat at rest. But when danger threatened he became a ball of lethal energy ready to explode, and woe betide his enemies! She loved having him at her side in times like these, and not just for the hot sex.

One problem with the light spell was the size of the illuminated circle. They could see up to eight feet away from them in any direction, but the light destroyed their night vision and anything beyond the circle was obscured in darkness. Bernadette wished, and not for the first time, that she knew a spell for that power the Gatti were said to have for seeing in dim light.

They found many interesting and unfamiliar plants as they travelled through the forest in their little circle of brilliance, and Bernadette gathered some of these. There were few sounds around them, suggesting that not that many creatures made this creepy place their home – or perhaps, happy thought, the glaring light globe was frightening them off. Predators that normally hunt in darkness or the crepuscular light of dusk and dawn might well shun prey that was carrying around its own little sun.

The forest was composed of various sorts of trees and a few smaller shrubs, many of them with fungus growing on them. Some of the trees were scarcely taller than they were, while others towered over their heads. The ground between them was damp and spongy, not really a swamp but a lot wetter than what the two Iscandia residents were used to.

Bernadette was walking along, then stopping after half a dozen paces to scan the next section of forest that had appeared in their circle of light. Left to right, looking for anything hanging, then down to the ground for fungus or lichens or whatever. She was going to have weeks of research ahead of her, identifying all the possible chemial ingredients she'd collected on this trip.

She was beginning to get discouraged and was thinking of calling a halt. Assuming they could survive the night it would be much easier to search in the morning. But as Bernadette paced forward again, her personal sun staying on point, Erik suddenly grunted. "What was that?" he said, half to himself. Bernadette spun, reaching for her bow. He smiled at her. "It's all right, love. Something just brushed my face, that's all." She stepped closer to him, the globe coming along. Just behind him, something was dangling down out of the branches of a tall, spreading tree. Moss!

Bernadette slapped her forehead. It hadn't occurred to her that the stuff might be growing too high for her to notice. She'd been expecting it at around the five foot level, for no particular reason. She'd likely walked right under the moss, but Erik at nearly a foot taller had felt it brush his head. He reached up into the branches with his khopesh, the globe floating among them and casting crisscrossed shadows that made it hard to see. A swipe, and several wispy, fibrous hunks of grayish-brown moss dropped to the sodden ground.

"You've done it, Erik!" Bernadette crowed. Relief flooded her. They could go home! Soon, anyway. She reached into her pack and took out a water skin that was almost empty, unscrewing its cap. The opening was more than an inch across, and she was able to poke clumps of the moss down into the skin. Meanwhile Erik was continuing his sword strokes, bringing more down. When Bernadette had crammed the skin nearly full of moss she put the cap back on and shook it up, distributing the moisture evenly.

Quite a few bits of the moss were still lying on the ground here and there under the tree. The ground was awfully damp, though. "Before we leave," Bernadette told her companion, "we'd better make sure." She picked up a goodly clump of moss and set it on a medium-size boulder that was standing amid the trees a few feet away. Then she and Erik stood there watching it. Talk about watching paint dry! Bernadette let her light spell expire and did not renew it. She was getting tired of squinting into the glare, and doubted anything was going to attack them in the few minutes she planned to remain here.

Thus both she and Erik noticed it when the moss began to heat. Severed from its parasitic connection to the tree it had been growing on, it had initiated a chemical reaction that would end with the production of spores, creating the next generation of moss. In the dank darkness in among the trees, it began to glow faintly. Sneyagflug had not mentioned that. Of course, the moss wouldn't be glowing when it was still attached to the trees, so perhaps he hadn't thought it a useful key to identification.

The light was not the bluish white of the glowing mushrooms in caves throughout Iscandia, but a dull reddish glow as from a nearly-extinguished brazier – similar to that of the mushrooms they'd gathered for the Destroyer of Magic potion nearly seven years ago. They leaned close, and could feel the heat. Erik stepped close to Bernadette and threw an arm around her, squeezing her tight. "That's it, baby," he said quietly. "Let's get the hell out of here."

Chapter 55: Drakespring Farm, Year Six

They arrived not long after night had fallen, probably the same day. Drakespring Farm was many hours to the west of the area of Darkreach where Bernadette and Erik had been, so that the time spent in fast-traveling was almost balanced out. Filled with glee to be home, their mission accomplished, they went in the front door and found the family hanging around the main living area. With the exception of their new hired hand, every current resident was there.

Andrion and Andi sat across from one another at the now-cleared dining table, playing Bjorn's card game. The boy was beginning to learn his ABCs and could now read a little, but no reading was required for this game. He seemed as bright as his parents, and picked it up quickly. They'd be needing something more challenging for him before long.

Christine Lamonte sat on a throw rug with Riki, playing a game with dolls and toy horses. Of late their little one had begun to take an interest in horses, and had been to visit with Sigrandil and Reshiva a time or two. They were thinking of getting a pony to keep here at the farm for both children, if one could be found. Most horses in Iscandia were enormous.

Ekka sat in a rocking chair, nursing baby Merelle to sleep. Everyone in the room except those two started up when Bernadette and Erik came in, welcoming them happily. Ekka smiled and nodded, but was trying not to wake the infant at her breast. Riki rose to her feet crying "Mama!" and demanded to be picked up. When Bernadette had hugged and kissed her daughter thoroughly she passed her to Erik, who snugged her up, tickled her belly to make her laugh, and eventually put her up onto his shoulders so he could hug Andi, after Bernadette had had a turn. Then Bernadette hugged Christine and gave her a kiss on the cheek, before moving on to Andrion. She was still wearing armor, so hugs were not as thorough as she would have liked.

"We did it!" Bernadette announced, her face aglow with joy and satisfaction. "Just let me drop all this stuff and take a bath, then we'll tell you all about it."

"I'm for a bath too," Andrion and Erik said almost simultaneously. Erik needed one, Andrion just wanted one.

"We'll be back out before long," Bernadette promised, looking around at the rest of the family.

Bernadette and Erik dropped their packs in the crafting room, where most of those chemial ingredients would be stored. Then they went to the master bedroom to remove their armor and get into robes. Andrion had already done so, and was waiting for them when they came in. When all were robed he threw his arms around Erik and gave him a bear hug, then did the same for Bernadette but with rather more pelvis in it.

She looked up into his eyes and saw hunger there. It had been awhile. The three of them bathed together, close to the maximum number of bodies that could fit in there at one time. They talked a little about the trip, but saved the full story for after they'd emerged, dried off, and changed into some comfortable clothing for hanging around the house.

The kids stayed up way past their bedtime, their eyes round as saucers at the exciting tale. Andi got a lot more from it than Riki did, of course; and meanwhile Merelle had been tucked into her crib for the night. Ekka was an avid gossip, and the tale of their adventures would probably be all over Waterdon by noon tomorrow. Eventually they all turned in for the night, Bernadette and her husbands all together in their huge bed. Andrion was happy to share.

It was days before Bernadette even began to think about crafting that Potion of Dragon Transformation. After getting back into the swing of things around home and catching up on her smithing (her business partners, Alessia and Wolaf, expected a certain quantity of arms and armor from her weekly for sale in their shop), Bernadette spread out the contents of her pack on the work table beside the chemia station and began going through them.

Andrion had come up with a wonderful illustrated book on the useful plants of Agena from his personal library, and Bernadette was able to put names to many of the things she'd collected. The book even included a list of each one's chemial properties, enabling her to craft a few potions with them. Any she didn't need to use herself would find a ready market at Adele's in town, and the more exotic ones fetched a good price. Each ingredient was placed in its own lidded earthenware jar, neatly labeled.

He promised to see if he could find a similarly illustrated bestiary when next he traveled to the Academy. Bernadette wanted to know the true name of the cat that attacked them in Remus, and those bizarre-looking pack predators in Darkreach.

All of them found they really enjoyed the freedom that having a full-time farm hand gave them. There was time to spend with the children, and time for their own projects. Andrion preferred not to do magical experiments at home because of the risk, but he always had a backlog of reading as well as his experiments with dypalfar technology. He and Erik spent some time sparring, too, getting a little exercise. As Andrion was close to entering his fifth decade, he found he needed to put in more effort to get off his backside and move, lest he lose the ability to do so.

Bernadette was intrigued by the changes in Merelle just since she had come to live with them. With the exception of the "changeling" leukalfar, all races of the alfar were very nearly as human as any Norseman. They looked like humans, spoke like them, had cultures very similar to those of humans, and could interbreed with them. She herself, as Galise, likely had alfar in her ancestry – which was supposed to account for her natural affinity with magic. But the leukalfar stood out. Had the poisoning or whatever it was that turned them eyeless also affected other aspects of their humanity?

After spending some hours observing and interacting with the baby girl, Bernadette was beginning to believe that the non-physical differences between leukalfar and the other human races were cultural: their silence, their curious living habits, their ingrained hostility toward all non-leukalfar. Now she had the opportunity to prove or disprove her theories. Merelle had appreciably put on weight since she arrived, and Ekka reported she "had a good appetite." She was sharing meals with the rest of the family, her portions cut into tiny pieces, while continuing to suckle at Ekka's breasts. And she was beginning to be more verbal, cooing, gurgling, babbling – all the signs that show a human baby is preparing to learn to speak.

What floored Bernadette the most was Merelle's reaction to a rattle. They had a little wooden rattle shaped like a darning egg, with dried peas inside it, that had been Andi's and then Riki's at that age. With Merelle sitting steadily before her as Bernadette sat cross-legged on the throw rug in the nursery, she shook the rattle. It was painted in bright colors. The baby started, turning her head to the sound. Bernadette shook it again, and Merelle gasped, broke into a grin, and giggled! Bernadette could hardly wait until she could talk, so she could ask her how her sense of vision worked.

As the week was nearly ended, Bernadette finally concluded that she could put it off no longer – it was time to craft Sneyagflug's potion. Using a long pair of tweezers, she extracted a fairly large clump of the Fire Moss from the water skin in which she'd stored it. It seemed un-deteriorated, living on within the vessel somehow. Capping the skin to preserve the rest of her samples, she blotted this one's excess moisture on a towel and then hung it on an herb-drying rack to dry the rest of the way.

While the moss dried Bernadette assembled the other ingredients, the book propped open on a stand atop the workbench. Never had she crafted a potion with this many ingredients! She had enough of them to make perhaps ten batches of the stuff. Maybe she could fill up Iscandia with sex-changed dragons and really give the race a boost. Though that didn't actually seem like such a hot idea.

The medium for this potion, like the majority of those she had made, was spring water. Some potions were alcohol-based, or like the one she and Erik had used to ward off sunburn in Remus, oil-based. The non-aqueous ones were usually those intended to be applied rather than ingested. Though, she thought, perhaps brandy could be considered an alcohol-based Potion of Get Drunk and Fall on Your Ass for internal use…

Bernadette kept checking the moss, and when it began to give off heat she knew that it was time to begin. Carefully, following the instructions to the letter, she concocted the ingredients in the order specified, transmogrifying them into a slightly heavy liquid that was a surprising deep red color when finished. After it had been poured off into the clean bottle she'd prepared for it and tightly sealed, the sides of the bottle felt slightly warm. It was as if the Fire Moss's action were continuing after it had been turned into a potion.

Hmm, Bernadette wondered. If this warmth persisted, one might use a flask of the stuff as a bed-warmer on cold nights. Much less likely to catch your bed on fire than a copper pan full of glowing coals from the fireplace! But after several hours, when she checked the bottle again, it had cooled to room temperature. The thermogenic reaction must have run its course.

The following morning, once again, the entire family was assembled for the calling of the dragon. Christine, Ekka, the three children and Umberth were gathered in the master bedroom, watching through the windows, while Bernadette, Andrion, and Erik stood at the edge of the farmyard near the road. The men were armed and armored. Sneyagflug might be their theoretical ally, and they were working to aid him in his quest; but both of them had fought too many dragons to be completely relaxed in their presence – especially one the size of Sneyagflug.

"SNE-YAG-FLUG!" Bernadette Called, and this time it seemed to take a little longer for the red dragon to appear. Eddies stirred the dust of the road as he came in for a landing.

"*Laude, Fjurblut,*" The great creature rumbled. "You have succeeded." His sharp eyes didn't fail to note the bottle she held in one hand. He turned his head to look at her men, arrayed in a defensive posture on either side. "You have nothing to fear from me…"

"You have recovered your strength?" Bernadette asked him. Sneyagflug seemed to radiate satisfaction.

"I am strong once again," he replied, "which is needful for I must now take you to obtain the *furml* I spoke of." The dragon spell! Caught up with her daily life and her own concerns, Bernadette had forgotten he had mentioned it. Was this quest ever to be at an end?

"So, this *furml* is not one you know?" she asked. Where else but from dragons had the Old Ones, and people like the ancient Norse heroes and herself, learned to use dragon spells? Of course, Sneyagflug had scorned Ehrgeizig and disciplines, so perhaps some of the *drachen* were deeper into these mysteries than others. She wondered where Ehrgeizig was, these days. She hadn't seen him for nearly seven years.

"This one has been lost to us for thousands of years, and none sought it as it was not needed. It is recorded on a wall graven with words of power, buried deep in a labyrinth where *drachen* cannot go. No *sterblit* has gone there in many generations either, because it can now only be reached from the air. But I will take you there, as I did to Todenstor."

"I'll need time to ready myself for an expedition," Bernadette told him, feeling faintly annoyed. He might have mentioned this earlier. "And I'll expect to bring a companion. But what about the potion? Don't you want it?" Humor rumbled in the dragon's tones as he answered her.

"Oh no, *einkliin*, it is not for me but for you! You must drink the potion in order to absorb all four words of the *furml*, so that you can use it to effect the full transformation. Only with this potion and your *Fjurblut* heritage can this spell be learned and used."

"And the stone for the spell? I will find it there?" Bernadette asked.

"I believe that will be the case," the dragon answered thoughtfully. In *Bergenfest* the dragon priesthood kept their mysteries for many centuries, and those who would learn the *furml* would travel there. But in any case the potion should enable you to learn the spell, after which you can tell it to me and I can form the stone for you."

Bernadette had a moment of doubt. But Sneyagflug was unimaginably older than she was, and had been around back when dragon magic was at its pinnacle. And on at least one or two occasions, she had encountered a Spell Wall that refused to yield up all of its secrets – giving her only one word of power instead of the entire spell. She decided to take the dragon's word for it.

"You should drink the potion now, *Fjurblut*," Sneyagflug said rather pointedly. "Tomorrow I will return and take you to *Bergenfest*." Bernadette blinked, uneasiness welling up in her. But she wouldn't have gotten to where she was today if she'd let a little uneasiness stop her from doing what needed to be done. She pulled the stopper from the bottle in her hand and took a sniff. It had not smelled unpleasant while she was concocting it, and now seemed to have a light and pleasing fragrance that was hard to define. She couldn't see how it would benefit the dragon to poison her, so she took a swig.

The ruby liquid felt cool on her tongue at first, and considering the ingredients list it tasted surprisingly good. Indescribable hints of summer fruit mixed somehow with rare beef and… fire! It didn't burn her tongue, but it suffused her mouth and body with the essence if not the actuality of heat – and flames licked up in her mind. She wanted more, she wanted it all! Raising the bottle to her lips, she drank continuously, her throat working, until the potion was drained.

Andrion and Erik stood transfixed, uncertain what if anything they could do, as Bernadette downed the potion she'd concocted then stood there breathing hard, eyes wide and dilated. Was it their imagination, or did her hair glint redder than usual in the morning sunlight? "Berni, are you all right?" Andrion asked after a few moments had gone by and she'd done nothing but stand motionless.

Bernadette tore her attention away from whatever was going on inside her to assure Andrion and Erik that nothing was amiss. She felt odd, certainly, warmth coursing to every corner of her body, excitement sparkling in her veins. But in a couple of minutes, the sensations ebbed and she was none the worse for wear. No headache or nausea, no weakness. If anything, her vision seemed a little sharper. But there were no other lasting effects that she could detect, as her mind reasserted itself. Yet Sneyagflug assured her that she would now be able to acquire the entire Dragon Transformation spell.

"I will be ready here, at this time tomorrow, to travel to this *Bergenfest*," Bernadette told the dragon. Mountain Fortress, murmured a small voice in her mind. Had the potion somehow heightened her ability to understand the dragon tongue?

"I will be here at the hour," Sneyagflug replied, his deep voice conveying satisfaction. She had been obedient to his every request. What cause for complaint could he have?

Bernadette now felt that they were close to accomplishing their objective. She would acquire this *furml*, perform the transformation (she assumed Sneyagflug intended himself as the target, females of many egg-laying species being larger than males), and her obligations would be concluded. She longed for a return to normal life.

The senior members of the Drakespring Clan discussed the situation later in the day, and decided that Andrion would accompany Bernadette on her quest for the dragon spell. They expected an ancient Norse ruin, probably a few aptrgangr, nothing to worry about. And the children needed at least one of their parents here. After the grueling quest for the chemial ingredients Erik was more than happy to volunteer to stay home; and after holding down the home fort for nearly two weeks now without a break, Andrion was more than happy to volunteer for some action.

Last minute preparations were made, and goodbyes were said the night before to Andi, Riki, and the two older women who'd be mothers to their brood while Bernadette and Andrion were gone. In the morning it was only Andrion and Bernadette who stood in the road, while the rest of the farm's occupants went about their daily business. Sneyagflug showed up promptly, and soon carried them off into the sky.

Chapter 56: Northeastern Iscandia, Year Six

Bernadette had stayed up late crafting a sort of double saddle for them. It was designed to drape over the dragon's neck, made all of leather, and had two padded sections shaped to receive the legs and buttocks of a smaller (forward) and larger rider. It made riding on dragon back scarcely any more uncomfortable than riding a horse, and was worth the effort.

Andrion hadn't been on a dragon's back since he and Erik had sneaked a ride on Sneyagflug some seven years before, and he was both exhilarated and fascinated. He wished their relationship with the dragon were good enough that he could induce him to participate in a mapping expedition. Many maps, he knew, including the magic ones he'd crafted at the Academy, were not as accurate in their details as one might want. But from this viewpoint you could see everything!

The ride took several hours, and they were glad of the extra layers of warm clothing they'd worn. If flying high above Remus could be chilly, at this altitude in Iscandia it was freezing. Face masks and warm gloves prevented frostbite, and Bernadette spread her snow cat cloak around them both to cut the wind of their passage. Their butts and lower limbs were warm as toast, however, in contact with the hot flesh of the dragon through the leather of the saddle they rode on.

Finally, as the afternoon sun was hurrying toward the western horizon, Sneyagflug began to circle lower. Below them was a chopped-up, mountainous landscape of crags and spires interspersed with deep, ice-coated ravines through which glacier-fed rivers raged. The golden rays glinted on a massive edifice of stone, showing signs of heavy damage on the southern side. What might once have been a bridge stood in piles of tumbled stone on either side of a wide chasm.

Sneyagflug landed in a broad courtyard, which appeared (thankfully, no doubt) to be deserted at the moment. The resemblance to Todenstor was eerie, and Bernadette supposed this place had a Norse name as well as the dragon-tongue designation of Bergenfest. No doubt lost in the mists of time, as no one could have traveled here by ordinary means since whatever cataclysm it was that had destroyed the only bridge.

Bernadette and Andrion slid down from their perch on the dragon's neck, dragging their "saddle" along with them. They would take it along, in case it was needed again. "Good fortune be yours, *Fjurblut*," Sneyagflug rumbled. "When you have the *furml*," he continued, "I expect you will return to your home. Call me when you are ready."

"See you then," Bernadette replied. After the dragon had flown away, the two humans stood looking around at their surroundings. That old familiar feeling of danger shared had come over them, and they were grinning at each other. The things they'd been doing with their lives in recent years seemed so much more important, but there was no denying that sharp enjoyment they both felt, delving into scary old tombs in search of danger and reward.

By mutual unspoken consent Bernadette and Andrion faced east, enormous double doors beckoning to them as they stood in the central courtyard. To the west was a jumble of staircases and buildings climbing up, but nothing that looked as important. Over their years of questing together, they'd learned that the obvious choice was often the right one.

Bernadette strung her bow, keeping it in hand, and adjusted the hang of her quiver. Andrion had brought a few weapons just for the hell of it, and because he did enjoy playing with them; but he was relying on his battle magic to neutralize any foes they might encounter. That they might not encounter any was beyond consideration.

Chapter 57: Bergenfest, Year Six

Bernadette and Andrion approached the doors with their usual degree of caution when entering an ancient Norse ruin, which is what this appeared to be. It was far more massive than most, but the architectural details were telling. They had covered perhaps half of the distance from their starting point when an ancient Norse arrow whizzed past between them. Aha.

Bernadette spotted an aptrgangr armed with a bow standing on the battlements above the main gates of the fortress, taking aim on them for another shot. He fell dead as her arrow struck him. Then she scanned the edifice before them for any more undead guardians. Sneyagflug had said that this place had once been a bastion of the dragon worshipers. She hoped they wouldn't have to face one of those undead dragon priests. She'd killed one or two, but they were usually a severe challenge.

No more enemies barred their path, and they found the gates unlocked. They closed of their own accord after the pair had stepped through, the hollow booming sounding like a death knell. No doubt about it, a typical ancient Norse ruin. Sturdy stonework formed chambers and passageways leading down. Bernadette supposed that, had they wanted to go up, they would have had to find stairways on the outside of the structure where the aptrgangr archer had stood. But in her experience Spell Walls were either high on a mountaintop, exposed to the elements, or hidden deep within labyrinthine caverns. And Sneyagflug had said that this was one of the latter type. Down they went.

The place seemed to be a subterranean castle. With temperatures what they were this far north, delving into the earth where a constant temperature a little on the cool side of comfortable was naturally maintained, was a good idea. At least this meant that the pathways were clean, and lined with rooms that had once housed the activities of daily life. Bernadette particularly disliked questing through catacombs, lined on both sides with 3-high crypts that might at any moment disgorge an aptrgangr warrior.

Not that there weren't aptrgangr aplenty here. They roamed the corridors in their deliberate pace, generally making enough noise that if you were quiet and paying attention you could sneak up on them and kill them with a stealthy bow shot. Bernadette felt uneasy when she was killing aptrgangr. These had once been living human beings, brave warriors who had died giving their lives for their people or their king – or perhaps, if the dragon priest theory was true, for their gods. Now nothing was left of them but their skills in battle and a mechanical devotion to duty. It was almost a blessing to return them to the sleep of true death. Did their souls perhaps go to Asengard then? Or were the walking dead already soulless?

Andrion had little to do at first as they made their way through the labyrinth, trying dead ends, discovering rooms full of treasure (of which Bernadette took sparingly; she had more important things on her mind). He followed behind her and kept an eye out for anything threatening her from that direction, which she hugely appreciated. But most of the threats appeared to be coming from ahead.

After many turnings they passed through a set of wooden doors and proceeded down a stone ramp. Now their surroundings changed, and they came into an area of catacombs. Swell, Bernadette thought, as she redoubled her vigilance. Corpses flanked her on either side, stretching out into the distance. Which of them would come alive and attack her if she drew close?

Those that were completely skeletal and in repose, in Bernadette's experience, never walked. She had encountered walking corpses that were nothing but skeletons many times, but not any that had been lying down before they decided to go walkabout. Of more concern were fully fleshed, mummified corpses. Any she thought suspicious she put an arrow into before they got too close to them. She'd brought along a bow enchanted with a combination of lethal effects targeted to the undead, anticipating aptrgangr. Arrows shot into targets that were innocent of ill intent merely splatted, and she retrieved them.

The labyrinth was much more extensive than they'd anticipated, and they grew hungry and tired walking through it. After killing a couple of aptrgangr in a large room that seemed intended as a dining hall, Bernadette suggested they rest. She'd lost all track of time, but her internal clock was telling her it was bloody well time for a break.

They supped on ordinary trail food, but sitting in high style at a long wooden table. Handsome goblets stood along the board as if just abandoned by those who had drunk from them, and Bernadette in a puckish mood swabbed one out with a handkerchief dipped in wine. Then she poured a little wine into it from the bottle she'd brought along, and handed it over to Andrion, before doing one for herself.

"Cheers!" she said, grinning. Andrion smiled back at her. The wine actually did improve the flavor of the trail rations, which certainly fulfilled their duty as a source of calories and nutrition but were sorely lacking in elegance. They killed the bottle of wine between them, and were now looking at the world from a somewhat different viewpoint.

Andrion walked around to her side of the table and threw his arm over Bernadette's well-armored shoulders. "I feel like it's time for a rest," he said. "What do you say we throw our bedrolls down over there in the corner, and fuck like bunnies?" She gave him a look. "Before taking a nap, of course!" he went on. She grinned at him. Actually, his suggestion had produced a curious surge of heat within her, almost an echo of the feeling after she'd downed that Dragon Transformation potion. Was it really a love potion?

The love potion theory received strong support in the ensuing half hour. Bernadette and Andrion, two people who might well be counted in middle age, who had been lovers for more than seven years and were the parents of two children (three if you counted Merelle, which they were beginning to do), tore off their armor in a mad frenzy and humped like they were seventeen and had just met. Afterward, they lay there breathing heavily on their bedrolls and looked at each other wild-eyed.

"What the fuck was *that*?" Bernadette wanted to know. Andrion looked deep into her sea-gray eyes.

"That," he panted, "was… amazing!" She fell back, trying to get her racing heart under control.

"Aye," she managed after a while, "it was that." Why, she wondered, had she had an almost overwhelming urge to rip off her amulet along with her clothes? Her rational mind knew it would be a month or more before doing that would be likely to result in a pregnancy. But whatever obsession had gripped them both seemed to be narrowly focused on reproduction.

Bernadette snuggled into Andrion's side, running her hand down the smooth skin of his taut belly. "I think we're beset by more dangers than aptrgangr," she said quietly. "And I think we brought them with us…" Despite their misgivings, the two dozed for a while. It was fortunate that no enemies prowled nearby. When they awoke, they had no idea how much time had passed; but they now felt more alert. They dressed and found the door leading to the next section of the labyrinth.

They'd left the catacombs behind long since, and were once again in an area of the underground complex where people, thousands of years gone, had carried out the activities of daily life: cooking, sewing, smithing… They went through another wooden door, an ordinary-looking thing, and came into a long corridor flanked by a series of arches on either side. Bernadette put a cautionary finger to her lips and motioned for Andrion to go in through one of the arches on their right, while she took the left.

As she'd suspected, an aptrgangr sentry stood in the space behind one arch, intent on the central corridor. She ended its watch with a well-placed arrow, and it fell soundlessly. On the other side, she heard the crackling of battle magic as Andrion blasted her sentry's counterpart – hurling the smoking corpse out into the central corridor.

They met in the middle, slapping mailed palms in a gesture of mutual congratulation. Drakesprings rule! The corridor ended in the sort of double doors that, they had come to learn, usually presaged a serious fight. Andrion knew what to do, and as Bernadette pushed the doors gently open he hung back, waiting for her to signal their attack.

The doors gave on an enormous room, raised platforms on either side and a larger one, a sort of stage, toward the back of the room. Vertical sarcophagi lined the walls, and on the central stage stood an ominous catafalque on which rested a heavy sarcophagus. Oh crap, Bernadette thought. Gotta be an overlord at least… An idea occurred to her, and before she and Andrion parted ways at the door she handed him a potion.

This was one she'd been developing for years, and she'd brought a couple of them with her anticipating just this sort of situation.

Drink it, and for ninety seconds you were invisible to your enemies. She'd discussed it with Andrion before they left, a contingency plan she'd hoped not to use; and on her signal the two of them downed their potions before fanning out into the room.

Their proximity triggered a continuous crepitation as aptrgangr burst from their sarcophagi on either side of the room. They failed to see the human intruders who had roused them from their sleep, and fell one by one to Bernadette's arrows and focused bursts of battle magic from Andrion. When the two adventurers had passed the platforms and stood before the stage, all of the aptrgangr lay dead behind them.

The room was still and quiet. In the distance beyond the front edge of the stage, Bernadette could see three thrones on which aptrgangr sat. And beyond them, the Spell Wall. She came close to Andrion and murmured, "I don't like the looks of this. If those guys are overlords, who's in the coffin?" The figures on the thrones, sitting slumped at the moment, did indeed wear the elaborate helmets normally associated with aptrgangr overlords.

Andrion shared her anxiety. This looked like a four-against-two fight, with undead at the upper levels of ability and inimical resolve. "Can you even the odds a bit?" he suggested as quietly.

"I'll try," she whispered back. "Get ready, in case they all go up…" Applying a strong magical energy poison to the tip of the arrow in her hand, Bernadette took careful aim on the presumed overlord occupying the throne to their left.

She hit the slumped aptrgangr squarely in the chest, where its shriveled heart should be. The poison was probably unnecessary. The bow's enchantment caused the undead target to burst into flame when struck, and a gout of flame welled out briefly as the figure slumped still further in its chair. So far, so good. Bernadette caught Andrion's eyes and a look of triumph passed between them. Three to two, now.

Bernadette turned her attention next to the aptrgangr seated on the chair to their right. She figured it was best to have all their enemies in the same line of sight, if anything went wrong. This time, she skipped the poison. The shot from hiding (nothing more hidden than shooting at your enemies while they're technically dead, she thought) put an end to the aptrgangr in the chair. But a side effect of the enchantment, which only occurred randomly, created an explosion that leapt from the dying aptrgangr on the right to the one in the center – and the one on the catafalque near the front of the stage.

Those two, roused from their millennia-long slumber by the less-than-lethal attack, stood and began seeking their enemies. "Shit!" Bernadette said shortly, motioning for Andrion to head off to the right. They made a harder target, spread out – and aptrgangr had problems following moving foes. Bernadette began pouring arrows into the central overlord from the left, as Andrion began raining a combination of fire and lightning down on the creature stepping down from the catafalque.

After the fifth arrow had struck, the overlord Bernadette had been targeting fell – his connection to the magic that animated him broken by her unrelenting attack. Meanwhile, Andrion had been keeping their last antagonist at bay with a barrage of lightnings; but they seemed to have little effect on him, and he was drawing closer. He spoke, the words of the dragon spell high-pitched and lost in a sort of roar, and the sword Andrion was holding flew several feet away, to the floor of the cavern. Not that he'd really needed it…

The figure, which Bernadette was beginning to suspect was a dragon priest, was carrying an enormous sword. It glowed ominously in the dim light of the chamber, a sure sign of enchanted powers. Bernadette put an arrow into his back, and he spun moments away from bringing that sword to bear on Andrion to fix her with an arcane glare. She didn't wait for him to take action, but cast her own Repel Weapon spell. The sword flew from his hands.

Their enemy seemed stunned to be confronted with one who shared his abilities. His face was hidden by a mask, but his body language said nothing like this had happened in dying memory. Meanwhile, at his rear, Andrion hurled another blast of concentrated battle magic from close range. Using his actinic "plasma ray" technique, he carved a hole the size of his fist through the creature's back and out the front, angling it to avoid hitting Bernadette as it passed through.

The dragon priest, if that's what he was, collapsed like a puppet with its strings cut and dissolved, in a second or two, into a pile of ash. Andrion and Bernadette exchanged another look of triumph. They'd done it! "Good work, love!" Bernadette chirped, approaching the ash pile. "Any idea who this was?" Lore about some of the most famous of the dragon priests had survived to this day. Andrion stirred the ashes and came up with a few items including a magical staff and a heavy, stylized copper-colored mask. The sword Bernadette had stripped from him lay on the stone of the stage thirty paces away, and they retrieved it.

Andrion tried the mask on, then stood there perplexed for a while. "This wasn't any dragon priest I've ever heard of," he admitted. "This mask seems to increase magical energy, and partially shield against magical attacks. But there's something else." Bernadette gestured, and he handed it over for her to put on. She had an idea what the power might be, and turning to the corpse of a fallen overlord she tried the dragon spell that would turn your enemy to a block of ice briefly. Why this should not result in instant death she had no idea, but experience with it proved that unless you then immediately hit the frozen foe with a hammer or similar weapon, they would soon thaw out and resume attacking you.

The corpse turned gelid. A few seconds later it thawed, and she froze it again. "It's for dragon spells," she said. Andrion had not used a dragon spell in years, not since they'd defeated Tarragin. The stone he'd used, hung as pendant around his neck, had been exhausted and gone black. "It reduces the time it takes me to recharge my spell stones to nearly nothing. This'll be really useful, if it turns out I can capture this enchantment." Bernadette's abilities in enchantment had soared over the past few years, but not every magical artifact could be turned into knowledge. For a very few, whatever magic had been used to enchant them remained hidden.

Andrion grinned at her. "All right!" he said enthusiastically. He gestured toward the Spell Wall at the back of the enormous room. "Your dragon spell awaits, milady!" Removing the mask, Bernadette turned and began walking toward the familiar looking half-circle of rune-carved stone. But she spotted a large chest sitting on the floor up to one side of it.

"Let's see if the stone is here, first," she said. This already complicated quest would be even more complicated if she had to wait for Sneyagflug to form a stone for her. Ooh, there was some pretty good treasure in here… And yes, down at the bottom was a series of little casks like the one she kept jewels in at home. "Help me take these out, Andrion!" Bernadette said excitedly. No matter how wealthy they'd become, finding glittering treasures in the bottom of creepy old ruins still had the power to make her eyes sparkle with avarice.

There were twelve of the little casks in all. Bernadette set them out along the edge of the stone dais on which the three aptrgangr had sat, then opened each of them. Each cask, it appeared, contained stones for only one single spell – as many as ten of them, as few as none.

She had actually beheld the stones for every one of the dragon spells that had been available at the Edelmied seven years ago; but she was not sure that she could recognize them all by sight. In any case, some stones were pretty similar to one another. So she scooped out one stone from each cask (now wouldn't it just be ironic, if the one she wanted was the one of which those ancient dragon priests had run out?) to see if it would melt into her hand.

No, no, no… This was a treasure trove, but it was not proving to be what she'd hoped for. The sixth cask was empty, no hint of what its contents must once have looked like. But the seventh…! Light actually flashed in her eyes as she opened the lid, the stones within sparkling and flickering as if they were living flames – flashing red, then orange, then yellow. The one she plucked out vanished into her palm in moments, and a surge of heat came over Bernadette. It was very like the experience of taking the potion.

She rocked back on her heels for a moment, then plopped onto her bottom, eyes wide, and waited for the sensations to ebb. Andrion looked at her with a touch of concern. "Think that might have been it?" he asked. Bernadette drew an arm across her forehead, which was beaded with sweat.

"It's got to be," she replied, panting slightly. She dug a water skin out of her pack and took a long drink. Then, just for due diligence, she tried the other five casks. All had stones, and all were ones she already had.

Bernadette hauled herself to her feet. "Please pack up all these casks to carry home with us," she told Andrion. "Those are worth a fortune, if we can find a buyer for them." Now, she stepped within the curve of the Spell Wall. Yes! As Sneyagflug had promised, at her approach four rune words, side by side, lit with blue fire. And as she moved closer, they sank into her soul.

Bernadette was nearly staggered by the force of the four words of the dragon spell as they embedded themselves in her being, to the accompaniment of the familiar wordless chorus. She had seldom experienced this nearly-orgasmic process in recent years, and having it hit her fourfold was overwhelming.

Mon-Drache-Ein-Korp, man-dragon-one-body, the words of power penetrated her; and as they did, suddenly she understood all the words engraved on the wall. A wave of heat suffused her, again similar to the effects after ingesting that potion. Bernadette's mind flared with visions of flame, scaly wings spread wide, sharp teeth sinking into tender flesh with a rush of blood in the mouth.

What in all the hells was happening to her? Bernadette came to normal consciousness to find that Andrion was supporting her where she sagged before the Spell Wall, his face a mask of concern. "Berni?" he asked gently, as if not sure who was in there.

"I'm… all right, I think," she replied weakly. Her mind seemed torn to wisps, unable to hold a train of thought. What was it about the dragon spell that had seemed so wrong?

Andrion held a water skin to her mouth and made her drink, tenderly ministering to her until she began to show signs of returning to herself. Abruptly, she felt better. A lot better. That surge of heat was back, and whatever misgivings her mind wanted to throw up were swept aside. "Thank you love," Bernadette said, her eyes bright with desire.

Chapter 58: Drakespring Farm, Year Six

The door at the back of the dungeon in which they'd found the Dragon Transformation spell did not disappoint, and after a few twists and turnings the adventurers found themselves standing on a rock ledge above the same chasm over which this place's bridge had once stood, ages in the past. Something was wrong with Berni, deeply wrong, and Andrion hastened to wish them home with his map as she giggled and tried to pull his clothes off.

They arrived in the middle of the night and went in through the veranda door of the master bedroom. Erik had chosen to sleep in his personal space while they were gone, and Andrion got Bernadette to sit on the master bed before he let himself in through the connecting door and roused his brother. Erik awoke, taking a moment to get his bearings. Had Andrion been in his place, it might have taken twice as long.

"Erik," Andrion said, his voice fraught with anxiety. "We got the dragon spell Sneyagflug told us about, but something is wrong. Berni's not acting like herself." Erik's mind slipped into gear at once as he understood Andrion's urgency, and he rose to throw on a robe before returning with his brother through the connecting door. Bernadette was out like a light, lying limp in the center of the huge bed with her armor on.

Erik immediately confirmed that she was sleeping, then tried to rouse her. She gave no response, and his concern deepened. "I can't wake her, Andrion," Erik said, a tinge of despair in his voice. Never would he admit how deeply he loved her; but confronted with the possibility of losing her, he felt as if his strong core had collapsed and the only thing holding him up was naked resolve.

The two of them removed her armor and tucked her into the bed. All the while she slept, looking perfectly healthy, glowing in fact. A hand to the forehead revealed that she was hot, but there were none of the usual signs of fever. They tried forcing a few drops of a panacea potion down her throat, but it had no apparent effect.

Erik was naked but for a robe, Andrion in full armor. Finally Andrion stripped to his underwear and they flanked her on the bed, keeping watch as their beloved slept. There seemed to be nothing left to do. As the first rays of dawn penetrated the shutters, Erik stirred and realized that he'd fallen asleep. He immediately looked to Berni, and found her sleeping as soundly as before. He put a hand to her brow, and found it cool.

As he did so she roused, peering at him sleepily. "Erik? What..." Bernadette raised herself on an elbow and looked around, trying to make sense of her situation. The last she remembered, she'd been about to approach that Spell Wall... Erik engulfed her in a hug, planting a kiss on her forehead.

"You're all right?" he asked anxiously.

On Bernadette's other side, Andrion began to stir. He, too, wanted to know if she were all right. What *was* all this? "I'm fine," she told them, though she was still having problems connecting the dots of her history for the past several hours. "I need a hot bath, and some tea. Then maybe I'll feel more human..." They all got up, and Erik handed her a robe. Andrion accompanied her to the bathroom, as much in need of a soak as she was. Fighting aptrgangr and questing through dusty ruins was dirty work.

As Bernadette sat enjoying the hot water while Andrion washed her back and planted a tender kiss on the nape of her neck, she found herself still unable to recall anything of the time since she had approached the Spell Wall, beyond the vaguest of mental images and an overall sense of emotion. She had been hot with desire, it seemed, but why?

She recalled with a blush rutting with Andrion in the depths of the underground fortress. Sex with Erik had approached that level of mindless ferocity a few times early in their relationship, but it had never been like that with Andrion. He was a passionate but patient and skillful lover, not a bull elk! Thinking of their session sent warmth flooding through her from the crotch upward, but her mind wasn't getting with the program. It wanted to consider the evidence and figure out what was going on.

Bernadette dressed in everyday clothing and ate some breakfast prepared by Erik. Umberth had already eaten and was out seeing to the cattle, but Ekka, Christine and the children joined them at the table. Erik had fitted legs to the coach seat they'd had built for Andreas during their first trip to Auverne, restoring it to its original purpose, after Riki had been born. It had been sitting in storage for a couple of years, but they got it out again and dusted it off, and now baby Merelle was taking her meals in it.

Bernadette had the feeling that Merelle was going to be like no leukalfar ever since the fall of the white elves. From the coldness and formality of Duraenis, among the last of their kind still living unchanged in the modern era, she guessed they had been a constrained people even before they had been poisoned by their supposed allies. This little one, nurtured in a human family surrounded by love and laughter, seemed to be turning into a human before their eyes.

After breakfast Bernadette felt better still. She still experienced hot flashes, and along with the physical warming came surges of sexual desire that seemed completely out of context. Surely, at not yet thirty, she could not be going through "The Change"? Her own mother was in the midst of it now, and had told her of the heat surges and jangled emotions that accompanied menopause. But Bernadette should have another fifteen or twenty years before it began for her.

When everyone else had left the dining area, off about their business, Bernadette remained at the table with Erik and Andrion, conferring about the dragon quest. "I've got the dragon spell Sneyagflug wanted," she said, "so I suppose we should call him and get it over with. I'm more than ready to get back to normal life."

"What's the dragon spell supposed to do?" Andrion asked. He had not learned to read the Spell Wall runes as yet.

Bernadette got a sudden mental flash of the Spell Wall, the glowing runes, and the sense of a wave crashing over her. It was always like that to some extent, so perhaps her memory loss and sense of being overwhelmed was from absorbing four words all at once in conjunction with that potion. The meaning of the words on the wall eluded her, though. She seemed to think she knew them, but whenever she tried to pin them down in her mind they wriggled out of her grasp. She hoped that didn't mean she'd forgotten the dragon spell. That didn't seem possible, in her experience. So why couldn't she articulate them now?

"From what I've gathered, Sneyagflug's plan is to transform a male dragon into a female so that new baby dragons can be born. I'm not sure if he means to become the new mother of their race himself, or bring along some other male dragon for me to perform the transformation on. I assume he knows what he's doing – the effects of all the other dragon spells I've learned last only a few seconds. I doubt that'd be long enough to produce fertile eggs…"

This was more information than Erik and Andrion had so far gotten. They'd been supporting her in her desire to stop dragonkind from going extinct, without knowing any details. After thinking about it some more, Bernadette added, "I plan to extract a promise from Sneyagflug that these babies will be raised to stay out of conflict with humans. It's for their own safety, really. I don't know how long it takes dragons to reach full size, but even the biggest of them can be brought down by a group of determined humans with bows, the Dragonfall spell or no. Humans and dragons are both sentient species, and we need to learn to share the continent and get along. I think Sneyagflug realizes that our fertility trumps their immortality, and if dragons continue attacking humans they're eventually going to be exterminated."

She rose to her feet. "Might as well get on with it, I suppose," she said. "This should be interesting. I don't think you guys need to wear armor, but we might want to gather the family to watch." This time, they called Umberth along with the women and children onto the veranda while Bernadette and her husbands stood near the road. "SNE-YAG-FLUG!" she called, and in considerably less time than before the red dragon was circling, coming in for a landing. He radiated heat, his scales glowing red.

"You have the *furml*?" Sneyagflug rumbled eagerly. His plans were coming to fruition at last – and soon, he hoped, the next generation of *drachen* would be born.

"I'm to use it on you, then?" Bernadette asked, seeing he had brought no other dragons with him. The red dragon turned his gaze on her, eyes glowing, seeming almost to purr. She felt a wave of heat surge through her once again, and though she had no way of knowing it, her own eyes glowed for a moment.

"Very well," Bernadette said, taking a few steps backward. Sneyagflug was a big target. She knew as she said it, that though she could not call the words of power to mind, they would come at her bidding. She motioned to Andrion and Erik to stand back a little. She very much doubted "overspray" from the dragon spell would turn them into female dragons, but some other effect might happen that would be no more desirable.

Sucking in a deep breath, Bernadette cried "Mon-Drache-Ein-Korp!" And her world exploded. A blaze of agonizing fire shot through her, her arms stretching and claws sprouting from her hands and feet, leathery wings bursting forth from her back where a second set of shoulders had grown. Her clothing was shredded as her size increased, the cord on which her amulet hung snapping and the amulet falling to the ground. As her transformation progressed, Bernadette's confusion lessened and was replaced with white-hot fury. She had been tricked!

Erik, Andrion, and the rest of the Drakespring Farm residents (with the exception of Merelle, too young to understand what she was seeing), gasped and cried out in horror as the central figure in their lives transformed before their eyes into an enormous red dragon. She was much smaller than Sneyagflug but far larger than a mammoth, let alone a human.

Andi and Riki were shrieking in terror, Ekka and Christine trying to comfort them at the same time their own horror was too profound to do anything but cower in fear. Christine, recovering some presence of mind, threw open the veranda door to the master bedroom and shooed them all inside. They didn't need to witness this.

Their beloved wife had been turned into a horrific monster, apparently by her own dragon spell, and Erik and Andrion had no idea what to do about it. They stood there, pale with shock, as the scene unfolded. Sneyagflug's draconic heart soared with joy. "Perfect!" he cried, in dragon tongue. "Beautiful! I name you Schunmurte, Beautiful Mother. You will be mother to the *drachen* for all time to come!"

Bernadette found that with her dragon form had come a full and complete understanding of dragon speech, and it was in this language that she spoke to her would-be lover. "Betrayer! Deceiver! I curse you!" she let fly a gout of flames into his face, her mind a blaze of grief and anger. But Ehrgeizig had taught her this *furml*, and she knew that to a dragon it was nothing more than a customary greeting.

Her fury modulating, Bernadette considered the fact that Sneyagflug was nearly twice her size and decided not to try to kill him – though he surely deserved it. Her human mind and attitudes remained inside her dragon body, but she was experiencing other thoughts and feelings, strange urges. She turned her scaly head on her long, snaky neck and examined her wings. They looked functional.

"Schunmurte, I will have you! Your children will be mine!" Sneyagflug said in dragon tongue.

"Never!" she cried defiantly, but fear was overcoming her anger. She flapped her wings hard and took to the air. Then, in moments, she was gone – flying fast over the western horizon. Sneyagflug grunted an untranslatable curse and lifted heavily from the ground, going after her.

Andrion and Erik embraced, tears running from their eyes. They hadn't understood Sneyagflug's words about Bernadette being the mother of dragons forever, or their grief might have been greater. As it was, they were bereft of their wife, their lover, their friend and companion, the mother of their children. But as they broke apart and stood looking at each other, determination showed in both their faces. Somehow, they would get her back.

Chapter 59: Iscandia, Year Six

She had lost him, it seemed. Bernadette had flown like a bat out of hell, trying to put distance between her and Sneyagflug. Then she had begun taking evasive action. Her smaller size gave her a slight advantage, in that there were places she could hide that he could not go. Her nose told her that a dragon's sense of smell was not particularly keener than that of a human. They hunted from on high, and her vision was now far, far better than it had been.

Bernadette lay huddled under the eaves of an enormous, spreading oak tree, resting from her panicked flight and trying to make sense of it all. I was an idiot, she thought, as she considered the quest Sneyagflug had tasked her with. Thousands of years older than she, he had had access to lore she did not. He had known that, with the potion and the dragon spell, The Fireblood could transform into a dragon. And he had played her every step of the way. Putting her simmering fury at the betrayal aside, she had another thought: did this make her a were-dragon? But there'd been no full moons involved, and she had no idea how to transform back. Maybe the change was permanent.

At that thought, her heart sank. Her babies, her husbands, everyone she loved would now regard her as a frightening monster. Would she never know love again? She had sensed Sneyagflug's desire for her. He was eager to become the father of the dragon brood she was supposed to produce. And from a dragon's perspective, he seemed a likely consort. He was the largest and healthiest dragon she had ever seen, and wise in the ways of men. But she didn't think the *drachen* knew love as humans understood it. They had little in the way of social organization, as what need had a creature like that for cooperation? Their language and culture must be hard-wired, she suspected.

Dragon eyes and minds were not configured for tears, or she would have cried. Instead she tucked her head beneath one wing and slept. When she awoke, it was late in the afternoon and she felt a ravening hunger. Now she truly understood what Sneyagflug had told her. Her fires burned hot, and the urge to kill, to devour, filled her mind and very nearly overrode anything else.

She crawled out from beneath the oak branches, questing with eyes, ears, and nose for signs of danger. Little stirred in the quiet woods where she'd slept. Though dragons were in essence enormous lizards with wings, they lacked a lizard's agility on the ground. With an effort she launched herself into the air, catching a thermal and soaring in circles as she'd seen dragons do countless times in the past. She could just make out another dragon doing the same thing a long way to her north, but she knew instinctively to stay away from him. Dragons were territorial, she now realized.

But as currently the only young, fertile female dragon in the entirety of Iscandia – if not Agena – she might be welcomed where another male would not. Should she foil Sneyagflug's nefarious scheme by shacking up with some other dragon? But she feared he, as the larger, would just kill her paramour and get her anyway. Better to stay alone, at least until she'd had some time to get used to being a dragon. In the back of her mind was a vision of every dragon in Iscandia lining up for the chance to rape her. Ick.

As the sun fell toward the western horizon Bernadette saw movement below. She was determined not to hunt men (even if, as a human woman, she had killed dozens of human bandits and renegade mages in her career as an adventuress), but anything else big enough to be worth the trouble of a dive was fair game. Her hunger was like a fist, twisting her in its grasp and demanding that she act.

She was cruising above the foothills of Westmarch, she realized, and it was one of those bipedal cyclops creatures she had spotted moving below. She hoped they were tasty. Dropping from the sky, she hurled a gout of flame at the creature. As it cowered, beating at its head and shoulders and trying to take evasive action, she knocked it down with Gale and then stooped, claws out. Her talons pierced its body, killing it, as her jaws came down to rip a chunk of slightly charred meat from its shoulder.

Oh, yes! The rich flow of blood in her mouth as the creature's heart took its last few beats! The succulent flesh… it'd be better with a little more caramelization, she realized, and she stood over her prey, carefully applying Holocaust until it was sizzling all over and smelled wonderful. And she thought she had been the mistress of dragon spells before! For a dragon, the *furml* was no more difficult than breathing. She could cast spells over and over again, with scarcely any recharging period between.

Thinking back on all the *drachen* she had killed, and how few of them had used anything but Holocaust or Chill on her, Bernadette concluded that most were not well educated in the spells. Perhaps, if she had to stay a dragon, she would become Iscandia's foremost dragon scholar! Maybe she should try to find Ehrgeizig and form an alliance with him.

The idea of Ehrgeizig as a father to her brood of dragon babies did not appeal, though. As she eagerly devoured the cyclops until there was nothing left but a few bone fragments and some splashes of blood, she realized that her innate dragon sensibilities had their own ideas on the subject – and the ancient, much-tattered Ehrgeizig didn't fill the bill.

Bernadette rose in the air again, clawing her way higher and higher. She wanted to soar in the thermals far above the land, look things over, and think. Up here, the sun still shone. And freed from the hunger that had allowed no digressions, she could begin to take in the shape of her new life.

Chapter 60: Drakespring Farm, Year Six

The hysterics had long since subsided, and Andi and Riki were now playing together quietly on the dining room floor while Andrion, Erik, and Christine consulted at the dining table. Seeing his mother turn into a dragon, belch fire, and fly away had been traumatic for Andi, but it seemed to have triggered a protective reaction in him and he was now actively working to engage Riki, distracting her from the event and soothing her fears. Ekka was tending to Merelle in the nursery, not sure what to make of the morning's events. She hoped it wouldn't interfere with her employment – her family needed the money.

"She's not a monster," Erik said with quiet vehemence. "She's Berni. Dragons are as capable of rational thought as humans are, and she's human under that dragon skin. She was just afraid of Sneyagflug jumping her bones, and that's why she left. She'll be back, and when she comes back we'll find some way to return her to herself."

"I hope you're right," Andrion said. "But we need to be prepared with something to tell her when she comes back. I think I should return to the Academy, and start searching the library. Papa's been on his own up there for weeks, in any case." Christine nodded. She was starting to miss her husband. After years when he'd been a burden to her, before and after his major stroke, he had in many ways returned to being the man she'd married. Their relationship as lovers might be long in the past, but she still cared for him.

"Maybe…" Christine started, still trying to work out her thoughts. "Andi, maybe you should bring Francois back here. He can take along some of the books he's working on, and we could stay in your room together. We can help to care for the children, and look for answers here, while you're looking for them at the Academy."

Andrion considered. Inside, he felt the icy winds of winter blowing through his soul. Berni was gone, and neither he nor Erik had any sure idea how to bring her back. Going to the Academy, returning with his father, then going there again would take more than a full day of fast traveling, even if it only seemed like a couple of minutes. But come to think of it, he didn't need to do that. Francois had been with him when they went to Eisenstag using

Berni's original map. He could give Francois that map, and his father could fast-travel himself back to the farm.

Furthermore, Andrion realized, until such time as Berni got over her initial shock at the transformation Sneyagflug had tricked her into there was nothing but time. Berni's obligation to produce arms and armor for Valkyrie was an issue, but Erik might be able to fill in for her. He lacked Berni's skill with enchanting, but had gotten quite good at producing sturdy, serviceable, and well-made pieces at the forge. He was even better at jewelry than she was, actually; though in this still-bellicose province there was less demand for sparkling gems than there was for deadly swords and axes.

"I'll go to Eisenstag and send Papa back with Berni's map," Andrion told his mother and brother. Berni's shredded clothing had gone to the rag bag, her amulet carefully gathered up and placed on the chest of drawers where it had rested, off and on, during the time they'd been married. Her other possessions, including her magic map of Agena, had not been on her person when the change happened.

"Christine, Ekka, and I will look after the kids," Erik promised. "And I'll talk to Alessia and Wolaf. I'm thinking it might not be a good idea to tell everyone in Waterdon about this, though the gods know how we'll keep Ekka from spreading the news." He knew her well and liked her, but had no illusions about her character. "I think I'll tell Alessia that Bernadette had to go off on a quest, and see if she'd like some of my pieces. They've sold them often enough…"

"That's settled, then," Andrion said. "I'll gather some things, say goodbye to the nippers, and be on my way." The other two nodded and arose from the table. Trying to maintain a semblance of normalcy, Christine fetched a shirt she'd been embroidering from the nursery. While she was there she had a word with Ekka, who was just putting Merelle down for a nap. "I think," she remarked with asperity, "that it would be a bad thing if the news of this were to be all over Waterdon any time in the near future. I'll have to mention that to Umberth as well. There are certainly lots of *other* people in town who'd like to have a job here…"

Ekka eyed her, taking her meaning, and vowed to keep her mouth shut for once. The news was almost too good to keep, but she felt sure her eyewitness account would be buying her drinks for months to come, once the word was out.

Chapter 61: Iscandia, Year Six

Bernadette swooped and rolled, diving hundreds of feet with wings folded then clawing her way into the air again. This was so exhilarating! She'd been using her wings for more than two weeks now, the marvelous new abilities of her dragon form and the stirrings of her now-hot blood enabling her to forget, for hours at a time, her anger at Sneyagflug's betrayal and her grief at separation from her human family.

Her scales glistened iridescent red in the sun's late afternoon rays as she climbed once more, then leveled out and cruised. After days of searching she'd found a hunting ground, one not contested by any other dragon. She'd approached a couple, seeking some kind of companionship and perhaps the chance to discuss her situation; but evidently her fears that the sight of her would drive all male dragons into uncontrolled lust were unjustified. The reaction in each case had been one of hostility: "Get out of my territory or be prepared to do battle."

Bernadette/Schunmurte was at least slightly smaller than any other dragon she'd seen, making battle a bad choice. She wondered if all female dragons were smaller than males, which seemed unlikely – the falcon was larger than the tiercel, after all. Perhaps it was because of her youth, probably barely adult by the standards of dragon lifespans, or because she had been transformed to this shape from a creature still smaller. She'd given some thought to how the transformation had acquired the extra mass, but concluded it was a magical mystery she had no way of answering.

That sounded like a project for Andrion. She'd put him on it if (when!) she returned to her human form. She spotted a stag below, drinking from a woodland pool, and dived on it silently. Most dragons she had seen were always making a lot of noise while they were in the air, which seemed to her a stupid way to hunt. She supposed it was for the purpose of announcing their command of their territory, warning off competitors.

The rustle of air across Bernadette's leathery wings alerted the stag at the last moment, and it raised its head in alarm before gathering its muscles to bound away. Four legs are no match in speed for wings, though, and before it had gone a dozen paces she seized it in her talons and bore it to the ground. Her massive weight snapped the creature's neck.

Bernadette sank her sharp teeth into the stag's throat, savoring the hot blood. Then she backed a few paces and judiciously licked it with flames until the fur was singed off, the skin crackling, the meat hot and juicy. She hadn't been around feeding dragons all that much and wasn't sure if this was standard technique – but this was how she liked *her* prey.

As Schunmurte she had now sampled the flesh of deer, bear, smilodon, cyclops, and several others of Iscandia's wild creatures. She didn't care for the cats, which had a musky flavor; but most of the others were delicious. Bears were beginning to fatten up at this season, and their meat was rich and buttery. She seemed to have no desire at all for vegetable foods.

When nothing was left of the stag but its antlers, attached to a small chunk of skull, Bernadette licked herself clean. Then she moved in under the trees to rest and digest. Most dragons preferred to rest perched on high places; but mountaintop altars were favored roosts and competition for them was fierce. Besides, she was in hiding. She wanted to keep low, away from the eyes of Sneyagflug if he were cruising the skies on the hunt for her. He'd invested too much effort in tricking her into becoming his "Schunmurte" to simply give up and slink away.

As she lay there quietly, emotions churned in her mind. It was so hard to be rational and cool-headed in this body! Actually, there'd been times when she'd had as much difficulty ordering her thoughts in the body she was born to; but Bernadette was coming to realize that instinct played a much larger part in the mental/emotional life of a dragon than was the case for humans, and strange urges surged through her – urges she could not ignore.

With every passing day the desire to mate was becoming stronger. Had Bernadette still been in human form, and not gotten laid in two weeks, she'd be experiencing similar urges; but it would have been easily possible to ignore them, if there were no opportunities for sex. She could immerse herself in her work or caring for her children, masturbate…

She'd actually tried masturbation in this form, but the dragon anatomy didn't lend itself to self-pleasuring. As egg-layers dragons had a cloaca, not an anus and a cunt – and no clitoris, either. She had her forepaws, each with four long clawed "fingers." But they were no substitute for hands with opposable thumbs. Just another reason humans were pushing dragons out of the world.

In any case, Bernadette suspected that dragon sex had more to do with bringing on the next generation than with pleasure and social interaction. Even had she somehow been able to give herself an orgasm (did dragons, female ones anyway, even *have* orgasms?), she suspected that only copulation with a suitable male dragon was going to answer the instinctive desire that was pressing on her. She sighed, crisping nearby vegetation with her hot breath but fortunately not starting a forest fire.

The other urge that was bothering her was a very human one – the longing to see, to touch, to speak with her loved ones at home was become an unending agony. She missed them so badly she wanted to lift her head and howl at the moons; yet in her heart she was terrified of their reaction. Would they fear her, reject her as the inhuman monster she had become? She ripped some of Iscandia's largest creatures apart with her teeth and devoured them extra-rare and bloody on a daily basis!

While she lay thinking, the sun had set and night was falling. Bernadette had a wild thought – why not just fly home in darkness? Dragons were daytime hunters, needing to see their prey on the ground, so most of them rested during the night. Perhaps she could ghost across the two hundred miles of Iscandia that separated her from Drakespring Farm, and touch down unseen. Even if she were not able to see her loved ones, just to see home would be so sweet…

Bernadette crawled ponderously from her resting spot, to drink from the nearby forest stream. Her relatively small size, for a dragon, let her use resources larger dragons could not. Then she made her way on the ground to the edge of a large clearing, and launched herself into the air. Home was calling.

Chapter 62: Drakespring Farm, Year Six

The hour was getting late, and everyone had gone to bed but Erik. He wondered how Andrion was doing with his search at the Academy. It had been almost two weeks since he left, and the next day his father Francois had shown up, looking remarkably sprightly for a man approaching seventy. He'd brought along a satchel full of books from the Academy library, mostly on the subjects he'd been researching before Andrion sent him back to the farm. But he had an eye out for any lore on the subject of dragons and The Fireblood, too.

Francois was deeply indebted to his daughter-in-law Bernadette. Her healing magic had brought him back from a near-vegetative state and given him back his mind, his life, and his marriage. And his son Andrion, whom he loved so dearly and had nearly lost forever, was clearly hopelessly in love with her – to the point where he'd been willing to share her with another man rather than let her slip away. Andrion's relationship with his co-husband Erik was still somewhat mysterious to Francois and Christine, but there was clearly love there and the family dynamic seemed to work. Who was he to criticize?

Erik had washed up the dinner dishes and tidied the kitchen and living room, and was now engaged in the highly uncharacteristic activity of reading a book. There were many purely entertaining books in the household's growing collection, and he hoped that if he read for a while before trying to go to bed he would become sleepy. Too many nights over the past two weeks had been spent lying awake in his oversized bed, his mind in torment.

Erik felt a touch of thirst and set the book down, getting up to draw a glass of water from the tap in their kitchen. Then he heard a noise outside, cattle lowing uneasily. Might there be a wolf or something worse on the prowl out there? Their milk cows' calves, fattening for slaughter in the fall, were penned separately from their mothers behind a stout fence; but some of the local predators wouldn't find that an insurmountable barrier.

Erik drew an axe from a wall-mounted rack near the door and crept out into the darkened farmyard. None of the moons were up, and the only light nearby was the dypalfar lamp Andrion had installed beside the doorway. It burned continually, useful for finding the keyhole if they came home late. He stood for a few moments in the darkness, listening to the night sounds as his eyes adjusted to the dim light.

With the lights of the Bathing Maiden down the road and the lights of Waterdon to their west, it was never pitch dark around the farm. Their many outbuildings stood out as dark shapes against the lighter darkness, and Erik could see the calves in their pen moving about. Both they and their mothers seemed uneasy, as if they scented something. But what, and where?

Finally he smelled it – a whiff of brimstone coupled with musk, the scent of dragon. And down at the bottom of the farmyard, in the road, a dark shape. Not a very big shape though, not Sneyagflug. What other dragon would fly here silently in the middle of the night and just sit in the road looking up at the farm? "Berni!" he cried, and ran down to the road, the axe forgotten at his side.

Bernadette's night vision was better than it had been when she was human. She saw Erik coming and cringed back, pulling in on herself as if to become smaller. She should have realized the cows would have a fit! One of the major points of conflict between dragons and humans in Iscandia was their fondness for beef…

The fact that her beloved had seen her as a dragon, called her name, and was rushing to meet her was enough to forestall Bernadette's urge to flee. He threw his axe to the ground as he came close enough to see it was indeed her, his very own red dragon. To her astonishment, he hurled himself at her flank, trying to hug her. She curled her neck around and nuzzled his shoulder. Erik, being tiny by comparison to her. Now *that* was something.

"Oh, Berni!" he rumbled, his voice fraught with emotion. "I was afraid we'd never see you again!"

"Hush, love," she rumbled back. Her draconic voice was less deep than Sneyagflug's, yet in a range lower than any human woman's. The emotion of the moment was so sweet and painful at the same time she wished deeply and urgently that she could cry.

"I've been hiding from Sneyagflug," Bernadette told him. "Has he been around?"

"We see him flying overhead almost every day," Erik acknowledged. "I'm sure he's expecting you to come back home, and thinks to catch you here. That bastard!" Bernadette dipped her head, gazing into Erik's eyes, and he stroked her head. Oh, the loving touch!

"Is Andrion here?" Bernadette asked. She'd been missing him deeply, as well as Erik and the children.

"He left for the Academy right after you vanished," Erik said. "He's trying to find some lore that will point us to a way to turn you back." He stroked the silky, warm scales of her neck. Bernadette considered.

"I'm pretty sure that Sneyagflug lied when he said the potion was to enable me to get all four of the words," she said. "I think it was like a prerequisite, something that prepared me physically for the transformation that was completed by the dragon spell. I started feeling odd right after I drank it."

Erik's stern expression was barely visible in the dim light. He hated Sneyagflug for what he'd done, deceiving them all when they were only trying to help him. Bernadette went on, speaking as quietly as she could. The draconic vocal apparatus was not set up for murmuring. "I studied the chemia book during the week we were home after getting those ingredients," she said. "There wasn't any potion called 'Man Transformation' or 'Transform back.' I don't think there's anything that chemia can do."

Erik just hugged her head. He was relying on Andrion to come up with a plan to turn her human again while he held down the home fort, but he didn't want to let her go. He didn't care what shape she was. "Hmm," Bernadette continued. "Nerissa was cured of vampirism by a priest up near Normarsh. And I've heard that it's possible to cure lycanthropy by some kind of ritual that frees the beast nature. Then you have to kill the beast nature. But I'd have to be human already to do that. It's not like I turn into a dragon on the full moon – I'm stuck here. My only hope is that there might be some kind of a dragon spell that will reverse it."

Erik looked up, hope shining dimly on his shadowed face. "If Andrion could find out about a dragon spell, could you learn it from a book?"

"I could learn it," she replied. "but I wouldn't be able to use it unless I had the spell stone to power it."

"I thought dragons, uh, made their own stones?" Erik asked.

"You're right!" she said. "I have no idea how to go about it, but from what Ehrgeizig told us it just sort of happens. If Andrion can somehow find those words of power in a book, I can make my own stone and turn back!"

"But if he can't, mightn't you be able to find the spell on a Spell Wall?" Erik asked.

"The outdoor Spell Walls are all jealously guarded by dragons a lot bigger than I am," Bernadette replied sadly. "The spell to turn me into a dragon was on a wall deep inside an ancient place of the dragon priests. I wonder…" At this juncture a small voice spoke out of the darkness.

"Mama, I could get the dragon spell for you…"

"Andi!" Bernadette nearly jumped out of her scaly red skin. "How long have you been listening?" she asked, now seeing the dim outline of her son where he stood a few paces beyond Erik.

"I was awake. Then I heard the cows making noise, so I went out on the veranda to see. I was going to wake up Papa Erik if there was anything bad, but then I saw him talking to you…" The boy ran to her, trying to hug her snout. Hot, salty tears ran down his smooth cheeks. "We miss you so much, Mama!" he cried. Bernadette curled her neck around her son, the closest she could come to hugging him. He didn't care that she was a monster! His sorrow cut her to the quick, but still her heart soared.

After the tearful reunion Erik picked the boy up, hugging him close and balancing him on one hip so that their heads were at nearly the same level. "It could work," Bernadette said. "If the dragon spell exists, and it's at an underground Spell Wall, Andi could learn it from the wall and then teach it to me so I can transform back. But that would mean taking our five-year-old son into a den of aptrgangr…"

"I'm not afraid of aptrgangr, Mama!" the boy chimed in. In the stories he'd been raised on, his mama and two papas always beat the aptrgangr and came back out of the dungeon loaded down with treasure. Nothing bad ever happened to the good guys.

"He does have a good suit of armor," Bernadette admitted. "You could make him a sword, Erik, and Andrion could teach him some spells and load him up with potions so he could defend himself in a pinch. And with both of you there with him, there aren't many aptrgangr that could even get close. I think it might work."

It was hard to see Andi's face, but it was practically glowing with pride at this vote of confidence from his mama the amazing red dragon. Erik was looking more positive than he had a few minutes before. "I think I'd better teach this boy a few dragon spells, as well," Bernadette said thoughtfully. "You know Calm and Terror, and Terror is a good one to use on aptrgangr or the undead. But you need to promise me that you'll only use the dragon spells I teach you if something or someone is attacking you – never on your friends or family members. Do you promise?"

Andi nodded solemnly, then said "I promise, Mama. Only on bad guys or monsters. Or wolves?" Bernadette nodded her enormous, smoothly-scaled head, then continued. "Here is the Dragonfall spell. You must use it when a dragon is hovering in air preparing to attack you, and it will hurt him and make him fly away sometimes, or land where he can be killed with arrows. I'm the only dragon in Iscandia that knows this dragon spell, and I don't think it will have any effect on me. But if Sneyagflug gives you any trouble, or any other dragon does, be sure to use it."

She gave him that dragon spell, as quietly as possible, and Repel Weapon and Lightning as well. None of these would be lethal to a human, in case his promise wavered – there was only so much you could expect from a child Andi's age. But any of them would temporarily break up an attack and give help time to arrive.

"I have extras of the stones for all those spells, and Terror as well," Bernadette said. "When you were playing in my jewel box, you must have missed a few. But let's try out this dragon ability, shall we? If it's true I can make my own stones, maybe you won't have to go dungeon diving at all." Her spirits were rising by the minute, finally taking action to solve her problem.

Bernadette reached within her, focusing first on the Terror spell. This spell would strike fear in the hearts of your enemies, making them flee for the minute or so that the spell lasted. If you spent that minute running fast in the other direction, a confrontation might be completely avoided. A feeling arose in her innards, which in her human form she would have interpreted as the need to belch. "Stand back," she warned. "I'm not sure what's going to happen!"

Erik, still holding Andi, backed off a few paces. The two of them watched her with fascination as her sides heaved, her neck jerked up and then down convulsively, and she deposited a small stone in the road. It reminded Bernadette of spitting out a baby tooth when she'd been five or six. In the dim light the stone looked gray and colorless.

Erik came back and collected the stone from where it lay. "Ouch, it's kind of hot!" he remarked. "Looks almost silver, like it's a mirror…" He handed it to Andi when it had cooled enough, and the stone – large in comparison with the boy's little hand – vanished beneath the surface. It had worked!

Bernadette set to work regurgitating stones for the rest of the spells she'd taught her son, pleased with her new trick and hopeful it would enable her to become human again without sending Andi into danger. "Don't forget," she warned him, "once you say a spell, you won't be able to do it again for quite a while. So make it count." Andi nodded again.

"I know," he said in a small voice. "I… already tried it a little." Aha. He'd picked up Gale before they realized he was fireblood, and it didn't surprise her to learn he'd been experimenting. What child, especially a boy, didn't long for magic powers?

"It is possible to use a different spell right away, but you shouldn't do it," Bernadette warned. "I tried that once years ago when we were hunting for potion ingredients to stop Tarragin, and I nearly fainted from weakness because both stones were trying to recharge using my mana."

"I remember, Mama," Andi said in a tone of impatience. Of course, he'd heard the story a thousand times.

"I can't stay," Bernadette said reluctantly. "I'm afraid Sneyagflug will find me if I'm here too long. But I'll try to come back, at night, in a few days. If you find the dragon spell, I don't know if there's any way to contact me. I…"

"SCHUNMURTE!" the call rumbled out, riveting her to the spot. Shit, Sneyagflug had arrived! She took to the air in the darkness, orienting herself to the east.

"I love you! Give my love to Riki and Andrion!" she cried. Then she bolted into the night, the huge red dragon in hot pursuit.

Chapter 63: Eastmarch, Year Six

Bernadette led Sneyagflug in the opposite direction from the territory she'd staked out. If she managed to lose him now, she could circle around and he would never suspect she was hunting daily hundreds of miles to the west of here – or so she hoped. For him to be seeking her at her human home was pretty obvious, but she didn't regret having gone there. To know that Erik and Andi loved her in spite of her transformation meant the world to her, and the news of Andrion's hunt for a cure filled her with hope.

Sneyagflug's greater size made him less maneuverable in close quarters, but it gave him an advantage of speed in a chase. He had more wing surface, more muscle. Bernadette had rounded the slopes of the Hochstein and was moving southeast, in the area south of Coldstein, when he caught her tail in his jaws. Ouch!

The moons had been rising since early in Bernadette's conversation with Erik, and there was now more light to see by. As Sneyagflug released her tail, she spun and hovered in midair, confronting him. "I have you now, Schunmurte!" he declared. "We will make beautiful children together!" He was speaking in the dragon tongue, and she replied in kind.

"I hate you!" she declared, wings flapping. Looking at him, she was riveted by the sight of the yard-long, bright red penis he had unfurled from his cloacal opening, rigid in the moonlight. He wasn't kidding about his desire to make babies with her, obviously. It was her first sight of dragon dick, and her human mind was suitably impressed.

Out of options, still hovering as the huge red male did the same, Bernadette cried "Alt-Wach-Sterb-Tot!" As she did so, she suddenly recalled that she was not, as she'd thought, the only dragon in Iscandia who had heard this dragon spell and lived to tell about it. Ehrgeizig had heard it, during her first use of it in the initial battle with Tarragin. And she had used it on Sneyagflug, bringing him down out of the air before trapping him in Wyrmshalla.

A couple of experiences seven years ago had not inured Sneyagflug to the effects of this unique dragon spell, however. He wavered in the air, the familiar color pattern of the spell flaring about him. "No! Don't do that!" he bellowed. "We must mate, for the sake of dragonkind!" Bernadette hit him with the spell again. She still doubted her ability to kill him. The Dragonfall spell would weaken him and bring him to the ground, but her claws and teeth were poor weapons for dragon-killing compared with her enchanted bow and a quiver of daimonic arrows.

But at least she had halted his attack. Bernadette wasn't sure whether rape was technically possible among dragonkind; or conversely, if it might be the standard technique for mating. But she had the upper hand, now. Sneyagflug's wings went up and he fluttered to the ground, as she hit him with the Dragonfall spell for the third time. He collapsed on the ground, rumbling in pain, and she alit beside him, looking down on him with satisfaction. The bastard deserved it.

"I submit, Schunmurte," the red dragon groaned. "You have defeated me. What would you now?" Bernadette's dragon instincts veered from the kill in an instant. Submission to the dominant combatant seemed to be all that was required, as it was when dogs fought.

"You lied to me," she said coldly. "You turned me into a dragon and stole me away from the people I love, when I had trusted you and was trying to help you. What do you have to say for yourself?" Vindictiveness toward a fallen foe might not be in dragon nature, but history had proven it to be a well-established characteristic of humans.

Sneyagflug seemed to be in agony, though there were no marks of injury on him. "I need you! I want you! You are dragonkind's last hope!" he pleaded. "I knew that it was possible for a human who is fireblood to transform into one of us, and there was no other way. But I feared you would not agree if I told you the truth. I only deceived you a little…" at this, head lowered, he looked up at her sideways as if judging her mood. "I beg you, mate with me. If there are females among our offspring dragonkind will be saved from extinction, and I will tell you how to find the dragon spell for transforming back into your human form."

His words seared Bernadette's brain. Sneyagflug knew of such a dragon spell? Andrion had been searching for nearly two weeks and had found no sign of it. And all she had to do was submit to the desire that had been welling up in her for weeks? "What's the catch, Sneyagflug?" Trust was gone. "Are female dragonlings in a clutch as rare as adult females?"

"No," he assured her. "Usually one out four in a clutch of a dozen or more are hatched female. But the way of our kind is hard on females. In eons past, when last any mated and bred, they were left to lay, hatch, and raise the brood on their own. I have spent much time around you humans, though, and have seen that you have a better way. This is why there are a thousand or more humans for every dragon. If you will mate with me, I will stay by your side and provide for you and our children. Every one of them will survive! And the females will be mothers to dragonkind for ages to come."

Bernadette hated to admit it, but Sneyagflug was making a lot of sense. Her desire not to see dragonkind exterminated was as strong as it had been when she'd embarked on his quest, and her weeks of living as a dragon had only increased this desire. "So, if I mate with you, when the eggs hatch and there are females among them you will tell me where to find the dragon spell so I can return to human?" Bernadette was surprised to find the human nod of assent duplicated among the *drachen*.

"How long is this going to take?" she next wanted to know. Pinning Sneyagflug down on every last detail seemed to be her only hope of coming out the other side without regrets.

"We must mate once, which will tell your body it is time to make eggs. Then again, in a week or so, to fertilize the eggs. Another two weeks and the eggs will be ready for laying. During that time we need to find a suitable nest. If they are kept warm and tended, the eggs will hatch in a month. The dragonlings will be tiny and able to move about, but not sentient. At that point they must be provided with unlimited food, or they will fight and kill each other to eat. After another month their minds become developed, and they will be able to speak."

"Speak?" Bernadette asked, doubting this. "After a month of life?"

"The minds of dragonkind are largely a part of our nature, I believe," came the reply. "We live for many ages and over this time we learn many things; and this can change our attitudes. But a month-old dragonling is in some ways like a miniature adult, minus the years of experience an older dragon will have. We begin to fly about three months after hatching, and continue growing for as long as we live. But females start out smaller and grow more slowly. An enormous female would be unlikely to find a safe nest for her young, as caves are preferred and few have entrances the largest dragons could pass through."

Wow, Bernadette thought, discovering that her ire had evaporated. She was a lot like Andrion in this regard – give her access to some information in which she was interested, and everything else would recede from view. She had a decision to make. Could Andrion, after failing to do so after two weeks of study, eventually find the words, or the location, of the dragon spell she needed to turn back into a human? If not, Sneyagflug was her only hope. And then there was the issue of dragon extinction. She really did want to save the species if she could – all the better if the father of the new generation was a dragon who was willing to bypass instinct in favor of logic. Maybe the next cohort of dragonlings would be smarter than their elders.

After considering for a while, as the much-larger dragon groveled before her, Bernadette spoke again. "Sneyagflug, there is one more promise I must have from you before I will undertake this. I will leave when our babies are old enough to speak and understand, and it will be on you to raise them from then on. You must raise them to regard humans as allies, not prey, and be sure that they will not attack them – or their livestock. There are thousands of square miles of uninhabited land in Iscandia, and it is not needful that dragons and men should be in conflict."

"Gladly, Schunmurte, gladly," Sneyagflug said. "It would be of little use to bring new dragons into the world only to see them fall to the arrows and swords of men, and there is game aplenty in the wilds. I will teach them all the Common speech, so they can converse with humans. Our children will be at peace with men, and in time all of dragonkind will be forced to join them or see extinction. We will be the parents of a new dragon race."

It seemed inevitable. "Very well," Bernadette said sternly. She had not completely forgiven Sneyagflug for his duplicity, and possibly never would. But she was willing to extend enough trust to him to let him go through with his plan. It was just sex, right? And then laying eggs, raising babies for a little while… Imagine if human babies could speak at a month of age! Of course they'd probably just be saying something like "feed me now" or "I'm bored, entertain me"…

Sneyagflug rose from his posture of submission. During the time they'd been conversing, he'd recovered from the damage done by the triple shot of the Dragonfall spell. His gaze was locked on her, his penis once again protruding and ready. Bernadette felt a surge of draconic desire rush over her at the sight of it, though she had scarcely any idea of how to proceed.

"Um, Sneyagflug…" Bernadette said hesitantly. "I don't know how dragons do it…"

"I myself have never done so," he rumbled, his already deep tones seeming gruff. "But dragonkind are driven by instinct. You have coupled many times as a human, yes?" She nodded. "I believe it's the same thing, only bigger."

He approached her awkwardly, towering over her. No kissing, obviously, as they had no lips. But boy, could they neck! They entwined their necks together, rubbing heads, and long tongues came out to slide along scaly flesh. Bernadette's neck skin was covered with small scales but it was still surprisingly sensitive, and she found that the feeling of Sneyagflug's tongue running along it filled her with fiery desire.

Sneyagflug's gigantic red cock swelled even more, becoming longer and thicker. For his size, it was probably smaller than Erik's on a proportional basis. But it certainly looked adequate for the job. Bernadette suspected that dragons, like most four-footed animals (which they were, sort of), usually copulated "doggy style." One of her favorite positions, as a human.

But her dragon tail was enormous and quite thick through at the base. How could she hold it up out of the way enough to allow Sneyagflug to penetrate? Instead, Bernadette broke from their cervical clasp and rolled over onto her back, wings spread and head raised, powerful hind limbs with their clawed feet spread to expose her gaping, glistening cloacal opening. "Take me," she purred.

Sneyagflug looked down upon her, this consort he'd sought so eagerly. He had an idea that dragon instinct didn't cover this situation, but he had little mind left to think with in any case. A dragon with a hard-on is a dragon on a one-way mission, hang the consequences. Without hands to guide his member to the target, he might have had trouble inserting it; but fortunately it was prehensile, and it went there of its own accord.

Bernadette looked up at her draconic lover. Not exactly a big romantic moment, but her dragon instincts were driving her on. Her human outlook on sex, which had always been enthusiastic in the extreme, informed those instincts with some ideas they'd never had before. "Fuck me!" she roared. "Yeah, all the way in! And out, and in again! Keep doing it!"

Sneyagflug was at a loss. He'd had no idea what he was getting into, mating with a dragon who had the mind of a human. For this first mating, before eggs were present to be fertilized, he had expected to insert his penis as a spermipositer and simply leave his semen behind. The idea had haunted his thoughts since he had first beheld Schunmurte, the creation of his patient effort. In a lifetime that could be nearly endless, an individual male dragon was counted successful if he got his rocks off half a dozen times. Might there be something more?

The friction felt… wonderful! Balancing on his powerful hind legs as they were spread on either side of her tail and taking some of his weight up by flapping his wings, Sneyagflug began thrusting his cock repeatedly into Schunmurte's cloaca. Though she was on her back, she raised the lower part of her body up to meet his thrusts. No clitoris, alas, but the friction felt good as that huge, glistening red monstrosity pushed deep inside her.

The mating didn't go on for all that long. Far longer than it would have among ordinary dragons, probably; but had Bernadette been making love with Andrion (and oh, how she missed doing so!), they would barely have been past the foreplay in the time it took for Sneyagflug's cock to swell still more and convulsively drench Bernadette's interior with what felt like a couple of gallons of hot dragon cum.

As he came, Sneyagflug bellowed, flapping his wings furiously as his cock gushed within her. Whoo! Bernadette had not had what she would consider an orgasm, but the coupling had been quite an experience anyhow. Already she could feel a gathering heat and heaviness within her body, as the act of intercourse (and probably, she guessed, the presence of sperm) triggered a cascade of hormones that would lead to ovulation.

Sneyagflug stood looking down at her, on his hind legs with his wings spread in a curious pose that made him look like a heraldic animal. His cock shriveled and was retracted inside his genital slit. Bernadette took a deep breath and heaved herself backwards until she could roll over and scramble to her feet, oceans of dragon semen coursing from her cloaca. She shivered a little.

Having mated, the two found themselves in the grip of another instinctive reaction. They now suddenly felt much better disposed toward one another, rubbing together and showing signs of physical affection. Bernadette no longer hated Sneyagflug, though a hard, shiny part of her underlying human mind was never going to completely trust him again.

They groomed each other with those long tongues, then went down to the nearby stream to drink and rinse off. "Schunmurte," Sneyagflug said hesitantly, "I didn't know it could be like that. I wonder if it is your humanity…?"

"Probably just getting laid for the first time," Bernadette remarked matter-of-factly. "It's not like any other activity in life, that's for sure."

He had lived for eons, this little human-turned-dragon less than thirty years. But Sneyagflug felt awed in her presence. She had had experiences many of his kind never got the chance to taste, which somehow made her the older. He wondered idly, for a moment, if there might be a dragon spell to turn a natural-born dragon into a human.

Bernadette had concluded her toilet. "Well, that's it then," she said. "Where shall I meet you, in a week's time?" He looked at her blankly. "You're going to find a nest for us, right? And after I've ovulated we're going to do this again, so I can lay my eggs in the nest? I plan to spend the time in the interim with my family."

Chapter 64: Drakespring Farm, Year Six

Andi shared Erik's bed, snuggling up with his papa to ward off any bad dreams and make sure that Ekka, Riki, and Merelle weren't disturbed in the nursery. They talked quietly for a long time before dropping off. In the morning Erik was up before anyone and, as they gathered in the kitchen for breakfast he told the tale of last night's visit by the lady of the Drakespring Clan. Andi was quite proud of his part in it.

The adults were riveted by the news, Riki merely confused. She was too young to grasp Bernadette's transformation. Maybe Mama had ridden away on a dragon? "I think we need to tell Andrion about this, whether he's found anything or not," Erik said, and Francois was eager to volunteer. He'd enjoyed sharing a bed with his wife the past couple of weeks, but he'd exhausted the books he'd brought back with him and would be more than happy to exchange them for others.

"I suppose I'm going to let you get away again, you old rascal," Christine told him, "but you'd better be back a little sooner this time."

"I'll just get some more books, then come right back," he promised, smiling at her. "Maybe Andi and I will come back together, if he thinks he'd be more useful here." They had not all finished eating, though Umberth was already out and about his chores, when they heard a commotion outside.

In the slanting rays of the rising sun, the glistening red dragon touched down – not in the road, but in the farmyard between the forge and the house. Her heart sang with joy. Inside her body, she felt changes taking place and knew it wouldn't be long before the next instinctive imperative claimed her; but for a few days, at least, she could be with the ones she loved. Sneyagflug was seeking out the perfect place for them to hatch and raise their young, and their next coupling would (she hoped) be his reward for a job well done.

As the cattle lowed uneasily, the one Umberth was milking nearly kicking over the pail, the family boiled out into the yard to look at her in surprise. Erik and Andi were soon by her side, the rest of them approaching more cautiously. But in moments they were all gathered around her, exclaiming and murmuring and stroking her hot, scaly hide. Riki, held aloft by her grandmother, still seemed confused about why this huge beast spoke as if it were her mama; but she was coming to accept the situation.

Bernadette quailed at explaining the details of her bargain with Sneyagflug. She'd been hiding out, cut off from her family for weeks in an effort to avoid him, had threatened dire murder; and a day later she had fucked him and was planning to shack up and make baby dragons with him? It was pretty inconsistent.

But Erik didn't care a whit. Working with Sneyagflug offered the possibility of her return to human form? And it would only take two or three months? This was wonderful, and he didn't judge her for her decision. Andrion wouldn't either, he assured her. Privately, he hoped that was the case. Erik loved Andrion, but he knew that his elder brother could be bothered by some things that didn't faze *him* in the least.

Eventually the excitement subsided, and Francois embarked on a fast-travel expedition to the Academy, to report to Andrion. Likely they would return together late tomorrow. There was no point in Andrion beating his head against a wall looking for that dragon spell if its location was going to be handed to them; and he surely wouldn't want to miss Bernadette's visit before she had to fly away again to begin her brief career as a dragon mother.

Erik lingered at Bernadette's side, as if he were afraid she'd disappear forever if he lost sight of her again. He had other things he could be doing, like making some arms and armor for Valkyrie; but nothing seemed more important than this. The calamity that had befallen their family had shaken his easy-going attitude to the core, and he was now confronted with the devastation that would result if he lost her forever. They weren't just lovers, friends, family members – she was the love of his life. He leaned against her warm flank, ignoring the smell. It seemed to him as though Berni's dragon pong was less objectionable than Sneyagflug's had been. Could it be a gender difference, or was it just that he loved her?

Rumblings came to Erik's ear as he stood there. "Whoa, what's going on in there?" he asked. Bernadette looped her neck around to nuzzle his shoulder and look into his eyes.

"I'm sort-of pregnant, I fear. At least, I'm ovulating. That seems to require a lot of energy. And mainly, I'm starving! Bloody Stupid Animal is starting to look like lunch. I think I'd better go hunting…"

Erik didn't want her to fly off again, even though he knew she'd be back. For her part, Bernadette did not want to feed in front of the family. It was one thing for them to accept her as a rather handsome-looking red monster, and something else for them to witness the savagery with which she could devour an entire stag in a few minutes' time. Still, when he suggested getting a bow and coming with her, she agreed to give it a try.

Arming himself, Erik climbed Bernadette's shoulder and sat on her back just forward of the point where her wings joined her body – his legs hanging down on either side of her neck. She was so very much smaller than Sneyagflug! Bernadette spread her wings and leapt into the air with all four limbs, flapping her wings. But it was no use. Erik was just too heavy! She fluttered back down to the ground, swiveled her head around, and said "Sorry, love. I might be able to lift Andi, but you're just too solid."

He grinned at her, and slid back down to the ground. "Don't be gone long," he said. "I've been worried out of my mind about you." Wow, that was quite an admission coming from Erik. During the first few months of their relationship he'd scarcely acknowledged that they were together, and she hadn't admitted to herself that she loved him, either. Love takes different forms, and Bernadette loved each of her husbands in his own unique way.

"Sure miss fucking you," she said as she prepared to leave.

"I'm up for it if you want to," he suggested with a leer. She suspected he wasn't entirely joking though.

"With that little dick?" she laughed. Erik was better endowed than any other man she had met, but his massive cock would be lost in that cavernous cloaca of hers. "Besides," Bernadette added, "this body isn't really made for sexual pleasure. I have the urge, but it's related to reproduction and not enjoyment. Just wait'll I'm human again, and we'll make up for lost time."

With that, she took to the air and flew off to the east. The foothills on the far side of the Brightwater were rife with game, and she'd often hunted there with her bow. Erik watched her go with a smile on his lips and a longing in his heart. He'd been without his wife for more than two weeks now, and was looking at another couple of months before he'd have her, in her true form, in his arms again. His balls ached at the thought. He'd been beating off, but it wasn't the same thing. Nor did he want to seek comfort elsewhere. There were plenty of young women at the Maiden who'd have been delighted to tumble a stud like Erik, but for seven years there'd been no one but Berni and he intended it to remain that way.

That Berni had, in essence, been unfaithful to him and Andrion by having sex with Sneyagflug in her dragon form, didn't really register on Erik. She wasn't cheating on them, she was doing what she had to do to return to human and help save the dragon race from extinction. Horniness, even loneliness, didn't stack up as a motivation compared to that. He sighed as he watched the red dragon disappear over the horizon.

Over her days of freedom before resuming her dragon obligations, Bernadette spent many of her daylight hours hunting. It was clear that making eggs called for a lot of extra protein, and she'd eat an entire stag only to find herself thinking fondly of food within an hour or two. Andrion returned to the farm late on the second day, with Francois in tow. The entire family was glad to see them.

The evening was fine, and they'd set up a dining table on the veranda to enjoy the warm air and share the meal with Bernadette, so she could participate as part of the family. She'd flown back from her hunting trip late this afternoon with a goat in her talons, and they'd roasted the whole thing. She got one of the legs, which she endeavored to eat with more decorum than usual.

Andi and Riki had discovered that their mama could catch tidbits in her mouth, and after they'd finished their meals they were having a hilarious time tossing her bread rolls – each of which she downed in a single gulp. While a dragon's natural diet was meat, marrow, and whatever plant foods remained in the stomachs of their kills, Bernadette's human mind had an appreciation for veggies, potatoes, and bread – and her draconic stomach didn't seem to object. She suspected dragons could eat anything, as long as they got enough protein – and calories.

It was this happy domestic scene that Andrion and Francois beheld, as they shimmered into existence on the road at the bottom of the farmyard. Andrion immediately bolted up the hill. He may have been horrified when his wife underwent her transformation, but he was eager to embrace her now, no matter what shape she was in. "Berni! Oh my love!" she lowered her head and he hugged it, stroking her smooth scales. Then he stood back again so they could speak together.

"When Papa told me what had happened I couldn't believe it," Andrion said. "This is wonderful news! All of my researches have turned up almost nothing on The Fireblood, let alone the power of dragon transformation. It's almost as if the records had been deliberately destroyed." Andi and Riki had mobbed him, and he scooped his little girl up off the ground to give her a hug and kiss while his son clung to his leg.

Erik got up from the table and joined them, while Francois was having a reunion with Christine and chucking Merelle under the chin. He'd been a bit repulsed when he'd first seen her, but he had to admit she was an appealing little creature – in a butt-ugly kind of way. Ekka was taking it all in with avid eyes, storing up her impressions. When she was released from her vow of silence on this issue, what a story she was going to have to tell! Umberth had not joined them tonight. Like every other young farm hand the Drakespring clan had had over the years, he preferred spending his evenings in the convivial company at the Bathing Maiden – where all the good-looking single women were to be found.

Erik picked Andi up, so that the five members of the clan, including the current largest and scaliest of the bunch, were gathered close together in a circle in the farmyard just east of the veranda. "I think you may be right, Andrion," Bernadette said seriously. "The dragon transformation ability would have been a closely guarded secret, and there was a dragon priest involved at that lost temple where we found the spell. Most likely the whole business was known only to those who served the dragons – the ability might have been a reward for their most trusted servants. I'm sure now that Sneyagflug lied, and the potion had nothing to do with getting the dragon spell – just enabling its effects. So if you can find the dragon spell for changing back, Andi should be able to get the whole thing. I hope it doesn't turn out that we also need a potion to enable it..."

Andrion leaned in to kiss Bernadette's scaly snout. "It won't matter if it does, love. We won't rest until we have you back again, no matter how long it takes." Bernadette couldn't smile, but she purred a little. Being a dragon was a pain in the butt, but at least she was in the bosom of her family. And soon she would have another family. The thought of it filled her with anxiety. Would motherhood of a brood of dragonlings leave her forever torn between the two forms?

The next morning Bernadette took Andi on a joyride. She worried that he might fall off; but he was coordinated and athletic for his age, and scrambled aboard her with no signs of hesitation. She flew him up over the Maiden and the land to the north and east of it as he whooped with excitement. Even his light weight made a difference in the effort it took to fly, and she marveled that Sneyagflug had been able to carry both her 120-pound human form and Erik's 250, along with all their luggage, for those thousands of miles across the width of the continent. He was that strong, yet she'd forced him to submit with a dragon spell.

As soon as she'd dropped her son off in the farmyard again she took off, headed for the hills to the east and some hunting. Flying with a load really worked up an appetite! There was no local dragon patrolling this area, probably because there were so many humans nearby, and she mused it might have been a better choice for her than her now-abandoned territory in Westmarch. But if Sneyagflug had been on the lookout for her near her home, he'd have caught her that much sooner.

As the days went by another appetite began to grow in Bernadette. Her eggs were approaching the stage where they must be fertilized, and her body was responding with a flood of hormones that had her panting with eagerness to receive Sneyagflug's cock once again. The differences between human and dragon when it came to sex seemed amazing to her, the only living being on Terris (or so she assumed) who had inhabited both forms. Humans certainly got a lot more fun out of it, and the sharing of pleasure deepened their love for one another. She didn't think dragons even knew what love was, though perhaps there was something like it that they felt for their young. She would soon see.

Bernadette gathered her men together while the children were elsewhere, to warn them that their time together was drawing to a close. "I can feel that my eggs are ripening," she said. "I'm going to be in the throes of insatiable lust pretty soon, not that I'm going to get any enjoyment out of satisfying it." A line appeared between Andrion's eyebrows, and she could tell that he was not enjoying contemplation of her situation, or of her imminent sexual liaison with the dragon. She moved on.

"Anyhow, I told Sneyagflug to come here for me when he had found a suitable nest for us. I'll be getting too heavy to fly in a week or so, then I'll be relying on him to bring me food. After the eggs are laid I'll be incubating them and turning them and so forth, and then when they hatch and we see that there are females among them, he's supposed to reveal the location of the Spell Wall with the spell to turn me human again. I promised him I would stay around until the babies are talking, supposedly a month after hatching. But I want you to go and acquire the dragon spell as soon as possible. So I'm going to try to fly back here with the information. Or else send Sneyagflug to tell you in person. One way or another, you should look for a dragon here in about six weeks' time."

They nodded solemnly. Only a little over ten weeks, and they might have their wife back for good. But it was going to be a long ten weeks.

Chapter 65: Northern Darkreach, Year Six

Her goodbyes said, Bernadette flew off into the sky with her dragon consort. As sad as she was to be leaving her human family for weeks, the hormones surging through her body had her burning with anticipation for their joining. As a married woman approaching middle age, she had not experienced anything like this in a long time – the mind-wiping, whole-body urgency that demanded sex, right now, and to hell with anything else.

How ironic that dragons, so much less equipped than humans to truly enjoy the sex act, should be so powerfully motivated to perform it. With what remained of her analytical mind, Bernadette supposed that without this the nearly-immortal buggers would never get around to knocking it out, and the race would perish. That was almost, in fact, what had happened.

They flew side by side, Sneyagflug seeming solicitous of her. She was, after all, his chance at passing his essence on to the next generation. He was cutting his speed to maintain pace with her, and they talked together as they flew northeast. Bernadette felt odd and uneasy with him. His deception was something she would never be able to forget, and this was in some ways an arranged marriage. But she felt she needed to be civil to him, at least – they were about to make babies together.

"The place I have prepared for our nesting is the best I have ever seen," Sneyagflug said, satisfaction in his tones. Together they spoke in the dragon tongue as a matter of course, though both of them were fluent in the common tongue as well.

"How is that?" Bernadette replied. She was learning more and more about the natural history of dragons as a result of being one, but her consort had become her teacher for the details personal experience could not supply. If she had been able to track Ehrgeizig down she supposed she might have learned much from him – but Sneyagflug was here beside her, and no other dragon she had found would even talk with her.

"It is in a cave complex near a volcano," he explained. "It stands far north, yet the rocks and streams of the area are warm. Many creatures flourish nearby, to provide us with food. And the nursery is so warm that you will not have to stay with the eggs at all times, but can leave to hunt." Hmm, Bernadette thought, her wings beating. Dragons were hot inside, their normal body temperature hotter than a human with a dangerously high fever. Yet they had no insulative fur or feathers, to prevent that heat from escaping. Their huge body size helped with this, as did their high metabolisms – which led to voracious appetites. It stood to reason dragon eggs needed a high incubation temperature.

"Sounds good, Sneyagflug," Bernadette replied. "I suppose there's no chance the volcano will erupt and bury us all in hot ash?" The larger dragon's wing beats continued for several seconds.

"The volcano is active, obviously, but it has only erupted a few times in the past several thousand years. It would be ill luck should it choose our arrival as the time for the next eruption."

She had no answer to that. The flight was tiring her, and hunger for food was rising – competing with her hunger for sex. After enduring it for a long while, Bernadette finally said "Sneyagflug, I must rest and eat. The eggs growing within me are demanding more food." That got him. Clearly he had studied all this at some time (probably in the unimaginably distant past), for he knew far more than he might be expected to know for a dragon who had never before mated.

They circled down in the northeastern quadrant of Iscandia, some dozens of miles to the southeast of Eisenstag. Snow covered the ground, but after the warming effort of flying all these miles the cold was welcome. "Rest, Schunmurte," Sneyagflug rumbled, "and I will bring us prey."

"Thank you," she said weakly, then thought to add "No humans!" He chuckled, a sound like an enormous stewpot on the boil.

"Fear not, little one! I do not eat your former kind."

Bernadette sat resting, and when she'd cooled off from the flight she began to feel a little chilled. Some short hair, at least, would have been useful. Mammals and birds could raise their hair or feathers to trap warm air next to the skin. Then she realized that her scales were rising slightly. It wasn't nearly as effective, but it provided some heat conservation.

The long northern dusk was falling when Sneyagflug returned –
lugging around two-thirds of a mammoth in his talons. By the gods!
The bloody carcass was partially charred, and the two of them
cooked it a little more before digging in. Bernadette presumed that he
had already eaten the rest of it, recouping the energy it had taken him
to kill it as well as reducing its carrying weight.

They gorged until only a few uncrackable long bones remained.
The head, and its enormous tusks, had not been included. The dragon
feeding paradigm of starve and gorge, not dissimilar from that of
primitive humans, left them both feeling logy and in need of time to
digest. In a moment that was almost tender, Bernadette licked blood
and gobbets of flesh from Sneyagflug's scales and he returned the
favor. Then the two of them curled up together for warmth, and fell
asleep.

This far north, and so close to the summer solstice, the sky
lightened before they had slept more than 3 or 4 hours. The two
dragons roused and continued their journey, both of them driven on
by an irresistible desire. They must mate again, and soon. They flew
over open water to an island north of the Darkreach mainland,
dominated by an enormous peak.

"Og Vulanz," Sneyagflug said. "Assuming it refrains from
blowing its top while we're here, it will be the birthplace of our
children." There was an edge of sarcasm in his voice. Evidently he
regarded her concerns about the volcano as foolish. He led her to the
cave he'd chosen, which was well up the mountainside – out of reach
of almost anything without wings. It had a broad porch, and a tapered
opening big enough to let her go more than 100 feet in, though he
would be unable to penetrate more than half that distance. Far above
them, Og Vulanz' peak spewed smoke into the air.

"This will do," Bernadette replied somewhat shortly. Without
the bond of shared pleasure, she was finding it hard to warm up to
Sneyagflug as she would have done with a human lover. There was
something mechanical about their relationship, a duty not a joy. Even
so, she found that hard-wired demand surging within her. She wanted
him, and was not going to wait much longer.

"Let's inspect the water supply, shall we?" Bernadette
suggested, launching herself down the mountain. Herds of some

unidentified four-footed grazers fled at her approach. At least there was an adequate supply of game. At the bottom of the peak an alluvial fan was cut through by a stream. Despite its heat, the upper reaches of Og Vulanz were clothed in snow. They were very far north, after all.

Still comfortably replete from gorging on mammoth, Bernadette landed with a thump, ignoring the fleeing prey, and bent her head to drink. The water was clear and cold, refreshing. She spotted salmon in the stream, and snatched one out with a lightning strike of her head, then tossed it up and swallowed it in one bite. She much preferred them cut into steaks and grilled with butter and herbs, but this wasn't bad…

Sneyagflug watched her enjoying herself with a curious feeling, one he had never really experienced before. She was so beautiful, so desirable. His body had responded to her with a surge of hormones that made him as eager for their mating as she was; but there was an element of the situation that engaged his intellect as well. Dragons were eternal, aging slowly if at all, and usually dying only by misadventure. They had a reputation for wisdom that mostly had to do with the fact they had thousands of years' more experience than any upstart human.

All a sham, Sneyagflug knew. The average member of his race was little more than a savage beast compared with even the least intellectually-gifted of humans. They had the power of conscious thought, of language, built into them by their creator; yet they failed to take advantage of it. They built nothing, they fought among themselves, they lived like wild predators. Other than their size and their long lives, they had little advantage over a smilodon.

Since he had met the *Fjurblut* some years back, only a short time after Tarragin had returned him to life, Sneyagflug had studied the humans much. They ruled this modern world he had awakened in, and with every passing year they seemed to be gaining control over more of it. If his people kept living as they did, they would soon be no more than a memory, and after that only a legend. A boogeyman for humans to use, to frighten their children into obedience. He and Schunmurte must somehow bring about a new race of dragons, one that would act together as a people, and use their minds for something besides outwitting prey.

Sneyagflug's reverie was interrupted when the lithe young object of his desire, finished playing in the stream's sparkling waters, turned to him with hunger in her eye. "It's time, O my lord," Bernadette said teasingly. Her desire threatened to engulf her, but it was he who must make the moves. He rested on all fours, facing her with wings folded along his back, and she lowered her head, extending her long tongue to lick him from the center of his chest, up as high along his neck as she could reach. Then she gently seized his neck in her jaws, pressing against the scales but not breaking the skin.

Yeow! Sneyagflug felt a rush of desire, and his penis broke from within his genital slit, getting longer and thicker by the moment. He might want to use his brain and think things through, but his body definitely had other ideas. A shudder engulfed him, causing Bernadette to look up at him in surprise. "Everything all right?" she asked.

"I want you," he rumbled, "but I want to please you also – in the way of humans."

Bernadette was touched. Maybe the old *drache* wasn't so bad after all. "I don't know whether it's possible for us to experience what humans do, made as we are," she warned him. "Aderos didn't put as much store by sexual pleasure when He made dragons. But I could try a few things, if you like…" What was this creature doing to him? Sneyagflug suspected that no dragon in living memory (and that was a *long* time) had experienced anything like this.

"Rise up on your hind legs, as if you were going to fly away," Bernadette instructed him. He obediently raised his head and neck up, forelegs off the ground, wings slightly spread – balancing on two legs and his tail. His cock jutted, red and glistening, from his oozing genital slit; and she wrapped her tongue around it. Bernadette judged that an inflexible mouth full of needle-sharp teeth was ill-designed for fellatio; but that long, prehensile tongue was a tool she wouldn't have minded having as a human.

Gliding and squeezing up and down the shaft, Bernadette brought her draconic consort to the brink in seconds. Wham, bam, oh look we have kids – that seemed to be the theory behind dragon sexuality. Perhaps because they had little in the way of social structure or culture, even though they were sentient beings, they didn't need anything more?

Sneyagflug roared, and Bernadette released his member – falling back onto her haunches. It was no use, her urgency was too great. She needed to get that cock inside her and fertilize those eggs, or her instincts were going to drive her insane. He lowered himself onto all fours again, huffing and panting as curls of steam rose from his nostrils. His eyes were on fire.

"I don't think it's going to work, Sneyagflug. Dragons are not humans, and we are here only to bring about the next generation. Come on and fuck me." She expected him to be on her like a chicken on a torchbug, but he surprised her.

"No, Schunmurte," he rasped. "Not yet. Lie on your back as you did before, and I will try something."

Oh? The tension, the hot desire to be filled up with dragon sperm, was an unending pressure. But Bernadette's human curiosity got the better of her. She folded her wings tight and rolled over onto her back, then spread her hind legs to expose her gaping cloacal opening. Sneyagflug lowered his head on its long, powerful neck down between her legs, and extended his own long tongue.

He explored the area around her opening, tasting a musk that raised his desire to a fever pitch. It was not quite as overpowering as what she had been doing with her tongue, but he still felt in danger of depositing his sperm in an un-useful spot. He dipped the tip of his tongue into the opening, and began working it around the inside. It was not smooth in there, but had bumps and ridges within it; and when his tongue found one particular ridge and slithered along its inner side, she roared.

Fire exploded in Bernadette's mind. She couldn't believe it! The sensation was like the most powerful orgasm she had ever had as a human, but it seemed to go on for an unbelievably long time. Dragon anatomy apparently had hidden surprises! Concerned about her reaction, Sneyagflug removed his tongue and watched her in anxiety. This allowed her brain to resume functioning. Surely his cock was longer than his tongue – why had it not reached this spot during their previous encounter?

Perhaps it was the angle… "That was wonderful, Sneyagflug!" she assured him, since he seemed so worried. She had to remember that this ancient and enormous creature with whom she was coupling was a very recent virgin. "Now I want your cock inside me…" (the phrase doesn't translate well from the dragon tongue). Sneyagflug had recovered his equanimity and approached her eagerly, on two legs as before with his cock like a snake coiling in front of him, pushing inside her.

"Further, further…" Bernadette gave instruction. She'd never been shy about doing so, and found it maximized her enjoyment more often than not. "Can you lift the tip up a little?" she asked, looking up at him. His head was several feet above hers, helping to balance him so he didn't crush her with his weight. Unlike human males, who are playing with their penises before they can walk or talk, Sneyagflug had only the slightest acquaintance with his. It did duty only for transferring sperm, as egg-layers don't urinate. For most of his long, long life it had been tucked away, unnoticed.

"I think so…" he groaned.

Bernadette felt it move inside her. "Yes, yes, a little further up, that's it, YES!" she roared, as he hit the magic spot and began moving slightly back and forth. She lifted her heavy lower body up on her powerful hind legs, pushing with her tail, and began humping in rhythm with Sneyagflug's thrusts, each one brushing that ridge and sending a fresh wave of ecstasy through her body. He withstood a few seconds of this, then roared and shuddered as he released his load of semen with a feeling that was indescribable and wonderful beyond belief.

Sneyagflug collapsed for a moment on his consort's body, utterly wrung out and unable to string two thoughts together. Never had he had such an experience in his long life! Her struggles quickly roused him, though, and he heaved himself to his hind feet and backed off, walking like a human for a few paces until he could drop to all fours again as his penis shriveled and returned to its usual resting place. Bernadette remained lying on her back, her dorsal ridges pressing into the soft soil.

Sneyagflug nudged her gently with his snout when a minute had gone by and she hadn't moved. "Schunmurte, are you all right?" he rumbled. She sighed.

"Fine, fine. That was fantastic! I've never experienced anything like it." He was pleased. In some odd way, he felt he was in competition with her human lovers, her "husbands." A human concept that had somehow wandered into the dragon tongue.

"Nor have I," he said. "This sex human style is something I think might catch on if more learned of it." She detected a sardonic note.

"I'm just going to lie here for another minute," Bernadette told him. "I want to let your seed sink in and fertilize these eggs. I can feel them crying out for it." Crouching near her, Sneyagflug rested his head tenderly on her belly and purred.

During the days that followed, Bernadette found herself feeling surprisingly content. She missed her husbands and her children, but so much of her attention was taken up with the growing life inside her. She felt both weak and ravenous, and Sneyagflug was solicitous beyond belief. From hating him and wishing him dead for his perfidy, she was coming to feel fond of him. Perhaps this was as close as dragons ever got to human love. He hunted the area around the mountain, coursing far and wide in his search for meat. Some he ate, some he brought to her, and some carcasses he stashed in an ice cave near the summit. They'd be needing those later on, when the eggs hatched.

The feeling reminded her very much of pregnancy, except that she had no breasts to swell, and no living child stirred within her. Living baby dragons would start stirring inside the eggs soon after they were laid. In fact it was only nine days after fertilization that Bernadette felt contractions begin and knew it was time to lay. The nest they'd prepared was on the floor of an alcove within the cave, big enough for her to curl up in comfortably though too small to admit Sneyagflug.

He'd brought her mouthful after mouthful of grasses from the surrounding island, and Bernadette had busied herself tucking them into place to form a layer of insulative padding over the dirt of the cave floor. The surrounding walls were slightly warm. Other than this project she'd had little to do but think in the last week, and she'd done little enough of that. Instead she'd spent hours drifting as if in a trance, draconic hormones working to keep her calm – she guessed later.

Her wings folded tight to her body, Bernadette crawled into the nesting space and squatted, panting, as convulsions moved smoothly across her abdomen. This was not much like trying to push a human child through an opening in her pelvic girdle smaller than the baby's head. The eggs had developed suspended in a clear, slippery fluid, which served to lubricate their passage through her cloaca to the outside world. In addition to that they were far smaller proportionately to her body size, in comparison with a human newborn.

Once the first one had come out, the others followed in quick succession. After more than an hour, Bernadette felt a great lightening of her abdomen, and an empty sensation that told her there were no more inside. Moving with the greatest of care, she crawled out of the alcove and rotated in the large space beyond to see what she'd wrought.

Each egg was the size of a small human baby, but cylindrical with symmetrically rounded ends. Dragonkind had clearly adopted the reptilian rather than the avian approach to eggs – besides the shape, they were leathery rather than hard-shelled. There were nineteen of them. Wow. If Bernadette had repeatedly produced a child as soon as it were possible after the last one, managed to avoid the perils of pregnancy and childbirth each time, and had done this throughout the thirty years a human woman was usually fertile, she might remotely have had this many babies. Now she was going to do it in a few months.

Clearly if dragons, which she presumed had eons of fertile life, were all to care for their young as humans did, the world would be up to its eyeballs in dragons and the only limit to their population would be the food supply. She had a good idea of which large animals on Terris might go to feed them, too. Yet dragons had essentially been extinct for thousands of years before Tarragin returned from his pocket universe to resurrect them.

And they were well on the way to extinction again, except for Sneyagflug's nefarious plan to turn her into a breeding female. Well, how could she object? Extinction of sentient creatures as strange and magnificent as dragons was something she would not let happen if there was anything she could do about it, and she was sure she'd have felt the same even if she were not fireblood.

They had talked in the evenings before sleeping, snuggled together, and she knew much more of his mind now, understood that this scheme was for him what killing Lord Karazin had been for her. She had feared that humans would be killed or enslaved by vampires, and Sneyagflug feared dragons would disappear from the planet. He was a dragon visionary, hoping to save his kind by guiding a new generation toward a new way of doing things – a way more like the human way. She had come to realize that he was indeed no ordinary dragon – perhaps a genius among them – and no longer bore him any resentment for his trickery.

Now that she'd been relieved of her load, Bernadette was feeling restless. She hadn't been in the air in almost a week, and was longing for the freedom of flight. As she was thinking of this, Sneyagflug returned to the ledge with a pair of those creatures she and Erik had fought, down on the mainland of Darkreach, a few weeks ago. They didn't look as if they had much meat on them.

Bernadette went to greet her consort, eyes glowing, purring slightly. He took one look at her and knew. "They came! How many?" he asked eagerly.

"Nineteen," she replied with pride in her voice.

"Nineteen!" he crowed. "Excellent! That is more than usual for a first-time breeding female. How many years have you?"

"Twenty-nine," she responded. "I'm about twice the age at which human females normally become capable of breeding."

"And you've borne two young, as well," he mused. "As a dragon," he explained, "you are little bigger than the minimum size for breeding. It is more about size than age, and we keep growing throughout our lives. I am older than many of those lesser dragons Tarragin called back from death. But whatever the reason, you have produced a clutch as big as a female half again your size might do. I am proud of you." He nuzzled her neck.

Bernadette glowed at the compliment. What was coming over her? "So now what?" she asked him, trying to stay businesslike. She was *not* falling in love with this great, big, duplicitous, red dragon.

"We need to keep the eggs at a uniform warm temperature and turn them every day, so the dragonlings don't get stuck to the insides. The temperature in the nest now is warm enough, but at night you may need to curl around them. By sleeping in front of the entrance to the alcove I can help to heat the space and prevent heat from escaping."

"Then, either of us can look after the eggs during the day while the other one hunts?" she asked. Sneyagflug nodded. "If you want to go, I'll eat those" – he nodded with his head towards the spindly-looking predator corpses "and stay here to watch the eggs. I think I would like to just spend some time looking at them," he added, a smile in his voice. "Schunmurte, you have made my dream come true." Bernadette nodded to him, and flew out into the summer afternoon.

Chapter 66: Drakespring Farm, Year Six

"Now, Andi!" Andrion directed. His tall five-year-old son, clad *cap a pie* in gleaming armor, raised both hands and a joined bolt of fire and lightning flew toward the archery butt in a corner of the farmyard, punching a hole in it. The straw caught fire and Andrion hurried over to extinguish it with the bucket of water sitting nearby, as his son sagged in temporary exhaustion. Andi had natural talent for magic, both of his biological parents being Galise – even if he was born in Iscandia. But at his age, these high-level destruction spells were taxing his capacity to the utmost. He'd need to down a potion to recoup his magical energy in anything less than several minutes.

"That was amazing, Papa!" the boy gasped, admiring the daylight he could see through the fist-sized hole. His father's technique for combining dual-wielded destruction spells for a completely new and lethal effect had come to him with surprising ease. Likewise, Andrion was teaching him to fine-tune his spellcasting so that the effect could be concentrated like an arrow or spread over a broader area. Everything he tried, he seemed to grasp almost immediately. Compared with the slow hours of practice required to become adept with bow or edged weapons, battle magic was a snap for him.

Andrion's mouth formed a grim line as he shuddered mentally at the thought. His adorable, sweet boy was being transformed into a deadly killer. He hated what he was doing, hated the necessity. But Andi was their one hope for getting Berni back, and he was *not* taking the child into an aptrgangr-infested dungeon, likely presided over by a dragon priest, without giving him every protection it was in his power to provide.

We're stealing his childhood, Andrion thought morosely, destroying his innocence. He had sympathized with Berni's desire to help Sneyagflug try to prevent the extinction of dragonkind, had assisted in the effort. But the dragon's callous disregard for the effects his plan had had on Berni and her family filled him with a cold rage. And now the old monster was off making babies with his wife. He wanted to kill him.

Erik had been looking on, in awe that his little son had more magical ability than he did. Not that he'd ever really pursued it. He was ideally constructed for physically overpowering his enemies, and so far it had worked very well for him. Seeing that Andi was physically if not magically recovered from his effort, he guided him by the shoulder, over to the still-smoldering target for a closer look.

"That was a pretty big hole you made, wasn't it?" Erik asked gently. Andi stood on tiptoe and put his hand through the opening, getting soot on his bracers. "Think about what that would look like if it were a person." Andi looked stricken, his active imagination painting gory details. Life on a farm had a way of teaching you early about blood and sex.

"Eeeww!" he exclaimed.

"That's right, eeeww," Erik rumbled. "That's why you need to treat these spells as if they were a very sharp sword, or an arrow," he went on. Andi had experience using both blades and bows now, though his extreme youth made him not much of a formidable opponent for anything bigger than he was. "These are deadly," Erik said, wanting to be sure the lesson was not forgotten, "and deadly means final. They are much more dangerous than the dragon spells Mama taught you. When somebody is killed, they're not coming back. Just like that chicken yesterday."

When hens got too old to lay, or surplus cockerels big enough to eat, they went to the chopping block. Andreas had witnessed this fact of life since he was Riki's age, so he knew what death was. He looked up at Erik solemnly with his big brown eyes, a copy of his father's and grandmother's. "I'll never use it except on enemies that mean to kill me, Papa" he promised, reciting a mantra that had been drummed into him since he'd first picked up a weapon. Erik patted him on the shoulder, then crouched and enfolded the boy in a bear hug. Like Andrion, he had misgivings about turning a five-year-old into a deadly fighter; but with his typical upbeat attitude toward life, he was sure it would all work out. Andi was a great kid!

Andi's sparring sessions with Fjuri had been put on hold for the duration of the crisis. Lifa and Bjorn, the most intimate of their friends, had been informed of the true situation – but everyone else in the Waterdon area, even Drelos and Lev down at the Maiden, believed that Bernadette was off on a quest that had required she go it alone. In a way, it was true.

Instead, Erik and Andrion were working with Andi each day, teaching him ways in which to repel attack from adult-sized foes. They expected aptrgangr, including some higher-level ones, and he was being schooled mostly in evasion tactics. When you're fighting for your life you need to play on your advantages. For Andrion, it was his abilities with battle magic and his strong right arm. For Erik, his dazzling combination of strength, speed, and skill with weapons. For their son, his small size and agility were what they hoped would carry him safely through whatever this putative dungeon had to offer.

He learned to dodge, climb, and hide. Dungeons were full of the sort of decorative elements that could conceal a small boy. And in a pinch, he had the bow Bernadette had made for Anja before he was born. It was well made and just the right size, and he'd been practicing with it for hours every day. It didn't pack a lot of punch, but being riddled with half-sized arrows could be a serious inconvenience for any foe. And Andi now hit the target just about every time. It might be his mother's talents coming to the fore.

"It should be pretty soon, now," Andrion remarked to Erik later as they sat out on the veranda enjoying the warm summer evening. Waterdon's climate in the summer frequently brought showers, but tonight the weather was fine and they were sitting, feet up, gazing out a starry sky above the river and mountains to the east. "She's out there somewhere," he went on thoughtfully. This was the direction in which their beloved had flown, when she last bid them farewell.

"We'll get her back, Andrion," Erik replied softly. "You know we will."

Chapter 67: Og Vulanz, Year Six

Bernadette was asleep, curled around her clutch, with Sneyagflug sprawled sleeping across the entryway to their nesting alcove. On this northern mountainside, even high summer came with cold nights. Something woke her, and her mother's senses immediately began questing for the source. Small creatures similar to shria would be happy to creep into their cave and gnaw on their eggs, and they had killed several such.

There it was again. Not an intruder – one of the eggs was rocking gently back and forth, and a high-pitched chirping was emanating from it. Sneyagflug had not mentioned this detail! From the depth of his knowledge he must have gathered information on the subject of dragon reproduction somehow, but perhaps his sources had omitted this. Dragons could see in near darkness, similarly to cats. A curious ability, since it was useless for night hunting at the altitudes they usually cruised. Here in the cave only the faintest of red glows could be seen, reflected off the cloud cover from the volcano's constant inner fire; but it was enough.

Bernadette strained her eyes, watching the moving egg. There, a dark spot appeared on the surface! She uncoiled herself carefully, wriggling out of the alcove without touching any of the eggs. "Sneyagflug!" she called softly. She nudged him in the back, as he was curled up sleeping with his belly (not to mention his talons, teeth, and fire-breathing mouth) pointed toward the cavern's entrance.

The big red dragon was considerably quicker to arouse than either of her human husbands. In an instant he was on his feet, wings half unfolding, head winding here and there like a serpent's as he searched for any threat to Schunmurte and their brood. He saw nothing. Turning to face his consort, he asked "What is it, dear one?" This adoption of terms of endearment was a development since she'd laid her eggs, and Bernadette wasn't sure how to take it.

She had no real personal experience of the relationships between dragons, and only Sneyagflug's word for the way it had been throughout their history as a people. But it seemed he had been infected by his observation of, and contact with, humans. If these ideas were transmissible to the next generation, a new era had dawned for both species.

"One of the eggs seems to be hatching," Bernadette told him.

"Let me see!" he cried, as excited as any human father who'd just been told of the birth of his child.

"You'll have to get out of the way before I can let you in, dear," she pointed out with asperity. Humoring him in his notion that they were living as a human couple seemed the route to the best outcome for her and their children.

He hastily backed out of the way, allowing her to come out into the larger area of the cavern. Then he eagerly squeezed in to see. The bulk of his body would not pass the "doorway," but he could easily crane his long neck inside to survey the clutch. He immediately spotted the one that was moving, on the surface of which an egg tooth had already carved a notch. He'd possibly neglected mentioning egg teeth to Schunmurte. Having a consort who was a virgin, with no prior experience of raising a brood, was one thing. Despite his age he was in the same situation. But her additional lack of prior experience in being a dragon was something that often brought him up short.

He gently seized the egg in his mouth, his sharp teeth shredding the leathery covering and enabling their firstborn to emerge. The little dragon, no bigger than a human baby but a lot more coordinated, poked its head up and looked around in the dim light. It saw its father for the first time and chirped appealingly. Sneyagflug's heart melted. Pride and triumph and an indescribable nurturing instinct welled up in him. How could dragon fathers down through the ages have turned their backs on this?

All around the clutch, eggs were rocking and their inhabitants chirping, talking back and forth among themselves. Their brains would not grow into the language that had been built into them for another few weeks, but they already knew how to communicate with each other. Sneyagflug became aware that Schunmurte was crowding him from behind, trying to crane her neck around the bulk of his body. "What's going on?" she demanded, "Did it hatch?"

"We have one chick," he told her jubilantly, "and the others are coming."

"Let me see!"

Pleased by her eagerness, ever convinced in the back of his mind that his beautiful consort was only living out the days of her captivity while longing for her return to the life he had stolen from her, Sneyagflug backed out and let her come in to see. "By the gods!" Bernadette said, "They are so… cute!" Her own heart melted at the sight of her babies as they emerged from their eggs. They were by and large miniatures of the adults, but their heads and eyes were bigger in proportion, their faces shorter.

In designing humans, who must patiently care for their young for many years before they can fend for themselves, the creator had wired in responses that would turn those humans, especially female ones, into gooey blobs of motherly love at the sight of certain characteristics of the young. He or She had done their work too well – human females would fall in love with, and mother, babies of almost any species with nearly the same obsessive care they gave to their own. How much more, then, must Bernadette respond to these adorable, clumsy youngsters who had come from her own body, as they staggered around the alcove meeping, peering about them in the dim light in search of nourishment?

Bernadette regretted her non-mammalian body. These babies she could not take to her breast. Of course the idea of trying to nurse nineteen of them was absurd in any case. But instinct came to her aid. She had eaten a large meal not long before lying down for the night, and she now heaved and regurgitated the partially digested remains onto the straw covering the alcove floor. By now all the eggs had hatched, and the youngsters eagerly set to devouring what their mother had provided.

Oh, gross! Bernadette thought, appalled. If she let her human mind think very hard about what her dragon body was doing, she could not but be repelled. She shrugged it off. How else could a dragon mother provide a meal that her just-hatched infants could eat and digest? She wouldn't be surprised to learn that her digestive enzymes mixed with the regurgitated food imparted some other benefits to the young, just as breast milk did for mammal babies. Bernadette backed out of the opening, allowing Sneyagflug to return. "I think they've all hatched, now," she told him. "Why don't you poke your head in there and throw up for them, while I go eat some more?"

In the morning light, they allowed the little ones to come out of the alcove a short way. They still paddled like kittens or puppies, staggering around on their stubby little legs. Even adult dragons were far from graceful on the ground. But the danger of their toddling off the precipice that fronted the cavern was real enough. Sneyagflug spent most of the earlier part of the day hauling boulders from the mountain slopes below, which Bernadette nudged into place to form a barrier – a playpen, as it were, where their babies could flounder around and practice their locomotion skills, while prevented from coming all the way out to the ledge.

From boulders the dragon parents switched over to food runs, hunting live prey while they hoarded their supply of frozen carcasses for an emergency. Sneyagflug soon realized that his idealistic goal of raising their entire brood to full sentience and flight was a hell of a lot more work than he'd dreamed. The common approach in the time he'd been born in, with females raising their babies unaided, was to put down as much food as was possible and let them fight it out until only the largest, strongest dragonlings had survived. This as much as anything had led to their extinction thousands of years ago, as the female chicks were usually smaller and weaker to begin with and few survived. He himself was one of three survivors from his mother's clutch of twelve, all male.

By late afternoon Bernadette and Sneyagflug had eaten and regurgitated half a dozen meals each, and it seemed as if the chicks were growing and developing before their eyes. Bernadette was keeping an eagle eye on them, picking out individual characteristics, and already beginning to assign names to them in her mind. Following the usual convention of three syllables (representing two or three words), she called this one with the dappling of green scales down its flanks Zuunenwalt (Forest Sun), another with a body and tail longer than its fellows Langekiind (Long Child).

And those who seemed to come out the losers in the scrum for the slimy delicacies deposited at frequent intervals by their parents, she took aside and made sure they got their share. Just because a kid entered the world with a slight disadvantage, didn't mean they

409

should be thrown away. From her human perspective, such children should be given extra help in order to catch up with the others. Sneyagflug marveled, and approved.

The two of them sat in the entryway to their cavern, behind the impromptu rock wall, and admired their brood as they played, engaged in mock battles, searched the floor for overlooked scraps of food, or slept. "Sneyagflug, they are adorable," Bernadette said formally. "Thank you. I was very angry when you tricked me into this, but now I am glad that you did." He rumbled deep in his throat and nuzzled her affectionately.

"But I need to know something, and I don't know how to find the answer by myself," Bernadette continued.

"What is it, my dear?" he asked diffidently. He'd been a large, powerful, and dominant dragon for many years, but nothing in his life had boosted his self-esteem quite like acquiring Schunmurte as a consort and producing this large, beautiful brood of dragonlings.

"How do you tell the boys from the girls?" she asked. Oh.

This was it. He had promised her the information she needed to return to her human form when their brood had hatched and contained female chicks. It would probably take her human family days or weeks to acquire the dragon spell – it was buried deep in an ancient Norse fortress similar to Bergenfest, where the dragon spell to effect the transformation from human to dragon had been hidden. And she had promised to stay until their children were speaking.

But then she would go back to her other family, return to her tiny, weak and mortal human form and leave him all alone. To raise their babies, he realized. He would be busy for years, teaching them all they needed to know. Perhaps they could even develop techniques for cooperative hunting together. This thought bolstered Sneyagflug, though pain stabbed his heart at the thought of her departure. He was a misfit among dragonkind, and he felt that only she, more human than dragon but a little of both, truly understood him.

"Determining the sex of dragon chicks at this age requires a careful eye," he told her, waxing pedantic as he struggled to hide the hurt. "You can see much from the crest atop the head. The boys' are longer and spikier, see?" Sneyagflug gestured carefully with his head to a little red dragon who was standing, head up, watching them alertly in case they might be feeling nauseated. "That's a little male, and this one over here" – a stockier dragonling with a purplish cast to her red scales – "is a female." Sneyagflug, after looking around at the milling babies, selected one and lifted it carefully in his jaws over the top of the rock barrier. As he set it down on the cavern floor, it tumbled over onto its back, tiny wings flapping and talons erect, and squalled at him in protest.

"Sometimes the crest is not enough to be sure. Some females may have a little more than others, some males less. But the shape of the cloacal opening is definitive." The shrieking dragonling quieted as its mother blew a murmur of Calm over it. "See," Sneyagflug went on, "this is a female. Her cloacal opening is like a tiny circle." The little one lay there on her back, relaxed, as he selected another from the enclosure and displayed it on its back. "Here's that little boy. We already knew he was a boy from his crest, but look at his vent." Bernadette peered at the baby from the other side. It was a slit. No doubt there was a tiny penis inside there, biding its time for some long-distant year when it might arise and father a new generation.

Sexing the brood took them the rest of the available daylight to achieve. The little ones kept escaping, and they were not as yet all that distinct from each other. How many had they counted more than once? Finally Bernadette resorted to carefully stepping over the barrier and, as they determined the gender of each one, she deposited it gently in the alcove where they'd been born. A freshly regurgitated meal and her own massive body kept them in there, until eventually all Nineteen had been accounted for.

"Nine!" Sneyagflug seemed stunned. "I was hoping for five at most. This is most amazing."

"Perhaps it was the higher incubation temperature," Bernadette suggested, causing him to look at her in puzzlement. "I read it in a book," she explained. "There's a reptile in tropical climes that piles a bunch of composting vegetation onto their nests. The number of babies that hatch male or female depends on how warm it was while they were developing in the eggs. With you and I both helping to keep them warm at night…"

Sneyagflug was flabbergasted. This was certainly information to pass along to his young, especially the girls. It was they who would be the future hope of the dragon race, and he needed to provide them with everything he could to assist them in that effort. He was torn from these musings by a sharp look from his consort. But her words were gentler than her look. "I need to know, dear. I can't be Schunmurte forever."

Chapter 68: Drakespring Farm, Year Six

Erik was working at the forge, hammering a breastplate. During Berni's long absence, which was becoming harder and harder to explain to their business partners at Valkyrie, Erik's skills had increased with daily practice as he struggled to keep up with their obligations. Alessia, older than Berni by several years and now the mother of a girl Sintra's age, had cut back on the amount of smithing she was doing to enjoy motherhood. Valkyrie needed the Drakesprings' output to meet the demand at their shop.

Andi watched, fascinated. He was a bright boy, interested in everything and anxious to acquire new abilities. He found smithing and similar crafting activities less unsettling than the combat skills his papas had been training him in the past six weeks. Suddenly he felt a whoosh of wind and looked up to see a red dragon descending from the afternoon sky. "Mama!" Erik laid his hammer down and went out to look as Bernadette/Schunmurte touched down a few yards away.

"Andi," he told his son, "go get Papa Andrion!"

The boy jumped to do his bidding, yelling "Hi, Mama!" as he ran off.

Bernadette turned her serpentine head to watch him go, fond amusement washing through her at his manic energy. Then she turned to look at Erik. The afternoon was warm, and he'd been working shirtless with only a leather apron to protect him from sparks. Perspiration was running down his forehead, his blond hair hanging in damp strands, and he looked good enough to eat. Though, not in her current form.

Bernadette's human libido, much more a thing of mind than of body, flourished as strongly as ever. But without backing from her dragon body, she hadn't made any further attempts to engage Sneyagflug in sex. Even if he'd been willing and able, she thought it would be a bad idea. That dragon "magic spot" thing might be addicting, and she had no intention of leaving her human family to live forever after with Sneyagflug and their brood, no matter what.

She'd had to spend an entire day bringing in game and watching the babies in shifts, so that he would have enough food on hand (including their stash of frozen corpses, now defrosting inside the cavern) to feed himself and the little ones while she was gone for the time it would take her to bring the location of the dragon spell to Andrion and Erik. Luckily she'd caught a tail wind coming over, and had made good time without exhausting herself. In the time it had taken for the eggs to hatch she'd completely recovered her draconic fighting trim, and was strong and fleet once more.

Arguably it would have made more sense to have Sneyagflug run this errand. He could fly faster than she could, and she would need less food to eat while he was gone. But this was something she had to do for herself, had to know that the information had been delivered and was being acted on. Besides, she had a secondary purpose.

Erik hugged her head and stroked her neck as she nuzzled him and purred. "Oh love," she said, "if you only knew how good you look."

"You're beautiful too," he murmured. "But I can't wait until you have tits again…" She snaked out her long tongue and stuck it in his ear, which caused him to jump back crying "Augh!"

At that moment Andi returned, still on the run, with Andrion following close behind. He came to stand in front of Bernadette and jumped up and down as if he were on springs, saying "Mama! Mama!" She lowered her head for him to hug, and after he'd done so he clambered up over the top of it and scrambled up her neck to rest just forward of her shoulders. There he sat, looking pleased as punch.

The rest of the family had been roused too, and soon Christine and Francois, Riki, and even Ekka with Merelle came trooping out. Umberth might live with them but he didn't really see himself as part of the family, and left them their privacy while he continued his farm chores. It was high summer, and keeping up with the weeds in the fields was almost a full-time job in itself.

"I can't stay long," Bernadette explained regretfully. "The baby dragons have hatched, and nine of them are girls so I'm off the hook with Sneyagflug and he gave me the location of the dragon spell to turn me human again. But I promised him I'd stay with them until they're old enough to talk, and meanwhile he's trying to care for nineteen ravenous youngsters by himself. So I need to get back there right away. Andrion? Do you have a map on you?"

Though he wasn't planning any trips until they left to find the dragon spell, Andrion had taken to carrying his personal Agena map with him at all times, folded up inside his shirt. He pulled it out. Not for the first time, Bernadette deeply regretted the lack of useful hands, let alone fingers, in this form. "Could you lay it on the ground, please?" she said. Then she extended her tongue delicately and touched it to a spot somewhat northwest of Grabentief, in an area that had no markings.

Bernadette had to pull her tongue back in to speak again. Then it occurred to her, that given the nature of magic maps, there might be a better approach. "I'm doing it wrong," she said. "Just hold the map in your hands, Andrion." He picked it up again, looking at her questioningly. "According to Sneyagflug, and I believe him, the dragon spell is to be found on a Spell Wall deep inside the ancient underground tomb of Gunderthal. It's located between Grabentief and Mzalendtham, and a little north of either of them."

Andrion studied the map as a symbol like a dragon's claw appeared in the spot she'd described. "It worked!" he crowed. He hoped that fact meant that the location was a true one, though he supposed the place itself could exist, could even contain a Spell Wall, without being what they sought. He didn't trust Sneyagflug any farther than he could throw him, which was no distance at all.

Andrion came forward to hug Bernadette's head and plant a kiss on her warm, scaly snout. "We'll leave just as soon as we can pack up our supplies and make a few arrangements," he promised her. "You're almost back again!" She nuzzled his shoulder.

"Not for a few weeks yet, love," she said. "But I want the spell as soon as I can get it. Erik, I'm guessing you don't have your map on you…" He grinned at her. He wasn't wearing much besides trousers, apron, and boots. "Back in a minute!" he said, and dashed toward the house.

When Erik had returned with his map Bernadette checked it. Oh, she recalled. Their trip to Darkreach had not produced any landmarks. Rats! "Sneyagflug and I have made ourselves a nest for our babies in a cavern about halfway up the slopes of Og Vulanz, on the island north of Darkreach. It's on the western side. I want you all to come find me there after you get the dragon spell."

415

Both Erik and Andrion exclaimed at once, "There!"

Now both of them had received a quest and a quest marker had appeared on their maps, so they knew where to find her. But knowing where to go and getting there were two different things. As Bernadette stood trying to think of a solution to the problem, Andrion said "We can fast-travel to Coldstein, find a ship, and sail to your island from there in a couple of days. Then once we've given you the dragon spell, we can just fast-travel home."

"Wonderful!" Bernadette said. "You'll have to watch out for volcanic activity and some very odd wildlife, but it should be possible to find the place with your maps. I'll see you then!"

Hasty goodbyes were said then, and Bernadette was in the air not half an hour after she'd landed. She was beginning to get a little hungry, but if that became too much of a problem she could pick off a deer or something small on the way back. Nothing too heavy for flying on. As she soared through the air heading northeast, her heart was alive with excitement. Soon she might have hands again!

Chapter 69: North Central Iscandia, Year Six

Andrion, Erik, and Andreas fast-traveled to Grabentief, a spot on Bernadette's original map from the time Andrion and Lifa had accompanied her to that area hunting the Staff of Zauber more than seven years previously. Then they began trekking across country. It shouldn't be a very long walk.

Andi was clad in armor from head to toe, and Erik had had his friend Garimund, the court wizard up at Wyrmshalla, place interwoven enchantments on it to increase its armor value and boost the boy's health and stamina. Berni hadn't bothered enchanting Andi's armor in the past, as he was just using if for sparring with his friend Fjuri – and the boys regularly outgrew each set within a few months after it was made.

Andi was fizzing with excitement. He was going on a *real quest*! With his papas, the most famous, invincible warriors in Iscandia, for companions. Sure it was a little scary, thinking about going up against aptrgangr and walking skeletons and who knows what; but he was a bold boy for all his level-headed thoughtfulness, just like his father.

They had not been walking long before it became apparent that either Andi was going to run all the way to Gunderthal, or the entire party would be moving at a pace possible for a five-year-old to walk. So Erik swung him up onto his armored shoulders, and they continued on their way. "Keep an eye out for danger, scout," Erik warned him. "We're counting on you."

Andi had loved riding on Papa Erik's shoulders since before he could remember, and as he'd gotten bigger the view had only gotten better. He took the responsibility he'd been tasked with seriously, and was the first to spot the smilodon that was lurking a few dozen feet from the nearly invisible trail they were following. He squeezed Erik's helmeted head with his armored thighs and bent down to hiss "There's a smilodon over there!" as he pointed.

"Thanks," Erik murmured back, then spoke quietly to Andrion. "Smilodon at ten o'clock…" They halted and Erik drew his bow, scanning the waste. There it was! Little hampered by the armored boy riding his shoulders, Erik fired, striking the cat in the shoulder. Then Andrion knocked it flying with a blast of lightning.

"Awesome!" Andi squealed, impressed by the competent way his papas had dealt with the threat – and proud that he had been the one to spot it first. He'd seen his parents in action a few times, but in the two years his memories covered, there'd been little enough danger around their sleepy farm.

The party resumed their trek, Andrion checking the map from time to time to make sure they were on course. This ruin was out in the middle of nowhere, and it wasn't surprising that he'd never come across it. In the seven years since he and Berni had gotten together, he'd discovered that his belief before then, that after ten years in Iscandia he'd been everywhere and seen it all, was naïve. The place had a thousand hidden secrets, waiting to surprise you.

They very nearly missed it. Unlike some of Iscandia's ruins, marked by stone pathways through a series of arches or some similar feature that could be seen from a distance, Gunderthal was one of those sunken tombs – reached by walking down a circular stone staircase into a pit, then entering through a door. Without the map, they might have passed by fifty feet away and never have noticed it was there.

The heavy oaken door was locked, the mechanism rusted shut. No one had been here for a long time. But Andrion had spellcraft at his disposal, and over the years since he'd become Magister of the Academy his studies had unraveled more mysteries than the making of magic maps and the summoning of hot baths. A glow surrounded the locking mechanism, then they heard a faint grinding sound and the door swung open with a creak. The hinges were as rusty as the lock.

Erik had let Andi down off his shoulders before they descended the staircase, and he now took point with his bow while Andrion brought up the rear. As they stood in the entryway with the door behind them, Erik said quietly, "We're going to be very sneaky now. We don't want anybody to hear us coming. Can you do that Andi?" His son beamed at him. Sneaky and silent were two of his better tricks.

The entryway, flanked by large urns, gave out into a larger room with three doors leading out of it. Biers lined the walls on either side, with mummified corpses lying on them. Andi's eyes got wide. The smell in this place! It was if the air in here had been as dead as those warriors (he assumed that's what they were, from the armor they wore and the swords at their sides) for thousands of years.

Andi had never seen dead people before that he could recall, but he had seen lots of pictures of aptrgangr in the books Uncle Bjorn, his best friend Fjuri's papa, had made. Bjorn was the best artist he'd ever seen, and he had been a warrior before Fjuri was born so he knew what he was talking about. These guys (and some of them were women!) looked just like the aptrgangr in the books, except they were lying there and not moving. Then, as Andi and his papas moved further into the room, one of them did.

Erik's bow twanged and the aptrgangr, which had been roused from its eons-long slumber by the proximity of intruders, burst into flames before collapsing to the floor. He was fulfilling Berni's role on this expedition, killing by stealth before their enemies were even aware of their location. He might be one hell of a melee fighter, but a melee was something he did *not* want to get involved in with their son along on the quest.

Andrion had closed up the distance behind Andi, ready to shield him with his body or die defending the boy if that was what it took. Meanwhile Erik scanned the corpses laid out on their biers on either side of the room. Berni had shown him how it was sometimes possible to tell by looking, which of the mummified dead still possessed the ability to arise and fight for their long-departed masters.

Erik's daimonic bow had been enchanted by Bernadette with the Bane of the Undead enchantment years before. Not only did arrows shot from it set the target on fire, but when fighting undead it could sometimes cause an explosion that would damage any other undead in the vicinity. The perfect weapon for tombs, or vampire dens. He thought the corpse on the right at the end of the row looked suspicious, and put an arrow into it. It burst into flames, rising briefly before collapsing once more – this time permanently dead.

Erik retrieved his arrows from the corpses. Waste not, want not – and these were the best Iscandia had to offer, daimonic arrows crafted by his beloved. At the end of the row of catafalques the group drew together so that Andrion and Erik could have a discussion.

Which of the three doors should they take? "Might as well start on the left and work our way around," Andrion suggested. Nearly two decades of experience with places like this had taught him that most offered only one real route through the maze to the central burial chamber, where whichever head honcho had occasioned the building of the tomb would be laid to rest.

They tried the left door, and found it locked. Andrion quickly dealt with that, and inside was an unlocked chest. Andi's eyes got wide at the sight of the treasure inside – gold, jewels, and exotic weapons. But he had never wanted for anything in his short life, so it was more the setting than the value that impressed him. "Let's take the gold and jewels, and leave the rest," Andrion said. "We're going to need to hire a ship later…"

The second door led to a short corridor, then dead-ended in a medium-sized room that looked like it might have been a guard room. There was a long table with benches, plates, and other items from everyday life. After looking over the bookshelves Andrion tucked one of the books in his pack, but they left the rest untouched. The third door led them down a long hallway.

Erik, taking point again, halted abruptly. He gestured at a stone on the floor that seemed raised a bit above the others. Speaking very softly, he said to Andi "It's a trap! If you step on that stone I think arrows will come down out of the ceiling and shoot you." He gestured up to the stones above their heads, where Andi could see there was indeed a regular pattern of small holes. He followed carefully in Erik's footsteps as Erik stepped around the trap trigger, Andrion bringing up the rear.

At the end of the corridor it came to a bend, then opened out into a wide gallery with upper and lower levels. They could hear a creaking sound. Andi immediately spotted a walking skeleton carrying a bow, patrolling a stone bridge that ran from one side of the upper level to the other. He touched Erik's hand and pointed wordlessly.

Erik had been scanning for the source of the sound. It was convenient that walking skeletons hadn't yet figured out lubrication. You could hear them coming two rooms away. He picked that one off with an arrow that ignited it briefly even as it sent the creature flying in a shower of bones. With a small explosion, a second skeleton on the next bridge over also disintegrated.

The creaking sounds had ceased, and the trio crept carefully into the room. Stairs ran up and down, and on the floor below an aptrgangr with an axe was on patrol. Erik soon brought him to an end. They checked upstairs, then went down and out through double doors at the far end. And so it went. Andrion was beginning to feel a huge sense of relief at the progress they had made, and so far none of them had been in any danger whatsoever. Andreas didn't have a scratch, nor had he dissolved in fear like you might expect from some boys his age. Love and pride surged in his heart.

They were drawing closer to what Andrion was sure would be the main burial chamber, likely (considering the esoteric nature of the dragon spell they sought) the tomb of a dragon priest. Some, like one he and Berni had killed on a quest out near Sylvanian, remained awake – haunting their tombs with a terrible will that drove any who came there mad. Others he had encountered slept until awakened, like any aptrgangr, by the arrival of an intruder to the tomb. And Andrion was coming to suspect that the lore did not record every dragon priest who had lived. That last one, for instance, with the mask that reduced the time between dragon spells, was not mentioned anywhere that he had found.

Given his desperate but futile two-week search of the Academy's library for any further lore about dragons, The Fireblood, dragon priests, or dragon spells, Andrion was beginning to believe that Berni's theory, which Erik had mentioned, was right. At some point in the past, a systematic effort had been made to eliminate all traces of such lore. What little survived had only done so by chance.

They'd been wandering the corridors of the ruinous tomb complex for nearly two hours now, and stopped for a brief rest. Erik and Andrion could have gone on for hours more without a break; but though Andi could run circles around them normally he lacked the stamina for prolonged effort. They loaded him up with water and sweet trail rations, which soon had him looking perkier.

Shortly after the break they came through a pair of ominous-looking iron doors, heavily incised with runic designs. This must surely signify that they were now in the inner section of the crypt.

Before long Erik came upon a fire rune, pointed it out to Andi, and explained what it was. These could be cast by any competent mage, and would last until triggered. They wondered how long the mage who had put this one here had been dead.

Andrion showed Andi how casting the opposite battle magic would work to trip the rune without setting you ablaze, casting a frost spell at it. The rune exploded in a burst of flames, soon extinguished. "You need to keep your eyes wide open when you're questing in dungeons," Andrion told his son. "Those things can really hurt, and so can all the other traps."

"So if it's a frost rune, you use fire on it?" the boy asked.

"Right," Andrion said, "but for lightning you need to throw something iron at it. Lightning is naturally drawn to iron, but there is no 'opposite' spell for it."

Andi absorbed this information solemnly. He was finding this trip to be less of a thrilling adventure and more of a really long hike interspersed with deadly danger. And he needed to pee. After a while he couldn't stand it any longer, and he touched Erik's free hand. "Papa?" he whispered, "I need to go…" Erik smiled down at him. They were walking through a corridor, with no enemies in sight.

Erik took Andi by the hand and led him down the corridor a little way to where an urn stood in an alcove. Each of these likely contained a little gold, but they hadn't been bothering to search them. Erik stood guard close at hand as Andi removed his gauntlets and enough of his armor to be able to urinate into the alcove behind the urn. Meanwhile Andrion kept a more distant watch.

The mission successfully concluded, they continued their progress. At the far end of the hallway they were traversing they came to a chamber flanked by corridors on either side, which were mostly hidden from view. Andrion had a bad feeling about this. The walls were pierced at intervals, and anything hiding in one of those corridors might be waiting to pounce on you as you walked down the middle. Such passageways were a common feature of ancient Norse tomb complexes, and he and Berni had encountered one in Bergenfest a couple of months back.

They were bunched up, sizing up the passage ahead of them. "Erik, why don't you go right and I'll go left? And Andi, you can stay here and be very quiet." Erik nodded. It seemed a reasonable idea. Andi watched, big-eyed, his little sword at the ready, as his protectors vanished through openings on either side of the corridor. He couldn't see what was going on, but he could hear alarming noises coming from either side. Noises like Papa Erik shouting "Die, undead scum!"

Then, as he watched in growing terror, an aptrgangr slipped from a doorway on the left, down at the very end of the corridor. It was tall, taller than Papa Erik even, and it was wearing a big fancy helmet that made it look taller still. It was looking right at him! He had a couple of invisibility potions on him, but he didn't think they would work if you took one right in front of somebody. He brandished his little sword, trying to look bigger, and stood defiant. What else could he do? There was nowhere to run to, nowhere to hide.

The aptrgangr gazed down at him with blue-glowing eyes, perhaps wondering what manner of creature this tiny armored warrior was supposed to be. But it was carrying a sword, and he knew what to do about that. Halting for a moment he gave a raucous cry that sent Andi's little sword flying through the air to land a dozen feet away. Then he continued walking forward, his ancient longsword raised for the killing blow.

Andi spelled right back, knocking him tumbling halfway down the corridor with Gale. The aptrgangr couldn't believe it. A tiny warrior with the power of dragon spells? As he gathered himself and prepared to rise once again, a very much larger warrior popped out of a doorway on the other side of the corridor, swinging an enormous and evil-looking sword, and took off his head.

A second later and that enormous warrior was on his knees before Andi, hugging him tight. "Are you all right, son?" Erik asked, his heart in his throat. There had been more aptrgangr than they had expected, and they should never have left the boy alone. Andi returned his hug, then Erik leaned back to peer anxiously into his face. Andrion was there too, having dispatched the other two aptrgangr who'd been lurking on the left. Had the party simply walked down the middle, they'd have been surrounded.

His son's face, what he could see of it inside the helmet, was white as a sheet beneath his tan. "You did well, Andi!" Andrion exclaimed. "What a shot! That undead monster didn't know what hit him." This was just the sort of thing to give the troops, and in moments Andi was feeling a lot better about the whole business. That one aptrgangr hadn't knocked his head off, he'd sent it flying, and now all the aptrgangr were dead forever and he and his papas were fine.

A look of grim resolve seeming out of place on his handsome, childish features, Andi retrieved his sword and then rifled the fallen aptrgangr, keeping any small items like gold and gems they were carrying. He knew what adventurers were supposed to do, once they'd defeated the enemy. The men continued to congratulate him, building up his confidence, but they didn't want to overdo it. Soon, they knew, it was going to take more than a dragon spell to win the day.

The corridor led to more long-abandoned rooms where living men must once have carried out their daily business, then forged straight and true to another set of ominous-looking doors. "This is probably it," Andrion said quietly. "There's likely a big room on the other side of that door, with some coffins scattered around the sides and a big catafalque up on a platform near the back. I expect we'll find the Spell Wall behind that, but first we're going to have to get past a lot of aptrgangr. We're going to be very, very quiet going in there, and as soon as we get inside, Andi, I want you to start climbing. There will probably be some big stone dragon heads. Go up there and be very quiet, and they'll be so busy fighting us they probably won't even notice you. Okay?"

Andi felt a little let down, but relieved at the same time. On the one hand, he was not being treated as a real member of the team despite Papa Andrion's fine words earlier. On the other, he was not an idiot. Those aptrgangr were twice his height, if perhaps not twice his weight, and they had thousands of years of experience being warriors while he was just breaking into the business. Climbing high and staying out of sight seemed like a pretty good idea. Besides, if he got killed and couldn't get the dragon spell, Mama would have to stay a dragon forever. He kind of liked her as a dragon, but she was a lot softer as the Mama he had always known.

"Okay, Papa," Andi said in a small voice, and Erik pushed open the doors of the central burial chamber. Inside, it was pretty much as Andrion had described. The décor was Early Giant Stone Dragon, a familiar motif in places where dragon priests had once ruled, and seconds after they'd stepped inside Erik had boosted Andi up to climb atop a large stone head. There was one protruding from the wall on either side of the doorway, and the top of the dragon's head offered shelter from arrows. As long as Andi kept hidden and quiet, he was safe up there.

Erik looked Andi in the eye and put a mailed finger to his lips, and Andi gave him a cheeky grin and a thumbs-up before shrinking back down into his hiding place. Erik sighed. They were going to have to keep an eye on this boy. He was too fearless for his own good. Now the two men fanned out. They had quested together in such places, usually with Berni, many a time; and they both knew what to expect.

Erik hung back a little, and Andrion's stealthy progress on the other side of the room produced a series of cracks as aptrgangr, wakened by his proximity, burst from their sarcophagi. Unseen in the shadows on the other side of the room, Erik picked them off one by one with his bow. He was very nearly as deadly a marksman as Bernadette, if a little slower, and each of them dropped with a momentary gout of flame. The third one fell with an explosion that staggered the last, and Andrion finished that one off with a blast of lightning that hurled it through the air.

The two of them stood motionless, waiting to see what else had been stirred up by the noise of their brief battle. Andi peeked around the top of the stone dragon head to see what was going on, then ducked back down. All was quiet, and this time Erik did decoy duty while Andrion stood ready with his tight-beam intertwined battle spells. As Erik passed the first sarcophagus, it and three more burst open. Those ancient Norsemen loved their symmetry.

Erik unlimbered his khopesh and smashed the nearest aptrgangr to shreds, while Andrion took out the next two in the line with carefully focused beams of battle magic. The aptrgangr were lightly armored, and fell easily. By the time those two were down, Erik had drawn his bow again and sent the last of them to permanent sleep. Silence returned, and the brothers converged in the center of the room. Andi peeked out again, and they waved to him – making shushing motions, as well.

"I think that's all the lesser aptrgangr," Andrion murmured, "but look at the platform." It resembled a stone stage, broad and deep, with three throne-like chairs arrayed along the back. They were empty, but the elaborate central catafalque was flanked by two lesser ones.

"My guess would be a dragon priest in the middle and a couple of overlord deputies," Erik said as quietly. Andrion nodded. Friends for years before Berni had come into their lives, mostly because everybody liked Erik and Erik liked everybody, they had become brothers on the day of their wedding. They were now so close that their thoughts ran in the same channels, despite their differences.

Experience told them they'd be unlikely to pick these foes off individually. As soon as one burst from his slumber, the rest would join him. Overlords were nothing to laugh at, but the dragon priest would be the deadliest of the three. "Why don't you stay in the shadows," Andrion suggested quietly. "I'll go up on the left side until I trigger that first overlord. Then as soon as the dragon priest wakes up, hit him with arrows. He'll be a little disoriented when he first comes out. Meanwhile I'll take care of the overlord on my side, and we can both do the other one after the Dragon priest is down."

"Sounds like a plan," Erik rumbled softly with a grin. Up on his safe perch, Andi was spellbound. From here he couldn't hear what they were saying, but their coordination, their confidence, and their competence thrilled him to the core. This was what adventuring should be! It was much more exciting than any book he'd read, or story he'd heard. Yet he was safe up here, and sure with all his heart that his papas would soon defeat the bad guys and save the day.

He wasn't far wrong. Amazingly graceful and silent for a man of his size, Erik faded back into the shadows behind the last of the sarcophagi on the right. It stood at waist height, so didn't really hide him from view. But it offered a modicum of protection – and with Andrion making noise on the left, their enemies would be looking there first. Andrion strode boldly toward the stage, approaching from the left side. As he'd expected, he could see the Spell Wall tucked behind it.

Right... about... here. As Andrion stepped within an invisible perimeter, the sarcophagus nearest him cracked open, its stone lid flying to the side, and its occupant climbed stiffly out. That was the thing about aptrgangr – they were stiff and slow. As more loud cracks told him that the other two sarcophagi had released their occupants, Andrion took careful aim with a dual-wielded blend of fire and lightning. This spell combination could be as broad as a door or as finely concentrated as a pen point. At this close range, he was able to use it to punch a sizzling hole about four inches in diameter through the emerging overlord's chest.

Meanwhile, Erik had gone completely unnoticed in the shadows on the other side of the room. As the first overlord fell, the figure emerging from the central sarcophagus, the boss, focused his attention on Andrion and readied a spell of some kind. He was taken completely by surprise when one of Erik's arrows hit him in the side, passing straight through the ribs to lodge in the center of his chest. As he staggered, not knowing what had hit him, Erik put a second arrow in his neck. It blew his head off, sending his metal mask flying and causing damage to the last of the three, the overlord still climbing out of his coffin on the right side of the platform.

Andrion stepped past the bodies of their first two foes and converged on the third, as it cast a dragon spell at him. If he had been holding a weapon, he would probably have been disarmed. But no dragon spell could rob him of the ability that shot a burst of lightning coursing into the undead mage. Meanwhile, Erik had slung his bow behind his back and converged on the stage. As soon as the second overlord had expended its dragon spell, uselessly, he closed on it. And as it staggered from Andrion's burst of magic, he hacked it in two with his sword. He had to admit archery from hiding was effective, but Erik had always gotten the greatest satisfaction from dealing death to his enemies up close and personal.

After the last aptrgangr had fallen, silence reigned for several seconds. Then Erik and Andrion were suddenly riveted by a shriek coming from the back of the room, near the door. Andi?!

"Yeeeaaahhh! We did it!" the boy screamed at the top of his lungs. "Come get me down!" he added. Erik hurried over and held out his arms, and Andi hopped down nimbly to be caught up in a hug. "That was completely amazing!" he squealed.

They walked carefully around the room examining their fallen foes. Most of the aptrgangr had little of value, but the dragon priest had a grotesque-looking metal mask, a sullen blue-gray in color, that Andrion determined had some magical powers and was probably very valuable even if it were not famous. The ash pile that had remained after Erik had killed him also contained some armor and weapons worth thousands, and they lugged those along. You don't stay rich by passing up treasure when it's handed to you on a platter.

As they rounded the platform, Andi stopped and said "I hear the dragon spell noise!" Ah, Andrion realized. The boy had learned several dragon spells from Berni, but had never encountered a Spell Wall before. She had said that a very similar chorus accompanied the capture of a dragon soul – another experience, Andrion was glad, their little son had not yet had. Perhaps he never would, if the new era of dragon-human relations Berni hoped would be brought about by her efforts came to pass.

"It's the sound of the Spell Wall, Andi," Andrion told his son. "Mama told me about it, but I can't hear it and neither can Erik. Only fireblood can hear it." Andi looked pleased.

"Oh," he remarked shortly. "Cool." Every child longs to be special – almost as much as they long to be accepted into their peer group, just like everyone else.

Erik and Andrion hung back as Andi approached the Spell Wall. To their eyes, it was a cold half-circle of carven white stone, inlaid with runes across the entire inner face. To Andi, a series of runes near the lower right of the curve were written in blue fire, dazzling his eyes as he approached and the chorus rose to a crescendo before dying away. As it did so, the words Drache-Mon-Zur-Heim sank into his being, and he knew their meaning. "Dragon-Man-Return-Home." The other runes on the wall meant nothing to him, but then he was barely beginning to learn how to read the Common tongue as yet.

"From what Berni and I worked out," Andrion said, "for the Spell Wall to have provided the words of power the stone for that spell must be nearby. Let's check that chest." They rifled the nearby chest. There were no casks here, but down at the bottom beneath a collection of valuable larger items was a small tanned leather drawstring bag.

Andrion picked it open and emptied the contents into his left palm. Three little gemstones spilled out, all identical: glittering in the dim light from the ancients' ever-burning torches, they showed colors of tan, pink, copper, and olive green. "Should I…?" Andi asked, and Andrion nodded. He held out one of the gems and placed it in his son's hand, where it swiftly vanished from sight. Andi felt the disorienting rapture sweep through him as the spell took root, while his father tucked the two remaining stones back into the pouch and pocketed it.

Andi tried the dragon spell, but as he was not a human who'd been transformed into a dragon it had no effect. Still he and his fathers felt its power. This was the real thing. His face split in a gap-toothed smile. More than half a year from his sixth birthday, he'd already begun dropping teeth. "I've got it!" he cried joyfully. "Can we go tell Mama now?"

Chapter 70: Og Vulanz, Year Six

Bernadette and Sneyagflug were kept very busy supplying their babies with food over the next week. By the gods, the bigger they got the hungrier they were, and the more they ate the bigger they grew. From the size of human babies they'd grown, in less than two weeks, to the size of small foxes. And they were starting to show some signs of intelligence. Like the human hardwiring for language that leads to babbling and then speech between seven and eighteen months, the dragon babies seemed to have the same thing on a drastically compressed timetable.

Soon a piping chorus of "Murte! Murte!" greeted Bernadette whenever she returned to the cavern, or "Vaater! Vaater!" when Sneyagflug came in. Without his much greater contribution, she realized, she'd have been lucky to raise a quarter this many young. She began trying to give them simple commands, and found them surprisingly obedient. Well, she *was* many times their size – but she hadn't noticed that making much impression on her human children when they were feeling fractious.

Their individual differences were becoming more noticeable to her now, and she'd begun applying names to more of them. Sneyagflug didn't try to argue with her on any of these, seeming content to leave the job to her. A few were still just "that one, or is it that other one," though. There were subtle color variations, but by and large their brood were all red dragons like their parents.

At least they'd been able to skip the regurgitation for the last few days. The little ones had teeth now, sharp teeth, and as long as there was a steady supply of animal carcasses they weren't using them on each other. Bernadette was death on serious fights, breaking them up the moment any erupted. Human children fought all the time but they weren't equipped by nature to be killers, as these youngsters were. She applauded Sneyagflug's desire to see dragonkind have a more cohesive social structure, similar to that of humans, and it was on her to show the way.

It had been several days now since Bernadette's trip to Drakespring Farm, and she was growing anxious. Had they found the tomb where Sneyagflug had said it was? Was the dragon spell truly there? Were they all, especially Andi, all right? As engaging as her dragon family was, and as much as she had come to rely on her huge dragon consort, the longing to become human again, to hold Riki in her arms, to make mad passionate love with Erik and Andrion, was becoming an obsession.

Sneyagflug had just returned to the cavern with a creature the size of an ox but definitely not the same shape. It looked like it would hold their little dragon horde for a couple of hours easily, and she rose to her feet. He sensed her mood and asked, "Is everything all right dear?" His solicitousness had continued long beyond the time of her temporary disability, when she was gravid; and she believed that he truly cared for her. She cared for him too, in a way, finding many admirable qualities there. But he was not her husband, and never could be.

"I just need some fresh air," she said, and shortly launched herself off the side of the mountain. She had not told Sneyagflug that she'd asked her husbands to bring Andi here. She didn't think that he would really attack her loved ones, but if he did it would be him or them – and she didn't have to consider what side she would be on. Then, if he was defeated, she and her human family would be left trying to raise nineteen baby dragons who were halfway up a mountainside. Best to avoid the whole issue.

Bernadette cruised on a thermal up higher, soaring above the foothills and flatlands below. The weather here was often cloudy or worse, smoky; but today for a blessing was clear. Flying free calmed her, and helped her to let go of some of the aching need to be with her family again. But a flying dragon is soon a hungry dragon – and she began scanning the ground below with her eagle eyes, looking for movement that would signal prey.

There was a path of sorts from the coast to the fields around the foot of the mountain, screened by low forests. The forests in this region were so thin that one hardly needed a path to navigate through them, really. She spotted a flicker of movement through the trees, and circled lower. She was silent, and those moving below had no idea she was up there until she was almost upon them. But the trees grew close enough together to prevent her sweeping in for a pounce. Just as well – those were people. Andrion? Erik?

Backpedaling in the air Bernadette hovered, coming in for a landing in a clearing some distance from the trail. Then she began working her way in among the trees on the ground, an awkward progress. She spotted them coming toward her, and there was no mistake. "Erik!" she called. It would be better if they didn't come out into the open, where they might be seen by Sneyagflug.

Erik turned sharply at her call, and in moments the three of them had converged on her. "Mama!" Andi called eagerly, dashing the last few feet to hurl himself on her. "We got it, we got it, Mama! Can I do it now?" He thought his mother made a great dragon, but he really missed her human form. Erik and Andrion, hugging her from either side, looked down at their son.

"Will it work when he says it?" Andrion asked. Bernadette had no idea. Might as well try it.

"Go ahead Andi, tell me," she urged.

"Drache-Mon-Zur-Heim!" he piped. Nothing visible happened, but Bernadette felt the dragon spell penetrate her being. It joined her collection of many others, including the one that had gotten her into this mess in the first place. Erik and Andrion looked at her, disappointed.

"Wait for it," she said, "I feel something happening." There was a hot sensation within her, as if the spell had burrowed into her body as well as into her mind. She stood breathing quietly, attention focused within, for more than a minute. Then the heat subsided, and she sensed that the spell had become hers. "I think the stone has been created now," she told them. "Here goes. Drache-Mon-Zur-Heim!"

The form before them shrank in an instant. Disoriented, heedless of her nudity, Bernadette fell to her knees and hugged her armored son with her own two, human arms. Tears, the first she had been able to shed in weeks, rolled down her cheeks. But these were tears of joy. There were more hugs, real kisses, and an impromptu dance in among the trees before Bernadette came to her senses.

"Oh thank you, thank you! I can't believe I'm walking on two legs again!" Andi was a bit bug-eyed. The family often bathed together, so his mother's nudity wasn't all that big a deal; but it was a little disconcerting to have her dancing around naked out here in the woods with wild animals around, while the rest of them were wearing armor.

In another few minutes Bernadette became more subdued. "I've got to go back," she said. "The little ones are starting to talk, but it'll be another couple of weeks before I'll be able to leave Sneyagflug to handle them on his own. You wouldn't believe how cute they are!" She sighed. "Stand back," she warned, and after they'd backed off a few yards she cried "Mon-Drache-Ein-Korp!" Once again she morphed in a couple of moments from human woman to smallish red dragon, her scales glistening in the afternoon light.

Oh, good. Her plan for them coming here had relied on the untested theory that, once primed by the potion and possessed of both dragon spells, she'd be able to transform back and forth at will. Now, instead of being trapped in an intolerable situation, she had a great new power! The nudity thing was a bit of an issue, but perhaps she could rig up some kind of pack she could slip over her head in dragon form, that would hold clothes, armor, and weapons for when she went back to being human.

"This is great!" she cried. "I can come back to human anytime I want, now!" They all beamed at her. They were sorry to see her back in draconic form again, but now that they knew for sure she would return they were happy to see her fulfill her obligations. Soon they would all be together again, forever! Bernadette still had some time before she'd be missed, and considered going human again for a while. But standing around in this northern forest naked wasn't the most enjoyable activity. She had a thought.

"Andrion, do you happen to have my map with you?"

"I have the original one," he replied. "Your Agena map's at home on the dresser."

"The original should do nicely, if you can figure out some way I can carry it with me in this form." Andrion began rummaging in his pack. He pulled out some long underdrawers, soft knit fabric with long legs, and tied them around her neck like a knit collar. He tucked the map between the folds of the crotch, and held the flaps together around it with a decorative brooch he'd taken off one of the aptrgangr they'd killed.

"You'll have to go human to get the brooch unfastened, but once you do you'll have something to put on the bottom at least," he mused. She laughed, a curious hissing sound in her dragon voice. "I hadn't considered that," she said. "Do you have a spare shirt in there as well?" He pulled one out and tied it to the pants. Now she had cloth festooned down her front, and as soon as she got back to the cavern she was going to have to tell Sneyagflug what was going on.

Bernadette watched as her husbands and son shimmered out of existence before her, fast-traveling home. Pain stabbed her heart at the sight but soon, soon, she would join them. She heaved herself back to the clearing and labored up into the air, careful not to dislodge her getaway kit. It was time to have a talk with the father of her children.

Bernadette was hungry still, but she didn't want to try hunting while carrying the clothes and map. It would be bad enough wearing men's long underwear, and she certainly didn't want it charred or covered in bloodstains. So she soon arrived back in the cavern, the garments tied around her neck. Sneyagflug was watching contentedly as their greedy brood savaged the carcass he'd brought them. They were now able to understand much of what was said to them; but they were often like unruly toddlers, so the stone barrier stayed in place.

His head swiveled at her approach, and his heart sank like a stone when he saw what she had around her neck. Humans, and surely it was *her* humans, had come here to the island and talked with her. He stifled the urge to roar in protest, to attack her, to fly off looking for them so that he could crisp them with Holocaust. This feeling he had for Schunmurte was something he had never experienced before. He wanted her to be happy, even at his own expense. Was this what humans called love? Whatever you called it, it hurt.

"So," he said, in a voice like a tomb, "you will be leaving us soon?" She walked awkwardly across the cavern floor to his side and nuzzled him gently at the juncture of his neck and shoulder, which was about as high as she could reach.

"Not that soon," Bernadette said quietly. Her heart went out to the big dragon. What they had shared was something she would never forget – but fireblood or not, this was not the life she was meant to have.

The two of them turned to watch the babies. They had all eaten as much as they wanted, with no need to keep the bigger, stronger ones from edging out the smaller. Individual differences aside, the girls seemed to be growing apace with their brothers. Bernadette's insistence that everybody got fed had paid off, and Sneyagflug was convinced that she was right – a little extra help for the females at the start of life, and there would be bigger broods to show for it. Sooner, too, as it was size rather than age that determined a female's breeding readiness.

They were scattered around the enclosure now, grooming themselves after the meal. Without fur or feathers, dragons didn't have the need to keep themselves clean that other predators did. But other predators weren't sentient, and dragons had a conscious desire for cleanliness that went beyond necessity; as did many humans. Bernadette was considered unusually fastidious in the culture of Iscandia, nor did most Galise care to bathe as often as she did. Perhaps her dragon babies had somehow acquired the trait?

Bernadette turned her head to Sneyagflug and nuzzled his shoulder again, as he lay there lost in thought, gazing at their little ones. "Cheer up, Red," she said. "Our children are going to change dragon society, and their relationships with humans. And it's all because of you and your vision." He turned to look down at her, his body language unreadable.

She went on, "This is their next lesson." With that she said "Drache-Mon-Zur-Heim!" and shrank where she stood – the clothing that had seemed like a scarf around her dragon neck hanging down across the front of her human body. Sneyagflug flinched, and the baby dragons were in an uproar.

There was a chaotic chorus along the lines of "Who are you?" and "What did you do with our mother?" in lisping dragon language, and eighteen of the babies cowered back – some of them even retreating into the alcove where they'd been born.

But one dragonling, a little male with burnished deep red scales to whom she had not yet given a name, came forward. His eyes were shining and his tail was up at the tip, and he looked as pleased to see her as a puppy when its master returns from some time away. "Mother! You changed!" I'll be darned, Bernadette thought, as she stood there with her arms folded across the wad of clothing dangling from her neck. He was the only one who got it, and the only one who wasn't afraid at the sight of a human.

She climbed over the rock barrier with some difficulty. It was slightly above crotch height. Then she knelt and beckoned to her dragon son. He came to her at once, zipping along as agilely as a big lizard. She welcomed the little guy into her arms, lifting him up and then squatting tailor fashion on the grass-strewn floor. The babies had been taught to use a latrine trench their parents had dug with their claws over near one wall, early on. Now the floor of the enclosure was covered with the straw that had once lined the alcove, still reasonably clean.

Bernadette lifted the bundle of cloth off her neck and used it to pad her lap, and the little dragon climbed right up and curled up like a somewhat oversized lapdog. He wasn't as heavy as he looked. Nor was he going to sleep, just snuggling up while he eyed her with rapt fascination. Addressing him and the rest of her brood, Bernadette said "That's right, I am your mother. This is my other form, a human being. Before you were born, this is the form I lived in all my life. You have a brother and a sister who are also this shape, and when you go out into the world you will find that it is full of people like me. Your father will teach you how to talk to them, and how to live in peace with them, and we can help each other."

She turned to the little dragon in her lap, who'd been following her words intently. "You," she said fondly, "I name Drachmondien." In the common tongue, it was Dragon-Man-Serve. She had plans for this boy, and she felt sure he had the aptitude for his mission in life. Seeing Drachmondien's lack of fear, and Bernadette's lack of aggression, the others began to creep back until she was surrounded by them. The bolder ones were demanding to crawl up into her lap and be petted, and she was thankful of the cloth protecting her bare legs from their claws.

Sneyagflug stood bemused, watching his erstwhile consort with their children. While a dragon mother would fight with ferocity for her young and do everything in her power (usually, not enough) to ensure their survival, he could see that human nature and human culture made humans the better mothers. Perhaps it was the mammalian trick of supplying the young with food from within their own bodies. He sighed. She was beautiful, even in this tiny form, and he was losing her.

Bernadette spent the next two weeks in dragon form, as Sneyagflug needed help to restock their larder. Until the young could fly on their own and begin bringing down small prey, they would be needing ever-increasing amounts of meat to fuel their growth and mental development. The two hunted in shifts from morning to night, and in the evenings spent time together with the children before curling up to sleep.

While she was resting and watching the kids in the cavern as Sneyagflug hunted, Bernadette began teaching them the common tongue spoken by humans throughout most of the continent. The dragon language was falling into place in their minds, apparently by the design of their creator. But this was an ideal time for them to learn another language as well, and they were picking it up fast. Sneyagflug might not have much teaching to do in that department, by the time she left. She certainly hoped he was up to the task of teaching them how to be dragons, though. Having been a woman one moment and a full-grown dragon the next, there was a lot she couldn't begin to explain.

Drachmondien was her constant companion whenever she was in the cavern, and as his verbal abilities grew by leaps and bounds his questions became ceaseless. "What's it like being a human? What are my human siblings' names? Who is their father? When can I fly? Where is Iscandia?" By the gods, Bernadette mused. And I thought Andi was persistent. She took it as a sign of an eager, active mind and tried to answer all his questions as honestly as she could, within the limits of his understanding. She came to realize that dragonlings at this age (a month, more or less, after hatching) were at a level of mental development similar to that of a human five-year-old. Andi's new brother, though more than five years his junior, was a good match for him socially.

It was not just mental and verbal development happening among the brood, however. They seemed to be forming into social cliques, those dragonlings with more in common spending more time together. Their social intercourse furthered their verbal abilities, but she tried to maintain a fairly tight control over their interactions. Unlike human children, baby dragons possessed sharp claws and mouths full of potentially lethal teeth. Any signs of intra-brood aggression were firmly stamped out.

Andrion would have called this enculturation, Bernadette realized. She was adamant that her children should be raised with values that included protection of the weak, hanging together as a team, and "treat others as you want to be treated." Sneyagflug was in complete accord with this, a blessing since it was he who would be raising them. He saw, where she perhaps did not, that if dragonkind did not change their ways the immortal *drachen* would be nothing but a memory inside the span of one human generation. Humans were taking over the world, and they were nasty little buggers.

The babies had all been named, and were babies no more. Bernadette and Sneyagflug agreed on each name, then presented it to the dragonling in question with a sort of ceremony. From now on, those three syllables would function as a dragon spell, and no matter where the dragon was he or she would hear it spoken. Ignoring it, or coming to the Call, would be up to the dragon of course.

Sneyagflug was off on another hunting expedition. It was the later part of summer, and at this altitude and latitude the days were already getting shorter and cooler. Bernadette lay resting near the entrance to their aerie, enjoying the afternoon sun as it streamed in from the direction of Iscandia. Around her, juvenile dragons were engaged in a flurry of different activities.

Some were conversing, imagining hunts they would go on as soon as they could fly. They all spent a goodly amount of time each day flapping their wings, which were now growing longer. But as yet most of them could not lift more than a few feet off the ground before coming in for a crash landing. The rock barrier had been removed, the rocks allowed to find their own way to the level ground far below. Now parental warnings would have to suffice to keep the brood from falling off the edge.

Drachmondien left a group of his peers and lifted off the ground for a few feet, earning him the dragon equivalent of applause: heads raised in a cheer. "Very impressive, son," Bernadette said. "You're not supposed to be able to fly for another month at least, you know." He tucked himself close to her side.

"Are you going to leave soon, Mother?" he asked. The kid was sharp as a knife. Somehow he had picked up on conversations she'd had with Sneyagflug, and knew that she was going back to her human form and her human life.

Bernadette sighed gently. She loved her dragon family, had even found something to love in Sneyagflug. But the longing for Andrion, Erik, her human children and friends was more and more on her mind and she couldn't wait much longer. "Yes, love," she said. "Soon you and your siblings will be on your own with your father, and my human children will have their mother again. But we'll still see each other sometimes, I promise. I can't wait to see what you'll be like when you're all grown up."

The little dragon pressed into her side, then looked up into her eyes. "I want to come with you," he said.

The day dawned, and Sneyagflug knew it was The Day. Their young were all children now, no babies. Well on the way to flight, and fully possessed of the powers of speaking and understanding. Carcasses aplenty lined the ice caves on the slopes above them, enough to feed him and their brood for another three months.

Beside him, Schunmurte roused from slumber. She crawled out to the rim of their cavern and sat back, stretching her wings and yawning. Oh, for a cup of tea! Or maybe some of that kaf the Afrans drank… Sneyagflug moved to her side. "You're leaving, aren't you?" he asked. She turned to look him in the eyes. How had he known?

"Yes," she said softly. "My other family needs me."

He dipped his head in acknowledgement. "Schunmurte… I'm sorry… sorry that I stole you from them. It was not right, but I knew no other way…" Bernadette turned to look at him. Had tears been possible, they would have glistened in her eyes.

"I forgive you, Red," she said softly. "What you did, you did for a good cause. It would have been nice to have been consulted… but it's all worked out in the end. Look at that!" She gestured with her head to where their brood slept in several piles, like litters of puppies. "I laid nineteen eggs and we've raised nineteen babies to childhood! How amazing is that?"

He returned her gaze. "You're taking Drachmondien?" he asked. She nodded.

"I don't know how it's possible, but I think that boy is half human. Maybe he's the dragon equivalent of Fireblood, perhaps Manblood. He's going to be dragonkind's first and foremost ambassador to the world of men when he grows up."

Sneyagflug hesitated before he spoke. "Schunmurte… Bernadette… I was wondering if we could… for old times' sake…?" Bernadette looked at him in astonishment. Never since they had first met, which was only a few weeks after she'd met the men who became her husbands, had he ever acknowledged that she had a name other than her title of *Fjurblut* or the one he had given her. And he was suggesting… sex?

"Uh," she said, stalling for time to gather her thoughts. "You can do that? I mean, I thought it was all instinct… and would that make me ovulate again, so soon after laying eggs?"

"I don't think so," Sneyagflug assured her. "Besides, you're about to turn human so I don't think you need to worry about laying eggs. But our time together a few weeks ago was the most incredible experience I have ever had. I think maybe for males, it might be possible whenever a receptive female is near. I only know I want you, and… I think I love you."

Physically, in her dragon body, Bernadette had no desire for sex at all. She had an incredibly large brood of dragonlings around her, and in the normal course of things she'd have been busy raising them for the next several years. She suspected that, as a human, she'd already had sex dozens of times more than any female dragon in the history of the species.

Mentally, however… Her immense desire for mad passionate sex with Erik and/or Andrion (and no way she planned to exclude either of them for her first trip back home as a human) had been nagging at the back of her mind for weeks. Nor had the memory of her last time together with Sneyagflug faded. That had truly been something. Well, why not? He'd said he loved her. Bernadette doubted any other dragon had said that to anyone. Sneyagflug deserved a little something to remember her by.

The kids were still sleeping, and they were all well aware of the rules. No fighting, no going near the edge, and if anything besides Mother or Father comes into the cavern, attack and kill it. They should be okay without supervision for a while. Bernadette looked at Sneyagflug with a glance that a human might have had trouble interpreting, but it filled his heart with joy. When she leaned over and ran her tongue up his neck, he knew he was in.

A couple of hours later, Bernadette assumed human form. She donned her long underwear, which (with the map) had been stowed on a ledge in the alcove for the past couple of weeks. It was several inches too long for her, and she had to roll up the pant legs and sleeves. She kissed and hugged each and every one of her brood, calling them by name and admonishing them to be good, to listen to Father, and to always treat each other – and humans – with kindness and courtesy. Then she threw her arms around Sneyagflug's head as he lowered it within her reach.

"Goodbye," she said, tears running down her cheeks. "Take good care of our little ones. And come see me sometimes. You know where to find us." Sneyagflug, still quivering inside from their passionate liaison on the plains below, had not abandoned the hope that he might yet get her back again, his Schunmurte. As a human she would age and die, but as a dragon she could live forever. Maybe someday she would be his.

Chapter 71: Drakespring Farm, Year Six

Once again the extended family was gathered around the dinner table, everyone from Merelle (sitting in her high chair playing with pieces of bread roll) to Francois, holding forth on the subject of ancient runes while working on his third glass of wine, as his wife tried to suggest it might be time to be quiet and let someone else speak. He would never be entirely convinced that, once someone had been given a proper understanding of one of his many fields of study, anyone could fail to be as fascinated as he was.

The convivial family gathering was interrupted as the front door opened to admit a small figure clownishly dressed in oversized long johns, a good-sized juvenile dragon perched on her shoulder. She beamed at them and said, "I'm back!" Around the table, several people leapt to their feet. Cries of "Berni!" and "Mama!" jumbled together, before they mobbed her.

Bernadette spoke to the dragonling, saying, "Hop down, Drachmondien," and gesturing at the table near the door. He couldn't fly ten feet yet, but he was certainly capable of covering the distance from his mother's shoulder to the table. This was a human dwelling! And this thing he was standing on was a table! Drachmondien's young mind was bursting with excitement. Not for him, a life spent gnawing on slightly-toasted dead animals in the wild. Mother had told him about civilization, and he craved it.

Erik, Andrion, and Andi rushed to embrace Bernadette, and Riki joined them a few seconds later. Now *this* was her mama, not that strange giant creature that had spoken with her voice. Hugs and kisses went on for a couple of minutes, as Drachmondien watched with interest. "Did you bring us a new pet, Mama?" Andi wanted to know, and Bernadette turned serious.

"Pet? Of course not. This is your new brother, Drachmondien. He's going to live with us now while your other new brothers and sisters live with their father." Bernadette's four other clan members turned to stare at the little dragon. This... *creature* was going to be part of their family? But she'd schooled her youngest son well. Wings folded where he stood on the table, Drachmondien bowed his head to them.

"I'm so glad to meet you," he said in unaccented Common. "You must be my brother Andreas, and this must be Erika. And you," he said looking up at the men who towered above him, "are my new papas, Erik and Andrion."

Hours later, all four of the family's children were sleeping in the nursery. Drachmondien had a nest of pillows on the floor until something more appropriate could be provided for him, and a box of wood shavings to use for a toilet. They weren't sure if he'd ever be able to manage using the water privy, and in any case he was likely to be outgrowing it before too many years had passed. He and Andi were already becoming friends, like minds in very different bodies.

The other adults had gone to their beds, and Bernadette was alone at last with Erik and Andrion. They headed for the bathroom to soak in the tub, which she found blissful beyond belief after week upon week of washing herself with saliva. The hours that had elapsed as she and her dragon son fast-traveled to the farm had taken a toll on her, but her hunger for her men was so strong it overpowered any fatigue.

For their part, they'd been reduced to masturbation for nearly two months, two healthy men in their prime, and they couldn't keep their hands off her. She might not be the dewy, pert 22-year-old they had first met, but they had never seen a woman who looked more desirable. They made love together in the bath, then cleaned up and moved to the bedroom where they resumed their frolics. Bernadette's joy was transcendent, and in the morning they did it yet again. On arising, she found her amulet and put it on. It was already too late.

Chapter 72: Drakespring Farm, Year Seven

Bernadette sat on the veranda in a rocking chair, nursing her son. At three months of age, he was just starting to hold his head up. He gazed into her sea-gray eyes with his blue ones, flecks of amber sparkling within them. His hair was deep red, far darker than hers, and in her heart of hearts she was still not sure who had fathered him.

Were blue eyes hidden in Andrion's family past? Could Erik have somehow given her a baby with such dark hair? She couldn't shake the idea that Sneyagflug had had something to do with it, even if it were only to trigger her ovulation in time to be impregnated in her human form. It didn't matter. He was theirs, belonging to all of them, and he was loved. His name was Sigmund, but everybody called him Sigi.

He began to doze off and she lifted him up to hold him to her shoulder and burp him. He emitted a tiny "urp" and subsided peacefully into sleep. Christine and Francois had returned to Auverne the previous fall, but were talking of selling their home and moving to the Waterdon area permanently. Andrion was on the lookout for a home for them in town, where they would be close to everything and not too far from the family at Drakespring Farm.

Merelle (now usually called Meri) had long since been weaned, Ekka returning to her enormous family in Waterdon – where, they had heard, she had been entertaining audiences at The Flying Horseman with the tale of the transforming Fireblood for months. Now Larissa was once more helping Bernadette with the children, and at the moment she was minding Meri along with Riki, Andi… and Mondi, as they'd begun calling Drachmondien. Not that those last two much needed a babysitter. They had become inseparable companions, often joined by Fjurbund. The two human boys now spoke the dragon tongue almost like natives.

Andrion had volunteered to teach the three playmates to read and cipher, and they'd all taken to his lessons with alacrity. The two human boys had been read to since babyhood, of course, but Mondi seemed to have some kind of an inborn gift for reading to go along with his instinctive language abilities. Much to his surprise, Andrion had found the young dragon to be his most eager pupil; and any resentment he'd felt at Mondi's insertion into their household had long since vanished.

Dragons could not learn all human activities, of course. Their foreclaws could grip prey but were unsuited for delicate tasks and lacked thumbs; but Andrion had been experimenting with teaching Mondi healing magic (with which he himself had only a little ability) and reported that the dragon child had a natural affinity for magic as well as a fund of magical energy that was far beyond human.

Bernadette suspected that in time Mondi would easily learn every dragon spell she had to offer, as would Andi. Andi had also expressed an interest in chemia, and she'd been teaching him some beneficial potions. He was tall enough now to reach the chemia station's platform, an important milestone. She thought she would wait awhile yet before teaching him enchanting, though under Erik's tutelage he was already crafting some serviceable knives at the forge.

As Bernadette had been feeding Sigi, Andi and Mondi were chasing around the yard in some imaginative game – the boy running while his dragon brother flew. At a year-plus of age Mondi was five feet long from nose to tail tip, with a wingspan that would soon have him banned from the nursery. Bernadette had assumed that as her children grew older they would eventually need private rooms, ones with their own entrances to the outside world; she hadn't expected it would be so soon.

Bernadette smiled at them as she rose, Sigi in her arms, to carry him to his crib in the nursery for a nap. Five children, two of them not even human, and she was half-seriously thinking of having her amulet permanently embedded in her skin. Not that she regretted for a moment the birth of this sweet boy in her arms, or any of the others. Each of them was a joy in their own way, and she loved them all deeply.

After tucking Sigi in Bernadette returned to the veranda and put her feet up, picking up some knitting. It was late morning on a lovely midsummer day, and she had nothing very pressing to do but enjoy it. She set it aside a moment later and put her feet down, rising to peer out from under the porch roof. What was that clattering sound she heard?

Andi skidded to a halt in front of her, a hand shading his eyes as he looked into the sky off to the east. Mondi flapped in mid-air a few feet off the ground, as he gazed in the same direction with his much-sharper dragon vision. "It's Father!" he cried. Andrion and Erik were his papas, as they were to Andi and Riki and Meri, but Sneyagflug was Father.

Bernadette and Andreas watched as Mondi flapped his wings and flew off like a shot, heading east. They soon saw a big red shape flying toward them, surrounded by smaller ones, with Mondi joining them and flying around them in excited circles as they drew closer to the farm. "By the gods," Bernadette murmured quietly, her eyes shining.

She and Andi stood watching, soon joined by the rest of the family and Larissa, as the enormous red dragon touched down in the road at the bottom of the farmyard. The little ones (not so little now!) came swarming up to hover near the veranda, chorusing "Mama! Mama!" Their fluency in Common was complete.

Tears ran down Bernadette's cheeks unnoticed as she beheld them, these children of her other body. She hadn't taken on dragon form since she'd left them, though she often dreamed of flying. The milling swarm eventually settled to the earth, all of them eagerly looking to her, and she went around greeting each of them by name. As if those names were truly dragon spells, she would never forget any of them, nor would she fail to recognize her children though they had changed.

All eighteen of them were here! Sneyagflug had not lost a single one. Bernadette hurried down to the bottom of the hill and embraced his head, kissing him on the snout. "You made it, Red!" she said in dragon tongue. "You raised them all! I'm so proud of you!" He rumbled softly.

"There's a lot of work yet to be done," he replied. "But they're coming along pretty well. We miss you, you know."

Bernadette colored. She had thought of them a lot over the past year, but with the new baby and the demands of her everyday human life she had not truly missed them. "Come fly with us, Schunmurte?" Sneyagflug suggested. As he spoke the words, she suddenly knew there was nothing she would like more.

"It'll take me a few minutes to get ready," she told him. "I have another son now..." He ducked his head.

"I wondered about that. Perhaps I should have warned you, but I truly did not know what would happen."

Bernadette walked back to the house, asking Larissa to keep an eye on Sigi for an hour or so. She told the rest of the kids (though Meri was as yet too young to understand much) what she was planning to do, and Andrion and Erik as well. Andrion looked a little unhappy. This invasion of their home by his wife's former abductor and the brood he'd fathered on her was not something he looked on with joy. But he knew Berni. If she wanted to turn into a dragon and go for a joyride she would, and objecting to it was only going to cause unpleasantness. He'd long since stopped doubting her love and loyalty. "Have fun, love," was all he said. "We'll hold down the fort while you're gone."

Smiling broadly, her eyes sparkling, she gave him a hot kiss. Well, *that* was worthwhile... Erik, of course, was easy with whatever she might want to do. But he got a kiss as well, on general principles. Then Bernadette headed into the house to strip down. No point in ruining a perfectly good dress. The amulet went back onto the chest of drawers. Modesty struck, and she didn't want to parade around in front of the entire household (and anybody walking along the main road to the east) in her birthday suit. So she threw on a robe and walked out the front door and around to the back, currently unoccupied, before dropping the robe to the ground and transforming into Schunmurte.

Oh, what a rush! Bernadette stretched her wings, feeling the morning sun warming their silky membranes as its rays sparkled and glistened on her scales. As a woman, she was 30 years old and beginning to sag a bit after her third (and she hoped, last) pregnancy. As a dragon she was ageless, a creature of the air. Never would she leave her family again for this, but she had to admit to herself that it filled her with excitement and a sense of freedom.

Bernadette lifted into the air and looked down to the east, beyond the roof of the farmhouse to where her children were milling, beginning to rise. It occurred to her then that she might bring Andi along. He was bigger and heavier than he'd been a year ago, when she last took him for a ride – but she was only going out for an hour or so, and she felt strong. She flapped over the house and came down on the east side, in the yard.

Around her, her flock of dragon children hovered crying "Mama! Come fly with us!"

"Andi?" Bernadette called in her deeper dragon voice. She no longer saw him among the humans gathered on the veranda, watching. And where was Mondi? Oh, there he was, hovering in midair beside… "Ready, Mama!" Andi said. He flapped his deep bronze wings and took to the sky.

The End

The adventures of the Drakespring Clan continue
in the Young Adult Fire Scion series.